SPOILED MILK

DOUBLEDAY
NEW YORK

FIRST DOUBLEDAY HARDCOVER EDITION 2026

Published by Doubleday, a division of Penguin Random House LLC,
1745 Broadway, New York, NY 10019.

Doubleday and the portrayal of an anchor with a dolphin are
registered trademarks of Penguin Random House LLC.

Book design by Anna B. Knighton

Library of Congress Cataloging-in-Publication Data
Names: Curran, Avery, author
Title: Spoiled milk : a novel / Avery Curran.
Description: First Doubleday hardcover edition. | New York : Doubleday, 2026. |
Identifiers: LCCN 2025003834 (print) | LCCN 2025003835 (ebook) |
ISBN 9780385551595 hardcover | ISBN 9780385551601 ebook
Subjects: LCGFT: Gothic fiction | Horror fiction | Novels
Classification: LCC PS3603.U7657 S66 2025 (print) |
LCC PS3603.U7657 (ebook) | DDC 813/.6—dc23/eng/20250402
LC record available at https://lccn.loc.gov/2025003834
LC ebook record available at https://lccn.loc.gov/2025003835

penguinrandomhouse.com | doubleday.com

Printed in the United States of America
2nd Printing

The authorized representative in the EU for product safety and
compliance is Penguin Random House Ireland, Morrison Chambers,
32 Nassau Street, Dublin D02 YH68, Ireland, https://eu-contact.penguin.ie.

For Martha,

in this world and the next

The two little girls kissed in the kind darkness, where the visible and the invisible could meet on equal terms.

—*The Enchanted Castle*, E. Nesbit

DRAMATIS PERSONAE

Briarley School for Girls

The upper sixth

EMILY LOCKE, a schoolgirl

EVELYN HART, a schoolgirl

MARION THOMAS, a schoolgirl

DOROTHY JAMES, a schoolgirl

ALICE BINGHAM, a schoolgirl

SOPHIE SALISBURY, a schoolgirl

VIOLET KIRSCH, dead

The younger years

OLIVIA SINCLAIR, a schoolgirl

LACEY CLARKE, a schoolgirl

MILDRED ALLEN, a schoolgirl

ANN TURNER, a schoolgirl

SHIRLEY CARR, a schoolgirl

The staff

Miss Lewis, the headmistress

Mademoiselle Lefèvre, the French mistress

Fräulein Weingarten, the German mistress

Miss Stone, the Mathematics and Sciences mistress

Miss Parker, the English and History mistress

Miss Stevens, the Games and Comportment mistress

Matron

Cook

Outside Briarley

Reverend Fish, the local priest

Mrs. Soane, the organ player

Mr. Kirsch, Violet's father

Mrs. Kirsch, Violet's mother

Mrs. Anne Northcote, a medium

SPOILED MILK

ONE

THE BEGINNING OF THE END

1928

The night Violet died, we had just finished celebrating her eighteenth birthday. Being the darling of the lower years, upper years, and schoolmistresses alike (and rich on top of that), Violet had been given countless presents. She held court after dinner in the younger girls' playroom while she opened them. It was the sort of little kindness she liked to extend when it suited her; our common room was off-limits to everyone but the upper sixth.

One of the lower fourths gave her a posy of evening primroses and the last of the harebells, picked during afternoon break and tied with a ribbon. Violet gasped with delight and leaned forwards to drop the girl a swift kiss on her rosy cheek. Then it was our turn.

Three weeks before, when everyone had arrived for the new school year at the beginning of September, I'd persuaded the other upper-sixth girls to pool our allowances, meagre as some of them were, to buy Violet a pair of real kid gloves with pearl buttons at the wrist. That ghastly prig Evelyn Hart had gone to the village on Saturday to pick them up, and she'd come back full of stories about how the shopkeeper had allowed her to touch them before he wrapped the gloves in parcel paper, and how they were softer and more delicate than anything she had ever seen, and how it was a shame none of us with our grubby paws would be allowed anywhere near the cream-coloured leather so as not to stain them before they reached Violet's perfect hands. I loathed Evelyn more than I could express.

As Violet opened her present, we held our breath, waiting for her approval. She seemed to like them; at least I think she did. I never got the chance to ask her about it in private. I like to think she would have told me the truth. Either way, she thanked us all and slipped the gloves on, exclaiming at how well they fit and promising to wear them at chapel the next week, a bending of the rules that I felt dead certain she would be allowed. I gave myself a moment—just a moment—to think about how her gloved hands would look holding the hymnal, or clasped together during prayers. Naturally we were supposed to keep our eyes shut during that part, but I thought I might be forgiven a peek. If you were in Violet's orbit, the rules could bend around you, too.

After Violet had made her fuss over the gloves, she turned delightedly around to the pile of packages from her parents, which had arrived in that morning's post. She always opened gifts with such enthusiasm that it almost felt like getting something yourself. As her white fingers tore apart the lovely printed paper, I hoped that later she might give me one of the silk ribbons that tied the parcels together, pressing it into my hand before bed like a mediaeval lady giving a knight a favour to tuck into his armour. She inspired that sort of devotion, you know: the chivalric, courtly kind, where, if you never got anything else, it would almost have been enough just to wear her ribbon.

Violet's parents had gone all out. First, there was a matching silver-backed hairbrush and hand mirror, which came in a slim box from one of the better department stores in London. Then she slit open a parcel containing a peach-coloured silk slip that was miles away from regulation but might never be seen as long as she was careful not to let the skirt of her pinafore ride up—this came with a sly note from her father, who owned a textile business, about how it had been made in one of his own factories. There were biscuits from Fortnum's in a turquoise tin, a jar of lemon drops, a mountain of powdery pink Turkish delight. She promised to share it all, though she never got the chance.

My family didn't send anything like that for my birthdays. If they'd had the money, they wouldn't have spent it on me. Usually I received an ill-suited card decorated with kittens or balloons that looked like it was for a much younger girl, the contents of which only served to imply my inadequacy as a daughter. I'd have killed for sweets and trifles, but Violet was always so good about giving me hers, sometimes to the point of not leaving any for herself, even though she had a sweet tooth like no one else I knew.

This was the point at which Sophie chose to unveil what I considered at the time to be a great betrayal. She interrupted the proceedings with a curious mixture of shyness and glee, bringing out a slim, dark green book. Its cover was plain, but there was gold type on the spine, and from my vantage point that was all I could see.

Evelyn's face went white. "I thought we had agreed—the gloves—"

"Why, Sophie, whatever could this be?" Violet cooed, reaching for the book.

"I found it in a bookshop," Sophie said, "in London." You could hear her pause for effect before saying *London*, and to her credit, I would've as well.

"In London," Violet repeated, ever sharp to the little devotions we paid to her.

"I was down with Mumsy and Dad to see something at the theatre, you remember how I told you, and I went into one of the bookshops on Charing Cross Road"—very bold of her—"and I found this."

"Out with it, what is it?" I said, surprising myself with how loud my voice was. I felt the strange sense of unease that I sometimes had when Violet turned her attention away from me, like the slight chill that comes when a candle is blown out.

Violet studied the spine. "*Spiritualist Phenomena and Mediumship*, by A. L. Walden. Oh, Sophie, Miss Stone would have kittens!"

"I thought you could hide it in your trunk," Sophie offered.

Violet flipped through to the table of contents, murmuring as she went. "Crystal gazing, table tipping, movement of objects without contact, *materialisation*—"

A thrill ran through me. Supernatural exploration was the sort of thing one always hoped might happen at school, like in the books. We had midnight feasts from time to time, and Alice had played a well-timed prank or two, but it was always kid stuff, never the real thing, no romantic kidnappings or other proper adventures. I felt as though I was peering over a precipice, at the bottom of which were mediums, and crystal balls, and the mysteries of adulthood.

"I'm not sure this is such a good idea," Evelyn started.

"Rot," Violet said. "It's a splendid idea, one of the best anyone's had this term. Don't be an ass about it. Thanks ever so, Sophie."

At this, Sophie went scarlet, words failing her, and I got up to fetch Violet another present to break the moment.

It was the final one, a small parcel from Mademoiselle

Lefèvre, the very young and very pretty French mistress. Mademoiselle had arrived the year before, in April, after the previous French mistress had got married. She was tall and willowy, with strong eyebrows and a rosebud mouth; she looked like a proper woman, lovely and grown-up, wearing a white lawn dress with her hair in an old-fashioned Gibson Girl pompadour. I'd heard Violet's father remark when we were all dropped off on the first day of term that Mademoiselle was hardly out of girlhood herself.

She rapidly became an object of admiration for us all—but Violet, as always, was the exception, because Mademoiselle admired her back. She had taken a special shine to Violet on account of her lovely lilting French accent, which the rest of us were constantly trying and failing to mimic. It wasn't the custom for schoolmistresses to give us gifts, but in the run-up to that September evening, we had all speculated among ourselves whether Mademoiselle adored Violet enough to break with tradition. In the end, she had: she gave her a little bottle of scent with violets all over the label, stoppered by a heavy piece of cut glass. Violet took the stopper out and put the bottle to her nose, sighing happily.

"I'll wear it always—and when it runs out, I'll simply have to scrounge all I can till I can buy another. It's terribly cruel of Mademoiselle, to give me a scent I couldn't live without once I'd tried it for the first time," she said, preening. She pressed the mouth of the bottle to the base of her palm and upended it, then brushed her wrists together in a brisk gesture that made her seem older than she was.

By that time, the festivities were coming to an end. We'd had our fill of Violet's birthday cake and the cordial Cook had given us, and while Violet's relationship with the rules was particular to her alone, the bedtime bell waited for no one. The lower years streamed from the playroom, chattering loudly. There were a few minutes of peace, then. The room was left to us upper-sixth girls: me, Dorothy, Alice, Marion, Sophie, and Evelyn. And then there was Violet, next to whom all others paled in comparison. She had always seemed more real, more vivid than the rest of us.

As Sophie and Marion bustled around, folding up torn paper and stacking Violet's gifts into a neat pile, I asked Violet if she wanted her hair plaited before bed. She did—she always did—so I stood behind her and combed through her long blonde curls with my fingers. I thought that when she had her hair plaited, she looked like Maid Marian from an old illustrated version of the stories of Robin Hood I'd had as a child. She had the kind of hair you only saw in illustrations and advertisements, anyway. We talked the whole time in a low murmur. I can't remember what we spoke about now, though I wish I could. I pitied all the other girls, none of whom had been granted the privilege of proximity and intimacy with Violet in that moment, which I prized above anything else in the world. When I'd finished, Violet let her eyes shiver shut for a moment, and then yawned. "Time for bed, I think."

Without needing to be asked, Evelyn scurried to pick up the presents, ready to carry them upstairs. We all filed out of the playroom with its wallpaper of pink and yellow flowers to make the chilly journey up to the top-year dormitory.

"You go on," Violet said. "Evelyn, could you be ever so decent and put those on my bed? I'm just going to say goodnight to Mademoiselle."

I followed the others as they made their way up the stairs. Mademoiselle was waiting for her on the landing, in the dim electric light; her smile on seeing Violet was radiant. Alice whispered something to Dot, who was too sweet-tempered for her own good and said, "Don't!" in a scandalised gasp. Evelyn shushed them both with the self-importance that came from having been given a task to do.

I wasn't looking when it happened. I was a few steps up the narrow staircase, the last in the queue, when I heard Violet say goodnight to Mademoiselle. I could see her in my mind's eye, stretching up on tiptoe to kiss Mademoiselle on the cheek. She'd started doing it last June, and I'd seen it every night since term began again. They had a sweet sort of intimacy that had begun to shape the run of our days: Violet slipping out of the dormitory early in the morning to wheedle Cook into making a cup of coffee for Mademoiselle, Mademoiselle trying and failing not to favour Violet when it came time to practise dictation in French class, Violet kissing her goodnight before traipsing back up to the dormitory to close off the evening.

The night of Violet's birthday moved differently.

I remember it now rather like a picture reel that's got stuck, moving at a snail's pace and then, all of a sudden, speeding up past the point of possible intervention. I can feel every second when something might've been done, as if anything we could've done would have saved Violet, saved any of the rest of them, erased from history everything that came after. I even prayed for it, once or twice and very privately, in the days after she died. What I understand now, though, is that nothing any of us could have done would've headed off disaster. It was inherent in the foundations of the place.

I can't put off the inevitable any longer. Violet kissed Mademoiselle goodnight. I imagine her frozen in amber, perfect for the last time. I heard her light footsteps, then a strange, aborted cry, then nothing, then a loud crack-and-thump. I whirled around and ran back down as fast as I could, but my feet moved slowly, clumsy in my slippers. By the time I reached the landing, I could hear my own scream in my ears, high and piercing, a sound I'd never heard before and one I didn't know that I was capable of making. Before long, everyone else had clustered around me. We hung for a while in that suspended moment when it was just us and Mademoiselle and Violet's broken body.

The layout of that part of the school was like this: if you went in via the side entrance (not the front, which faced onto a large, grand flight of stairs, and was used for formal occasions), you saw the coat racks, corridors that led to the dining hall and classrooms and so on, and a smaller flight of stairs that led up to a landing. From the landing, there was the playroom, a narrow corridor that led to our common room, and a poky little staircase that went to the upper-sixth dormitory, which used to be the housekeeper's quarters. The landing itself was a roomy space with a neat balcony, ringed by a carved wooden balustrade. We used to play Romeo and Juliet from that balcony as children.

Violet hadn't fallen down the stairs—this was reported incorrectly in the few newspaper articles that were published about the incident, all of which I have tracked down and kept throughout the intervening years. She fell over the balustrade itself, directly from the landing onto the floor below. It was easily a fifteen-foot drop.

Blood was seeping from the back of Violet's head through the plait I had made a few minutes before, turning her golden curls nearly black in the evening light. Her neck was at a bad angle, and the bone of one of her shins had broken through her skin like splintered wood. Her fist remained closed, hadn't had time to uncurl yet, and I could see a trickle of red coming from her hand where she had been clutching the bottle of scent. Shards of glass glinted on the floorboards and the perfume pooled around her. The smell of violets wafted upwards, so strong it felt like it might choke me, with a metallic smell underneath that I didn't want to think about. There could be no question that she was dead. Another heavy sound came from behind me and I turned to see Mademoiselle, slumped to the floor in a faint. That, although I didn't know it at the time, was the beginning of the end of Briarley.

TWO

WAIT UNTIL SHE'S COLD FIRST

ONE WEEK LATER

I spent the entirety of Violet's memorial service utterly furious. It seemed obvious to me what had happened; the only questions were how long it would take before I could tell the others, and whether or not they would believe me. I even longed to tell Sophie, and her head was chiefly filled with the contents of magazines and the desire for a permanent wave. Miss Lewis, the headmistress, had seated me in the front row of chapel, granting me that uneasy privilege by virtue of my status as Violet's closest friend and, I suppose, the first one to see the body. This set me apart from the other girls and meant that I sat alongside Violet's parents, who each looked wretched in their own way. When the priest climbed into the pulpit, Mrs. Kirsch reached out and clutched clumsily at my hand. It took a few tries before she managed to grasp it fully and pat it with the soft fingers of her other hand. This left my handkerchief balled up in my lap, sweaty and creased, and I saw hatchet-faced Miss Stone at the side of the room glare at it in remonstrance before remembering to be more sympathetic on account of the sad occasion.

Fond as I was of the rest of the place, the chapel at Briarley was a rather unimpressive affair, considering its role in the spiritual lives of forty-five young girls. It was an awkward addition around the side of the dining hall. The school had been converted from an old manor house, but the Briarley family hadn't been wealthy or—more likely—pious enough to fork out for a chapel themselves when the place was built back in the eighteenth century. Instead, that job was left to the benefactors who started the school, a haven for upwardly mobile young ladies to learn such delights as French, Comportment, and Maths if they insisted. In their haste to get things up and running they had thrown the chapel together with little care for aesthetics, and no subsequent administrator had been willing to lose access to it for long enough to improve it in any really significant way. As a result, it was plainly whitewashed, with no means of heating it to speak of (prayers on winter mornings were a misery), and housed a meagre twelve rows of severe wooden pews. The whole effect was rather Calvinist, even though Briarley was a good Church of England establishment. Of course, as the well-behaved girls we were, we did our level best to hold God in our hearts and remember that we would be rewarded for our faith, despite trying circumstances, in the hereafter.

All this to say, when Reverend Fish climbed wearily into his pulpit, the scene was nothing much to look at. The Reverend was a pallid, wet sort of man who came in from Briarley Village on important occasions, and was hardly the right one to deliver any kind of sermon about the vision that had been Violet Kirsch. I longed to climb up there myself and deliver a fire-and-brimstone tirade so scorchingly sincere that her murderer—who, I knew, was in the room—would have no choice but to break down and confess then and there. Instead, Fish droned on about how sad it was to lose one of our number so young, and a girl with such potential too.

Potential—potential!—Violet was everything. Even with her life ended she was more than the rest of us put together. The whole thing stuck in my throat. I had never been more angry in my life, brimming with the kind of fury that seems to fill every corner of your body until there is no room for anything else. That was, I suppose, a blessing. Even being at the memorial service felt like an insult; you'd have thought I might have been invited to my own best friend's real funeral, but evidently in their wisdom the Kirsches had decided otherwise, and I was relegated with the rest of the upper sixth to the Briarley-only memorial. I hated all of them in that moment. I hated Fish, I hated Mr. and Mrs. Kirsch for burying Violet so far away, I hated my own parents for not even coming, I hated the lower-third girl I could hear sobbing, I hated the entire upper school, and most of all, I hated Mademoiselle Lefèvre.

Mrs. Kirsch made a soft noise. She was still holding my hand, but my knuckles had gone white and my fingernails were digging into the meat of her thumb. I made a conscious effort to relax but found that this only invited tears, something I was absolutely unwilling to allow.

"And so," Fish intoned, "we will hold the memory of Violet Kirsch within our hearts and hope that she will hold us in hers, now that she is among the angels. Let us stand and sing the hymn from page thirteen of our hymn books, 'Abide with Me.' "

With that, Fish descended from the pulpit, knees creaking as loudly as the wood, and gestured to Mrs. Soane, who came from the village to play the organ. As she bashed out those first familiar chords, and we all stood up in hushed unison, I felt scooped-out inside. Mrs. Kirsch had finally withdrawn her hand, and against my better judgement, I found myself wishing she hadn't.

I was glad, at least, that we hadn't been given one of the

truly saccharine hymns. I don't think I could have borne it. I looked around, searching for signs on the girls' faces. There was Evelyn, one row behind me and smarting that I had been given the pew at the front, singing loudly as though Violet could hear from wherever she was to be impressed by it. Her parents hadn't come either; Evelyn's people were Presbyterians and only barely tolerated Briarley's decent Anglican outlook, and usually they avoided any events that might involve chapel. Sophie had a lock of hair twirled around her finger so hard the skin had blanched. Dorothy and Alice leaned against each other for support, Dot's heart-shaped face pink and blotchy and Alice's serious. I resolved to find Alice after everything had died down. She had a way of providing a rough sort of comfort that left no room for sentimentality. Marion looked cool as a cucumber, as she always did; it was hard to see what might break through her shell, if not this (though—of course—the events of the following months would prove sufficient).

We were all wearing our black clothes, hastily sent for from home, rather than the usual uniform, which did its best to smooth out class differences and personal idiosyncrasies. Most of us had suitably sober dresses bought for grandfathers' and great-aunts' funerals over the years. Mine was too short, having been last worn when I was fourteen, and it was tight at the waist because there hadn't been time to let it out in the period between Violet's fall and the memorial service at Briarley. In short it was insurmountably plain, bought at a good department store, but several years before, so it not only didn't fit but was also well out of fashion.

I glanced over at Mademoiselle as the hymn reached its close, only to see that she was silently weeping, her mouth wrenched open. Her chest heaved and her eyes looked painfully red. Good, I thought. Let her cry. I hadn't seen her since she visited me in the infirmary in those bewildering, blank first days after Violet's death. I'd been landed in San with hardly the strength to raise a hand, stuck there for nearly a week, until she'd arrived. With all that had happened during her visit—my realisation, ultimately, of what had happened to Violet—I could have gone without ever seeing her again. But I didn't intend to think about that, just then. I was inordinately grateful for the distraction when the organ blared out its last note, heavy and ugly, and we paired up like good schoolgirls to file out of chapel.

I hoped for a friendly face. Unfortunately, I had lined up alongside Evelyn, whose pinched expression was the picture of sombreness and whom I wouldn't describe as "friendly" in a thousand years, not even now, when I know her much better. We were directly behind Mr. and Mrs. Kirsch, and Evelyn looked as though she was itching to reach out to them, to clasp their hands and tell them what a lovely girl their daughter had been. They walked, stiff-backed, at an agonisingly slow pace.

I longed to take Alice aside, if I could tear her away from Dot, or even to sidle my way up to Marion and ask her what she really thought. Marion always seemed to know the right thing to do, and she had the sort of iron-fist-in-a-velvet-glove personality that swept the others along without their even noticing. Really, with Violet gone, Marion was our natural leader; if only I could persuade her out of her reticence and make her see the truth about Mademoiselle, she might be a useful ally. Surely she was clever enough to understand, once it was explained to her, that contrary to everyone's assumption (and the coroner's report), what had happened to Violet couldn't have been an accident. When I twisted around and tried to make eye contact, though, her gaze remained inscrutable. Whatever she thought I was trying to communicate, she wasn't having it. Alice noticed my efforts and gave me a sharp look. Exasperated, I turned forwards again and misjudged the distance between me and Mr. Kirsch, but Evelyn snatched at my shoulder before I was able to fall.

"What do you think you're doing?" she snapped.

I barely had time to stamp on her foot before Miss Stone, who was stalking alongside the queue of girls, hurried up to silence us, glaring through her pince-nez.

"Well?" Evelyn had the good sense to be quieter this time.

I silently cursed the fact that she had ended up being the first one I could speak to about Violet's murder. A poor sort of help she'd be. Since I'd got back from San, they'd all been handling me with the utmost care, at times going so far as to seem like they were avoiding me. It didn't seem fair, not when I'd worked it all out so neatly and I was longing to explain it to someone. Alice and Marion were the obvious first choices, being the most intelligent, and Dot at least would've been able to take a message back to Alice. Sophie didn't usually have the guts to snitch, although her brave stunt with the spiritualist book on Violet's birthday left me in some doubt. Evelyn, though—Evelyn had been gunning for prefect as long as she'd been at Briarley, had finally made it at the beginning of this year, and there was no telling what she'd do if something struck her the wrong way. I knew she'd eventually agree with me, that was never in question, but she was riskier than I liked. The thought of getting this far—the first step on the path towards justice for Violet—and being thwarted by a goody-two-shoes tattling to the nearest schoolmistress was almost too much to bear. Still—no choice now.

"Marshalling forces," I murmured. "I can't keep an eye on Mademoiselle alone."

Evelyn put on a look of utter shock. "You can't possibly—" she breathed. "Mademoiselle? But she *adored* Violet."

I sighed in relief. This little act meant that Evelyn just felt she needed to be wooed into agreeing with me.

"Look, you're one of the cleverest girls in the year. You must have noticed there was something strange about the night Violet died. One minute she was there, kissing Mademoiselle goodnight, and the next she had fallen off the landing and broken her—"

"Emily!" Evelyn's face had gone white. Even she couldn't have faked that. I resolved to soften up.

"What I mean to say is, Violet was better than anyone but Alice at Games, and much as Marion wouldn't like to admit it, she was the best dancer as well. I can't imagine her simply pitching—simply falling like that. It doesn't make any sense."

"I *have* wondered . . ."

"Well, exactly, and it seems odd that Mademoiselle hung back so far that night."

"Hung back?" Oh God, she was taking some persuading to accept the obvious.

"Didn't Violet usually kiss Mademoiselle goodnight in front of us?"

"Yes, it was always so lovely," Evelyn sighed.

"Doesn't it strike you as unusual that the night Violet—passed on—Mademoiselle wasn't waiting for her at the bottom of the staircase up to the dorms as usual but instead she was on the landing? And then she stayed there while we all filed past, so Violet stayed behind to say goodnight?"

"Emily, I don't see—"

"And isn't it strange that it was only because Violet hung back to kiss her that we didn't see what happened? You know, Evelyn," I said, laying it on thick in desperation, because the walk from chapel to the front entrance was only so long, "I turned back as soon as I heard that ghastly scream and even then I only saw—"

"Oh, don't," she begged.

"It was unbearable, being the first one to know that Violet was gone."

"But you *weren't* the first one!" Evelyn exclaimed, too loudly, gaining a warning look from Miss Stevens, the Games mistress, whose bark was worse than her bite; she was mostly interested in Alice, who intended to play cricket for England, just as soon as that became a possibility for girls. "It was *Mademoiselle* who would have seen her first."

I felt like a detective in one of those novels we were forbidden to keep in the dormitory, ensnaring their target in an inescapable narrative, the pieces clicking together neatly.

"Precisely," I whispered, as we filed up to the big oak doors that marked the entrance to Briarley. Evelyn looked shaken. Still, if she hadn't ratted my investigation out to Miss Stevens or whoever happened to be walking past by now, she never would. Now she was implicated as much as I was.

When you entered Briarley, you first passed through a rather imposing ironwork gate ("To keep the boys out," Marion once said, archly). You then followed a half-mile-long gravelled drive until you reached a small fountain adorned with a stooped winged figure, holding a jug across his privates that poured out water. The water was cold all year long, and we were absolutely forbidden to go anywhere near it. Just past him—"Adonis," as we called him once we got old enough for play-acting at attraction to feel like a thrill—you saw the house itself. I know now that as English country houses go, it was hardly the most imposing tableau of its kind, but the first day I arrived it felt unimaginably huge.

Briarley had been built in 1768 of striking red brick. Its eight chimneys stood up ramrod straight, and it had a few little gable roofs, under whose points the schoolmistresses had their quarters. Those of its original windows that still survived were made of that old-fashioned crown glass, lead-latticed and bullseye-shaped, which distorted the view outside into muddied swirls of tree and gate and grass. The whole effect was stately and well-ordered; Briarley Manor embodied a sturdy English pleasantness and ought to have stayed standing for centuries yet.

The Briarleys had been a wealthy family, captains of eighteenth-century merchant capitalism, who had made a living off the thriving sugar trade. For a time, their plantations stretched across large swathes of Barbados, and a sizeable proportion of British molasses had been attributable to Briarley sugarcane. Briarley Manor was supposed to be the jewel in their crown, but it wasn't long after they had built the place, intended to be their legacy forever, that the abolition of slavery in Barbados upended the family fortunes. They staggered on for some years, trying and failing to take advantage of various loopholes in the law, but eventually an irresponsible great-nephew frittered away the payment that the British government had given the Briarleys in compensation for manumitting their slaves, spending it not on sensible investments but instead on gambling and liquor. By the turn of the century the family had finally given up due to lack of funds and sold the place off. That was how Briarley School for Girls began.

The first time my parents had left me there at the beginning of term, without so much as a backward glance as they went down the gravel drive, I simply howled with grief. I can't have made a good first impression in that state, but Violet took pity on me anyway, petting me and soothing me even as my face got redder and my hair escaped from its pigtails with how hard I was crying. Even at eleven she looked like a picture of an angel on a chocolate box. She told me, as she stroked my hair, that I ought to feel grateful for the opportunity to make something new of myself. Before long, I learned to think of it not as exile but relief.

I loved the place. It had, after all, been my truest home for six years by that time. At best, my mother and father showed little interest in me, preferring me to be neither seen nor heard. At worst, my sullen face and lack of charm were displeasing enough to bear the brunt of harsh tongues and the back of a hairbrush, or sometimes my father's belt. No matter how hard I tried to be the model of a pleasant schoolgirl who spoke French prettily and could dance without kicking anyone in the ankles, it seemed to make no difference. If I'd had siblings, I suppose it might have been easier, unless—more likely—I became more of a disappointment by comparison. It wasn't as though I didn't get my fair share of whacks from a ruler or being sent to bed without supper from the schoolmistresses, but the difference was that it happened only when I had really done something to deserve it.

All in all, Briarley was an easy place for my parents to leave me and not think about me between September and Christmas, and, if I was lucky, I could stay there right through Easter until the summer holidays began in July. And, most importantly, there was Violet: Briarley, to me, meant Violet.

Walking up the curving steps that led to the grand front entrance had always felt like coming home, but today, as Evelyn and I followed Mr. and Mrs. Kirsch through the monumental front doors of Briarley, I found myself hesitant to step over the threshold for the first time in years.

The school was strangely quiet, strangely empty. We couldn't whisper anything in there—sound carried like you wouldn't believe—so we descended into silence as we walked to the dining hall. There, I could at least take someone off to the side if I needed a moment of privacy. Which I did, in abundance.

In the dining hall, the usual table settings were gone, in favour of two trestle tables, one laden with cream buns and one with tea. Miss Lewis began to speak, her voice resounding through the hall with its comforting boom. She had a way of filling a space so entirely that there was no room for uncertainty.

"Thank you, everyone, for being here," she said. "It is a painful occasion for us all, but I'm certain that our Violet would have been glad to see the whole school come together to mourn her."

"Yes, thank you," Mrs. Kirsch added, in a timid, wavering tone. "It means more to us than we can say to have you all here."

I noticed at this point that the lower school had been shepherded out somewhere along the way, culling the school's population down to twenty or so. Fifteen and older only for post-memorial socialising, I suppose.

"Please let's celebrate Violet's life and forget for a moment the awful—the—" Mrs. Kirsch pressed her handkerchief to her lips and turned away.

Mr. Kirsch didn't step in; he was too busy staring into the middle distance. Uncharitably, I wondered whether he was thinking about how his grief would affect the running of his many factories; he had, under normal circumstances, a businessman's self-importance.

I decided to take pity on Violet's mother myself and made my way to the refreshments table, starting a general movement that broke the silence and allowed Mrs. Kirsch to retreat to the corner, alone.

Marion came over and looked me up and down. I wished she'd stop examining me as though I was liable to collapse; she was the eldest of four sisters and had a way of getting right to the heart of what was bothering you. I didn't want to be peered at just then.

"How are you feeling?"

"Right as rain." I thought briefly about broaching the topic of Mademoiselle, but something in me balked at the thought that she wouldn't agree.

"I'm sure you are," she said, with the tone of someone who wasn't sure in the least. "But if you need anything, you can ask me. In fact I'd rather you did than—"

"Really, Marion, I don't need babying." She gave me a look under which anyone less headstrong than I would have withered. I imagine she was referring to the days I had spent in San the week before, which I thought was awfully unfair of her. I'd told her, when I returned to the dormitory, that I didn't want to talk about it, and anyway no one should be expected to be at their best under the direst of circumstances. "I'm better than ever," I said, and without much ceremony went to find Alice and Dorothy, who were usually in one another's company.

They were standing across the room, far enough away that as I approached them, I no longer had to feel the concern radiating from Marion. They made an odd pair: Alice red-headed and freckled and Dot with her dark curling hair and skin the colour of milk and roses, Alice tomboyish and Dot endearingly pretty, Alice stocky and Dot plump.

"Alice, can I speak to you for a moment? Nothing against you, Dot, only you might rather not."

"If this is about Violet I think you ought to wait until she's cold first—sorry, Dot," Alice said, looking over at Dot, whose lower lip had begun to quiver.

"Look, the longer we leave it the worse it gets. Sunlight's the best disinfectant and all."

"Doesn't need any disinfecting; I disagree with your entire proposition. And yes, I did hear you and Evelyn, which means you were far less quiet than you thought you were, particularly being right behind the Kirsches. Not on, Emily."

I couldn't take that one lying down. "If someone murdered their beloved only daughter, don't you think they'd want to know? Don't you think they'd want someone to do something about it?"

"Oh don't, don't," Dot wailed, forcing Alice and me to look at her—we'd been arguing quite over her head. "It's horrible, she's dead and I don't want to think about it any more!"

"Don't be a child, Dot, it doesn't do us any good to stick our heads under the covers and pretend it isn't real," I said.

"Don't bully her," Alice said bluntly. "I won't have it. You can try and persuade me later—we'll talk after lights-out. And leave Dot out of it." She slung an arm around Dot's shoulders and looked away from me, making it obvious the conversation was good and over. I scuffed the heel of my shoe in frustration and went to get a cucumber sandwich.

It felt a bit awful, eating. I mean it would anyway, because I had felt sick to my stomach every day since Violet's death—but more than that, cucumber sandwiches had been a favourite of hers. I'd teased her about it once. For someone whom I had always considered consummately cultured (she knew about scent, and fashion, and had been to the opera) she ate like a child. She liked bland, plain foods best. More than once, when Violet had a toothache, I'd trooped down to Cook to persuade her to spare some of the rusks being given to homesick lower thirds.

All around the dining hall, people moved into clusters. I tried to divine which of them felt as miserable over Violet as I did. As if to spite me, there was a loud cry from across the room. When I looked over, Mademoiselle had slumped over the mantel, her slender body bent like a reed. Her hair had escaped its chignon and her skin looked sallow and ugly against her black serge mourning dress. I only wished I could've derived more satisfaction from the sight. Instead, it felt like watching her spit on Violet's fresh grave. Thinking about all the times I had admired Mademoiselle's slight, shy smile and old-fashioned way of dressing made me feel unwell. So, too, did the memory of her only weeks before, asking in what I now assumed was a well-practised girlish tone how long Violet and I had been friends and did I think she might enjoy being taken for tea in the village one Saturday.

Fräulein Weingarten, the German mistress, was always a soft touch; she bustled over to lay a gentle hand on Mademoiselle's back. But Mademoiselle wrenched violently away. You could see her streaming eyes and scarlet cheeks from across the room, and her fingers were bone white where they clutched the corner of the fireplace.

"Hush, hush, Élodie," I heard Fräulein Weingarten say. (Isn't it funny how she was Fräulein Weingarten to us, referred to formally even though I knew she was the favourite teacher of at least a few of the girls, and yet Mademoiselle was always that—just Mademoiselle—despite everything?) "Think of the girls."

I couldn't make out Mademoiselle's response, just garbled, distressed sounds, and then Fräulein Weingarten, all dull blonde hair and caring demeanour, was draping a shawl over her shoulders and hurrying her out of the dining hall. I hadn't a jot of sympathy for her. If she wanted sympathy she should've left Violet well enough alone.

Evelyn sidled over to me. "It does seem a bit suspicious, how Mademoiselle's acting," she admitted, winding the curly end of her plait around a finger.

"Doesn't it just," I said, seething.

"Do you think," Evelyn said, as though she wasn't sure I'd like what she was about to say, "do you think there was something wrong with Violet and Mademoiselle?"

"There was nothing wrong with Violet," I responded, perhaps a little too sharply. "Violet was sweet and innocent. She cared for Mademoiselle a great deal. Mademoiselle, on the other hand . . ." Evelyn looked at me in that way she had where her big eyes quickly narrowed, like a hawk lighting on its prey.

"Mademoiselle on the other hand, what?"

"Well—"

THREE

THICK AS THIEVES

Offending Evelyn's delicate sensibilities proved worthwhile. It took some explaining; Evelyn hadn't been paying as close attention to lurid accounts of suicides and court cases in the papers as I had. But she was a bright enough girl despite her faults, and she did work it out eventually. I suppose the Calvinist streak in her upbringing helped. Her eyes grew round again as I spoke.

"And you think Mademoiselle might be one of *those*? Trying to—corrupt Violet, or whatever it is you said they do?"

"As far as I'm concerned it's the only explanation. They're criminals, you know, deviants; it'd hardly be any difference at all for Mademoiselle to . . ." I trailed off. "Lose her temper, or become jealous." Evelyn worried at a hangnail for a while, and we lapsed into silence standing by the platter of cream buns.

"And so you think Mademoiselle pushed Violet?"

"It can drive you mad," I told her, trying to sound matter-of-fact. "It is madness. Violet had a pash for Mademoiselle, something completely normal that eons of perfectly healthy schoolgirls have had. Mademoiselle is ill."

At that, Evelyn's expression melted a bit; I caught a distinct wobble of the chin. *She* had had a pash for Violet, that much was obvious: following her about, turning down her bed without being asked, most crucially the general lack of reciprocation. Nothing wrong with a pash—but at least Violet had cared for me back.

"Do you think any of the other schoolmistresses know? You don't suppose they're—they're covering it up because of the scandal?"

I have to admit, that floored me. I suppose I'd felt so dreadful over my bone-deep instinctive knowledge that Mademoiselle had killed Violet that I hadn't thought much about any of the rest of it. It had felt so important I persuade the others that I hadn't got much further.

"It'd be awfully cold of them," I said, playing for time.

"Well, if these people are as sick as you say . . ." Evelyn trailed off.

I didn't answer. She fiddled with the buttons on one of her cuffs. I didn't like her, and never had. Evelyn was incorrigibly sanctimonious. Her hand was always the first to shoot up in class and the way she wore her curly red hair in plaits seemed such a cheap imitation of the way Violet wore hers that I had been incensed about it long before Violet's death. She was a hopeless try-hard, and I always felt faintly embarrassed to look at her. But now, Evelyn and I were comrades, the only ones in on the plot, forced together by circumstance. Almost involuntarily, I leaned towards her. Her pointy little shoulder connected with mine, and she rested her weight on me for a moment.

"I wish she weren't dead," Evelyn said.

"Me too," I replied, because that was all there was to say.

We stood like that and watched the room for a while. Fräulein Weingarten had returned at some point and was shifting about disconsolately, waiting for someone to need looking after.

Miss Lewis presided over the occasion as she presided over every room she entered. She was a big woman, with tightly pinned hair. Violet, in an unkinder moment, had once described her as "mannish." It wouldn't do for a headmistress to be fashionable, anyway. She held a certain sort of power in her mass and crisp starched shirts.

Then a movement caught my eye at another corner of the room. Alice and Dot had retreated there, Dot all red and puffy and Alice looking stone-faced. It was the motion of Alice putting her arm around Dot's shoulders that I had noticed. It was a familiar gesture, sweetly protective. Before I could look away, though, I saw Alice—my eyes fixed on her as though they were prised open and held to the spot—lean down and kiss the corner of Dot's mouth. They drew their heads together and murmured to one another, and I felt a queer tingling sensation in my hands, as though all the blood had rushed out of them at once. It was over in a second, and then they were their ordinary selves again. I looked over at Evelyn, but she was absorbed in the little buttons at her cuff, doing them up and unbuttoning them all over again. She didn't seem to have seen a thing and I detested her for it. It was as though something dense and hard had grown in the pit of my stomach, a ball of sickness that threatened to spread and spread, and without anyone else to see, I had absolutely nowhere to put it.

It might not mean anything, I told myself, closing my eyes and concentrating. I was thinking too hard about such things; I had allowed Mademoiselle's behaviour to affect how I viewed the activities of innocent schoolgirls who had done nothing wrong. It was a coincidence: I was sure I'd seen a friendly kiss between them before, in among Alice fetching things for Dot or lifting her up in her strong arms or Dot resting her head on Alice's shoulder when she was tired. I was only thinking about it like this because I'd spent the past few days steeped in thought about what happened when a pash went too far and became something else entirely.

I had to do my level best to forget what I had seen, and hope to God that whatever it was wouldn't get in the way of their believing me about Mademoiselle. Lying behind that hope, coiled, was the terror that it was some sort of infection spreading among us, changing us one by one; but that I pushed aside as unproductive. I couldn't allow myself to get caught up and lose sight of my ultimate, righteous goal of getting some kind of justice for Violet.

By the time I looked up again, the room had thinned out somewhat. It's funny; I suppose if you had asked me at the beginning of that term what the relationships were like among the girls of the top year at Briarley, I should have said something like: pleasant, collegial, some of us thick as thieves. Aside from Violet, whom I had always assumed would be the mainstay of my existence for as long as we both lived, I thought of the others as perfectly good company with whom to spend seven years of cricket matches and school dinners. I didn't think I was much like any of them: I wanted to go to university, but not with Marion's single-minded zeal, which had driven her to persuade her parents to let her go to school rather than be taught by her sisters' governess. Nor had I much interest in babies, unlike Sophie or Dot; mostly I thought it would be nice to find a way out of my family's house, for which I would need some kind of occupation. With Violet gone, my understanding of the future had been replaced with something like a howling black void. But I liked Alice very much, and I thought Marion had decent odds of becoming a lady authoress or something equally impressive if she could avoid her parents' attempts to marry her off, and while I had less time for Sophie and Dot, they were sweet enough. And, of course, there was Evelyn, but the less said of how I felt about her, the better.

What I'm getting at is that before Violet died, I was unaware of how shallow and schoolgirlish our feelings towards one another had been. I can't say whether I would choose to give back what we became to each other, if I could. The point is moot, anyway. What happened to Briarley is a fixed point in our past.

I get ahead of myself. Back in the dining hall, just when I had almost managed to push what I had seen between Dot and Alice out of my mind, Miss Stone laid a hand on my shoulder and I flinched violently.

"Emily, dear," she said, the endearment sounding awkward and uncomfortable coming out of her thin mouth. I don't think I'd heard her use my Christian name in years. "You look terribly pale. Ought you go to the infirmary?"

I knew she meant it as an instruction rather than the gentle suggestion it might've been. I did consider it—after her collapse earlier, there was a decent chance that Mademoiselle would be in there, giving me a prime opportunity to confront her alone. But that hard feeling in my belly, provoked by what I'd just seen, had left me cowardly. If she could have pushed Violet over the balcony in the coldest of blood, as we all stood scant metres away, what could she be capable of alone, in the chilly solitude of San, after being confronted with what she'd done and—that settled it.

"I'm all right, Miss Stone," I said, choosing to interpret her overture as a question after all.

"Are you quite sure?" she asked, her eyes narrowing. She was a woman accustomed to getting what she wanted.

"Yes, thank you," I said firmly. "I'm sure I only need a strong cup of tea and I'll be good as new."

Miss Stone sighed. She looked weary, and I considered for

the first time that the schoolmistresses themselves had lost Violet, too.

"All right," she said. "Hart, could you be so kind as to fetch Locke a cup of tea?"

Evelyn, ever a teacher's pet, scurried off to the tea table immediately. A curl had come out of her plaits and bounced as she ran; I vaguely thought of pulling it, like a schoolyard bully.

This left me and Miss Stone standing together in discomfiting silence. The thing about an awful tragedy happening at the age of seventeen or eighteen was, it seemed, that you hovered halfway between childhood and adulthood and no one was quite sure what to do with you. Did they stroke your hair and coddle you? Did they fail to meet your eyes and tell you to buck up? Miss Stone had been rapping me across the knuckles for being a duffer at trigonometry since I was a babe of eleven and now here we were, neither of us sure what to say. As if to illustrate the point, she cleared her throat and adjusted her pince-nez in a definitive manner.

"If you're certain—"

"I'm quite certain, Miss Stone, thank you."

Without another word she strode off to confer with Miss Lewis. I hoped she wouldn't talk about me.

Evelyn was taking her sweet time with that cup of tea. I had to admit that I was feeling more than a little wobbly, and it would've done me a world of good. Something about being sympathised with always set me off. Mrs. Kirsch was leaning heavily against Miss Stevens, who looked distinctly uncomfortable but who was at least a sturdy support, given that she was nearly six feet tall. Judging by the way she had crushed my hand in chapel, Mrs. Kirsch was not holding up well at all, and even from a distance I could see that her handkerchief, clutched in her fist, was pickled with tears.

Really—where was her husband? I spotted Mr. Kirsch making a circuit of the room, heading towards Evelyn, who stood at the tea table measuring out what must have been history's most specific quantity of milk.

From this distance I could see the whole of her black dress, a rather childish number with a big frilled collar. The dress hovered at her knees, which would ordinarily have been frowned upon but none of us could have expected to need a funeral dress, and we were still at the age when you could shoot up and gain an inch in a month or two. The backs of Evelyn's white knees where her socks didn't quite reach looked strangely vulnerable.

Mr. Kirsch was next to her now, bending to match her height. He was an austere man, never as tall in person as you remembered him being. I couldn't hear what he was saying but he had put his mouth right up to Evelyn's ear. Her back stiffened, rigid as a ruler, like you could snap her in half. His hand slid around her waist for a second before withdrawing; she stood utterly still. Her hand was resting on the milk jug. A moment later, the jug upset, flooding the table with milk.

As soon as the teachers heard the *thunk* of the falling jug, a few of them rushed over to try to limit the damage done. Miss Stevens detached herself from Mrs. Kirsch, scooping up the teapot and sugar bowl so that Miss Stone could ball up the soaked tablecloth and bustle it off to the laundry. Mrs. Kirsch looked on, and Marion, level-headed in a crisis, walked over to her to place a hand on her shoulder.

All the while Evelyn just stood there.

Somewhere in the hubbub, Mr. Kirsch had moved away from her, and was watching the scene as though he hadn't been a participant in it at all. Evelyn still hadn't moved an inch. She was in everyone's way. I held my breath, wishing she would do something, anything; I didn't think I could relax until she moved. After several long seconds of stillness, she came to herself and walked off.

I looked down and noticed that I was digging the heel of my left shoe into my right ankle. My stocking had laddered there. All of a sudden I felt the sting where I'd scraped off a layer of skin and nearly lost my balance. I still didn't go to her, which I feel ashamed of now. What you must understand is that, whatever I thought of myself, I was hardly more than a child. I didn't know, as I do now, the many ways it is possible to be hurt. So I let Evelyn leave the hall at her steady, dreamlike pace and did nothing.

The rest of the afternoon went off without a hitch. I gathered my courage and said something vague and kind to Mrs. Kirsch, and avoided making eye contact with Mr. Kirsch. I forced down a cucumber sandwich and spread clotted cream and jam on a scone for Dot as a sort of peace offering for Alice. Evelyn was nowhere to be found, and Mademoiselle never returned to the hall.

When all had been said that could be said and the Kirsches went home, we were left with the truth of it, which was that the best of us, the golden girl of the upper sixth, was gone. We filed out in silence, our steps faltering as we crossed the landing where she had fallen.

By the time the dinner bell rang at six o'clock, we were in the dormitory, absorbed in whatever task allowed us to avoid making conversation. Alice was scrubbing at her tennis racquet with a violence it couldn't have deserved; Evelyn had a book and was turning the pages, though I suspected she wasn't taking much in. I chanced a glance at the others, but no one stirred.

Schools like Briarley thrive on orderliness, routine. The

bells governed our lives, and we responded to them on instinct. Morning bell told us to splash cold water on our faces and brush out our hair. Breakfast bell summoned us down for the first meal of the day. The bells between lessons allotted us five minutes to make our way from the airless room where History lessons were given to the small gymnasium with its sprung floor, or to the games field. Then there was the lunch bell, the end of day bell, after which we had an hour to ourselves, and the dinner bell. Finally the evening bell sent us to bed.

I had been at Briarley for six years, and I had learned to respond to these bells as a soldier does to the whistle. From time to time, when at home for the holidays, I found myself waiting for the bell to call me down from bed in the mornings, lying uncomfortably among the covers with an aching sense of being lost. This isn't to say that we didn't groan and fling our pillows over our heads, or dawdle more than we ought on the way to classes. To ignore them, though—to ignore the bells altogether—was anathema.

The day of Violet's memorial service, I didn't even feel the itch under my skin, the longing to take action, that I usually felt when the bell rang. We could hear the thunderous footsteps of a herd of lower-school girls making their way through the corridors, but we simply sat on our narrow beds and carried on with whatever meaningless things we were doing. Dot's needlepoint, Sophie's magazine, Marion's mending. Strangest of all was that at no point did any of the teachers storm up the steps to punish us for failing to appear. Our decision was taken in silent unison and accepted across the board.

Twilight turned to dusk, and then full dark, and still none of us had said a word. Eventually, at nine-thirty, the evening bell rang, and this time we did respond, traipsing out across the chilly hallway to the bathroom.

Fiddling with her tooth-brush, Alice spoke first. "God, but that was awful," she said, her voice strong and clear. I loved her for it.

"Thoroughly," I replied, relieved that someone had come out and said it. "Miss Stone being all sweet and gentle—it can't be countenanced."

Sophie broke in. "And Fish's dreadful sermon!"

"Oh, don't remind me," Marion groaned. "I thought it would never *end*. And we thought he was bad enough at Lent."

Alice grinned through a mouthful of tooth-powder.

"Stop it, stop it, you look absolutely frightful," Marion said, laughing. "I thought this was a school for well-bred young ladies!"

"If you judged on Alice alone you'd consider it a zoo for wild animals," I said, and Alice made a face at me.

"Maybe we should do something ourselves," Sophie said. "For Violet, I mean, to celebrate her. We could do it tonight, even. What if we had a séance?"

Half a dozen heads snapped towards her. It had come out of nowhere, but her twisting hands told me she had been thinking about it for some time.

"I kept the book I gave Violet, it's got instructions and everything. We could, we could talk to the spirits, or to Violet, or—" And here she stopped, because no one else was helping her.

"No," Evelyn said, voice strained. She had blanched so much her freckles stood out like pinpricks. "No, we can't do that—"

Marion saved us. "A midnight feast," she said. "We'll have a midnight feast."

Violet had been the best of any of us at preparing a midnight feast, every schoolgirl's favourite pastime. It helped to have her on board. The teachers were so inclined to be lenient with her that if they caught her wrapping up breakfast scones in her handkerchief they were more likely than not to look the other way. She always had the most extravagant sweets, too: tooth-rotting delicacies like piles of rose-flavoured Turkish delight so covered in icing sugar that it clotted at the back of your throat, or shortbreads stamped with the Scottish thistle. These she kept under a floorboard near her bed and brought out only for special occasions, like birthdays or broken hearts. Violet could eat mountains of chocolate in one go and never have to worry about her figure. I envied her this, although I could never bring myself to tell her so. Anything like that tended to result in her saying something breezy about playing tennis till she dropped and how she'd really rather be like one of those elegant *Vogue* fashion plates who looked almost like a boy. "Or like you, Emily," she once said, which was so outrageously silly that I couldn't say a thing in response.

We set about making the feast. Marion took things in hand, as the oldest and by far the most authoritative. Her birthday had come at the very beginning of September, the first by several weeks. She produced a butter knife from her trunk and used it to pry up the loose floorboard where Violet kept her treasures. It was somewhat depleted in there; our beginning-of-term feast had been lavish. Violet hadn't had time, before she died, to hide any of the sweets she'd been given for her birthday. Ultimately it had all gone back to her parents, never to be seen again. But Marion unearthed some cold tongue and a tin of chocolate-flavoured Horlicks, which was bounty enough. We sent Dot down to the kitchen to find milk and apples and bread, as the member of the party, in Violet's absence, least likely to be punished for sneaking downstairs at night. She put on her gym shoes first, the usual way of muffling one's footsteps down a series of creaking staircases.

By the time Dot returned, Sophie had spread out one of the

camp blankets that lay on our beds onto the floor. Alice lit the kerosene lamp we were absolutely forbidden to use with a match she had squirrelled away for lighting cigarettes with when we were unchaperoned in town (our lack of access to cigarettes in the first place didn't deter her from keeping the matches around, just in case). The lamp, placed riskily in the middle of the blanket, threw a circle of warmth about us and cast the corners of the room into pitch darkness.

When we were younger, those dark corners took on a spooky quality, and it was a dare among the lower years to run to the side on quiet tiptoe, touch the wall, and run back. But that evening they surrounded us in a way that felt almost cosy, pressing in until all that existed was the circle of the six of us, huddled together against the oncoming October chill.

Marion was a genius to think of a feast; even Evelyn looked close to contented, bathed in warm light. She had draped a quilt over her shoulders and the effect made her look smaller than usual—more like a child. In the last year or so some of us had started to look more like women than girls. Marion, certainly, had the willowy figure and the self-possession that were so in fashion in those days. Evelyn had been caught rather in the middle. She was all elbows and the combination of her big eyes and pointy nose gave the impression of a cygnet midway through turning into a swan. I hoped, privately, that she stayed ungainly and awkward forever.

I was as plain as I had always been, but Violet had assured me that once I'd managed to persuade my mother to let me shingle my hair I'd look the picture of modern womanhood. I protested that nothing on earth could drive my mother to countenance the loss of what she insisted was my crowning glory, my only real claim to femininity—in reality nothing more than a dull heap of dark brown snarls. This only spurred Violet on until she'd even offered to do it herself, and brandished her sewing-scissors with a delighted grin. I thought now, looking around at the others, that I didn't know how to be pretty, and without Violet I wasn't sure how I could possibly learn.

Sophie poured us mugs of milk and stirred in spoonfuls of Horlicks; it wasn't hot, but it would do.

"To Violet," Marion said softly, raising her mug in a toast.

"To Violet."

"Is the milk off?" Dot said, interrupting what had felt like an important moment.

It was just like her to be a baby about it, but in the interest of keeping the peace I took a sip and considered. It did taste as though it was edging towards sour. Funny, I thought, in the vague and abstracted way that the most important thoughts sneak into your consciousness: funny, considering that Evelyn had upset the jug that had sat on the table all day, so this one had been in the cold larder since the milkman had delivered it.

"It won't be good by tomorrow but it won't make you ill, either," I told her, and dropped another spoonful of Horlicks into her mug to console her.

"I suppose someone ought to say a few words about Violet," Marion said.

Evelyn's reedy voice piped up. "She was brilliant and very beautiful. She was the best at everything."

"Emily thinks she was murdered," Dot said.

A chill settled over us.

"Let's not discuss that now," Alice said, giving me a significant look as if to say *Look what you've done.*

"I think Mademoiselle had something to do with her death. It makes no sense otherwise, none at all—you said it yourself, Evelyn, she was the best of us, when did you ever see her trip over or do something clumsy? And she fell over that balustrade like it just didn't exist. Mademoiselle obsessed over Violet, we all saw it." I was making my move whether I ought to or not, and once I'd started, I felt as though I couldn't stop. It was pouring off my tongue and I tasted bile. "And—Mademoiselle said something to me. When I was in San. Look, I just know it was her."

I did stop there, because I didn't want to tell them what had happened, how she had appeared by my bedside like a ministering angel missing only her halo, the things she had implied. Things about Violet—about herself—about me.

Sophie looked aghast. "We all thought it was an accident, a really horrible accident—it sounds so awful."

"It is awful! Violet was special. I don't know how else to put it. She had *it*, whatever you want to call it. Charisma, charm. Her being gone is all wrong."

"So you're planning to pin Violet's death on Mademoiselle, to what, to stop yourself having to face up to her being gone?" Alice said, staring across the blanket towards me. Her voice was rising above the customary whisper.

"Settle down," said Marion. Her tone was final. "I'm not having us all given lines to write because you can't control your temper—either of you. Be quiet and eat up."

She opened the tin of tongue as if to punctuate the conversation. I decided to go with my better judgement and shut up when she told me to, although I didn't like it. My heart was going like a rabbit's. Taking the hunks of bread that Sophie held out, Marion laid the cuts of tongue across them. They glistened wetly in the lamplight. In a gesture that tugged at the heartstrings, she took the knife and scraped the gelatine off the tongue for Dot.

Dot spilled the tea towel filled with apples onto the floor. The apples were the first of the season. If you hunted around the small orchard of apple trees behind Briarley you could sometimes snag slightly wrinkled discards, which were nonetheless delicious. These, however, were perfect, leftovers from the fruit bowl at Violet's memorial.

I raised an apple to my mouth and bit into it. The skin was taut and red but once I'd broken through I felt my teeth sinking into soft, mealy flesh—too sweet, with a bitter edge—and then something moved inside my mouth, crawling against my tongue. Whatever it was, it was alive. My whole body roiled, throat working, tongue curling in on itself as my stomach revolted. I gagged, spitting a mouthful of brown mush into my hand.

The others recoiled; I must have looked possessed. But there in my palm, in among the rancid, chewed-up apple, was a frantically wriggling white maggot. It shone against the apple flesh, oddly clean as though it had never come from inside my mouth. I flung it off my hand in one motion and fled to vomit in the corner.

When I crawled back, the taste of sick burning my throat, the cluster of girls looked back at me with saucer-wide eyes.

"What *was* that?" hissed Evelyn.

I could hardly speak, could hardly so much as take a breath without getting a shocky, tight feeling in my chest. "There was something—in the apple—" I said weakly, pointing at where it had fallen onto the blanket in my scramble.

We crowded around the apple. It looked utterly normal from the outside: red, smallish, shiny. But the inside was a mess of larvae, all alive and flailing, set into deep brown flesh that was so soft as to be almost syrupy. With the skin broken, the smell of fermenting fruit had begun to permeate the room.

Marion grimly picked up the knife she had used to scrape the gelatine off the tongue and cut another apple in half. It was exactly the same. Stuck in the aspic on the knife was a maggot, severed in half but wriggling feebly; this proved too much for me and I had to run off and be sick again.

"I swear I looked to make sure they were all right," Dot whispered, aghast. "I wouldn't have brought them if they looked bad, I promise."

"You didn't do a thing wrong," Marion said. "Emily couldn't tell until she'd bitten into one, could she? And the skin looks perfect on the one I cut open."

I'd never seen a rotten apple look like that before, whole and shiny.

"I'm trying the rest of them," Alice said. With a single-minded zeal, she cut each of the apples in half, revealing that every single one, regardless of how polished and delicious it looked on the outside, had rotted completely. I couldn't for the life of me understand how they didn't give under our fingers. The whole thing made no sense.

By the time Alice finished, the camp blanket was crawling with maggots. We all backed away, even Marion, who had nerves of steel. The scene looked like one of those Vanitas paintings warning the viewer of the risks of youthful hubris: worms, spoiled fruit, the warm glow of the lamplight.

"Well," said Alice, baffled. "Can't understand how this happened. The milk wasn't exactly fresh—maybe there's something wrong with the larder."

"What do we do with it all?" said Sophie, her voice rising into a wail.

"We can't *tell* anyone," Evelyn said hollowly. "We weren't supposed to be out of bed, we weren't supposed to steal, we'll—"

"I'll tip it into the incinerator and burn it," I said. I didn't want it to sit there festering any longer if I could help it.

Sophie looked at me, uncertain. "The incinerator's all the way down in the kitchen, Emily, are you sure?"

"I'm not going down there again," Dot announced, crossing her arms in front of her chest.

"No one asked you to," I snapped. "I'll go, I'm not a *child*."

I regretted it instantly. Both Dot and Sophie shrank back a little, and Marion glared at me. It was too late to take it back, so I gathered up the camp blanket, trying not to touch any of its contents. Without a word, I crept out of the dormitory and carried the squirming bundle of rotting apples and maggots down the servants' stairs.

When I returned, everyone else was speaking quietly, huddled together around the lamp. I didn't want to deal with them and to be entirely honest I didn't want to deal with myself either, so instead I crawled into bed and pulled the covers over my head. It took me what felt like forever to fall asleep, and when I did I dreamed of Violet: her golden hair curling over her pink-shell ears, the amethyst ring she often wore on her little finger, the smell of her perfume—rancid now, and rotting—wafting upwards from where the bottle had shattered on the floor.

FOUR

GOD KNOWS THIS PLACE NEEDS A LAUGH

The next morning I dressed hastily, on account of the sudden October chill that ran through the air. Our winter uniform consisted of a grey serge pinafore with a severe square neck and a belt at the waist, worn over a blouse and neatly knotted tie. Whenever we left the school, the whole ensemble was covered by a long and rather shapeless blazer that had the school's crest embroidered over the breast pocket. I always felt surpassingly awkward in that blazer, and once Violet had told me in a kind voice that it wasn't my fault it made me look a bit lumpy. "Miss Lewis chose them to stop us getting *looked at* in the village," she had said, gleefully. "Even Marion can't carry it off!"

That morning, my tie was akimbo and I hadn't done much of anything with my hair. Evelyn came up to me right before we headed downstairs, managing somehow to look entirely put together.

"I'll do your plait for you, if you want," she said. I couldn't think of anything that sounded less appealing, and moreover I couldn't think of why she'd offer, which was faintly disturbing. Her devotion to Violet was an exception: with anyone else, if she did something for you, you could expect her to cash in the favour sooner rather than later.

"I don't need help, thanks. I assume we've got a little longer before Miss Stone returns to the warpath so you can leave it be for now."

I said it as sweetly as I could manage, but I suppose it wasn't the nicest tone in history, because Evelyn sniffed and said, "Fine" very loudly and turned on her heel. The thought that this was exactly what I had done for Violet on innumerable occasions never even occurred to me. I was so indistinct, so unlovely in my own eyes, that the comparison would have felt laughable. And in any case, I didn't care to be fussed over.

Marion sidled by me on the stairs and said, a little coolly, "I think you ought to be a tad more generous with the others."

"Generous how?"

"They all know how much you cared about Violet. We're not trying to patronise you, we're trying to help."

"I just—" I felt myself about to say something unpleasant and stopped, with effort. "I don't need anyone feeling sorry for me. It doesn't—I don't—"

"I know, I know. But you can't snap at Dot like you did last night and expect her to understand. She's upset enough as it is and she thinks she's helping."

"Look, I'll try," I told her. "Evelyn, though—"

"Oh, well, Evelyn," she said, in a way that told me it was a full sentence.

"Well, Evelyn," I said, trying not to raise my voice. "She's being so unbelievably . . ."

"Like herself? We can't fault her for that, either."

"A leopard can't change its *annoying* spots," I muttered.

"Quite," Marion said, and we went down the next few stairs in silence. Then she took a breath, and paused. It was a rare hesitation on her part; she was usually so sure of herself. "I know you and Evelyn were vying for Violet's friendship," she said, carefully. "And that it's left a sort of vacuum now that she's gone. I think it might be worth considering that Evelyn's going through the same thing that you are, but she hasn't got the . . ." Marion searched for the right thing to say, again. "She isn't as strong as you are. It's difficult for her."

Now, I *didn't* scream that it was difficult for me too, that I felt hollow and brittle every waking moment and that the only thing keeping me upright was the thought of proving Mademoiselle's guilt. Nor did I remind her that if there had been any competition between me and Evelyn, I had won. For my restraint I thought I should receive some kind of prize, a lovely cup with my name engraved at the bottom. Instead, I made a sort of neutral noise and kept on walking.

"Listen, I'm not saying you need to be her best friend, or even to like her particularly. But for all our sakes, go a bit easier on her. The last thing we need is for you two to have some dreadful row that tears the whole group apart, because it's bad enough as it is."

"Did Dot put you up to that?" I said, as soft as I could make it. Dot could never stand when any of us were fighting.

"She didn't," Marion said, "but even if she had I would've agreed with her. Think about it, will you?"

"I'll think about it," I allowed, and she reached out a hand to clasp at my shoulder for a second, before we stepped into the dining hall.

Evidently we had taken longer than usual to get ready; by the time we got downstairs everyone was already there, and some of the youngest ones had started on their porridge. Our table sat empty.

The dining room was organised by year. Long oak tables

were set out like church pews, each presided over by one of the schoolmistresses, on hand to coax lower fourths into eating their vegetables and to chide us for putting our elbows on the table. Ours, by virtue of our age and supposed maturity, was the only one without a teacher at the head. The rest of the mistresses—barring Mademoiselle, who was nowhere to be seen—sat at high table, so called in the Cantabrigian fashion, to grant the whole endeavour an air of academic officialdom.

I was famished all of a sudden, so I reached for my spoon, but Miss Lewis cut in. "*Grace*, girls!"

It was probably louder than necessary, considering that everyone else had clearly done it before we'd got there, and it was only our table that had failed in its piety.

"For this and all we are about to receive may the Lord make us truly thankful. Amen," we recited, the words worn soft and smooth with continual use. As soon as the "Amen" fell from our collective lips we scrambled for our spoons, the familiar noises of breakfast starting up again from their temporary lull.

It was then that we heard the scream.

It came from a few tables down, and was shrill and piercing in the way only a child's scream can be. Everything went silent except for the clank of silver hitting the floor, and the scrape of chairs as Fräulein Weingarten and Miss Lewis rushed over.

"Pull it together, Sinclair, whatever are you screaming for?" Miss Lewis exclaimed.

Somehow I hadn't considered that it might not be something catastrophic. Eight days after I had leaned over the balustrade and seen Violet's ruined body, I simply assumed that someone had died or at the very least ended up horribly bloodied.

Hearing Miss Lewis take control of the situation seemed to break the spell; everyone at our table glanced at one another, and then I found myself moving again, walking over to the table where Sinclair—Olivia, all of twelve years old and frequently homesick—was sitting. She had finally shut up, her scream trailing off into a mewl.

"What is it?" Fraülein Weingarten said, her voice shaky. She grasped her by the shoulder, perhaps harder than she meant to, her knuckles going white. "What's wrong, Olivia?"

At last, Olivia spoke. You could barely hear it, even with everyone else in the dining hall dead silent. "Miss, there was something in—" She stopped, collected herself, and tried again. "There was something in my porridge?" she finished, tone drifting upwards at the end even though it couldn't possibly have been a question. The room seemed to deflate all at once. A false alarm; an unneeded injection of terror into the peace of the morning.

"And what," Miss Lewis said evenly, "did you find in your porridge, Sinclair?"

"Well, it's . . ." she faltered.

Then she plunged her fingers into the porridge, fishing around for a moment before pulling back, her hand closed in a fist. Opening her now-sticky palm, she revealed a large dark beetle. Unexpectedly, it was alive, but flipped on its back so it couldn't go anywhere. Its legs wriggled in the air; a blob of porridge was caught on its carapace. I watched, entranced, as it slid down onto Olivia's wrist.

Miss Lewis sent me to dispose of the beetle, wrapped damply in Olivia's handkerchief. Feeling obscurely that I wanted it destroyed, rather than just removed, I took it down to the incinerator, and for the second time in twenty-four hours, I set alight a thing that seemed to have grown spontaneously within what I had believed to be the safe walls of Briarley.

The thing about the beetle was that it wasn't miles away from normal. Briarley Manor was an old house; it was kept up decently by the school, but it was agreed upon by the foremost educational establishments that a little deprivation was good for the character, and so pains weren't exactly taken to keep the place pristine. The furniture was austere and unwelcoming; there were cobwebs in the corners of some of the lesser-used rooms from time to time; the food was never first-class fare. And Briarley had its share of unwanted visitors, too: ladybirds sometimes collected on the windowsills in spring and summer, and we were used to the occasional sighting of ants and mice. Dot always cried when she saw the mouse-traps. Once, memorably, Miss Stevens had to chase a squirrel out of the dining hall with a broom, galloping about entirely without dignity while we watched, hooting with laughter and cheering her on.

So the beetle seemed to me, at least, to be a coincidence, more like a bad joke than a threat. Perhaps that was stupid of me; I have never been good at discerning the contours of exactly what I ought to be afraid of. But I felt then that it just proved how on edge we were. Briarley had felt safe and impenetrable, and then Violet died, and whether we believed it was an accident or something more nefarious, we had all been made aware of the vulnerability of life. The rotten, squirming apples had been a shock. The beetle, by that measure, was more like a relief.

Even so, the atmosphere was tense. In the interest of collective peace and calm, over the next week or two, I worked and worked at making myself gentler towards the others, particularly Sophie and Dot. They were both especially tender and needling them felt like poking a bruise. I tried, several times, to bring up what we ought to do about Mademoiselle, in the hushed, steady tones you might use to coax a frightened horse across a stream. But Dot's lower lip wobbled at the slightest provocation, and Sophie had developed a tendency to let a girlish vacancy settle over her if she heard something that upset her. The nastier part of me thought that honestly—honestly!—of all of us, they had been the least close to Violet. Of all of us, they had related to her more with hero-worship than with friendship. I had been *special*. Even Evelyn had been a bit special, as much as I hated to admit it. And yet, in the interest of sisterly camaraderie and Marion not cutting me out entirely, I went above and beyond to be soft with them, and not push until they broke.

Evelyn didn't have such luck. It was something of a zero-sum game, wherein the softer and gentler I was with the others, the harder I was with her. She was on my side about Mademoiselle, and for that I had to be grateful, but the thaw that had come to our relationship during Violet's memorial service had frozen over again. I longed for a distraction: my attempts at getting the others on side regarding Mademoiselle were going nowhere, and I felt cooped up and bored, which meant I began picking fights.

Evelyn's constant stream of sniping and disapproving got the better of me one afternoon in the classroom where we were to have our History lesson. We were waiting for Miss Parker, a mousy woman who was reliably late and tended towards lenience. Evelyn was sulking while the rest of us chatted idly. I kicked at the leg of my desk without thinking, sort of scuffing my toe against it, and Evelyn turned around in her seat to glare at me.

"Will you stop that," she said.

I rolled my eyes. "Honestly, Evelyn, it's as though everything I do is wired directly into your brain."

"There isn't much I can do about it when you're making awful noises and disrupting everyone," she snapped.

"If you haven't noticed, you seem to be the only person bothered by—"

"I saw in the newspaper that there's a medium in the village," Sophie said, interrupting me. In retrospect, it's miraculous that a comment intended mostly to stave off yet another argument between me and Evelyn wound up being so important in the end. Sophie, as I so seldom understood back then, had a way of putting her finger on the pulse of a thing.

"A what?" Evelyn asked.

"A medium, a spirit medium, they're women who can talk to dead people. Like in the book I gave Violet."

"That book," Evelyn said, barely disguising a sneer.

"I saw one of them in London once," I said, feeling sickeningly sophisticated for knowing about it. "Really truly. It was in a lecture hall, she spoke with a man's voice and told a woman in the audience that she was her dead fiancé."

"What did he say?" Sophie asked.

"Oh, the usual, *My darling I love you but you must find happiness without me*, et cetera et cetera."

"So he was telling her to get married to someone else? That's not very romantic," Sophie said, wrinkling her nose.

"Well, if you imagine that ghosts are real people, then it stands to reason some would be more romantic than others."

"I think the whole thing is foul," Evelyn announced.

"Well, good for you, you can leave the fun to the rest of us, then," I said, and deliberately scraped my chair away so I didn't have to look at her.

"It's un-Christian."

"So is Marion, and you don't call her foul, do you?" I said, turning back around.

"Leave me out of it, thanks awfully," Marion said, rolling her eyes. I felt like a prize idiot for bringing it up; none of us had talked about Marion's family being Jewish since an enormous row years before, and I didn't want to breach the peace.

"Anyway it's not un-Christian, lots of mediums are Christians," Sophie persisted. "They sing hymns at the beginnings of séances, don't they? The book says that spiritualism actually started with Christ."

"Oh, what," I said, "like Lazarus?"

"Yes, exactly! Maybe we should go and see the medium," Sophie said, a flush in her cheeks. I hadn't realised how much time she had spent reading the book since Violet died; I didn't understand, then, how much her desire for a distraction would change the course of things.

"Ripping," Alice said, from across the room. "Next village trip?"

Evelyn looked furious. "You're all making an awful mistake and you'll be lucky if I don't tell."

"Listen, Evelyn." Marion gave me a warning look but I carried on, seething. "By all means: remain as much of a goody-two-shoes as you like. The rest of us intend to make as much as we can out of this year, and I won't have you ruining it. Stay home! Practise your German! I don't care what you do, just leave it alone."

Without saying a word Evelyn turned in her seat to face the front, even though Miss Parker hadn't arrived yet. She bent over her exercise book with such violence that her narrow elbows swung out to the sides, and she began scribbling, clutching her pencil so tightly I thought it might break.

"Anyway," Sophie said, worriedly.

"Let's go," I said. "Next week-end. It'll be a laugh, won't it? And God knows this place needs a laugh."

We were interrupted, then, by the arrival of the errant Miss Parker, and the concurrent necessity of paying at least half attention to the dry lecture she was giving us on the glory days of the East India Company. Keeping my mind on tea or saltpetre was difficult enough, without the gleaming possibility of mediums and séances and spirits just a few days ahead.

Our craze for spiritualism provided, for the first time since Violet's death, an effective distraction. Mademoiselle was in San, and had been since the day of the memorial. French lessons were taken by Miss Stone, who had a rotten accent and—whatever Mademoiselle's crimes—was much less nice about conjugations. Mademoiselle, stuck in the draughty old infirmary in God only knew what state, loomed large in my imagination every time I wasn't involved in a discussion about whether we'd prefer the spirits to bring us fresh fruit or lilies. There was a cowardly part of me that was relieved we had a diversion—that my failure to muster a force ready to confront Violet's murderer was no longer the only thing I had to think about.

If I didn't persuade the others, I'd have to go alone, and the thought frightened me more than I care to admit. I hadn't been anywhere near San since the days I'd spent there after Violet's death, which I can only remember as a grey blur, right up until Mademoiselle came in and I felt that sudden, certain clarity of purpose. I was grateful for that purpose now, but it had created a whole new set of fears. The thought of going back there was bad enough already; now it housed Violet's murderer, which made it rather worse. Her isolation meant I didn't have to look at her, which I didn't think I could bear. *Emily*, I imagined her saying, soft and gentle and full of hidden malice, *what do you think I got up to with Violet when you weren't looking?*

So I let the others carry me along in their enthusiasm. We tended to discuss things in the common room, which was reserved for our use only. I suppose it spoke to what nicely brought up young ladies we were that none of us ever thought to take real advantage of this privacy. Instead we just found ourselves sitting as we liked, limbs thrown over the sides of armchairs and shoulders hunched; talking about topics absolutely forbidden, like spiritualism; and making interventions to the décor. I had never before had a place that felt as much like mine.

The room itself was barely more than a glorified closet with a fireplace, but we cherished it nevertheless. Violet had persuaded her father to send enough ribbon and velvet and silk from his textile factories for us to decorate it. I can't say in retrospect that it looked any good; Violet's upholstering was in a rather outdated arsenic green that was lovely on her milky complexion but always made me look ill. Dot had contributed a little decoupaged box that we kept sweets in, and Sophie put up a sampler she had made the year before, which read *As many hands make a house, so many hearts make a school.*

Without even mentioning it, we had all avoided the place like the plague for the first few days after Violet's death, as if we might run into her ghost there. In fact, the first time we ventured back, Sophie had sat on the squashy little sofa and, making a face, fished around under the cushion to find a compact hidden there. She popped it open, the gold-varnished metal making a satisfying *thunking* sound, and we all stared awkwardly as she revealed Violet's rouge compact. I had seen her with it a thousand times: the scalloped shell design on the top, the engraving inside the lid that said *To Violet, who is growing up too fast.* On seeing it, Evelyn hopped out of her seat and said, "I'll take that, no need to worry about it." Before Sophie—or I—could do anything, she had pocketed the compact. I never saw it again.

"Do you think we could get a Ouija board?" Sophie asked one day during afternoon break. The book about spiritualism lay open in her lap, to a chapter about automatic writing.

"How?" Marion said, grimacing. "Remember when I tried to bring in a copy of *Ulysses* and Miss Stone threw it on the fire?"

"*Miss Thomas here thinks she can sneak the tawdriest filth into a good clean school like Briarley right under our noses!*" Alice said, pinching her nose shut and doing a passable imitation of Miss Stone's nasal shriek.

"We'd just as easily get a crystal ball. Sophie, what does your book say about those?" I don't know when it became Sophie's book. The thought of distributing Violet's possessions had never come up; her trunk had simply been taken away by the Kirsches the day of the memorial, and we never saw it again, only the book hadn't been packed yet when she died. Sophie had hidden it away to avoid confiscation, and in doing so kept it for ourselves inadvertently. Perhaps it had been so little touched by its intended owner that it never gathered an aura of Violet around itself like her other things had, the hairbrush we would never borrow without permission, or the boxes of chocolates no one ever dared steal from.

"Oh, the crystal ball stuff isn't anything much. But there's a bit here about going to a medium that's *really* good." Sophie began to read aloud. "*In order to conduct a séance, the parties must sit in a circle, fairer sex next to rougher—*"

"Well, that's out," Alice said.

"Hardly fairer, are you," I replied, and she stuck her tongue out at me.

"*Fairer sex next to rougher—*" Sophie continued, giving us a stern look. "*Lights ought to be dimmed; a single candle will provide sufficient illumination. At this stage, the party may choose to sing a hymn to begin the séance. Many circles have had success with 'On Jordan's Stormy Banks I Stand,' with its references to 'that happy place' where all will be 'forever blest.' If in possession of a Ouija board, it may be brought out once the hymn is sung. If no talking board can be obtained*—"

"Yes, that bit, you can skip all the Ouija parts," I urged.

"*If no talking board can be obtained, then a traditional séance can be conducted merely by clasping hands around the circle. The medium will call out to the spirits and await a response; if no response is forthcoming the sitters may sing another hymn.*"

"What larks," Alice said, satisfied.

Evelyn sat in the corner, practically vibrating with fury. I chose to take the high road and ignored her, as the rest of us eased into a comfortable discussion of which hymns we thought would be the most atmospheric.

She had forgotten to be ostentatiously annoyed with us by that evening, when she burst into the dormitory with news. As much of an irritant as she could be, she was a valuable ally and I wasn't about to throw that away. So when she swung open the door, panting slightly, rather than telling her to spit it out, I waited until she was ready.

"Mademoiselle," she said, leaning against the door frame. "She is not well."

"Last I saw of her she was collapsing at the funeral of a girl she murdered, so I suppose that's to be expected," I said. Evelyn looked at me, wide-eyed. Then she shook herself free of it, red plaits tossing about.

"As I was saying, I went to San because I was looking for a—well—a sanitary belt, and I thought Matron would be in there but she must have been down in the kitchens with Cook, and so

I looked around—you know all the little corners that San has, it's impossible to find anything . . ."

"Yes, go on," I said tightly.

"Anyway," Evelyn said, finally coming to the point, around which she had been circling for what felt like hours. "While I was in there, I saw Mademoiselle. She looked awful. Her hair was like a rat's nest and her eyes were all red and puffy, with such dark circles underneath it looked as though she hadn't slept in weeks."

Which, I thought with grim satisfaction, she probably hadn't.

"Her bedside table was stacked with all kinds of pills and bottles—I squinted to see if I could make out any of the labels but I didn't want to get too close to her because, well, you know," she finished lamely.

Alice kicked at the leg of her chair with surprising force, and left the room, twisting her handkerchief between her hands. Dot shot an anxious glance over her shoulder at us and looked as if she wanted to follow.

"Did she say anything?" Sophie asked, her eyes wide.

"No—not anything useful, anyway. She said she was sorry about Violet—"

"The *nerve!*" I interjected.

"And then she said she hoped I could forgive her. It was awful. I'm sure—" She looked at me, I suppose for moral support, but all the blood had rushed to my head and my ears were ringing, so I wasn't much use. "I'm sure she meant—you know."

"I don't think you have any reason to be sure of that," Marion said icily.

I had recovered somewhat. "Come off it, Marion, don't be deliberately obtuse. She's *sorry* and she wants *forgiveness*. That's as good as a confession."

"Perhaps more pertinently, why is she still there? Surely she's got somewhere to go other than San," Marion said, in a clear attempt to change the subject. I thought to myself that again it seemed like the teachers possessed internal worlds into which we couldn't see. I didn't know anything about Mademoiselle's life beyond Briarley. The decision to allow her to stay in the infirmary was opaque to me, and I couldn't put myself in the mind of Miss Lewis or Matron to work it out.

"P'raps she's not allowed back in France," Sophie wondered.

"Hasn't the funds, more like," I said.

Evelyn had that canny look on her face that I hated. "Well, isn't it possible the other teachers knew all along about Mademoiselle's—predilections? Weren't we saying they might be in on it?" And here she looked to me, as if I was going to back her up.

"I certainly wasn't saying that, Evelyn, don't put words in my mouth," Marion said, tartly. "I think a grand Lesbian conspiracy among the teachers is a fantasy and you'd do better to drop it."

"How do you know about Lesbianism?" I asked, for no reason I could discern.

"Emily, I *read*, for heaven's sake. Baudelaire. The papers. Honestly, it isn't difficult," she said. "I may as well ask how you know."

"Oh, well," I said, "you know, I just—"

"Eloquently put," and she tossed me a pear drop from Dot's decoupaged box on the occasional table to appease me.

"Mademoiselle, though," Evelyn started, and even though I knew she was on my side, I longed for her to shut up. Marion disapproved of our speculation; she was more diplomatic than Alice but she had a way of broadcasting her feelings without saying a word. I could just imagine the grateful look she'd give me when I successfully turned the conversation onto anything else.

"When she's better I think we should confront her," I said. (Well—I never claimed to make good decisions.)

"Come off it," Marion said.

"I do! It doesn't do us or her any good to sit around wondering and simmering and hating her. Better to get it all out in the open."

"I have—a bit of a bad feeling about it," said Sophie. I turned to her.

"What do you mean?"

"Well, just, a sense that we oughtn't," she said, hesitating.

"All right, all right," I said, trying to bring a joking tone back to the proceedings. "No confrontations yet. We can wait."

Thank you, mouthed Marion.

"That way maybe we can ask the medium's advice," I said, and watched as Evelyn sputtered between gratitude that I was part of her crusade and horror that, despite her best efforts, she was getting involved in spiritualism anyhow. Two birds, one stone.

"I think going to the medium should be a *nice* thing," Dot said stubbornly, which punctured the moment a bit. "I want to ask her about what it's like in the spirit world and if she has a crystal ball and things. Not—all of that."

"I was only kidding," I told her, and mostly I meant it.

When we talked about spiritualism, which we did very often at that point in the year with the zeal shared by the young for discovering something new and controversial to believe in, none of us ever seriously countenanced discussion of trying to contact Violet herself—except for Sophie, that one time, and then we left her floundering before changing the subject. The thought that our fascination with spiritualism might have been to do with Violet all along feels uncomfortably tender, even now—easier to remember instead the faddishness of seventeen- and eighteen-year-olds, the thrill and romance of it all. I have never quite been able to put my finger on why we didn't discuss it from the start. Why wouldn't the shocking—and, I thought, suspicious—death of one of our peers be at the centre of our desire to see what happened if we spoke to the dead? Perhaps, as I have often suspected, Sophie was the cleverest of us all; she knew where we were going from the beginning, and those of us too frightened to square up to our feelings found it easier to ignore her than to listen.

FIVE

MRS. ANNE NORTHCOTE, 14 DARLEY LANE, BRIARLEY VILLAGE, SUSSEX

"Well, Evelyn," Alice called behind her, as we crossed the country road that led away from the Briarley estate. Breakfast had gone smoothly, no screaming or rotting, thank God, and we had been freed from the confines of school to go to the village, where we intended to see the medium. "Have you changed your mind? Coming with us after all?"

"Certainly not." Evelyn's nose was in the air. "I'm going to the haberdasher's for some darning thread, that's all."

"What a bundle of fun you are," I said.

"Are you sure you don't want to come with us? I think it's going to be awfully thrilling," Dot said, her arm linked with Alice's.

"Ever so," Sophie agreed. "You don't have to *do* anything, you can just watch."

I didn't understand how the others couldn't see that trying to accommodate Evelyn was pointless. She kept walking and didn't say a word, so I rolled my eyes and ignored her: leave her to fiddle with her prefect badge and worry at the tip of her plait all week-end if she liked.

It was a long walk to the village, but not a disagreeable one. I find it, years later, still fixed in my mind. I can see the entire route, picture exactly where the road curves and where the view opens out to an idyllic panorama. The country around Briarley was for the most part arable, alongside the occasional grassy field populated with sheep and cows and the like. It was all very "green and pleasant land," as they say. If you were so inclined, you could climb the narrow steps up to the little turret that was a long-ago governess's quarters back at the manor, and look out the window there to a view spanning miles and miles of gently rolling hills, punctuated by the steeple of a church or the low brick structure of a farmhouse. It was altogether a wholesome place in which to grow up, with fresh air and the type of climate to put roses in any English girl's cheeks. That was rather the point of a place like Briarley, I suppose. To pluck us from grimy cities or dull suburbs and flush us with the glow of country living, to raise us healthy and strong for the good of the Empire.

The village itself was small and unassuming, one main road with a grocer's and a butcher's and a sweet shop (which seemed to exist solely to provide for the girls of Briarley School; how it maintained a profit I couldn't say). There were smaller streets branching off that main thoroughfare, all higgledy-piggledy and cobbled. It was on one of these side streets that the medium lived, a Mrs. Northcote. The advertisement had listed her address as "Mrs. Anne Northcote, 14 Darley Lane, Briarley Village, Sussex": no frills or furbelows to suggest much of a commercial enterprise or, for that matter, the mystical.

"We could go to the sweet shop first," Dot suggested, hope beyond hope.

"We are reserving *all* our pennies for the séance, thank you very much," Marion said, steering her by the shoulders away from the pink-fronted sweet shop. Evelyn had already marched off towards the haberdasher's. I watched her red plaits swing back and forth and longed to dip one in my inkpot.

Mrs. Northcote's rooms were in an unassuming brick house around the corner from the village post office. Marion knocked. There was no unearthly echo into another world: all I heard after a brief silence was a quiet voice coming from inside, announcing her arrival at the door.

When the medium opened the door, we must have been a sight. Five girls, dressed identically, slightly pink-nosed from the chilly walk. We goggled back at her. Mrs. Northcote was a small woman, perhaps in her sixties, with an out-of-fashion mauve dress and lank, greyish hair. I'm not sure what we had been expecting. Perhaps an old crone, or—better yet—a glamorous young thing in a turban and jewels. Instead she could have been any of our grandmothers, or possibly an ageing aunt.

"Well?" she said, peering down her nose. "How may I assist you young ladies?" Her voice was thin but firm, and she spoke very properly.

"We'd like a séance," Sophie said, almost shyly. "We read about you in the newspaper."

"We can pay," I added.

Mrs. Northcote looked rather fagged, but she pulled the door open to reveal her drawing room. It had the air of Victorian stuffiness that one might have expected from a woman of her age and demeanour. The wallpaper was dingy flock in a floral pattern, and the chairs were covered with crocheted antimacassars. Light didn't seem to filter in the way it ought; then I noticed that the windows were partially covered with special curtains.

"You need darkness, for a séance," she explained, though I hadn't said anything aloud. "Can't have sunlight peeking through. My old wrists are too delicate to pull those heavy curtains all the way each time, so I have had to grow used to the dark."

"I could pull them open for you," I offered, but she waved her hand and walked to the settee. We all looked at each other, trying to work out if this was an invitation. Alice chose to read it as one, taking off her hat and sitting herself down on a spindly armchair, which creaked loudly. I followed suit, and soon enough we were all seated in a shallow half-moon around Mrs. Northcote. She reached out to sip from a teacup.

"The séance," Alice urged. "Could we have one now?"

"Ordinarily I work by appointment," she said. "That advertisement included my address to send letters, not to visit out of the blue."

"You're right, of course," said Marion, swiftly. "We would hate to be any bother, only sometimes it's difficult to get post up at the school."

"You mean the schoolmistresses would confiscate it, more like," Mrs. Northcote said, her eyes sharpening. I wondered whether she would think about us being Briarley girls and mention Violet; I didn't think I could bear it.

"Well, yes," I said. "But our money's good either way, and if you can't give us a séance now we could come back this time next week."

I held my breath, hoping I hadn't spoken so far out of turn that she would tell us to leave her house altogether. I felt an unaccountable desire to see the thing through to the end. Whether it was so that I might have an experience that was new and untainted by Violet's death, or because I anticipated something was going to happen, I don't know.

"You're very persistent. Make me a fresh cup of tea and draw the curtains, and I'll see what I can do."

When Marion and Sophie had boiled the kettle, and the rest

of us had made miserable small talk, Mrs. Northcote began the séance.

"I have been a spirit medium since 1902. One thing I have learned in all those years—nearly thirty years—is that you cannot guarantee a thing. I have felt the most sure and auspicious about a séance as I have felt anything in my life, but that means nothing when measured against the vastness of the spirit world, the mysteries it continues to hold for us." Her speech sounded practised, but it was effective anyhow, and I shivered. "I can offer no refunded payment for a failed séance, but if we make no contact with the spirits you may come by next week-end for another try."

"Bit prosaic of her," Alice muttered to me.

"Another thing," Mrs. Northcote said, looking Alice right in the eye. "Scepticism has no place in the séance. The great mediums of the nineteenth century exhausted themselves—physically, spiritually—in the service of tests from sceptics. They were tied to their chairs with strips of calico, sewn into their clothes, and held fast with iron shackles. Young women were forced to stand on glass, with electromagnetic currents run up through their feet. Many of them ended up dying alone and in poverty. I consider it my duty to other mediums not to allow any such testing in my séances, for we are a delicate breed and will not take rough treatment."

"We wouldn't dream of it," said Sophie fervently.

"My final warning is that my clients do not always like what they hear. Their time in the spirit world often softens the rough edges of the spirits, and you are likely to find any loved ones contacting you from the beyond to be unusually kind and gentle. But this does not preclude pain, or the expression of uncomfortable truths. I understand that this can be difficult. I would only ask that you remember my position in this: I am only a messenger. Now, with all that out of the way—" The slight portentous tone vanished from her voice, leaving her with a business-like edge. "We may begin. It can be challenging with only girls—"

"Told you," Alice whispered.

"But it is more your temperament than your sex that determines your relation to the spirit world. Most mediums are women; our passive nature bends itself well to becoming a vessel for the spirits. But there are women who maintain an active, out-going relationship to the world around them, and this must be taken into account for them to become valuable members of a spirit circle. And conversely, there are men whose gentle, submissive nature allows them to serve as the link between worlds."

Marion arched an eyebrow; I thought of her reading Baudelaire.

"With that in mind," Mrs. Northcote continued, "I'd like you to arrange yourselves however you see fit. If you've done your research, you'll know that the ideal arrangement for a séance alternates between men and women. So make of that what you will." I caught a glimpse of mischief in her eye. Clearly, she expected this to cause some tension.

Alice moved to sit between Dot and Sophie, and I placed myself in between Sophie and Marion, and Marion sat equivocally next to Mrs. Northcote herself. This left a slightly awkward space between Dot and Mrs. Northcote, and all of a sudden, I could almost see their natures repelling one another, like the matching poles of two magnets. It threw the whole room off to a degree that felt almost disturbing. We had been sitting perfectly happily before, but the ritual of arranging ourselves caused something to *happen*, some shifting in the stifling air of Mrs. Northcote's front room. While there was much to come—much more impressive things, things I considered unequivocal proof of life beyond death—it was this unassuming presence that planted the seed of belief within me.

"Not quite right, is it," Alice said. Without much further discussion we rearranged ourselves, trying things out until it no longer felt like the balance of the room was off. Sophie and Dot stood together for a moment—something I had seen them do a thousand times, naturally, but in the atmosphere of Mrs. Northcote's it felt all wrong. In the end Alice and I ended up flanking Mrs. Northcote, with Sophie sitting next to me and Marion between Dot and Sophie. I took brief pride in the idea of being considered active and out-going, in the absence of any marked success at passivity or gentleness.

"With a group of girls it's never likely to be perfect," Mrs. Northcote said, "but I think this will do well enough. Join hands, please. I understand it's old-fashioned, but I still prefer to begin with a hymn."

"'On Jordan's Stormy Banks I Stand,'" said Sophie, her eyes shining.

"Yes, that is a common choice," she sighed. We began to sing, following her lead. I had heard everyone sing before; it's impossible to spend several years with one another and not to become intimately acquainted with the sound of each other's voices. In that room, though, hushed and tentative, we all sounded quite different. Even Marion's strong, steady alto faltered, until we reached the refrain:

"*I am bound for the promised land, / I am bound for the promised land; / Oh, who will come and go with me?*"

At that point our voices melded together, becoming one strong fine chorus, and then if there was any light left coming through the curtains I could no longer see it. The small, staid room was plunged into unnatural darkness. Mrs. Northcote broke off her singing and the rest of us stopped as well. My hands felt full of some kind of energy, like the flickering buzz when an electric light comes on.

"Is anyone there?" she asked. "Is anyone there?"

I held my breath. When I squeezed my eyes shut, I could see pink and white starbursts behind my eyelids. Far from the supernatural chill I had been expecting, the room felt warm, warm for October, warm for the dark; a drop of sweat ran down the length of my back until the waistband of my pinafore caught it.

"Is anyone there?" she asked again. Then: a knock. It came from somewhere behind us. Sophie gasped. Mrs. Northcote gripped my hand, hard. "Knock once for yes, twice for no. Are you here to speak to us?" The knock came once—twice—three times. My heart banged against my chest.

"What does three times mean?" Dot whispered, in agony.

"I think it's—hang on—" That was Marion. I heard a fumbling sound and the circle broke; the electric feeling that had run through our clasped hands subsided. Then the door opened, and a flood of afternoon light came through. I squinted. Evelyn was standing outside, her mouth pinched.

"Might I join you?" she asked.

"I thought you were going to the haberdasher's," I said from across the room, feeling the loss of whatever had been going on before she knocked. I wanted her gone, out, as quickly as possible so we could get back to it.

"I've finished at the haberdasher's, and now I'm here," Evelyn said.

"I'm sure it's not appropriate to have someone quite so hostile to spiritualism in our séance." I turned to Mrs. Northcote with a pleading look, in the hope that she'd agree. Mrs. Northcote looked at Evelyn appraisingly.

"Let her join us," she said, in a tone that brooked no discussion.

I abruptly shut my mouth, and Evelyn slotted herself into the broken circle next to me.

"We begin again, from the hymn," Mrs. Northcote announced.

Evelyn reached out her hand; I hated the thought of holding it. When she slipped her palm against mine it was clammy, slick with sweat. She hung onto me hard, which felt like an imposition, given that she had quite literally inserted herself into what I had without intention begun to consider *our* séance circle.

We sang, and the harmonious, humming feeling from before didn't quite return. Instead there was something pricklier, crackling between us.

"Is anyone there?" Mrs. Northcote asked. "Is there a spirit presence here? Knock once for yes, twice for no."

And there it was, a single, resounding knock that seemed to come from nowhere and take up the whole room. My grip on Evelyn's knuckles tightened involuntarily, and she whispered, "It wasn't me." Her eyes remained fixed on Mrs. Northcote, and I could see the gleam of fear in them.

"Is your presence strong enough to speak through me?" Mrs. Northcote called out. A pause, and then another single knock, louder this time. "Very well," she said. "You may."

When she next opened her mouth, an entirely different voice spoke through her. I had never seen—or heard—anything like it before, that fundamental disjunct between one sense and another. Gone was the old woman; this was the voice of someone a great deal her junior, light and lilting. It said: "Good morning. I am Penelope."

"That must be her spirit control," Sophie murmured. "It said in the advertisement." She cleared her throat and put on her most authoritative voice. "Penelope, please will you tell us about the spirit world?"

"Our life in this higher sphere is filled with joys. Our world is sweet; we have no more illness, no more death, no annihilation."

"Will you tell us something only we would know?" Alice asked.

"I have not come to be tested," Penelope said, a warning note coming into her voice.

"No, I—we understand," Alice said.

"Only I've read so much about the power of the spirits," I cut in. "I know you can see beyond walls, move anywhere, hear anything."

"Flattery," Penelope said, a smile in her voice that ghosted onto Mrs. Northcote's face as well.

"Please," Evelyn said out of nowhere. "Will you tell us about Briarley?" Her voice shook. It sounded like she wanted to ask about Violet, but felt, as I did, the unspoken taboo against the subject. Briarley, I suppose, was the next-best thing.

"Briarley," Penelope said. We all waited, but she didn't say anything else. Things seemed to be veering off-pattern; the pause went on and on until it could hardly be considered a pause any more.

"The school," Alice urged.

"Briarley—Briarley—" And here Penelope's lovely voice disappeared, and we were left with something altogether different, the dry clicking sound of Mrs. Northcote's throat, a wheezing coming from deep inside her lungs.

She made a move with her left hand as though to bring it to her chest but Alice held it fast. Inarticulate sounds started coming from her mouth; I would have said she was speaking in tongues but it is closer to the truth to describe it as what speech might sound like without recourse to a tongue. It was garbled and guttural, and it made me shudder. Then the sounds took on a grinding quality, like shaved metal. I had never heard a person's voice sound like that before.

It brought me back with sudden violence to a moment when I was a child and a train had derailed from the tracks behind my parents' house. I had been playing (alone, as I so often was) in the garden, and was startled by the squeal of metal on metal and the sound of hissing steam, the punctuation of chaos into suburban stillness. I'd rushed to the wall at the end of the garden and peered over, hoping to see something bloody and horrible, which would have given me an excuse, for once, to cry and not receive a walloping for the imposition.

And then Penelope returned, sweet and lilting for just a moment. "Briarley—Briarley—something is coming," she said. "The worm in the bud, the fly in the ointment. Something's coming—something's coming—"

Mrs. Northcote's hand tightened in my own, crushing my bones together. I cried out in pain and tried to pull away but her grip was too tight. And then Evelyn wrenched her hand from mine, and the circle was broken. I felt scalded with the loss of the power that had thrummed through us.

"Well, girls," said Mrs. Northcote pleasantly. "Did you manage to speak with anyone?"

SIX

SOMETHING'S COMING

After the séance had ended, Sophie paid Mrs. Northcote with our collected sixpences and shillings. Mrs. Northcote didn't say a word once her initial enquiry was met with silence. The stricken looks painted across our faces had been enough of a response. Probably she had known about Violet after all, and had been too polite to say anything. News like that—a death up at the school—certainly travelled. Whatever her motive, she watched us without speaking as I drew the curtain for her and we filed out of her house. Sometimes I wonder if we became a story she brought out at dinner parties: five and then six insane girls showing up, demanding a séance, then trudging out disconsolately as if they were the ghosts rather than the living. And then, of course, what came after: the punchline to an already sad joke.

Miss Lewis watched us gravely as we trudged back up the front steps of Briarley, but she didn't say anything either. What I could not have predicted prior to Violet's death was the extent to which adults would be willing to chalk just about anything up to youthful grief. They seemed to pity our inability to handle our uglier, more difficult emotions, or at least they were so uncomfortable around them that to say nothing was preferable. Violet's death hadn't been swept under the rug, not exactly, but if the mistresses discussed it among themselves, they never did it where we could see. It was part of the atmosphere of a school like Briarley, I suppose: to coddle us in our grief would only give us unrealistic expectations for the rest of our lives.

We split up when we got back. Evelyn disappeared without saying a word to the rest of us; I assumed she was going off to say whatever the Presbyterian equivalent of a Hail Mary was, in penance for our idolatry. Marion went after her wearily, and Alice and Dot went back to the dormitory, presumably to discuss what they'd seen in private. I think a collective discussion would have made it all feel too big, too significant just then: we needed time to think, to let what we had experienced sink in.

This left me and Sophie. In a way I was glad it was her, with whom I had never had a really serious conversation in my life. We sat together on the common room sofa. I think now that, despite everything, we were very innocent then.

"It was real, wasn't it?" Sophie said, wonderingly.

"Of course it was real. How could it have been anything else?" It was funny that she was unsure, given that without her we wouldn't have gone to Mrs. Northcote's at all.

"No, I know, I wasn't—it's not that I thought it *wasn't*, only, how can it—" She let out a shocked little laugh. "I thought it would be fun."

"Oh, God, well, it looks like we're not in for much fun, if we go by what Penelope told us. She might as well have come right out and said it was Mademoiselle. If Evelyn hadn't ended things when she did, who knows what else we might've heard, that awful cow—"

But Sophie didn't seem to be listening to my worries;

instead, she clutched one of those—if I'm honest, and my apologies to Violet's memory—hideous green cushions to her face and went into absolute gales of laughter.

"It's just that—oh, Emily, I can't believe I'm saying it, but I *stole* the book in the first place. I didn't have any money and I could hardly ask Mumsy and Dad for however much it cost to buy a *magic book*, and now here we are."

At this point I could no longer keep a handle on myself, and I let all my fear and anger slide momentarily away; together we laughed so hard we wept.

When we had sufficiently recovered ourselves, Sophie and I went to bring the others down to the common room so we could discuss things. I felt rather hesitant about it; I didn't want petty disagreements to get in the way of something that felt so important. Unfortunately, I tended to attract so many petty disagreements that trying to avoid them was impossible.

"You're obsessed," Alice said, when I tried to explain to her how certain I was that the spirit had been warning us about Mademoiselle. "You're trying to hide the fact that you haven't got any proof by going on and on about it to wear us down."

"I think that's patently absurd. Are we supposed to consider what happened a coincidence?"

"Well, I don't know, why are we all acting as though Mrs. Northcote couldn't just have been saying things for the effect?"

"It wasn't like that," Evelyn said, sounding hoarse. I turned to stare at her. "It was as though she could—see into me." She had the tip of one of her plaits in one cold-chapped hand and was twisting it so hard I thought it might start splitting and unravelling.

"So what do you think, was it Mademoiselle she was talking about? The danger in Briarley?" I couldn't help asking; Evelyn was the last person I expected to have actually believed in the séance.

"I don't know. Yes. Probably."

"I wish you'd stop," Alice said. "Marion, tell them to stop."

"I'm staying out of this, thank you," Marion said, conspicuously picking her novel up off the arm of the sofa and opening it. "I don't know what I think happened at Mrs. Northcote's; I only know I didn't like it."

"The spirit was warning us," I said. "She wanted us to know something. She wouldn't have said what she did if it wasn't important."

Sophie spoke up, and I felt very warmly towards her just then. "The spirits know things. I read it in the book, how sometimes they can see into the future. They do warn people. There was a man in Blackpool, the book said, who woke up in the middle of the night to see a ghostly woman floating above his bed. And she pointed at the door, and the man was so terrified he ran to get away from her, and then he had just made it outside when the kerosene lamp shattered and set fire to his curtains and the whole house went up." She broke off there, sounding almost embarrassed. I seized on it.

"So it's happened before!"

"She could've been warning us about anything," Alice protested. "If she meant Mademoiselle, someone we all know and have known for months, she wouldn't have been so vague."

"Good Lord, Alice, when did you become the world's expert on the supernatural? Isn't Fish always saying the Lord works in mysterious ways? Why can't the spirits?"

"You still haven't even managed to persuade me that what happened to Violet wasn't just a terrible accident," said Alice. "I'm sorry, but you're a long way from convincing me that the spirits were trying to tell us something about her."

"Either way, they were trying to tell us *something*. Why don't we have another séance and ask them again?" Sophie suggested.

"You know, that isn't a poor idea at all," I said. "We could ask Penelope directly, really pin her down."

"I'm not going back to Mrs. Northcote's. I couldn't," Evelyn said.

"Couldn't we do it here?" Sophie asked. "Right here, in the common room. We could do it ourselves. The book tells you how."

"Sophie, you're a brick. That's an excellent idea," I said, at which she preened, tucking her long yellow hair behind her ears.

"If it stops you harping on about Mademoiselle then Dot and I are in," Alice allowed.

"One question," Marion said, because as much as she liked to stay out of our arguments, she could never resist being in on the action. "Who would play medium?"

"It's not *playing*," Sophie said hotly. "It's *serious*."

It was days and days before we were able to try again. It wasn't long, that Saturday, before the dinner bell rang and we were all herded into the brightly lit dining hall full of chattering girls. And Sunday was for prayer, and chores; the schoolmistresses kept a watchful eye over us and would certainly have brooked no secret meetings. I suppose that for all our protestations to Evelyn about the good Christian nature of what we were planning, something didn't feel right about doing it on the Lord's day. In the intervening time, some of the shock of the séance in the village leached away. Teen-age girls—what can I say?—our memories were short and our appetite for mischief endless. I like to think of our capacity for frivolity as being still intact, at that point: what a wonder.

By Monday, we were whispering about the upcoming séance between lessons, as if it were a midnight feast we were planning to have rather than a rendezvous with the dead. I suggested Friday night, because I happened to know after overhearing them at dinner that Fräulein Weingarten was planning to walk to the village after dinner to see a young man, and Miss Stone was insisting on chaperoning her, so the number of teachers able to catch us would be diminished. Ordinarily Fräulein Weingarten's visit to the village would have been quite enough gossip to sustain us for weeks on end, but this time we had bigger fish to fry.

On Friday night, we all went to bed at the bell. If you had looked into our dormitory you would have seen six girls snug in their beds, blankets folded neatly around them and the window open to let in the good cold air. We stayed like that for what felt like an eternity. I tried to pass the time by counting, at first, and then when I got to two thousand I gave up and started on world capitals, British colonies, the works of Shakespeare, anything I could think of that would keep me awake.

"Do you think it's time?" Alice whispered.

"I think I'll go mad if I wait another minute," Dot whispered back.

Trying my absolute hardest not to make a peep, I got out of bed. The floorboards were icy cold and it occurred to me as we crept down the staircase to the common room that we could simply have held the séance in our dormitory, where we had managed to hold midnight feasts before without ever being found out. But the thought made me shiver. If we were to be told some dark secret, I wanted it to happen far away from where I slept, thank you very much.

The common room looked unfamiliar at night, but Marion had absolutely forbidden us any lights, saying it was too much of a risk, and séances were meant to be held in the dark anyhow. At the time, I'd been firmly on her side. But now, stepping into the common room, lit only by thin moonlight, I wished I had argued with her. The furniture threw eerie shadows against the walls and the familiar curtains that Violet had chosen. But I could not accept the entirely reasonable accusation of yellow-bellied cowardice that would for certain have come with backing out. Instead, I took my place in the circle on the floor, trying to move lightly so the floorboards didn't creak. We were wedged between the sofa and the fireplace, with hardly enough space to stretch out an arm.

"We can't sing, like the book said we should," Sophie started. "But perhaps we could do the Lord's Prayer, that one sounds all right whispered."

I hoped the spirits would notice us even if we weren't singing. It occurred to me that no one had ever really made it clear what part of the hymn at the beginning of a séance was the operative part: the singing? The religion? The sense of ritual? Whatever it was, as we murmured our way through "Our Father who art in heaven," my hands began to tingle. I sat between Evelyn and Alice. In Mrs. Northcote's absence, the balance of the room wasn't quite right, but we were just going to have to make do. Alice's grip was firm and solid—that, I thought, was the hand of a champion cricket player. Evelyn's nails were overgrown and dug into the back of my hand. I didn't know why she continued to take part, if she felt such disdain for the whole thing.

"For thine is the kingdom, the power and the glory, forever and ever, amen."

I tried to settle into the silence that followed, but it was difficult. I felt every irregularity in the floorboards and Evelyn's fingernails were honestly getting a bit much. After a minute or so, Sophie closed her eyes with a great sense of purpose, and whispered, "Are you there? Penelope? Is anyone there?" But instead of any sense of otherworldly power I got the most unbearable urge to scratch my nose.

"We could each try," Marion said. "Asking if anyone's there, I mean, to see if anyone in particular gets more of a response."

"Marion, you go first, maybe they'll listen to you."

"Right—is anyone there? Spirits?" She only waited a moment before tossing her hair and saying, "Well, clearly it isn't me."

"Spirits, can you hear me? It's Dot, are you there?" I looked over at Dot's sweet face, but aside from the wind whistling through a gap in the window there was nothing.

"Honestly, it's not going to be me, is it," Alice whispered. "You heard what Mrs. Northcote said, and, well, look at me."

I felt like it must be my turn, but I was dreadfully frightened all of a sudden. On the one hand, I was half-certain I'd be useless at it. Without question the exercise at Mrs. Northcote's had suggested as much. But on the other, if it was me, if I was a medium, what would it feel like? I hadn't considered it before. The thought of something else taking over my body, or my mind—speaking with my mouth—sent a crawling feeling down my spine. I could be made to say anything.

"Emily?"

"I'll go, I'll go," I said. I closed my eyes. "If you're there, spirits, say something. Give us a sign." I held my breath for what felt like a thousand years. A breeze passed over me and I went cold; my hair ruffled with it, then settled back down on my forehead, which had broken out in a sweat. I froze still, waiting for whatever was coming, my throat working. Then—nothing. "Spirits?" Nothing. The air was dead again. "Not me, then," I whispered, and forced a laugh.

"I'll try again," Sophie said. "I'm not sure I did it right last time, I wasn't ready." She stilled herself very deliberately. "O spirits," she intoned. "Dear spirits, please will you make your presence known to me, your servant, Sophie Salisbury. O spirits, is anybody there?" Her eyes were closed but she cracked one open after a moment to see absolutely nothing happening in the common room.

"Evelyn," Marion murmured. "Do you want to try?" Evelyn went red.

"Not particularly."

"Please will you," Sophie pleaded. "It's our only chance, none of the rest of us could do it."

"I don't—it's not right," Evelyn said, looking rather desperate. "I don't know what I'm supposed to do."

"Empty your mind," Sophie said. "Think of yourself as a vessel, like an empty jug waiting to be filled. That's what the book said."

"An empty jug," I muttered. "Honestly."

"Just try," Marion said. "You don't have to keep at it if you don't want to."

"A vessel, an empty jug, I'm not Evelyn, I'm waiting for the spirits to fill me," she almost chanted, her eyes screwed shut. "Just an empty jug. I'm not Evelyn. If there are spirits out there, I give them permission to take control of me, if they need it, which they oughtn't because I'm *not Evelyn*—"

It wasn't a traditional call to the spirits by any means. But almost as soon as she'd finished speaking, the old kerosene lamp in the corner came on of its own accord and flared a brilliant orange, and the curtains flapped hard with a stronger gust of wind than there had been all night.

"Is it happening?" said Dot, redundantly.

Evelyn's eyes weren't shut any longer but there was something unfamiliar about her face. She opened her mouth to speak. And then it opened wider, a little too wide, as if the voice inside didn't fit through. The hinge of her jaw drew back and back, beyond the point where it must have been painful. I held my breath, waiting to hear it click out of place, dreading the sound of bone moving against itself.

Nothing came, though—instead, there was a single cracking noise. It was louder than the rapping from the spirits at Mrs. Northcote's; it seemed to ripple through the room. I felt as though I might jump out of my own skin.

"Can you hear us?" Sophie said. "Knock once for yes, and twice for no." Her ability to keep it together in the face of the miraculous was, I had to admit, very impressive. One further resounding crack sounded. It didn't come from anywhere in particular—not against the wall or the table—instead it seemed to hang in the air.

"Who killed Violet?" I asked, surprising myself. I heard Dot draw in a breath; I suppose the question had come out of nowhere for everyone else, too. "Do you know who killed Violet?"

Evelyn's mouth shut abruptly, her teeth *thunking* together with a painful sound. The curtains, still being buffeted by the wind, made a sharp snapping noise.

"Evelyn?"

There was no answer. I wanted to curse aloud with frustration but before I had the chance, the poker from the fireplace began to rise unsteadily into the air, as if held aloft by a weak hand. It reached a position two or three feet up and hovered there. I wanted to look at the others but I felt held fast, like if I broke away it would come clattering to the ground and wake up the whole school. Whether it was holding me there, or I was holding it, felt immaterial. Sophie whimpered from across the circle. The poker feinted in one direction and then another. I winced. If it meant us violence, it could probably kill one of us with a single blow. I thought of Violet's skull, and of how easy it was to obliterate a person.

"It's difficult, for us," said Evelyn, out of nowhere. "It's like looking through the wrong end of a telescope. Everything seems terribly far away."

I realised partway through that whoever was speaking wasn't Evelyn at all. It sounded much more grown-up, nothing like her scratchy, precocious voice.

Her hand, which was holding mine, had grown chilly, and her thumb started to stroke the back of my hand. I shivered violently, but she didn't stop. All my senses electrified along the path of the pad of her thumb. One of the armchairs jerked, seemingly of its own accord, the sound of its wooden legs grinding against the floor like a groan. I came over in a sweat.

"Who killed Violet?" I said. "Please, I have to know, was it Mademoiselle Lefèvre?"

At that, the poker fell to the ground, denting the floorboard closest to the fireplace and making an awful *thwacking* noise. It seemed to ripple through the room: all I could think was, *Knock once for yes.*

I gasped; from across the circle I heard Dot sob, and Alice whispered something to her that I couldn't make out. I looked over at Marion, whose face had gone ashen. Evelyn's thumb was still tracing a lazy arc across the back of my hand. I couldn't take any of it any more, and a wave of nausea came over me. I tried to yank my hand away but Evelyn, or whatever was possessing her, held fast. Her nails dug into my flesh so hard I could feel the skin breaking.

"Please stop," I said. I was making a fool of myself. Tears were running into my mouth and my voice had come out strangled—that was how I realised I was crying—but I couldn't help it.

"Something's coming. Something that wants to hurt you," the spirit said, and then, almost as an afterthought, "Something's coming—no—it's already here—" With that, Evelyn's hand went limp in mine and she fainted.

The séance circle broke. I knelt over Evelyn's supine body; she was breathing shallowly and there were bright spots of colour high in her cheeks.

"Evelyn? Evelyn, wake up," I said. I couldn't think of anything to do but to slap her across the face, at which point she flinched with sufficient vigour that I felt pretty well assured she wasn't dying.

"What happened? Did anything happen?"

"You haven't a clue," Sophie breathed.

Then we heard footsteps coming up the stairs, and a silent panic overtook us. I scrambled under the sofa, dragging Evelyn with me, and prayed that the others had the sense to do similarly. There we lay, pressed together, her heart pounding so hard I could feel it in my whole body. She was trembling. It was, I think, the most I had ever touched her, Evelyn who was always so awkward and reticent about getting close to people. I hoped she couldn't feel how covered my face was in tears, hoped even more she couldn't tell that they were all over her hair.

The door to the common room opened. The sound of the spirits saying "Something's coming" rang in my ears. But nothing came in—I chanced turning my head to look at the sliver of the doorway that was visible to me, and all I could see were Miss Lewis's sturdy black leather boots. She stood there for a moment, and then closed the door.

I held as still as I could, with Evelyn's hair covering most of my face and her cold, sweaty wrist clutched in my hand.

SEVEN

A SHOCK TO THE SYSTEM

After the séance ended, we didn't have time to talk about what had happened. When Miss Lewis could no longer be heard, we hurried up to bed as quietly as we could, exhausted and frightened. I couldn't stop looking at the back of my hand, into which Evelyn's fingernails had scored four neat vermilion marks.

When we woke up the next morning, we were shepherded to breakfast with the brisk efficiency that Briarley did so well. All of us were careful around each other, treading lightly; I thought the falling poker was as good as proof but even with my certainty reinforced, I felt aching dread every time I thought about the séance. We agreed over our porridge that we needed to find a time to debrief in the common room. Marion suggested that none of the teachers would think twice about us hiding away to work on our Hallowe'en costumes, and we would be able to discuss things freely.

Hallowe'en was always much more of an event at Briarley than any of the schoolmistresses (or the prospectus sent to our parents) would have liked to admit. During my first Hallowe'en at Briarley, there was slightly more pretence at official disapproval. In an early display of the influence she had over the school, Violet had managed to persuade the schoolmistresses that good Christians could still put up bunting and wear costumes. This year, there had been quiet speculation about whether or not the traditional celebrations would go ahead on account of Violet's death. Marion, mostly at Dot and Sophie's behest, had a quiet word with Miss Lewis about it. I would never have asked her to—I fancied myself too grown-up to go about begging Miss Lewis to let us have a party—but I was glad she did; Hallowe'en and Violet, in my mind, were linked forever.

That afternoon we all made a public fuss about sewing our costumes, and decamped to the common room with relative certainty that we'd be left alone. At this point it became clear that I was actually expected to sew something, which felt laughable to me, but in the interest of collective peace and unity I kept my mouth shut.

I was never a good seamstress even at the best of times; I didn't have the patience or the eye for detail. Aware of my own limitations, I had gone for a sort of plain black sack with a witch's hat. I looked over, seething with envy, at Dot, who was merrily hand-smocking away. She had helped with Alice's costume too, doing the difficult bits of sewing for her, and seemed perfectly cheerful. I longed to be like her, only a bit. Dot was like a child; she upset easily, but it never took long before she was right as rain again. After the séance, I had heard the distinct sound of someone crying themselves to sleep from the direction of her bed, and the next day she was eagerly discussing whether she ought to be a shepherdess or a fairy for the costume party. I, on the other hand, was both easy to upset and difficult to console.

Evelyn had always disapproved of Hallowe'en for religious

reasons, though she was willing to dress up and bob for apples with the rest of us. She had made it very clear that she considered Sophie's Spanish dancer costume too risqué, Alice's Pierrot too masculine, and my witch too heretical. I suppose she couldn't think of much to object to with shepherdesses or ballerinas. Evelyn's concession to the occasion was a dress with a large appliqué cat splashed across the front, hissing and arching its back. It looked like something one of us might have made years before, only she was, unfortunately, a jolly good seamstress and so it was done perfectly. I could just picture her kneeling over the apple-bobbing tub. For several years she had made Violet's Hallowe'en costumes for her, and they were lovelier than anything she ever made for herself: one year, she spent about a week sewing little beads to a pair of butterfly wings she'd made by stretching tulle over a wire frame. As much as I loathed to admit it, Violet had never looked so beautiful. The beads glittered in the light and made her seem otherworldly, as though at any moment she might take to the air.

Evelyn didn't offer to help with my sewing, naturally; instead I caught her looking at me from across the room as she worked. The bones on the inside of her wrist pressed whitely against her skin. My hand had circled that wrist just the night before.

"Do you think Mademoiselle is going to come to the party tonight?" Sophie asked. It was the first foray into anything like discussion of the séance; we had, I suppose, to ease ourselves into it with what felt almost like gossip.

"She wouldn't need a costume, being a witch already," I said.

"Do you think she'll be well enough?"

"It's Hallowe'en! When demons abound and magic-doers gather to perform their evil deeds . . ."

"Be serious about this, will you?" Marion said. "I don't want you—I don't know—causing a scene. Anyhow, the party is four days before Hallowe'en itself, the veil can't be that thin so far in advance."

"If Mademoiselle blithely shows up to the Hallowe'en party dressed as Marie Antoinette or what have you, there is nothing in this world that could stop me making a scene. After last night—after that *single knock for yes* the poker made *just after* I asked the spirits if it was her who killed Violet—"

"I heard Fräulein Weingarten telling Miss Stevens that Mademoiselle was a bit better, actually," Dot offered. "After the German lesson yesterday, when she asked me to clean the blackboards. I was just leaving when Miss Stevens came by."

"Dot," said Alice, looking wounded. "You said you weren't going to tell."

"Better how?" I demanded.

"I didn't hear much more than that, only that she's better. I was glad, that's all, because it was horrid thinking of her sitting all alone in San."

"When were you planning to tell us about this?" Evelyn said, with a shrill tone to her voice.

"Leave it," Alice said, "leave her alone, I don't want her dragged into this."

"Just because you share some . . . some *sympathy* with Mademoiselle," Evelyn said, "I don't think you're in any position to keep things like that from us."

I winced.

"Not sure what you mean by that," said Alice, squaring up.

I cut in. In a way, it was my fault that Evelyn was on this track, by goading her into the investigation, and I didn't want her blowing up the rest of us as a result. There were some topics that felt too tender to broach; Alice-and-Dot was one of them.

"She didn't mean anything," I said, perhaps with a touch too much haste.

"No, she didn't, did she," Marion said. She glared at Evelyn significantly.

"Forget whatever nonsense Evelyn's saying," I said. "If Mademoiselle's better now, we need to decide what to do tonight. Sophie, what do you think?"

But Sophie wasn't playing along. "I think we oughtn't do anything at the Hallowe'en party. Even if Mademoiselle is there. I think we should try to have a nice evening. I want to look pretty and dance to the gramophone and bob for apples. It's all been so horrible and I don't want to make it worse." Her voice wavered a little.

I was taken aback; I knew she agreed with me about Mademoiselle, even more so after the spirits had as much as confirmed it. I couldn't understand the idea of knowing that the person who killed your friend was out there, feeling swell and attending your party, and not feeling like you couldn't rest till you'd done something. If Mademoiselle came to the Hallowe'en party, it would be an insult to Violet's memory and a mockery of what we had all been put through. Then again, Sophie was Sophie: she was artlessly easy-going, and so when she put her foot down you felt too guilty to try and contradict her.

"All right," I said. "We'll leave it, for now. Even if she's there. But I can't act like we don't know what she did, not after what happened last night."

"Later," Sophie echoed, vaguely. "We can deal with it later."

The dining hall had been decorated with orange and black streamers, bought in town by Miss Parker and Fräulein Weingarten. For her part, Miss Parker had shown up, in a moment of indulgent dramatics outside of her ordinarily retiring character, wearing an enormous velveteen dress and a piano shawl draped over her shoulders, as though she was longing to be an eccentric Russian dance mistress out of a novel. Cole Porter was playing on the big old gramophone, which always sounded rather fuzzy but was good enough for us, considering there wasn't a wireless in school.

Alice immediately swept Dot out to dance a clumsy waltz, and I tried not to pay too much attention. Instead, I watched Evelyn. She walked solemnly over to the chairs set out along the side of the room and sat down. When I followed the line of her gaze, I saw Mademoiselle, slumped in a chair behind high table, ostensibly watching over the refreshments. It looked as though she couldn't have stood for more than a few minutes if she'd wanted to. She was wan, and when she reached up to pin back a stray strand of hair, her hand shook. At least she hadn't put on some kind of vulgar costume to add insult to injury.

When I caught her eye by accident, she glanced away furtively, as though she'd been caught doing something she oughtn't, and it seemed like she was very glad indeed that we had high table between us. The last time we'd spoken, in San all those weeks ago, she'd had the advantage, weak and miserable as I had been in the creaky ironwork bed. What she'd said to me—the things she had implied—I couldn't understand it as anything other than deliberate, mocking cruelty. That scene seemed miles away from the fragile woman in the dining hall, and even so I was relieved not to have to be too close to her.

I went through the motions of the Hallowe'en party until I felt myself relax somewhat. I straightened the tam o'shanter that Lucy, two years below, was wearing when she asked me to, I ate an egg and cress sandwich, I had a little foxtrot with Sophie, who was always content to be led even rather badly. And if I looked over my shoulder every once in a while to keep an eye on Mademoiselle, who could blame me?

“Gather round, girls,” Cook said, from a corner. She had an apron full of apples from the barrel that had been brought in from the cellar, which she dropped into a tub of water.

“Bobbing for apples!” one of the upper fourths squealed, and then there was a mad rush to queue in front of the tub.

“Don’t think you lot can get away with standing at the sidelines!” Cook called to us, collected as we were in a semi-isolated clump towards the mantelpiece. I loved hearing her speak; the schoolmistresses were hand-picked to sound as prim as we did lest they infect us with any lower-class sensibilities. But it was practically mandatory to have a kind, countrified cook with a large bosom and ruddy cheeks at a secluded girls’ school, and Briarley was never one to break with tradition. Cook was easier with affection than the rest, and she had loved Violet.

Alice, taking charge, herded us all towards the tub.

“It’s time to ritually lose our dignity,” Marion said to me.

“At least your hair’s already pinned up. Mine’s everywhere, it’s going to get soaked.”

“An unkempt witch suits your character.”

“Ah!” I said, clutching my chest. “You wound me!”

“Go on, girls, don’t leave the little ones to snag all the best apples first,” Cook said to us. She shooed a few upper fourths out of our way. All joking aside, I felt rather apprehensive about the prospect of plunging my face into the tub when the last time I had encountered a Briarley apple it had been chock full of maggots. But the pressure of tradition weighed on me; I had never once in six years failed to bob for apples at Hallowe’en, even when I was so small that my mouth could only fit around the littlest, most withered ones.

"All right, all right," I said, and took off my misshapen witch's hat in preparation. I knelt down in front of the tub and took a deep breath.

Wouldn't it have been nice, if we had been able to have a good time? It would have felt like a gift, an unexpected infusion of normality into a world that had all of a sudden become very strange. I would have been grateful for it, anyway. Plunging my face into the cold water was a shock to the system. I opened my mouth to snatch at an apple, and water flooded in.

The problem was, I hadn't been expecting it. If the apple had sunk unnaturally under my teeth I had already planned to let it go and not even look at what I'd left behind, but the apple itself was fine. Instead, the water that went into my mouth didn't have the cool, sweet taste of the stuff that usually came from the well, but was bitter and thick against my tongue. I panicked, took a sharp intake of breath, and aspirated a stream of scummy water. I tried to sit up but it was like I was being held down, forced to stay still; it wasn't long before I began to feel light-headed. My throat and nose burned with the nasty bitter taste of the water, though that along with everything else felt muted and distant. It was as though I was down there for hours, swaddled in thick darkness.

I remember once as a child I took a bite of my biscuit after it had fallen into the dirt and immediately started wailing. I didn't calm down until my nurse had rinsed out my mouth and given me a lemon drop from her carpet bag. The taste of the soil was awful; it had the distinct feeling of being something I was *not supposed* to be eating. It was alkaline, almost like the soap my mother washed out my mouth with when I had been nasty, and it filled the whole mouth at once.

I had a sense, fuzzy lights popping behind my eyelids, that Mademoiselle must be doing this somehow. Then I heard something faint and unformed. It wasn't words: just sounds, echoing and rebounding under the water. Silvery, bell-like, and, most of all, familiar. It sounded like Violet.

All at once my muscles unlocked. I pulled my head up out of the water, and noticed I had the apple caught between my teeth. I heaved and sputtered awfully, dropping it into my hand. Cook looked at me, baffled.

"What's that all over her face?" It was the voice of one of the younger girls, a shy whisper that was perfectly clear in the drawn silence of the hall.

No one rushed to see if I was all right. I realised it must only have been a few seconds that I'd been underwater, certainly not long enough for anyone to have become worried. From their perspective I suppose they had only seen me plunge my face in, stay there for a while, and then come up spattering water everywhere.

The apple hadn't sunk under my teeth like the rotten ones from before; as far as I could tell it was as good inside as any normal apple. But the outside was covered in a slimy brackish substance, and I soon realised that whatever it was had coated my face and tongue as well. I spat and hacked and came up with more of it until my stomach began to heave and I had to squeeze my eyes shut and ball my fists until the urge to vomit had passed.

When I opened my eyes again, Sophie was crouched next to me with a glass of punch in one hand and a tea towel in the other, looking worried. I swigged the punch in one long gulp and scrubbed at my face with the tea towel, which came away covered in something resembling algae. I dreaded to think what I looked like; it was in my hair as well, which had swept forwards into the water.

"Cook, how did this happen?" Miss Lewis demanded.

"I don't understand it," Cook said, bewildered. "That's well water, we drink it every day and it's never been anything but pure and clean."

I smarted on Cook's behalf. "It looked all right," I added, hoarsely.

"This isn't some sort of prank, is it, girls?" Miss Stone asked, looking hard at me, which I thought was just typical of her.

"I didn't do anything," I protested, though my voice came out thick and I wasn't up to being persuasive. Miss Lewis sighed.

"Best to check the well, Cook. We can't have unwholesome water here. I suppose we'll have to leave the rest of the apple bobbing until next year."

I scratched behind my ear and my fingers came back filthy, greenish scum collected under my nails. When I looked over at Evelyn she hadn't moved. Her eyes were open wide and her lips were pressed together so hard they were going white, as if when she opened her mouth she wasn't sure what would come out. She was staring dead on at Mademoiselle, who looked barely conscious. I thought, briefly but quite intensely, that I didn't know when everything had become so complicated.

The party returned gradually from the rather hushed lull it had descended into. I wasn't adored enough for anyone to be shocked into sympathetic silence for long, especially over a bit of grime. But nerves were frayed thin, and so a gasp or a thinly veiled argument between Cook and the teachers was enough to rattle everyone. It wasn't until the gramophone had been put on as loud as it would go and Marion had pointedly started a banal and very public conversation with Sophie that the usual volume of chatter returned.

Over in the corner, some of the youngest girls were playing pin the tail on the donkey, and I watched them idly as they scurried about. I reflected that we were all there, in that room, because of Violet; without her, all those years ago, Miss Lewis might never have relented and allowed us to have a party. She'd had a way, even at twelve, of persuading anyone around to anything. By the time she was done with you, you'd not only do whatever she wanted but you'd think it had been your idea all along. Someone who had loved her less might have called it calculating. I thought of her voice, and the painful absence of it. I thought of Violet, who had loved me, and who was giving me a warning.

EIGHT

A THIN THREAD OF HORROR

When I brushed my teeth that night, the tooth-powder I spat into the sink was grey and dirty. The taste of the water still lingered at the back of my throat. I slunk back into the dormitory, feeling terribly sorry for myself.

"Dot, have you got any sweets? I only want one. I can still taste all that muck."

"'Course," Dot said—she could be relied upon to have some manner of sweets in her bedside table—and scrabbled around till she found a tin of bonbons. I took a pear drop and popped it in my mouth.

"Thanks," I said, and lapsed into silence. I sat down in my bed, and twisted around to look out the open window. It faced onto the grassy fields surrounding Briarley, cushioning us from the rest of the world. There were the apple trees, casting spidery shadows onto the lawn. There was the winding road that led to the village. There was the hedgerow, where Violet and I had picked blackberries days before she died, staining our fingers purple and eating until our stomachs hurt and we didn't want our dinner. *Something's coming*, I thought.

"Emily, I was watching Mademoiselle," Evelyn said, from across the room. I started. Evelyn addressed me so rarely that it felt like an event whenever it did happen. "She was staring at you."

"Staring at me? When?"

"When you had your head in the tub. She was slumped over but she was *staring*."

"Probably wondering why you were in there so long. Honestly, Evelyn, not everything needs to be a conspiracy," Alice said. She had a spot of tooth-powder on her chin, but I didn't want to puncture her pride by mentioning it.

"No, she had this strange expression on her face," Evelyn insisted. "As though she was afraid."

"Afraid?" I said. I thought about what I had heard under the water. It sounded stupidly far-fetched, when I tried to imagine saying it aloud. "When I was in the tub," I started, and then faltered. Once we had accepted that the dead could speak through the living—which it seemed, undoubtedly, that they could—where was the limit? There had to come a point at which I drew a line, after which I could dismiss things as insane, or ridiculous. Or, perhaps, I was worried that there was a line after which everyone could dismiss *me* as insane, or ridiculous.

"Well?" Alice said.

"When I was in the tub," I started again, "I felt something—odd."

"Odd how?"

"Odd like . . . well, there were two odd things about it, I suppose. The first was that I couldn't get my head out of the water when I first realised it wasn't right. All I wanted to do was pull myself out, but I couldn't move at all."

"Some kind of—neurotic attack?" Alice suggested. I recoiled.

"No," I said, perhaps too vehemently. "It wasn't like that. My body froze up, like it was completely out of my control."

"So what are you saying?"

"I don't *know*," I said. "Alice, I don't know what I'm saying. All I know is it felt unnatural."

"You cannot be telling me you think Mademoiselle did a—what, a spell on you?" Alice's voice began to rise.

"Keep it down," Marion said tightly. She had, perhaps wisely, been lying in bed reading and being very careful not to pay attention.

"I'm sorry, but that is absurd," Alice said. She was nearly shouting now. "That is completely insane."

"The other thing was," I said, dreading every word, "that I thought I heard Violet's voice when I was under there." Evelyn stiffened.

"What was she saying?" she said.

"I couldn't make it out. I could hardly hear a thing. I just knew it was her."

"Did she sound frightened?" There was a thin thread of horror in her voice.

"No," I said. I wished I had some kind of control over the situation and that I wouldn't keep on saying things that made me sound like I was losing my grip. "It sounded like she wanted me to know something. Like she was warning me. I mean, I suppose that's settled things, then, hasn't it? If we were warned by the spirits and now Violet herself . . ."

"Why did she speak to *you*?" Evelyn said, but it didn't sound like she expected an answer. "I had to go through that awful séance, sitting there and feeling this horrid presence in my body, like it wasn't mine any more. You have no idea how it felt, none of you—and then Violet goes and talks to *Emily*.

As if I didn't—as if I was some rubbish to be thrown aside—when I went through all that and you'll make me do it again—" Abruptly she threw the covers off and ran to the door. As she slammed it shut, I heard something that might have been a sob.

"Should I go after her?" I asked Marion.

"I can't imagine she's going to want to speak to you," Marion said. Her book lay abandoned on the bedspread. "Best to leave it, I think. Let her cry it out and come back when she's ready."

"It's beside the point," I said, fiddling with the fringe on my blanket, to have something to do with my hands. "Who gives a toss who Violet chose to warn? Surely all that matters is she wants us to know something. Something important."

"Are you telling me you wouldn't have minded if she'd chosen Evelyn?" Marion asked, looking at me steadily.

"No! Obviously I wouldn't have! I'm not *possessive* about it."

"Right," Marion said.

"What really matters is that we have to—heed Violet's warning, or whatever it is. I think we should confront Mademoiselle."

"Do you mean you think we should harass a weak, ill woman? Who you don't even know has done anything wrong?" Alice said.

I looked to Sophie in the hopes that she would back me up, and this time she got the message.

"Alice, Violet is trying to talk to us. If the spirits were warning us at Mrs. Northcote's, and then here, what else could it mean?"

"I don't know what happened," Alice said. "But I think it's bloody suspicious that you took us to Mrs. Northcote and Evelyn's the one who said all that rubbish about how it wasn't an accident, and now Emily's hearing warnings from Violet in the apple tub. It's just funny, isn't it, that it's you three, who hate Mademoiselle and think she's some kind of—some kind of sick menace, who happen to be hearing voices telling you the same thing."

"You can't pin what happened at Mrs. Northcote's on Sophie," I said. "How on earth could she have had any idea what the spirits were going to say? And Evelyn—you didn't feel her after that séance. She was freezing cold and clammy all over, and I thought her heart was going to come right out of her chest. There's no way she could've faked that. And you still haven't answered Sophie's question."

"What question?" Alice said, too loudly.

"What else could it mean?"

At that moment, Evelyn slipped back into the dormitory. Her eyes were shining and her face was scrubbed pink and raw.

"I don't care what anyone else thinks," she said. Her voice was tense and low and had a distinct crack in the middle of it. "I'm confronting Mademoiselle and you can't stop me."

She sounded so utterly flat and miserable it frightened me. For a second I longed to have the old Evelyn back, the one before Violet died. I had hardly known her as anything but an irritant, someone to whom Violet turned when she and I had rowed and she wanted to make a point of how easily her affections could change. I didn't like having these occasional waves of sympathy for Evelyn; it was all so much easier when I could hate her for being sanctimonious and prissy. But there she stood in front of the dormitory door, her hair escaping its plaits and her knobby wrists sticking out of her nightgown sleeves. I admired her for it despite myself.

Her pronouncement worked on Alice, who fell back and stopped arguing. Dot was crying. She hated when we fought. She always said it reminded her of her mother sniping at her. I hated it too, especially now, but I always seemed to find myself saying things I couldn't take back.

"Thanks, Evelyn," I said, distantly. She didn't say a word, only walked over to her bed and blew out the candle on her bedside table.

We decided to confront Mademoiselle at Monday breaktime. Alice and Dot were nowhere to be seen that morning. I suspected they might've risen before the bell so they could brush their teeth and get dressed without having to talk to anyone. Evelyn and Sophie and I whispered about what we were going to do while Sophie brushed her hair, over breakfast (very quietly), and in Fräulein Weingarten's German lesson. It was all I could think about, the anticipation rising in my head like a shrill buzz. When the bell rang, instead of going to the common room like we normally would, we took the other staircase up to San.

I suppose I ought now to explain what had happened, the last time I was there. The thought of those days unnerves me, and I don't much like to think about it, even now. I spent several days in San after Violet died. No one had been able to get a word out of me, or so I'm told. I was hardly a person at all, as though so much of myself had been carted away in the ambulance along with Violet's body that there wasn't enough left to speak.

What brought me out of it was, ironically, Mademoiselle. She came to visit me one afternoon, soft concern on her face and something I couldn't quite see in her hands. She glided down the aisle between the lines of beds as though her feet hardly needed to touch the floor. Her big brown eyes were wet with tears and she worried at her lower lip with gleaming white teeth.

"Emily," she said, in her low, soft voice, accented only lightly. "I'm so sorry I didn't come sooner. I couldn't bear it. Having to give these dreary lessons to a room that ought to have Violet in it—and then I couldn't stand the thought of looking you in the eye. But I found this, and I thought perhaps you might like to have it." She brought out a handkerchief, of a pale lilac colour and scalloped around the edges. I looked helplessly at it, and at her. She thrust the handkerchief towards me. My hands moved to take it almost of their own accord, and my whole body felt like it might shimmer apart into pieces if I didn't concentrate on keeping it together with everything I had. The handkerchief was soft, made of a finely spun cotton lawn that was more expensive than anything I owned myself. There, on the corner, in pale blue thread, was embroidered the letter *E*, in stitches so minute you could hardly see them.

The trouble was, I had seen the handkerchief before. More than that, I had given it to Violet. It was the nicest thing I had ever bought in my life, and I had given it to her on her seventeenth birthday. The embroidery was Violet's; I hadn't seen it before but I recognised the perfect, tiny stitches. I thought for a second that the *E* might be for my name, and then I remembered that Mademoiselle's Christian name was Élodie. All at once my chest seized up: foolish, to assume it might have been for me.

"I know you loved her," Mademoiselle said. Her voice came to me as if through water. "Like I loved her. Our feelings, I think, were the same, and—"

She reached out and touched my hand. Her skin was soft and cool.

"Our feelings," I said, my voice creaky with disuse.

"I am sorry if I ever let on that I was jealous of you, Emily, or gave you reason to feel jealous yourself. Violet's attention could feel like the warmth of the sun, and to lose it even for a short time—well. She cared for you very much; she always told me so. Haven't we all wished that a rival for our loved one's affections would cease to tempt them—haven't we all wished that our loved one would choose us, above all others? But it doesn't matter now."

All at once, the pieces fell into place and I felt freer than I had in days.

"If you imagine," I said, growing stronger and stronger as I spoke, "that you and I have anything in common where Violet was concerned, you're even sicker than I thought."

San was a big airy room with six ironwork beds and larger than average windows, which Matron kept open at all times to promote circulation of the air. She felt this was good for the blood, though she never did explain why. The beds were arranged in neat rows like in a hospital, their covers tucked in severely at the corners. There was little concession to childhood comfort, and I remember going to San feeling like the worst kind of nightmare when I was in lower fourth and had to stay there for weeks when I was ill. I had been so unwell that anyone else would have been sent home to recuperate, but I simply refused to be sent back to my parents, so San became my temporary, inhospitable home.

It was a chilly, clean place with none of the cosy familiarity of the rest of the school, and it always smelled of strong cleaning fluid. It wasn't the sort of place you wanted to stay any longer than was strictly necessary. If I totted it up, Mademoiselle had been here for a month, with the brief and unpleasant exception of Hallowe'en. I couldn't understand why she hadn't just gone home by now.

Evelyn had timed our visit so that Matron would be about to take her break; to buy us more time I promised Lily Henry in the upper fourth that I would bring back tenpence worth of sweets from the village the next week-end if she made a big scene about falling over and skinning her knee. It was perfect timing, and Matron met us as we came up the stairs.

"You're ever so kind, girls, to visit her."

"Wouldn't dream of leaving her all on her own," I said. "She and Violet were so close, you know." Evelyn kicked me in the shin.

"Yes, awful how it's affected her—imagine, her not having people of her own to look after her! A month shut up in the infirmary can't be good for anyone."

"I suppose she hasn't anywhere else to go," said Evelyn, her voice cold. Matron didn't seem to notice her tone.

"Precisely—all the way from France and not a soul willing to care for her, the poor pet. We wrote to her family but they sent word back that we were to look after her and they'd send us funds if we insisted—but I shouldn't be telling you about all that. I was so glad to see her up and about at the Hallowe'en party. Do leave the door pulled to so as to preserve the good air, will you?"

"Of course, Matron," Sophie said. With that Matron bustled past us down the stairs, her starched hat tipping dangerously to the side. All there was left to do was open the door to San.

Mademoiselle was in the bed furthest from the door. She looked terribly small all the way down there, sitting up with a book in her lap. Her bedside table was a mess of pill bottles and tonics. I felt enormously relieved that San was empty of all other patients; this wasn't a conversation I intended to have with onlookers. She looked up at us as we approached and cringed, drawing back.

"Mademoiselle!" I called.

"What do you want from me?" she said. Her voice was weak.

The book fell from her hand onto the floor, its pages folding badly underneath.

"What do you think we want?" I said, striding through the room till I reached her bedside table, where I could tower over her.

Sophie and I stood on one side of the bed, Evelyn on the other, till Mademoiselle was well and truly boxed in. It felt good, the best thing I'd felt in weeks, as though a groundswell of energy was rising beneath me.

"We want you to admit that you killed Violet," I said.

"I don't understand why you hate me so," she said. "I don't know what I ever did to you, to make you think I could do a thing like that."

She sounded defeated. I took her in from my vantage point above her: lips dry and cracked and nearly bleeding from a split, hair tangled and ugly, skin pallid. I wish I could say that at that moment I felt sympathy for her. With everything that came after it would be a relief, to know that deep in myself I had enough compassion that standing over her and seeing her utterly broken would allow me to see sense and behave with decency. Instead, I looked at her diminished beauty and recalled all the times Violet had turned away from a conversation to steal a moment with Mademoiselle, the evening when I had seen Mademoiselle's hand toying with the tip of Violet's plait, the unfamiliar soft look in Violet's eyes after being kissed goodnight. So I slapped her, a feeble slap that barely connected with her cheek.

"Emily," Sophie said, stricken, and grabbed my arm. I had never in my life done anything so outrageous.

"Don't be a coward, Sophie."

She hung back, then, hurt, and I didn't have time to feel badly over it before I turned back to Mademoiselle and the sight of her crumpled, pathetic face filled me with fury again.

"Just admit it. I can't see why you won't admit it. You pushed her off the landing and broke half the bones in her body." I felt Evelyn go rigid at that, all the way from across Mademoiselle's bed.

"Please just tell me," Evelyn said softly. "Why did you do it?"

"Come on, Evelyn, you know why she did it," I said, not looking at her, my eyes fixed instead on Mademoiselle's blanched face.

"Please tell me," Evelyn said again. "I loved Violet. Why did you kill her?"

Mademoiselle stared back, her eyes glassy. Then her bony hand shot out and snatched me by the arm, tighter than I would've thought possible. I yelped in pain and tried to step back; it felt like she would break my wrist. My mouth went dry.

"Stop it—stop it—" Evelyn said, frozen in place. The bed seemed to telescope until she was very far away from me.

Then Mademoiselle began to speak, all her quavering gone and replaced with a steely self-assurance. "Your friend did not die by accident," she said.

"Yes, we're well aware, thank you," I said, through a fog of dizziness, trying again to pull my arm away. Mademoiselle's hand held me fast.

"She was only the beginning," she added. Then Mademoiselle appeared to get control of herself, only to burst into a flood of tears. "What is happening to me?" she pleaded, her grip on my wrist going slack. "I wouldn't do a thing to Violet, she was a darling girl and I loved her, I didn't want her to die!" Her voice slurred and shrilled, a hysterical shriek.

I dragged myself away from her and fought the urge to scramble out of San altogether.

Mademoiselle's mouth twisted again. "When your friend fell from the landing, her last thought was confusion," she said.

"Her last act was to reach for her beloved. Her last feeling was pain as the perfume bottle shattered in her palm and her back broke on the floorboards." The split at the centre of her bottom lip had opened in earnest, and now her tears were mingling with blood at her pointed chin. "She will not be the last. Tonight—tonight—"

Something in Evelyn broke. She made an inarticulate noise of fury, and I watched as she flew at Mademoiselle, her face scarlet with rage. Evelyn hauled her up from where she lay, arranged against the pillows, and shook her hard by the shoulders. Mademoiselle's head lolled back, knocking against the headboard, and her voice stopped droning. At last, Evelyn collapsed over Mademoiselle's still body, sobbing and shaking, in an awful parody of an embrace. Sophie reached out to her tentatively but she didn't respond at all.

"Evelyn," I said. "We should leave. Matron won't be away for much longer."

"We need to get to the village," Sophie said, sounding perhaps more decisive than she felt. "We have to go to the police, tell them what we know."

"She as much as admitted it," I added, trying to bolster her. "Even if in her—her conscious mind she didn't mean to do it, she's clearly mad and dangerous and we'll be putting everyone at risk if we don't do something."

"Evelyn, please." Sophie rested her hand on Evelyn's shoulder. She was still draped over Mademoiselle, silent now but shaking.

"I can't tell if she's breathing," Evelyn said, without moving.

"What?" Sophie said. Her voice was high, full of nerves. "Let me—Mum was a nurse in the war, she showed me how to check."

I couldn't have been more grateful to see Sophie circle

the bed, grasp Evelyn by the waist with all the authority of an expert, and move her out of the way. Evelyn allowed herself to be shuttled about without resistance. Sophie leaned down to put her ear by Mademoiselle's mouth, and then rested two fingers on her wrist, which lay limply in the bedclothes.

"She's breathing, but her pulse is weak," Sophie said.

"Is she in some kind of faint?"

"I don't know if it seems altogether natural."

"Get the smelling salts, will you?" I said, touching Evelyn on the shoulder. Evelyn looked at me blankly. "Matron keeps them in the cabinet over there, it's the unlocked one with the bandages and things she doesn't mind us having. Evelyn!" This jolted her out of her stupor and she walked over to the cabinet, her movements jerky like a puppet's.

The smelling salts did nothing. Nor did splashing Mademoiselle's face with cold water from the basin, and nor did slapping her quite hard (my idea). She just lay there, breathing slowly but utterly still and silent. A mad tension skittered up and down my arms and I itched to do something, but finally we had to formulate an alternative plan. We sent Sophie out, as the most innocent and gentle-looking of the three of us, to fetch Matron back early and tell her with the utmost concern about Mademoiselle's faint. In the meantime, Evelyn and I pulled up chairs and sat by Mademoiselle's side, looking the picture of concerned schoolgirls while watching her like a hawk.

She didn't stir the whole time, not even when Matron arrived, flustered and out of breath, to fuss over her. Matron gave us some kindly platitudes about how she was sure Mademoiselle would be fine in no time, but there was a furrow between her brows that told me she was more concerned than she was letting on. Her gentleness and worry for us was sweet, and I cannot bear to think about it, or how little we deserved it, for long.

What I felt then, though, was triumph. I was vindicated. I was certain that even Alice couldn't hold it against me any more: Mademoiselle speaking in that awful way and nearly crushing my bones to dust was proof enough that she was capable of having killed Violet, but the veiled threats to the rest of us—those were evidence, real conclusive evidence, the sort of thing that ended those detective novels I was so fond of.

With Mademoiselle unconscious, I thought we had a little more breathing room before we needed to fetch the police, and I intended to tell the others what we had seen, very cordially, and march to the village first thing the next morning, damn and blast whatever Miss Lewis might have to say about it. As Evelyn, Sophie, and I walked to our English lesson I felt my step grow lighter and easier than it had been in weeks.

I couldn't bring Violet back; that was impossible. But perhaps now that the danger had passed I could try to find her in a séance, call out to her spirit in heaven or Summerland or wherever it was. I knew she would want to see us—see me. I had earned her some measure of justice, or at least I would have as soon as Mademoiselle had been sent away somewhere terrible. The world felt full of possibility again and I was swimming in it. I had, for once, a sense of generosity—towards my friends, towards myself. I could even feel generous towards Mademoiselle, poor mad broken Mademoiselle who couldn't have meant to hurt Violet, even if her unnatural desires were rotten through. Things weren't ever going to go back to normal, not without Violet there, but Briarley might feel like home again.

We stepped into the poky classroom where the top year English lessons were held. I watched as the late morning light filtered in through the bullseye glass windows, dust motes leaping up into the air. Alice's back practically vibrated with tension, but it wouldn't be long before I could tell her everything and watch her relax into the inevitability of what was to come. Dot leaned her curly dark head on Alice's shoulder as we waited for Miss Parker to come in and tell us about *Middlemarch*. Marion fiddled with a pen, her sleek hair neat in a chignon. I thought, then, that I had never loved them all more.

I have held that image fast in my mind ever since. It's become something like one of those old stereographs: the sort of Victorian artefact you dig up in your attic and spend a rainy afternoon poring over. In my imagination, the scene doesn't look like a flat photograph at all. There's a tangibility and depth to it, as if I could reach out my hand and touch someone's shoulder, insert myself back into that moment like nothing happened at all.

NINE

OCCAM'S RAZOR

Marion and Alice and Dot took being told about Mademoiselle surprisingly well, even Alice, who really just looked desperately sad. She and Marion told us they didn't want to be involved in going to the police but they wouldn't stop us doing it either, which felt to me like the coward's way out, though I didn't want to push my luck by saying so. I was so convinced that given time they would come around. I tried to ignore the doubtful note in Marion's voice when she said she supposed that what Mademoiselle said could have been a threat, but couldn't it also have been a warning? From her, or from—and I could hear the uncertainty when she said it—the spirits?

"Occam's razor," I replied, almost surprised by how quickly I was putting the pieces together, and with such clarity. "She was the only one with Violet when she fell. If we're putting it in the politest terms possible, she was obsessed with Violet, and now she's telling us more of us will die. It's simple; if you strip out all the rest of it—séances, or diagnoses, or anything—it starts to seem inevitable."

"Yes, I suppose I can't much argue with that," Marion said,

and absent-mindedly stirred her tea. I don't mean to paint Marion as stupid here, because of course I am aware that I come across as stupid as one could possibly get, and here she was halfway to agreeing with me. But I knew that Marion, although not exactly a hard-headed sceptic, wasn't the type to be taken in by mysterious hunches. I think, despite myself because it hurts to remember it, that it was the crack in my voice that persuaded her I wasn't lying or exaggerating, when I said Mademoiselle had claimed Violet's last act was to reach for her.

Worst of all, I felt a sort of thrill. It couldn't be easy, to be a detective in one of those novels; you were always having to hurt people in your search for the truth. Marion wasn't wholly on side but I thought I'd made real progress, and anyhow the most important thing was that the next day, all of us who were willing would go into the village and fetch the police and the whole nightmare would be over. The fact that looking at Marion and Dot and Alice provoked a curl of shame deep inside me wasn't something I wanted to linger on.

"We've done the right thing," Evelyn said. I couldn't tell if she meant it as a question. I thought I'd act as if she hadn't.

"Yes we have, haven't we. If you think about it—really think about it—we could've saved someone's life today. Who can tell how seriously we should've taken all that mad ranting—but clearly she thought someone was going to be killed and if she was going to be the one to do it then, well. She can't now, can she?" I said.

"Yes," Evelyn said, not sounding sure at all.

"Consider it a relief," I advised her.

I was so convinced I had everything figured out, had cut right to the heart of things and allowed all the distractions—vague warnings, sour milk, things that couldn't be pinned down and understood—to fall away. It was freeing like nothing

I had ever felt. I was weightless, unfettered. My own feelings, my own fears, had receded far enough that I didn't have to look at them if I didn't want to. Nothing mattered except the truth I had discerned, which was clean and simple and whole. Sometimes I miss that moment of certainty, brief as it turned out to be.

That evening, I stepped outside to sit and think to myself for a few minutes before dinner. It was a quarter to six and the sun had already set. The sky felt low and quiet, like something hanging over us, hushing the world.

"Violet?" I said aloud, surprising myself. "Are you there?" Nothing answered me. A chilly breeze rustled the leaves on the apple trees. "If you can hear me . . . I'm glad we found out what happened to you."

I sat there for a minute or two longer, waiting for some kind of sign—a shooting star whizzing across the sky or something equally saccharine. Whatever it was, it didn't come, and so I turned tail and marched back up to the manor to sit down with everyone else for dinner.

The dining hall was warm and bright. I watched as a herd of girls clattered in, their feet on the flagstones like little hooves. I thought, fondly, that they were safe now, and I had played no small part in it. Glowing with a rare generosity of spirit, I stood to the side and watched them filter through the narrow doorway, and then explode back out again as they headed to their tables. When I caught sight of the others, I felt terribly proud of us all: Sophie and Evelyn, obviously, but Marion and Dot and even Alice, who had allowed reason and justice to triumph over pettier things.

"Wotcher, Locke," Alice said as I approached.

"Hullo," I replied, a little cautiously.

"Listen, I wanted to say. I know I didn't make it the easiest, your whole thing with Mademoiselle, and I just wanted to say sorry." She sent a penitent glance towards Marion, who had obviously put her up to it.

"That's frightfully decent of you, Alice, thanks. And, you know, for what it's worth I'm sorry too. I know you didn't want it to be her and I wish it didn't have to be a sort of wedge between us."

"Apology accepted. Friends again?"

"Yes please." She stuck her hand out across the table and I shook it. Marion looked extremely pleased with herself.

"Don't you think it'll be ever so nice," Dot said, "not to have to talk about this any more? It's all been too dreary, and now we can get back to talking about—whatever we talked about before. Whether we want humbugs or sherbet lemons for our penny sweets, or if there's anything we want to see at the pictures during the holidays."

"I've wanted to discuss getting a Marcel wave for weeks and no one would let me get a word in edgeways," Sophie said solemnly.

I like to imagine a version of that evening where we had a normal dinner, with jam roly poly for pudding and going to bed early, and all the things that our lives ought to have been. Instead, I took a bite of the stew and made a face. Something was off with it: a queer sweetness at the back of the throat that seemed to coat one's tongue and stick in the gullet. "Does this taste odd to you?"

Alice, who was even less polite than I was, muttered something about Cook forgetting everything she'd ever known about dinner.

"It's not ideal, is it," Marion admitted, pushing her food about on her plate.

I chanced a look over at high table and, sure enough, no one appeared to be eating with gusto there, either. Miss Lewis had a piece of potato speared on her fork, but she wasn't eating it; the fork lay abandoned on her plate as she spoke to the other teachers.

"I hope there isn't anything wrong with the pantry," Evelyn said abruptly.

"Why would there be?" Dot asked.

"Just—the milk, the apples, now this. It'll be difficult to make it through the rest of term if the pantry can't keep things fresh."

I thought that was typical Evelyn: parsimonious, overcautious. "You worry too much. Look, I'm eating it," I said, and ostentatiously took a piece of carrot. It tasted distinctly unpleasant, but I chewed and swallowed like a champion.

"I don't know if I think it's gone off, per se," Marion said doubtfully. "It doesn't look mouldy, it's just . . . odd."

"Odd," Evelyn echoed, folding and re-folding her napkin in her lap.

There was a loud *thunk* from somewhere across the room. Then: gasps, a child screaming, the clatter of silverware. I felt a powerful wave of déjà vu but it was as though I was stuck in place as everything erupted around me.

Marion and Alice shoved their chairs back in an instant and ran off. I heard loud crying, from more than one person; worst of all, some of the crying was clearly from whichever schoolmistress had made her way across the room fastest. The weeping began to spread, as people in a wider and wider radius got wind of whatever had happened. I still hadn't moved, my legs aching and leaden.

Evelyn and I were the only two left at the table, the only two left anywhere nearby, in fact: everyone else had rushed behind us to one of the lower school tables. I heard familiar voices above the crying, Marion's tone sounding more distressed than I had ever heard before, Miss Stone barking something I couldn't make out.

My back was to the drama unfolding across the room. I couldn't even see what people were doing, I was going on sound alone, but there was a rising ringing in my ears that threatened to drown the rest of it out. All I could see was Evelyn sitting still in front of me, her plate untouched and her face deadly white.

"Evelyn," I said.

"Yes," she whispered. It was an answer to a question I hadn't asked. "Yes, she's dead."

It was enough. My legs still felt heavy as anything but with enormous force of will I dragged myself out of my chair. Most of the school's population had circled about the upper thirds' table, where Miss Stone and Miss Lewis were hunched over, at the epicentre of the hubbub. I edged closer but it was nearly impossible to see beyond the cluster of girls and teachers.

"Ring for an ambulance," Miss Lewis said to Dot, who looked stricken.

She nodded vigorously, glad for an excuse to leave the room, and pushed her way through the crowd.

"There isn't any point," I heard Sophie say, and realised she was in the circle too, dipped down out of sight. "It's too late."

I remember thinking in an almost abstracted way how bizarre it was that in a crisis, we were old enough to be drafted in as honorary adults. Ordinarily we were as much subject to uniform regulations or raps across the knuckles as anyone else, but in this state of chaos, all distinctions had blurred. The fact that Sophie's mother had taught her what she'd learned from nursing during the war was no longer something Sophie bragged about whenever she got the chance, but something that could be put to real use.

For my part, I stood there, pointlessly. It didn't seem possible to move; my limbs were as useless as a toy soldier's. I looked over at Evelyn, who was staring into the distance back at our table, her mouth pursed together, creased like it had been sewn shut.

"Emily, would you—" Marion called, and I felt myself being dragged into the situation. I moved through the crowd and finally saw it.

It—she—was one of the upper thirds. She was face-down in her stew, but a growing puddle of foamy pink was spreading out around her head and she wasn't moving. I stared at her hair, which was dark brown, neatly brushed, and tied back with a black ribbon. I remembered seeing that hair a hundred times before, and I thought her name might be Lucy, or Lacey. Sophie was sitting on the bench next to what had five minutes ago been a child, her hand on Lacey—it was Lacey—Lacey's back. She'd pushed the cuff of her jumper up to expose her wristwatch but she wasn't looking at it, because it was clear that Lacey wasn't breathing.

"Will you check on Mademoiselle?" Marion said, urgently. I looked up at her, trying to work out what she meant. She grabbed my shoulders hard, her fingers digging in. "If this is her, I want to know. I don't intend for there to be any doubt."

"Why me?" I said.

"Because if it's not her, I want you to see it for yourself." I felt hot shame at the thought that I couldn't be trusted otherwise, but I couldn't fault her.

Just then, Sophie pulled gingerly at Lacey's shoulder. Her body flopped back, undignified, and revealed her face. Lacey's face had been round and sort of pointed at the chin, like a love heart. Now it was distended and purple. A thin stream of bloody foam trickled from her lips. I felt my stomach turn and said "I'm going, I'm going" to Marion, to no one in particular.

I ran, feeling like I might push over anyone who was in my way, till I reached the staircase, and then I dragged myself up till I got to San. My lungs burned and my legs felt like jelly but not being in that room any more made the air taste cool and sweet. I leaned against the door for a second. I had no idea what I was hoping to see inside. Would it have been better, I wonder, to see Mademoiselle upright, cackling, in whatever state of consciousness she was still capable of, holding—I don't know—a vial of poison in a taloned fist? Would I have preferred to see San empty, her bed in disarray?

I'm sure it's been obvious for a long time, to anyone less blinkered and stupid than I was, what I found there. I swung the door open, breathing hard, and there at the far corner of the room was Mademoiselle. She was lying in bed, unmoving. Her fingers didn't twitch evilly, she didn't look at me with malice in her eyes, she just lay there exactly as we had left her, pale and still. I knew this was my only shot at knowing the truth one way or another, so I forced myself to cross to her bedside. Gingerly, I touched her forehead. She was clammy, but not from exertion. I moved to her neck, right over the pulsing artery there. Her heartbeat thudded steadily, much slower than mine. Under the covers, her feet were bare and clean. She hadn't been anywhere. I thought madly of all the ways she could've slipped downstairs to poison the stew, but Matron was always in San during lunch, and she didn't leave till dinnertime. There was no way Mademoiselle's absence could've been missed. I thought and thought and came up with nothing. The sense of contentment I'd felt earlier evaporated, and for the first time I considered just how badly I had ruined things.

I contemplated lying. It would've been easy, to tell everyone that Mademoiselle had been breathing hard as if she'd run up the stairs minutes before, or I hadn't seen her at all. We could still go to the police in the village. We would never need to have a séance again, I thought. No need for any ghostly voices to opine about how there was a liar in our midst or what have you. We would have a concrete story to hold onto, that Mademoiselle had killed Violet, and she had made threats to the rest of us and that same day another girl had died. Perhaps it would even come out in the end that Lacey's death had been some horrible accident—an allergic reaction, or a garden-variety choking—but by then the mystery of Violet's death would already have been neatly solved and her killer brought to justice. Then I thought about Lacey's bloated face, and I remembered the look of surprise Violet had worn after hitting the ground, and I steeled myself to tell the others the truth.

TEN

PERFECTLY BEASTLY

I stood in the doorway to the common room, not quite willing to meet anyone's eye. All of us had gathered there once Lacey's body had been driven away. It was late, perhaps eleven o'clock. It had taken some time to regroup. Ordinarily we would never in a thousand years have been permitted to stay up so late, but there seemed to be a tacit agreement that night that we should be allowed to do as we liked. I suppose the six of us were a special case, which on the one hand I appreciated, but on the other was disturbed by. It felt as though years had passed since Violet died and we were a group of horrified adolescents in need of comfort.

"You ought to know that Mademoiselle was in bed when I went to see her."

"Was she," Alice said through gritted teeth, and Dot's little hand in hers appeared to be the only thing holding her back from throttling me. Dot had rung for an ambulance and then spent an hour and a half comforting Cook, who was absolutely disconsolate and convinced that she had been responsible. Cook had always had a particular fondness for Dot, giving her extra cake and letting her help in the kitchen and so on; the thought of the tables being turned, and Dot looking after her instead, wasn't right at all.

"Yes, and she was still unconscious." I didn't have the energy to try and spin anything in my favour. "It didn't look like she'd moved in hours. I checked her pulse—I even checked the soles of her feet. They were clean."

"And Matron would've been in there with her all afternoon," Marion said, two fingers pressing at her temple. Her skin blanched at the pressure.

"Couldn't Mademoiselle have slipped out just for a minute? She could've gone down to the kitchen and poisoned Lacey then?" Sophie said, a pleading note in her voice. Her hands looked scrubbed raw. Sophie had needed to be gently extricated from the scene after Lacey was taken away. Miss Parker had steered her out by the shoulders, told her to wash her hands thoroughly, and made her a strong cup of tea.

"Matron never leaves San between break and dinner," Evelyn said slowly. "I'm a prefect—"

"Thanks, Evelyn, we're aware," I snapped, and then felt like an idiot. Her face fell, just for a moment, but she collected herself. She rolled her eyes with an exasperation that looked a little heavy-handed.

"I was going to say I'm a prefect, and one of my duties is to bring Matron lunch once a week. Because she's always in San. She has to be there, in case there's an emergency. Miss Lewis stays in her office during break so there's someone to go to if any of us breaks an arm, or something."

"So there's no way—"

"No."

Sophie bit her lip. "Mademoiselle's warning," she said. "It wasn't her saying all that, was it? It was something else."

I didn't want to say anything. Sophie, lucky simple Sophie, hadn't put it together yet: she hadn't realised what we had done.

"Let's get everything straight," Marion said. "Violet dies; none of us saw what happened. Mademoiselle's there. We hear a warning from the spirits at Mrs. Northcote's. We hear a warning from the spirits when Evelyn does a séance. Emily hears Violet when she's in the apple tub. Mademoiselle—or something speaking through her, which I'm beginning to think is more likely—gives us another warning today."

Alice interrupted. "And there's something wrong with the food."

"Quite. Lacey dies; Mademoiselle is still in bed."

"It was never Mademoiselle," said Evelyn, distantly.

"She wasn't ever mad, she was just—being a medium," Dot said. "Like Evelyn." Evelyn flinched.

"I owe you all an apology," I started, still not willing to look directly at any of their faces.

"You owe Mademoiselle an apology," Alice said, "except—hang on—you can't apologise to her because she's been unconscious all day after you and Evelyn and Sophie harassed her half to death."

"Stop it," Evelyn said, her voice high and quaking. "Stop it, it was Emily who made me think it was Mademoiselle in the first place, why don't you leave me alone?"

"Oh, for Christ's sake, Evelyn, you rotten little snitch. You took about five minutes before you started inventing cover-ups, and in the end you went along with all of it. You hated Mademoiselle just as much as I did, only you were too cowardly to show it." I was trying not to shout and not entirely succeeding. In the absence of our shared mission, something had shifted between us. Evelyn and I were no longer allies, we were something else altogether, and I found I no longer quite knew what to do with her. "You wanted it to be her, I know you did, because—"

"Will you two stop arguing, *please?*" Dot wailed.

"Dot's right," Marion said. "You need to put away whatever is going on between you. This is serious. We need to do something about it, and we can't if you two are shouting at each other all the time."

"What are we supposed to do? We can't exactly go to Miss Lewis and tell her Violet and Lacey were both murdered, maybe, and we don't know by whom, but we do think there's something wrong because a ghost told us so." Saying it aloud made the entire situation feel significantly less sane.

"We've got to tell them something, haven't we?" Sophie said.

"Do we even know that Lacey's death wasn't just a horrible accident?" Dot asked, hopefully.

"No," Evelyn said. "It wasn't an accident. I can feel it. Something—something about the—oh, I can't explain it, can't you just understand me and let it be?"

I was startled by her outburst. Evelyn was usually so wedded to the ordinary that the idea of her giving herself over to the numinous was faintly disturbing. It was so surprising that I found myself defending her.

"More things in heaven and earth, et cetera. If Evelyn says she knows that Lacey was murdered, then it's up to us to decide whether or not we believe her. I for one am inclined to, considering that only a few days ago I heard a voice that shouldn't have been possible come out of her shrill little throat."

"Agreed," said Marion, which was also a surprise, considering how careful she usually was.

"I saw Lacey's face up close," Sophie said, hesitantly. "It didn't quite look natural, somehow."

"Do we agree that it seems like Lacey didn't die by accident?"

Marion asked, looking around. We all nodded, with varying degrees of confidence.

"It's picking us off," Evelyn said out of nowhere, with a chill in her voice that made my spine ache.

We held our third séance that same long, grim night. I felt as though I'd been awake for a week; it was the best I could do not to yawn during the hymn. I hadn't forgotten that it was the séances that had felt to me like ultimate proof of Mademoiselle's guilt. But a supernatural situation demanded a supernatural solution: even if all we got was a warning that someone else would soon be next, that was preferable to stumbling pointlessly forwards in the dark.

"Are we all ready?" Sophie said. In place of Evelyn, who wasn't willing to stoop to any theatrics, she had clearly appointed herself master of ceremonies.

"No," Evelyn muttered.

"Are you ever likely to be readier than you are now?" I asked.

"Hardly."

"Then buck up, there's a good girl, and let's get on with it."

We arranged ourselves in a circle. I didn't think the teachers would bother us, not tonight, but it was still worth keeping quiet. I didn't want to have to explain why we were doing pagan chanting or whatever else Miss Stone would take the séance to be.

"O spirits," Sophie intoned. "Witness your servant, Evelyn Hart, waiting before you, and grace us with your presence."

"That's quite enough, thank you," Evelyn snapped, and Sophie fell silent. Evelyn shut her eyes and squeezed my hand hard. She looked a bit like she did during German lessons, when she was on the spot and couldn't remember how to spell something. I thought, quite sensibly, that if the idea was to allow yourself to be filled, vessel-like, by spiritual presence, screwing yourself up like a discarded piece of paper wasn't the right approach. But more fool me, because just then Evelyn relaxed. She went almost limp, in fact, and flopped over to lean on my shoulder, useless as a ragdoll.

"Evelyn," I whispered. "Are you there?"

"No," replied a new, childlike voice. "Who's Evelyn?"

Dot made a sort of nervous whining noise. Even in the dark I could sense Alice knocking their shoulders together for comfort.

"Can you tell us your name?" Sophie said, proving once again that she was far more prepared to handle the reality of a séance than the rest of us were.

"Something's coming," the voice said, pondering.

"Oh God, please stop saying that," Alice said. Then Evelyn sat up sharply, her back straight but with a certain looseness to the shoulders that I recognised. Her eyes snapped open.

"Emily, is that you?"

I froze. I knew that voice.

"As I live and breathe—so to speak. It *is* you."

My mouth went dry.

"Don't tell me you don't remember me. It hasn't been so long."

"Violet," I said.

"The very same. Come all the way from the afterlife, my dear kid." Looking at Evelyn—Evelyn's body, that is, with Violet *inside* of it—was like looking through a stereoscope that hadn't been put together right. Rather than naturalistic depth, the two images overlapped one another, slightly askew. Their outward differences were minimal, once you stripped back the details.

But Evelyn's posture was always tense, with a hunch at the top of her shoulders that only disappeared when she was being particularly supercilious. Violet had a feline grace to her, a loucheness; seeing it in Evelyn's body was unbelievably peculiar.

"It's you—really you?"

"Don't play the fool; it doesn't suit you. You know it's me. I won't be charmed by a damp-eyed act." I tried to regroup, but she got there first. "Did you expect all my hard edges to have been sanded off in Summerland? Ascending through the spheres, becoming purer and sweeter? No such luck. I haven't got a real body any more. I was murdered. I feel all hard edges now."

"You were murdered," I said. "Who did it?"

"That's better. That's my Emily." Evelyn's red hair tossed; I could practically see Violet's curls shining in the dim light. "First—I can't see too well like this—who's your medium? It couldn't possibly be Alice. Even a more experienced spirit than I would have trouble penetrating all that broad-shouldered strength of hers . . . and Emily, I'd recognise you anywhere. Dot—too soft, sorry, Dot. Marion? Sophie?"

"Evelyn," I said tightly.

"Am I *in Evelyn*?" Violet giggled. "Gosh, how awful."

I managed to look away from her—not an easy feat. Violet was dazzling. I don't know why I had bothered to hope the others hadn't been listening. Dot's chin was wobbling like she was trying her hardest to hide it, and Alice's face was stony. I saw Marion's mouth twist the way it did when she watched me being unpleasant to someone and felt a strange flash of shame on Violet's behalf. She'd said that sort of thing all the time when she was alive, and I couldn't remember it ever bothering me before.

"Don't," I said.

"Oh, you know perfectly well she'd love it; it's a terrible shame she won't remember." I focused quite hard on not listening. Instead, I watched her. Evelyn's white face, with the freckles on her forehead I'd once caught her trying to lighten with lemon juice. The elegant arch of Violet's eyebrow. Evelyn's narrow shoulders, Violet's ease. Her hand was holding mine and I reminded myself it was only because of the circle.

From time to time Violet and I had linked arms when walking to the village. Once Marion teased us that we looked like girls on the cover of an Angela Brazil novel. I don't know if I had ever held her hand in earnest, though, not since we were twelve and had to walk hand in hand in a crocodile every time we left the school building. Violet's grip was casual, careless.

"If you're quite finished insulting Evelyn, I think we ought to get down to business," Marion said, clearing her throat.

"Yes, madam," Violet said. Evelyn's mouth curled into a smirk.

"You said you were murdered."

"Didn't I just," Violet purred.

"Who did it?"

"Not Mademoiselle, if that's what you're asking," and she looked directly at me. I wilted a little under her gaze. "You little schemers! You and Evelyn, working yourselves up into a frenzy, and dragging poor impressionable Sophie with you. And now she's all alone in horrible old San, with nothing but the draught from the window for company. Mademoiselle didn't lay a finger on me—not like that, anyhow."

I smarted. "I don't think that's a fair way of putting it, Violet—"

"I'm dead, dummy, I'm not in the business of sugar-coating any more. Like it or lump it. You got the wrong woman."

"Then who did it?" Alice burst out. Evelyn's eyes went blurry.

"Honestly, I'm not sure. One moment I was kissing Mademoiselle goodnight, then I stepped away, and before I knew it, I was falling. Terribly uncanny, that feeling. Did I ever tell you, Emily, about my father?" The about-face startled me.

"Your father," I said.

"The gentle and upstanding Robert Kirsch, yes. You've met him a thousand times. Never tried to . . ." She trailed off. "Did he?"

"Tried to what?"

"Never mind. It's not important. Priorities, here . . . they're a little difficult. Nothing looks quite the same."

"You're not saying Mr. Kirsch had anything to do with it, are you?" If I could only pin her down about it—nothing was more appealing to me then than finding out who it really was, and making some sort of reparations to Mademoiselle.

"No. No, it wasn't him, I'm sure of that much. I'd know if it was him—I know what it would feel like. I just wondered if you'd ever noticed—but it doesn't matter now. How's Briarley, dear old place?"

"Don't you know?" Marion said, with an acerbic tone that I couldn't imagine Violet would appreciate. "I thought you knew everything up there. It's why we're here; little Lacey Clarke died earlier tonight while we were eating dinner."

"Oh," Violet said, and shrank back a little.

"We were hoping you might know something about it. If it wasn't Mademoiselle, then someone else must be—picking us off," I said, unable to think of anything other than Evelyn's term for it.

"Someone," she said. "I'm not sure it is someone, you know. Maybe some*thing*. I wonder." Her hand felt a little limp in mine. I hung on, desperate not to break the séance off by letting her let go.

"There's something wrong with the food," Dot offered. She

sounded nervous. "There was this thing with the apples, the night of your memorial, and the milk's been going off, and then tonight dinner tasted really awful. Lacey—"

"She looked like she'd been poisoned," Sophie said.

"Yes, I was wondering whether something like that might happen," Violet said, pondering. "It isn't right down there. Little things—then bigger. I'm afraid you're all rather in for it."

I couldn't bear it any more. "You're so *vague*. Something's coming. Someone's going to die. Something isn't right. I'm sick of it, Violet, I wasted so much time over Mademoiselle, I was so sure—it's all real, it's real people's lives we're talking about. Lacey was just a child. Who's next? One of us?"

"You'll forgive me if being dead hasn't also given me clairvoyance," Violet snapped. "That's rather wishful thinking on the part of the books, unfortunately. It's hard to describe. There's something very big here; you can't look beyond it even if you try and try to peer around the corners. It simply fills your whole field of vision until you give up and stop straining your eyes. But it doesn't look like anything, it just is, it's too big even to see the shape. More like a . . . feeling." Her voice softened, at the end.

I remembered the times when she had sounded like that in life: once in the upper fourth when she confided to me that she was homesick, once when I'd broken my arm and she came to sit with me in San for hours on end, the time days before her sixteenth birthday when I caught her crying for no apparent reason, even though her parents were coming to visit in just a few hours. I had tried and tried to draw her out, but she just kept telling me it wasn't anything for me to worry about. The thought made me feel sick; almost worse was the memory of how tears made her eyes look bluer than ever, her lashes clumping together thickly, the way the skin underneath was almost translucent.

"I'm sorry, Emily. I'm being perfectly beastly. Only—you don't know what it's like. I'm at such a remove. I feel rather like . . . do you remember when you and Alice got into that catfight when we were fourteen? Hitting each other and pulling each other's hair over nothing? You told me afterwards that your ears were ringing and it felt as though there was a delay between your body and your brain. You didn't want to be fighting Alice, you just *were*. That's what it's like, Emily. I'm not being dreadful on purpose. I can't help it. It's like there's something suffocating me. I thought being dead was supposed to be pleasanter than this. You know how they say the veil is thin—well, it feels very thick—only I did want to talk to you ever so badly—"

"You made anything you ever wanted happen," I said, stupidly, and I found that I was crying. I tried not to think about how the others were still there, circled around, listening.

"Yes, well," she said hazily. Evelyn's grip tightened, a little twitchily, and I felt her thumb trace across the back of my hand. Just like last time. "I'm not sure I'll be able to come back. I'll try." Evelyn turned her head to look out at the circle, and so did I; they all looked as furtive as I felt, as though they shouldn't quite be seeing this.

"Violet, wait," I said. "Can you tell me—"

She leaned in, closer than I'd expected. Evelyn's lips were cold and dry as they brushed against my ear, but her breath was hot. "You were right about me and Mademoiselle, you know. Only I'm afraid I rather seduced *her*. Don't tell Evelyn, she wouldn't like it."

At that, something changed. A certain pressure left the room, and the curtains rustled. Evelyn was herself again, but she was barely conscious. Her mouth had gone white and her hand in mine was damp. When her eyes flickered open I was almost surprised to see their ordinary grey colour, not Violet's cool blue. She looked as though she could barely hold herself up, so I grasped her by the shoulders to try and rest her against the armchair, but she flinched away from me before I could get a good grip.

"Honestly," I said. "I'm trying to help."

"Violet came, didn't she," Evelyn said. It wasn't really a question. Her voice sounded dull and lifeless.

"Yes, but don't get your hopes up, she didn't say anything of much use."

"She came and I wasn't *here*," Evelyn said.

I couldn't work out where she was going with it. All at once I remembered that Evelyn and I weren't alone in the common room. No one was speaking, and the room had a distinctly shellshocked air to it. I caught Marion and Alice glancing at one another out of the corner of my eye, like they were trying to decide how to deal with us: us, I suppose, meaning me and Evelyn. It wasn't company I particularly cared to be in.

"Why don't you come onto the sofa," Sophie suggested to Evelyn, an instinct of hers towards caring in the face of crisis I had come to recognise. There was something pacifying about her manner, I had to admit; some of the tension dissipated as she fussed over Evelyn. "It must've exhausted you. Sit down and we can tell you everything."

"She's right, you look awful," I told her.

"Thanks," Evelyn said, aiming for sarcasm and landing somewhere well short.

"Really, we're ever so grateful, you look so tired out *and* you had to miss all of it," Sophie said, and while I thought for Evelyn's sake she oughtn't press the point, it was sweet of her. "It doesn't seem fair."

"Tell me what I missed."

"Oh, it was incredible—it was really her—she was just the same as when she was alive, but then she said something—"

"Ominous," Marion supplied. She didn't seem to be having any of the fun that Sophie was.

"Yes, that's it, and then she and Emily spoke for a while."

Everyone went quiet at that. I felt as though I was supposed to be jumping in, given that almost the entire rest of the séance had been a conversation between me and Violet alone. But the secret Violet had told me right before she left had me burning guiltily—for knowing things the others didn't know, for keeping a secret from Evelyn that would overturn her view of Violet altogether, for knowing how unforgivable what I had done to Mademoiselle really was. I was re-imagining Violet from the beginning; it was as though she was changing in front of my very eyes. I thought back to my worry that something was spreading among us, something catching, but even then I couldn't think of Violet as anything but fearfully and wonderfully made. In the face of all that I didn't know where to begin, so I let the others take over.

"Violet told us that Mademoiselle wasn't responsible for her death, and she told us that Lacey's death wasn't an accident either. She didn't know much more than that; apparently there's something blocking her. She said it was suffocating." Marion didn't say another word, and when Sophie opened her mouth to add something she gave her a significant look and Sophie decided against it.

Evelyn nodded weakly. "Did she—We're not really any closer to understanding about Lacey, then," she said.

"Violet did say something about Mr. Kirsch, though," Alice said. "Didn't understand it and she wasn't saying he'd killed her, she just brought him up and dropped it again. It was odd."

Evelyn blanched at that.

"What?" I said.

"What do you mean, what?" The brittle, snippy tone was coming back to her voice. I found that I had almost missed it.

"Is it to do with Mr. Kirsch?" I asked. "Do you know something we don't?"

Evelyn protested, "I don't know a thing."

"Yes you do—look at you—what is it?"

"Please will you leave it?" she said, and looked steadfastly away.

"P'raps we'd better go to bed," Dot said coaxingly, reaching out to stroke Evelyn's hair.

"I don't intend to leave it at all," I said. "I think she knows something—don't you, Evelyn?"

"Fine!" She pushed herself further away so none of us could reach her. She was shoved against the armchair now, backed quite literally into a corner. "Mr. Kirsch made a sort of pass at me after Violet's memorial. He tried to grab me round the waist and he . . . whispered some things to me. It's when I upset the milk. Are you satisfied now?"

"Satisfied! Not in the slightest," I said. "I saw him paw at you a bit. What did he say?"

"Evelyn, that's awful," Dot whispered.

"Leave her be, Emily," Alice warned. "She doesn't need to tell us."

"She absolutely does, don't be silly."

"Alice is right," Marion said, sceptically. "Violet said it wasn't him. I think this is Evelyn's business, and Violet's, and none of ours."

I smarted at this. "Violet was my *best friend*, Marion, if Evelyn knows something important about her I think it very much is my business to—"

"He told me he'd always thought I was pretty like Violet," Evelyn interrupted, in a flat, blank voice. "Which—I know it wasn't true, but he said it anyway. And he said if I needed a shoulder to cry on, his was always available. He said Violet had spoken highly of me and it wouldn't do for a girl as charming as me not to have anyone to teach me the ways of the world."

"Thank you for telling us, Evelyn, I appreciate that it must have been difficult—" Marion started.

"I'd like to go to bed now," Evelyn said. "I'm tired. Goodnight." She stood up abruptly, a little shaky in the legs, and left the common room.

Alice checked her wristwatch. "It's past midnight. We probably ought to go too."

"Leave it for a while, I think," Marion said. "I don't think she wants our company right now."

We stayed in the common room for another twenty minutes or so, mostly in silence. I was exhausted. Lacey had died six hours or so before; it felt like it had been days. If I'd had the energy to be introspective, my mind would have been whirring. I had spoken to Violet and it had been horrible and wonderful at once. She had told me her secret and Evelyn had told us another; I had learned new, frightening things about the world around me, which had until recently felt solid and predictable. We were in danger, terrible danger, and we hadn't the first clue where it was coming from or how to stop it. But right then, I mostly felt so tired it was as though I was thinking through molasses, and when I fell asleep I don't think I had a single dream.

ELEVEN

COMPANY WITH ANGELS

For days and days after Lacey's death, the younger years looked shellshocked, and great swathes of them were let out of lessons on account of crying so hard it interrupted dictation or arithmetic. You couldn't walk down a corridor without seeing a little cluster of them, unmoored from the daily routine of school life, weeping loudly or heading to San.

I felt a flicker of frustration, perhaps, or resentment, that after Violet had died there'd been an unspoken expectation that we would keep a stiff upper lip and carry on, as though by virtue of being a few years older we had lost some capacity for feeling. Lessons had gone on as normal, the bell had never stopped ringing; it was only in our extracurricular investigation of Violet's death that we strayed from the rigid bounds of order that defined our lives. After Lacey died, this changed. We had all been tenderised by the double tragedy.

There was a police investigation into Lacey's death, but as any of us could have predicted, it turned up absolutely nothing. Mademoiselle remained in San, failing to wake up even to be questioned, and no one brought up her name in connection with Lacey's death. I felt as though I ought to confess what I had put her through to someone, but even if I'd had the courage to do it, there was no one I could tell.

In the end Cook was mostly exonerated, which was such a relief I had a little sob of my own about it. Dot went down to the kitchen after we were told and, when she came back, she reported that Cook had been put through hours and hours of questioning, and, worst of all, she had been so convinced that she had somehow been responsible for what happened to Lacey that she had almost certainly made things worse for herself. The trouble was that no explanation made sense: Cook had eaten a portion of the stew herself for dinner and all the rest of us had experienced no ill effects. They had gone so far as to test the salt at Lacey's table, to no avail.

Lacey was poisoned, by the way; the local coroner determined as much as soon as he saw her body. What he couldn't identify was the nature of the poison that had killed her. He said, in a statement that spread through the gossip grapevine within a day, that he could identify no evidence to suggest that her death had been caused by intention or misadventure, but that in his decades-long career in the Sussex Coroner's Court he had never seen a case quite like this. In deference to the police investigation that found no suspicious activities whatsoever, he ultimately ruled it to be an accident. I envied then, as I envy now, the simple experience of life that rendered his judgement possible.

We were the only ones who knew better. A few of the adults who drifted in and out of our lives during this period remarked on the coincidence of it all: a police officer, Lacey's devastated mother, an inspector from the local council. But ultimately none of them could come up with any connection between the two incidents. A teen-ager who fell fifteen feet to her death, even though no one had any idea how she'd managed to do so. A preadolescent girl who seemed to have been poisoned by a plateful of disagreeable but otherwise non-lethal food. All the incidents had in common was that they shouldn't have happened, and in Lacey's case, at least, shouldn't have been possible. With the benefit of hindsight I can't even blame the authorities for their oversight, though at that time I felt constantly, furiously aggrieved that somehow all of the hard work was being done by a gaggle of girls barely past childhood themselves. But what could we have said? It all sounded insane—it *was* insane.

Lacey's memorial service was a smaller affair than Violet's. My black dress was as shabby as ever, and there seemed to be less energy for extravagant mourning. A few of the girls had already been whisked out of school, a steady trickle that started only a day or two after Lacey's death. Nevertheless, I spent the entire service feeling vaguely relieved that everyone was gathered in one place. If anything happened, it was out in the open. No room for interpretation, no possibility of catastrophic error on my part like with Mademoiselle. Just me, almost the entire school population crammed into the pews, many of the lower-school parents, and Fish, droning on from the pulpit.

"Has he got worse since Violet?" Alice whispered into my ear. Her attitude towards me had thawed since the séance a few days before, for reasons I didn't quite care to examine.

"Infinitely," I said. "He used up all his pretty phrases and sad paeans to lost, youthful potential last time."

"We mourn little Lacey's tragic death and look to the heavens to imagine her with the angels," Fish intoned, as if to illustrate the point.

I considered that image: thus far the spirits had been rather unforthcoming about the nature of the afterlife, and Sophie's book tended towards the philosophical rather than the descriptive, full of musings on the spiritual telegraph and the ascension through the spheres. Was little Lacey sitting at God's right hand on high in a white toga after all? Had she sprouted wings? Violet certainly hadn't sounded as though she was keeping company with angels.

Fish ended his eulogy with something about how Lacey was lucky to have been spared from the mortal world of sin so early. That may be unfair of me; I was barely listening. But it does sound like the sort of thing he'd have said, as if choking on poison at the age of twelve could be made up for. Miss Lewis ascended the pulpit once he'd left, cutting a much more impressive figure in her funeral black than his weedy frame in a dull, under-laundered surplice.

"Girls," she said. "Ladies and gentlemen." She left a long pause there. I was troubled by how thin and weary her voice sounded. I was worried she wouldn't be able to start again, when she collected herself, booming out, "It is a hard task, to hold a position such as headmistress of a school like Briarley, a school with a reputation to uphold, growing minds to shape and nourish, and, above all, a consideration for the safety and security of one's charges. Every day one is met with challenges, from the pedestrian to the complex. I dare say I have never before, in all my sixteen years as headmistress of Briarley School for Girls, faced such a challenge as this."

The whole room was silent. "Two of our girls have now been lost to us in the span of less than two months. I pay tribute to the life of Lacey Clarke, short as it was; she was a charming girl, kind to all who encountered her, a diligent pupil with a bright future ahead. I pay tribute also to the bravery and resilience of those Briarley girls who, in saying goodbye to Lacey, say goodbye to the carefree innocence of youth, which is the preserve of those who have not yet experienced grief. I had hoped this double loss would be confined to those who mourned most closely the recent untimely passing of another Briarley pupil, but it seems we are not so fortunate. More is to come regarding any action the leadership at Briarley intends to take to ensure the safety of our pupils. For now, I would ask you only to come together and celebrate the life of our friend, Miss Lacey Clarke." She turned immediately, waiting for neither applause nor the first few blasts of the chapel organ, and walked down the steps of the pulpit to take her seat.

I hardly heard a word of the hymn. Evelyn, sitting beside me, was a still, stiff presence; she wasn't singing at all. It wasn't like her, but I didn't think much of it. I was too busy tossing what Miss Lewis had said around and around in my mind. "Action"—what could she mean? I hoped to the point of distraction that there was no risk of us being sent home. I'd beg at Miss Lewis's feet before it came to that; I didn't think I could bear it. I imagined my mother and father waiting at the gates, disappointed to see me again so early, not even bothering to ask me about what had happened to Violet. At the end of term I used to make bets with myself over how long it would take for me to be administered a hiding, and usually I would lose them, because no matter how hard I tried I couldn't maintain the fiction of being nice and well-behaved, the sort of girl you could be proud of, for more than a few hours on end.

I thought of all the others, whom in Violet's absence I had only just begun to know properly, scattering across the country to whatever awaited them. And if the thing that had killed Violet, and now Lacey too, followed us home, I would be entirely alone: I would have nothing and no one. There could be no doubt that something was very badly wrong at Briarley, but not having a family that loves you will lead you to do the strangest things. *Please*, I said to myself. *Please, don't make me leave.* In retrospect, if I believed less firmly that by then we were already heading towards our inescapable denouement, I would think that my silent prayer had cursed us.

After the service we found ourselves, once again, in the dining hall. The spread was considerably less impressive this time around. Cook had asked to recuse herself from preparing any food, so Dot and I had put it together ourselves, which proved unexpectedly difficult. The tea had to be served without milk; Cook told us the pantry couldn't seem to keep things cool enough despite the frosty weather outside. Even milk kept in the icebox was spoiling after a few days. The sandwiches had an odd assortment of fillings, because half the produce had gone bad. Only the store-bought tinned food remained good with any reliability, so we were left with sliced tongue, luncheon meat, green beans that were greyer than they were green, and peaches in syrup. It was a grim send-off for Lacey, particularly considering how she'd died.

"These sandwiches are rank," Alice complained.

"Don't I know it," I told her. "Try one of the tongue ones, there's only so bad a tongue sandwich can be."

"I'm forbidding you from doing the cooking from now on. If it's more complicated than buttering toast you're not doing it."

"Oh, come off it. Do you really think Sophie or Marion would've done a better job of turning all this into something edible? It's luncheon meat, Alice, it is what it is."

We fell comfortably silent for a moment. I picked meditatively at a bowl of peaches in syrup. It was an incredible relief that Alice was warming up to me again. It was never pleasant when she was cross; she was so blunt and honest that she really let you know it, and it meant Dot was wary around you as well, which hurt like the dickens. I thought I'd go a step further towards mending fences.

"I wanted to let you know," I started, "that I'm sorry about what happened with Mademoiselle."

" 'S all right," she said, gnawing at a hangnail. "I get it now, after that séance."

"What do you mean?"

Alice looked uncomfortable. "Well, the way you and Violet were talking."

"What about it?" I asked her. Whatever Violet had said didn't need to mean anything about me, didn't need to mean anything at all except that I had been wrong about Mademoiselle. My legs were itching to carry me away just to head off whatever direction this conversation was going.

"Nothing really, just—sort of felt familiar. Like me and Dot." Alice, reaching down to kiss Dot. A second, no longer than that, when they thought no one was looking. I'd worked so hard over the past weeks to forget it.

"Emily?" Alice said, sounding concerned.

I pushed her away ineffectually. My throat was seizing up and I felt as though I was looking down from a great height, like Alice in Wonderland eating the cake and growing so tall her head hit the ceiling.

"I'm fine," I managed to choke out, and then whether I liked it or not I was running, trying to get out of the dining hall altogether. I dodged out of the way of Alice, who was reaching for me, and then Sophie, who appeared at my elbow to ask what was wrong. I made it all the way to the door when I was forced to pull up short, realising that someone was already standing in the doorway. It took me a moment to recognise him, but there he was, plain as day.

"Miss Locke," said Mr. Kirsch. "Certainly in a rush, aren't you?"

I couldn't speak. He took up more space than his actual physicality seemed to warrant. It seemed perverse to have invited him, but I suppose it would have been rude not to include the similarly bereaved in Briarley's latest memorial service.

I remembered what Evelyn had said—*made a sort of pass at me, teach me the ways of the world.* My line of vision felt very narrow. I thought, unbidden, of an uncle who had always liked to corner me when he and my aunt were around, tugging at my pigtails to watch me squirm.

"I need to—" I gasped.

"You know, I always liked you. You were such a good friend to my little Violet; she always spoke very highly of you. It's rather a relief, to see that Briarley carries on even in her absence; the place always felt special to me. You'll tell me, won't you, if you ever need a shoulder to cry on?" For just a moment, there flickered onto his face an expression of what I can only describe as hunger. Just as soon as I noticed it, it disappeared, and he was back to his regular oily self. "Anyway, I won't stand in your way. You'd better get going before that harridan Miss Lewis catches you. I know how much decorum matters to her."

He stepped almost entirely out of my way with a friendly wink that I felt right to the back of my spine. It was, I thought, almost exactly what he had said to Evelyn. I wanted to say something cutting, or to spit in his face, or any number of things I thought Violet would have liked me to do. But I bottled it.

"Thanks," I said, my voice ringing in my ears, and I sidled past—I had to flatten myself all the way sideways to make it through the narrow doorway without touching him.

As I rushed away, I heard him strike up a genial conversation about shared business interests, more cheerful than the occasion warranted, with Lacey's mutely despairing father. It was as though nothing he'd said to me had ever happened, and he was just an ordinary man with a fleet of profitable factories and a dead daughter.

By this point I was so distraught, whether because of Mr. Kirsch or by what Alice had implied about me and Violet or by the cumulative effect of the entire wretched term, that I can't say for sure if what I saw next really happened. It feels absurd to suggest, given the pattern of events thus far, that it was a hallucination. This, however, happened to me alone, and the thought that it might have been some kind of awful delusion has preyed on me ever since. It's important to me that I explain it all truthfully.

After I ran from the dining hall, I went straight to the old Long Gallery. The gallery was, appropriately, a narrow room lined with paintings that had belonged to the Briarleys. It was a condition of the family's sale of the place that the benefactors who started the school maintained the collection. I suppose it was a way of offloading an expensive aspect of the family legacy onto another party without selling it off or consigning it to the scrap heap. Most of the paintings were awful, a lesser Stubbs with docked-tail horses and some allegorical nonsense about Britannia, and so on. There were a few newer ones as well, ugly portraits of ex-Briarley girls who had gone on to do something impressive: a lady novelist who had written about the Viceroy's wife in the Raj, a minor aristocrat who was known to be an accomplished horsewoman.

Despite the lack of quality in the paintings on display, we were nevertheless absolutely forbidden from going in there unsupervised, which is why I was certain it would be empty. I stole into the room and lay flat on the floor, letting the cool wood soothe my sweaty skin. I was alone, but it was the good kind of alone: I was somewhere that belonged to me, somewhere that I thought wanted to keep me safe.

And then I heard it. A sort of curious metallic scraping, not unlike the sound of a knife being sharpened.

I didn't need to look to confirm what I knew in the back of my skull to be true, which was that the source of the noise was the old suit of armour that stood at the far end of the Long Gallery. It had always been there, hulking and obdurate, as long as I could remember. The Briarleys, as a family, didn't go back far enough for something so old; it had been bought at auction decades before, and had belonged to some Sussex lord in the fourteenth century. It ordinarily stood to attention, visor drawn, its sword pointing downwards.

When I finally forced myself to look up, the sword was trembling where it was clasped in a plated gauntlet, its tip scraping across the stone pedestal on which it had always stood. Just trembling, at first, moving infinitesimally back and forth, until it swung with undeniable intention, rising up and up and wavering in the air.

It came to point directly at me: I imagined it piercing my chest, cutting me to ribbons. The only thing stopping it was the space between where I lay by the door and the pedestal at the other end of the room. I couldn't stop picturing the suit of armour's empty feet stepping off the pedestal and making their way towards me. I felt pinned in place, chest heaving to no effect. With an enormous effort of will, before it could confirm my fears and move any further, I scrambled to my feet and through the door, plastering myself against the wall outside.

I never told anyone about what I saw. It's stupid—I know that. The first time we felt the power thrumming through our circle at Mrs. Northcote's I should've given up entirely on whatever ideas I had about propriety or the limits of sanity. But I felt throughout that term that my grasp on reality was loosening, entirely separate to whatever was happening to us as a group. I was teetering on some vertiginous cliff's edge too precariously to open myself up to the others' disbelief. So I kept it to myself, let it fester, felt sure beyond anything that it was a warning to me specifically, for some unknown sin that only I could have committed. I decided then that I would never return to the Long Gallery again. When I look back, the closest I have ever been able to come to explaining what happened that afternoon is that whatever was hunting us was marshalling its forces, closing its ranks.

TWELVE

I FELT AS IF I OWNED THE PLACE

That evening, Marion proposed the idea of having another séance. Sophie nodded gravely, looking up from *Spiritualist Phenomena and Mediumship*, which had become her constant companion, even though she must have read it three times over by that point.

"The spirits help, sometimes," she said. "It says here that there was a woman who kept hearing these strange noises in the night, and she had a séance where the spirits told her it was someone who'd been murdered in her house decades ago. They helped her put it to rest, and she never heard the noises again."

"I can't exactly imagine Violet being *helpful*," Marion said, glowering.

"We could try, anyway. Maybe they can warn us about what's coming next."

"I can't stand being in the dark about it." Marion stalked around the dormitory, tidying furiously. She picked up my pillow (while I was sitting on the bed, mind) and shook it out with the utmost aggression until it stood proudly at the top of my bed like the stiff peak of a meringue.

"Thanks ever so," I said. She pulled her hairpins out viciously, as if they'd wronged her, and yanked her glossy hair into an even tighter knot, before moving on to Alice's bed. It was a mess, so there was plenty for her to do. Alice moved over obligingly to let her shake out the moth-eaten Swiss army blanket.

"Didn't Violet say it was hard for her to talk to us?" Alice mused. "What if she needs rest?"

"She's in the eternal kingdom of rest, Alice, if she can tell us who's going to be mysteriously murdered next I'm perfectly happy to call her down whenever we like," I told her. I meant it, but also I thought it probably couldn't hurt to avoid being too sentimental about Violet, given the encounter I'd had with Alice earlier. It put my hackles up to think about it.

"Mrs. Northcote," Marion said. "Maybe we ought to visit her again next week-end. If we somehow combine her and Evelyn's mediumistic access, or power, or whatever we're going to call it, it might get through to Violet more easily."

"I'm *not* going back there," Evelyn said. She was perched on the end of her bed, her arms crossed like the very picture of priggishness.

I rolled my eyes. "Come off it, Evelyn, if you wanted to be our special favourite medium you only had to ask."

"Sometimes you're insufferable, Emily, do you know that?" she said, turning on me, which startled me into silence. "I'm not going to see Mrs. Northcote, I'm not doing another séance, I don't want any part of it. I'm through. You can do whatever you like but don't expect me to be involved."

"Oh, no, but Evelyn, you're so talented, you can't give up now," Sophie said, pleading.

"I can and I will. It's a filthy horrible business and I wish I'd never let any of you drag me into it." There was a strange, fragile quality to her voice. Her hands were twisting in her lap, dragging white lines of pressure across palm and knuckle.

Marion sighed. "We won't force you."

"Oh, we might," I started, in case threats worked on her. But aside from a flicker of something in her eyes, she held fast.

"You couldn't," Evelyn said primly. "I have to let the spirits in, don't I?"

"But Evelyn, we're in danger," Dot said. Her big, round eyes swam with tears. It was hard to say no to her—I never could—but Evelyn, the hard-hearted little minx, managed it beautifully.

"It's disgusting, it's *sinful*. I don't care what Sophie says her book told her about it being Christian. I've felt it and it's not, it's—idolatry, at best. If my parents heard I'd been doing any of this, they'd—the fact that I can do it at all just shows that I haven't yet been strong enough to fight it off."

"Evelyn," Marion said, her voice softening. I was glad she'd interrupted; I abhorred the thought of Evelyn going on about temptation and weakness.

"I won't do it."

All at once I was tired of humouring her. "Fine!" I exclaimed, flinging Marion's carefully arranged pillow to the floor. I wanted to throw something else, something solid and more likely to make a dent, like my water glass or the box with shells pasted to it that Violet had given me years before. "Suit yourself. I don't know why anyone should be surprised that you're happy for us all to choke to death or break our necks to save your precious, pure soul. I've never met anyone as selfish as you in my life."

"Don't," Marion started.

"No—sorry, Marion, but I can't take it any more. You're right, Evelyn, we can't force you to help us with a séance. If you want to leave us all at the mercy of whatever's killing us, that's your prerogative. But you should really mean it, and you should know what you're abandoning us to. Did you see Lacey, or did you just sit at our table like a coward the whole time? Did you see her face? It was the worst thing I've ever seen, worse than Violet even. She'd gone purple, I didn't even know faces could go that colour—"

"Stop it!" Evelyn shouted. "You think you're the only person ever to find something unbearable. You think you're special, you think no one else feels anything like you do, but look around you, Emily—Dot's crying because of what you said, Sophie looks like she's going to be sick, you lash out and you've never once considered the consequences for everyone else." I looked around. She was right; Dot had curled up on her bed and Alice was holding her around the shoulders. Sophie looked stricken. Even Marion had gone pale.

"You've never *once* thought what it might be like to feel some alien presence in your body, only it's not alien, it's Violet, knowing it's—she's—in there but not being able to control yourself, going blank and waking up aching as though you've run miles and miles. And then everyone around you gossips about what your body did, what your mouth said, and you don't remember a word of it. It tells people things that ought to be secrets and you can't stop it. And you know all the while that you're going to hell for letting it happen. That's your problem, Emily, you haven't thought: you never do."

Evelyn was white and shaking, but in an odd, contained sort of way. She was sitting very still, exactly in the centre of her bed, and it was as though all the blood had drained from her except for those two points high on her cheeks. I wanted to throttle her. Everyone else in the room was staying as far away from us as they could. I thought fuzzily that I didn't know how this had become so personal between the two of us.

"At least I try to do something," I told her. I couldn't stop myself. "I make mistakes but I would never sit around twiddling my thumbs while something—God only knows what—picks us off, to use your words. I'm sorry to Dot and Sophie and the others but at least if I had the power to *do something* I'd die before I threw it away. I wouldn't let that happen." The tension between me and Evelyn stretched taut across the room, both of us going quiet. I didn't know what I was going to do next. I was frightened it was going to be something I couldn't come back from.

The bell rang, puncturing our brief silence, and then there was a knock at the door. It was the sort of knock that represented the barest courtesy rather than any concern whatsoever for privacy, and Miss Parker came in without hesitation.

"If you could all come downstairs, please," she said, "Miss Lewis has an announcement to make in a few minutes." She shut the door and left us to come down of our own accord.

"She can't make us leave," Evelyn said hotly. "I don't want to go back home, term's only just started. I thought I'd have until Christmas before I had to go back."

Our row shrivelled into nothing. All at once, it ceased to matter.

Miss Lewis gathered everyone in chapel. It felt wrong being there only a few hours after Lacey's memorial; we hadn't even had a Sunday service to even things out. She stood in front of the pews, looking grave. I had never liked chapel, but with the threat of leaving Briarley hanging over my head I felt terribly fond of its ugly whitewash and cramped pews. It was rather as though I was heading for the guillotine. Miss Lewis folded her hands under her bosom. I couldn't remember the last time I'd seen her out of her black clothes.

"Girls," she started, then took a long pause before trying again. "It has been an unprecedentedly trying time for us all. I appreciate you may be feeling frightened and unsure, and your families are concerned for you. I have heard from several parents who believe that Briarley should close for good."

I held my breath. Chancing a glance over at the others, I saw that Marion was sitting up ramrod-straight, her arm resting on the back of the pew with a casual air belied by her posture, whereas Evelyn had curled in on herself as though she wanted to become as small as possible. I had never considered Evelyn's family as anything more than a faintly unpleasant oddity, but I couldn't imagine they were any better to be around than mine.

"I do not intend to describe the various discussions that have been held in recent days, but rest assured this was one of the most difficult decisions I have ever had to make as headmistress of this school. I have come to the conclusion that any girl who wishes to go, and any parents who wish to bring their daughter home, may do so; you will be welcomed back with open arms next term. I encourage anyone feeling uncertain to think on the matter for a few days. This week-end, I would ask you to contact your families and discuss the matter with them. The telephone in my office will be made available for you to do so."

Dot reached over to squeeze my hand, and I felt awful about every time I'd been short with her. In that moment I could've slapped Violet for calling her soft; she was as frightened as the rest of us but here she was, brave as anything. There was a low murmur about the room, which Miss Lewis silenced with a stern look.

"I would emphasise," she said, her tone sharpening, "that I expect standards of behaviour to be maintained to the utmost degree among any of you who remain at Briarley. I will not have the good name of this school and the girls who attend it sullied by anyone choosing to use the losses we have all experienced as an excuse to let standards slip. We will carry on as normal. I am certain that this is what Violet Kirsch and Lacey Clarke would have wanted." With that, she nodded curtly and stepped away from her place at the head of the room. I couldn't help thinking that Violet would've wanted the whole world to stop for her.

Over the time I'd been at Briarley I'd developed a view of Miss Lewis rather on a par with, if not God, then an archbishop: she had a way of making events bend to her will with a stern look. It never occurred to me that one of her plans might go awry. But go awry this one did.

We weren't ordinarily allowed to use the telephone—if you wanted to contact your family you had to wait until post day on Wednesdays. It had been installed two years before and was strictly for emergencies only. This, naturally, qualified as an emergency, so the plan was to form a queue outside her office on a year-by-year basis so that all the girls could have a private talk with their families about whether to go home. The queue formed, of the littlest girls first, but it never diminished.

The telephone had stopped working. Anyone picking up the receiver was met with a harsh, constant sound, like the crashing of a waterfall.

We Briarley girls had been taught the values of resourcefulness and resilience, though, and this setback didn't faze Miss Lewis. Swathes of the school population decamped to the village to queue for the telephone there. Miss Stone and Miss Parker took them year by year, youngest first, and as each year group returned, large quantities of suitcases and trunks began to pile up near the entrance. Having felt like my march towards the guillotine was halted by Miss Lewis's announcement, the upwards movement through the year groups was a bit like the tumbril had jolted forwards, and was now once again trundling on towards its destination.

There wouldn't be time before dark for the upper sixth to walk into the village, so our exodus was put off until Sunday. I spent the whole of Saturday unsettled. I left lunch, begging for permission to use the water closet, but mostly I wanted to be alone: I was unable to think or talk of anything but the set of bad choices that lay before me. Once that permission was granted, I intended to hang around for a few minutes in the darkest corner I could find. That happened to be the vestibule into the side entrance, which on a normal day would have been empty.

But it wasn't a normal day, and Miss Stone and Miss Parker came through the door while I huddled in the corner.

"Oh, I don't know," Miss Stone said. I flattened myself against the wall, trying to make myself invisible. Her voice sounded wearier than I had ever heard it. "I've hardly slept in weeks."

"I know exactly how you feel. My feet feel as though they're made of lead," Miss Parker murmured. "As though another trudge into the village might kill me."

"I can take the third years for you—"

"No, no. No. It's not even the walk, it's looking at them, somehow. The older ones especially. They seem like different people altogether, since Violet. As if they're living in their own little world and we can't see in."

"It's everything at once, you know. Standards slipping." Miss Stone paused, then continued, her voice bitter. "All the things that made this place a constant, going down the drain."

"I told Evelyn Hart the other day that her tie was done up wrong and she just stared at me for a moment, before wandering off. Hart, who'd dob in one of her friends as soon as look at them!"

It was a relief, though only a momentary one, to hear someone else as tired of Evelyn as I was.

"Well, it's just—you spend years of your life maintaining discipline, trying to keep some kind of order, broadly succeeding, and then before you know it, it all winds up so far out of your control that you can't imagine why you tried in the first place." I couldn't see them, but I thought I heard a thin tremor in Miss Stone's voice.

It wasn't that I thought the adults were going to save us from anything, far from it. But it felt like a crossing of the Rubicon to hear them admitting—if not openly, then at least on the sacred school grounds, where they were all we had besides ourselves—that they were in over their heads.

"The younger girls cry through half my lessons these days and there isn't anything you can say to stop them, not even telling them off or sending them out of the classroom. Even the building itself seems to be going to pieces—there's mould all over the walls of my room and I keep waking up with a cough," Miss Parker said.

"Elizabeth, honestly, I don't know how much longer I can bear it. Two deaths in one term—accidents, I know, but—" Miss Stone began, and then the worst thing happened, which was a sniffling sound coming from someone I had only known, for years, as a tyrant. All the punishments doled out by her unforgiving hand fell flat, in the face of one afternoon's tears.

I started in horror, and took off before I could stop myself, my shoes clattering on the floorboards. As I ran full tilt back to the dining hall I heard Miss Stone's voice, a shell of what it ought to have been, calling out to ask who I was and where I thought I was going and didn't I know eavesdropping was a sin.

In the end all the first- and second-year girls left, which I suppose wasn't a real surprise. You couldn't pass Lacey's death off as a teen-age drama. I'm sure plenty of their families assumed Violet had been drunk when she fell, or something scandalous like that, and disapproved of her quietly. But Lacey—she was unquestionably innocent.

Only three out of all the younger girls stayed. Mildred Allen, three years below us, whose father was in the colonial service and who had hung around Alice for a while before Alice and Dot became so close; Shirley Carr, whose mother was off being an actress in Hollywood and who appeared to be uninterested in multiple deaths at her daughter's school; Ann Turner, the youngest of all the stragglers, who played the piano very well but couldn't string a sentence together to save her life.

Sunday afternoon came, and I sat in the common room feeling grim while the others prepared to go to the village and telephone their families.

"I'm not going anywhere," said Marion. She looked worried, and that frightened me. "University exams. Miss Lewis would have to drag me out before I gave up on them."

"The mater and pater still threatening to marry you off, then?" I asked.

"More and more every time I go back home. I don't know what I'd do if I had to sit in the drawing room and listen to them prattle on about dresses and prospects."

"I don't want to leave either, but if it's not safe . . ." Sophie was winding a lock of hair around and around her finger.

"We can't leave." Everyone turned to me as if they were bracing themselves for what I'd say next, but I didn't have much to offer. "Briarley's our home, isn't it? I mean our real home, not like—"

I faltered, desperate not to talk about it any more. I felt as though, with everything I said, I was peeling off layers of my skin and revealing tender muscle underneath.

Marion rescued me. "I suppose there's no point dwelling on it just yet. I want to stay, too; more than that, I don't want to leave anyone here to bear it alone."

"I've got to tell them Miss Lewis said we could go home," Dot told me apologetically. "I couldn't not tell them, I'd only blurt it out as soon as I saw them at Christmas anyhow."

"No, it's all right, Dot. You don't have to stay, you know."

"Silly," she said, "I don't want to go back home either." She threw her arms around me for a second before running off downstairs to find Alice.

Dot had always complained about her mother. From what I'd seen of the woman, she was right to protest. When Mrs. James, a miserable woman with a colourless face and a lemon-sucking mouth, had dropped her daughter off for the start of term in September, she'd pinched Dot's cheek so hard it left a bright red mark for ages afterwards. "Watch your appetite," she'd said, by way of goodbye, and got back in the car that had brought her up. Mr. James hadn't even got out of the driver's seat. Dot's sweetness seemed to have generated itself out of nothing. As far back as I could remember, she had gone to stay with Alice's family over the Easter holidays. Alice lived in a huge country pile in Nottinghamshire with her brothers, one older and one younger, both of whom shared her bluff, cheerful demeanour and whom you imagined playing constant games of Sardines. Dot had told me about them once with affection, but when she'd finished she had an odd little look on her face and said, "Not quite as good as one's own, though, I suppose."

"I'll have to explain things to my parents too, I'm afraid," Marion said, setting her jaw.

"I'm not worried about *you*," I told her. "I don't think wild horses could drag you out of here."

"I hope we can all stay," she said, "for your sake, if nothing else."

I couldn't look at her after she said that. She didn't seem to mind. It was just like Marion, not to need a profusion of gratitude to understand how I felt.

Sophie went more quietly—I wondered if I had been wrong about her being willing to stay on. I didn't like how conspiratorial all this had made me feel. Wanting everyone to remain at Briarley as long as we could felt like a betrayal of them, somehow. I didn't want anyone else to get hurt. I didn't want them to feel afraid, or regret that they hadn't gone back home to sit in on their little siblings' lessons and play the piano till everything had died down.

But I couldn't help myself; I wanted us all together. I knew—as I think we all did, if we were being honest with ourselves—that there was something very badly wrong pulling us closer to Briarley, even when the most rational thing to do might have been to get far away from the place. I thought we might have a better chance of surviving it together. Going home had never been an option for me, and the thought of being left one by one—left, perhaps, with only Evelyn—made me sick. And on top of that, in a deeper place that felt too delicate to touch, I knew we were the closest thing I had to a real family. I'd grown accustomed to the six of us existing as a unit, and I couldn't bear the thought of it being broken apart.

I'd never have thought such a thing before Violet died. If I had been pressed in the old days, I'd have said that Violet and I existed like a sun and its closest orbiting planet. My world circled around her, and those other, lesser planets could never matter as much as we did. Things had changed, since then, almost without my noticing.

So there I was, that Sunday afternoon, alone with Evelyn in the common room in studied silence. She didn't need to tell us all that she didn't intend to speak to her family. Frankly, I'm not even sure they had a telephone; they must have had some money, to send Evelyn to Briarley, but they were strict and seemed to distrust anything that smacked of the modern. And there were ever so many little Harts running about. When her mother came to pick her up at the end of term she never came in a motorcar, but rather came up the drive on foot with a host of Evelyn's siblings trailing behind her like a family of ducklings. The change that came over Evelyn when she spotted them was immediate: she looked older somehow, and set to wiping noses or tying shoelaces. I had always considered it faintly disgusting, and thought it was just typical of her that she would spend all term cleaning up after Violet and following her around trying to fiddle with her hair—which I considered my job—just to go home and do the same for a pack of sticky children.

That afternoon, she was reading something characteristically pretentious—*Jane Eyre*, I think, which suited her sense of drama. I had my legs crossed over the arm of my chair with one of Sophie's magazines open on my lap. It was open to an advertisement about how Lux soap flakes wouldn't damage even the airiest georgette, but I was only pretending to read; I felt as though I wouldn't be able to relax for a moment until everyone had come back from the village. I sat, flipping the pages back and forth idly and failing to take anything in.

"Will you stop that," Evelyn said, audibly struggling to remain civil.

"What?"

"Will you stop that," she said again.

"This?" I said, and loudly flipped over to an article about how short hemlines were being worn this autumn.

"Yes, that."

"Awfully sorry to bother you with something as unbearable as turning the pages of a magazine, I'll go then," I replied, and felt grateful for the excuse to get out of there. I glanced over my shoulder. Evelyn's queer, pinched little face stared back at me. I rolled my eyes and went for a wander.

There had been no question whether I would or wouldn't go to the village with the others. I had no intention of leaving and as a result, I felt there was no need at all to alert my mother and father to the possibility. It's not as though they would have wanted me home, anyway. At the beginning of term I had lugged my trunk, alone, all the way to the train station in the poky suburb they lived in just to get half an hour's peace from them. I suppose I ought to have been grateful to be fed and clothed and given a roof over my head, but I often felt when I was among them for long periods of time—chiefly during the summer holidays—that I was some kind of alien creature.

I looked just like my father, broad-shouldered and dark-haired, and I'd inherited his lack of grace and permanent scowl. But we were nothing alike in our characters. I used to play games as a small child where it turned out I had been found in a basket of reeds like Moses and my real parents were miles away up the river. I would walk for ages, pretending to be searching for them, until I'd stayed out too late and had to rush home so I wouldn't get a hiding. I thought for a time that I'd eventually accept that the failings were mine, and learn to appreciate the comforts of family, but I never managed it. In fact, as far as they know, I have been dead for some time.

I had everything I needed right here, in Briarley. The orchard, my bed, Adonis, they were all I knew and all I cared to know. Despite the circumstances, it was with a sense of contentment that I wandered the empty upper floors of the manor. The sun was about to go down and without the electric lights on, things looked bathed in purple, casting long, thin shadows.

Violet had once chased me through these very corridors on the same sort of day, a smoky autumn twilight and an emptier than usual school. We laughed and shrieked at the tops of our lungs, wheeling around corners with abandon. She could be fast when she tried, her hair streaming behind her like a golden pennant. At those times her smile was so wide you could see her one crooked tooth, a canine that crossed in front of its neighbour just slightly, impinging on its territory. I always thought it gave her face character. She caught me as I slowed to round a corner, barrelling into me and reaching out to grab at my hair and the waist of my pinafore. It was only a second before she took off again, still smiling, too swift for me to have any hope of catching her.

I felt as if I owned the place. It was mine, everything in it was somehow mine, and no one could make me leave. Lost in my daydream, I rounded a corner, and nearly ran into Miss Lewis.

"Locke," she said.

"Yes, Miss Lewis?"

"I notice you aren't on your way to the village with the other girls." She didn't seem to be telling me off or anything, just presenting the facts, so I responded in kind.

"You notice correctly, Miss Lewis."

"And what if I were to insist that you hurried along after them to make a telephone call of your own?"

"I would ring up my mother and father and inform them, accurately, that I have no desire whatsoever to leave Briarley. I wouldn't expect them to ask any further questions, as they haven't given me any sense that they're much interested in my education beyond the fees they pay every term." This, perhaps, was imprudent. I stood up very straight and didn't make eye contact, though I was absolutely champing at the bit to get out of there. Miss Lewis always brought out a rather military instinct in me.

Contrary to my fears, she flashed what could almost be called a smile. It was unnerving to see; her face didn't look used to it in the least. But I know that's what it was, because there was at the corners of her eyes a slight softening, a look that might have been fondness. "Very well, Locke. I hope you understand that if directly asked, I will explain to your parents why half your chums will be leaving school in the next few days."

Her words didn't betray a thing, but in the face of all that came after I have always remembered that on that day, she wanted me to stay.

"Wouldn't dream of anything else, Miss Lewis." God, I hoped half of the upper sixth wouldn't leave. I didn't care about the rest. Miss Lewis grasped me by the shoulder, only briefly, before leaving me to my own devices.

I had been wandering for an hour or so when the others came back. I caught them near the entryway, barely speaking, as if Miss Stone would somehow understand everything that was going on if they said even a word. All their faces were flushed from the cold. The tips of Dot's ears had gone scarlet and Marion was flexing her hands to get the heat back into them. November was slipping away from us; the chill in the air was turning to downright cold and within a month we'd be sent home for Christmas anyway.

"Emily!" Sophie cried, noticing me. "We're all staying," she whispered.

"Really?"

"Really really—we talked about it all the way there—meet you in the common room once we've got our coats off?"

"Please," I said, feeling a sort of pain in my chest from relief and fondness for them. They clattered into the cloakroom and hung up the regulation coats we wore all winter—big ugly boiled wool things that swallowed up every one of us.

When we had all gathered in the common room, Alice stoked a fire in the grate using some balled-up newspaper and the big iron poker. I hadn't felt inclined to touch the poker since our second séance, so I was grateful to her for doing it. Everyone who'd been to the village huddled in front of the fireplace, with me and Evelyn hanging back so as not to take up more than our fair share of the heat.

"So we're staying," Marion started.

"I had to beg my mum," Dot added, proudly. "She said she wanted me home with Mary and Ruth where she could keep an eye on me, but I told her I couldn't bear to leave early."

"I heard it, it was dreadful. Dot's mum can tug on the heart-strings like no one I've ever seen," Alice said.

"So it's all of you—no one's going?"

"Not one," Marion said. "I had to promise my mother all kinds of things before she agreed. Buying a white coming-out dress with her as soon as I get home for the holidays—luncheon with my third cousins—all manner of agonies. But we're staying."

"And we're not leaving you here on your own," Alice added.

"Thanks," I said, trying not to sound too pleased about it.

"You too, Evelyn," Marion said, and Evelyn looked up sharply. She didn't say a word. I hadn't noticed till now but she was looking unwell; her hair was lank and she was pale as anything. I didn't want to pity her, but I did.

THIRTEEN

FOR A GIVEN VALUE

Evelyn's birthday came the next week, on Friday. All week the gravel drive up to Briarley Manor had been full of parents coming to whisk away their daughters. By Friday we were mostly alone. It was just us, the stragglers from the lower years, and most of the schoolmistresses. Some had taken Miss Lewis's offer to heart and left when the younger girls did; Fräulein Weingarten had gone, and so had Cook. Mademoiselle, of course, languished in San, in the absence of anyone to take her home—wherever home was.

I had never seen the school so quiet in all the six-and-some years I had been there. Cook wept during all her goodbyes. I wish I could've told her that we knew for certain she hadn't been responsible for Lacey's death—that as far as we were concerned, she was utterly absolved. When I think about it now, I feel nothing but relief that she wasn't there to see the rest of it.

With Cook gone, meals were prepared on a rota. Supplies seemed to go off as soon as they were brought in, and the entire home economy of the school had been thrown off. Every night at dinner there was tension running through the air till we'd finished, and you could feel everyone thinking, though no one said anything aloud, that they hoped there wouldn't be a repeat of what had happened to Lacey.

Evelyn's birthday, however, was different. In a stroke of bad luck, it was Marion's and my turn in the kitchen, so aside from the usual, rather depressing fare, we had sent for fresh eggs and milk and butter from the village. We had noticed after the last few weeks that tinned food was best, and all fresh food had been going off at an accelerated pace, but things from the village lasted better than anything grown on the grounds of Briarley itself. With these provisions, we made Evelyn what had to pass for a birthday cake. One of the eggs had to be thrown out anyway, because the yolk had gone an unpleasant greenish colour, and the white was cloudy and diseased.

Sophie or Dot really ought to have been in charge. Marion and I, far from dab hands in the kitchen, had to depend on Cook's battered old copy of Mrs. *Beeton's*, lacking any instincts of our own. As a result it turned out stodgy; you could tell the recipe had been written by the Victorians. The oven must have been uneven because the top had a dangerous tilt to it and the icing was liable to slide off at any moment.

"Not exactly angels in the house, are we?" I said to Marion as we tried to transfer the cake from its baking tin to a platter.

"Poor Evelyn." She leaned down like a billiards player lining herself up to take a shot. I held up the platter while she used a knife to glide the cake on.

"Mm," I said. I didn't want to start a fight but considering that I'd spent all afternoon slaving over a cake for the girl, I wasn't particularly inclined to sympathise with her on top of it.

"I know it's difficult."

I squirmed. "Mm," I said again, as if that would do anything.

"I wish she'd give in about doing another séance, too. It's—

frustrating, knowing there's a way we could get in touch with Violet, but we can't use it."

She was pushing, so I let myself be pushed. "I feel completely powerless and Evelyn's standing in the way of the only chance we have to do anything," I said, and turned to wash up the cake tin so Marion couldn't see my face.

"I know. I *know*, Emily. But we can't force Evelyn, you know that. She has to come to it in her own time. I think she will, you know; she's not really selfish, she's frightened."

"Wish I agreed." I moved on to the mixing bowl, which I scrubbed harder than it perhaps deserved. "I feel like she doesn't want me to talk to Violet," I said, slowly, "because she's jealous."

Marion looked at me with that penetrating gaze I could usually do without.

"Interesting" was all she said.

"She was always jealous of me and Violet, you know. She couldn't stand that it meant something to Violet when I did things for her, and no matter how many times she brought Violet flowers or turned down her bed she was always left out in the cold. Maybe it wasn't fair, but it isn't fair to any of us either, for her to behave like this."

"It's very big of you to say so." Marion was being arch; I could never quite read her when she was like that. It made me nervous.

"I'd do it, you know. A séance. If I could."

"Of course you would. So would any of us—but there's something special about her."

"Maybe that's why she's so *irritating*."

"Oh, probably," Marion said, which made me snort. "How about this: if Evelyn hasn't agreed to do another séance by next week-end, we'll all try being mediums again. Sophie's desperate to do it, she'd love that. Maybe it's just that Evelyn's a natural, but the rest of us could learn with a bit of work."

"Thanks awfully," I said, thickly. She'd stuck eighteen candles into the cake, so I struck one of Cook's long matches and lit them, before carrying the platter with care into the dining hall.

The hall had become unfamiliar. It was colder, for being so empty, and there was a plume of mould climbing up one of the walls, with the insinuative creeping look of ivy. *Bad air*, I thought, *unwholesome*.

High table was still there, with its remaining complement of teachers. Matron had stayed behind to look after Mademoiselle, who, Sophie reported, had been moving about restively. Everything else in the dining hall had been moved. Most of the long tables had been shoved to the sides of the room, leaving two, crowded close to high table. We'd had no privacy at dinner all week, with how quiet it was; the usual ringing chatter had vanished with the departure of most of the school's population. On a pettier level, you couldn't put your elbows on the table for even a second without Miss Stone shouting at you.

The three younger girls who were left sat clustered at the end of one table, leaving the rest of it empty. Alice, Dot, Sophie, and Evelyn sat at the other table, with spaces left for me and Marion. It looked like no one was making much of an effort towards integrating the years, and selfishly I had no plans to change that.

Marion turned the electric lights off at the wall. Evelyn started like a terrified rabbit, bewildered, then relaxed when she realised what was going on. Even by candlelight I noticed how ill she looked. Her hair was greasy and dull, and there was a crack in her bottom lip that looked liable to bleed. I remember thinking she'd hardly have the strength to do the candles.

She leaned forwards as we finished singing "For She's a Jolly Good Fellow" to blow them out. Her hair swung as she moved, slipping over her shoulders and going right into the flames.

Immediately there came the acrid scent of burning hair. Evelyn jerked back as the curly ends of her plaits fell back towards her shoulders, smoking. I ran over as fast as I could, heart in my throat, acting without thought. In a split second I had imagined her reduced to ash. I reached out and grabbed Evelyn's tightly braided plaits and pulled downwards (perhaps harder than I should've), extinguishing them. She whirled around.

"What are you *doing?*"

"Your hair was on fire! I don't know, I was putting it out!"

"Sorry," she said. "I'm sorry, Emily. Thank you." It sounded like it took a terrible effort to get the words out.

"Just eat your cake, will you?" I said, taking my seat and waiting for a slice to be handed around to me. My heart was still pounding.

I kept an eye on Evelyn all the rest of the evening. She was quiet. This wasn't new; she had seldom been herself since Violet died, which I frankly considered a relief. I'm not sure I could've handled her usual energetic level of snitching and sighing. But on the night of her birthday things were different, as though something was causing her to expend enormous, constant effort. I just couldn't see what it was. The last thing I wanted was to be concerned for Evelyn's welfare but my attention was fixed on her; it was like witnessing a train wreck. She seldom spoke, and when she did it was as if she had to arrange her words very carefully before they left her mouth.

I can't tell whether I fell asleep that night or not—all I know is, it felt like it was only seconds after I closed my eyes that Evelyn cried out. It wasn't a scream—not quite—I thought unless she did it again the teachers might not hear. Then, of course, she did do it again, and louder.

I sat up in bed; Sophie had already scrambled over to Evelyn's bedside. Evelyn had thrown her blanket off, which was now lying crumpled on the floor, so her body was covered in just a sheet. She thrashed about, wrapping herself up in the sheet until she could hardly have moved at all, and then thrashed some more as if to try and free herself. Footsteps came urgently up the stairs.

"Girls?" came Miss Stevens's voice through the door. "Girls, I heard a shout, what's going on?"

"Nothing," Marion called. "Evelyn had a nightmare. She's all right now, I'm getting her a glass of water. Nothing to worry about."

Marion's eyes were wide, and the wrongness of that alone forced me to Evelyn's bedside. She had stopped writhing, but then she went rigid—absolutely stiff as a board. I laid a hand on her, thinking I might try and soothe her, but the second I touched her she snapped into an arc, bending further than she ought to have been able to go. It looked like she might come apart. For all I knew it was because she hated me.

"Are you sure everything's all right?" Miss Stevens called.

There was a nervous edge to her voice. It wasn't right at all, coming from her; she was usually so solid and brusque. I don't know why we didn't tell her the truth. Somehow we understood that our problems were our own, now. We could no longer be considered children to be looked after in any meaningful sense. Alice made a face as though she wanted to say something, but that was only because she liked Miss Stevens for making her cricket captain.

"Really, everything's fine," I shouted.

"Very well. I don't want to hear another sound out of this dormitory."

The footsteps retreated, and with their echoing clicks I felt a thrill of panic. What if Evelyn was having some sort of fit? Should someone bring Miss Stevens back, or go to San and get Matron? I thought about putting a belt between her teeth like I'd read about in books and then thought better of it.

"Evelyn, Evelyn," Sophie was whispering, panic in her voice. "Are you all right? Can you hear me?"

Evelyn's body bent still further, till I thought her spine would break clean in two. At last, she went limp.

"Thank God," I muttered, and then I shut up, because she had begun to rise into the air.

"What's going on?" whimpered Dot. "What's she doing?"

It was by inches at first. She hovered just above the surface of the bed. You could only tell something was happening because the sheet she had wrapped herself in had begun to move. But she kept going, rising steadily till she was a foot in the air, then two feet, the fabric hanging off her so she looked like one of those old statues draped in a marble winding-sheet that occupied the churchyard near my family's house.

I couldn't bear watching it. I called on Alice. "You take her ankles, I'll take her shoulders," I said.

She acted fast, starting on Evelyn's ankles with a hefty tug that felt like it should've pulled Evelyn back down to earth. Alice was strong, really strong. She was the only one of us who could go up the climbing-rope in gym with any speed, and I had seen her haul massive bags of flour for Cook into the pantry as a favour. But our attempts to pull Evelyn down did nothing. Her body continued to rise until the sheets lifted off the bed altogether, revealing the empty hollow underneath where she should've been.

"Evelyn, wake up," Sophie whispered again.

"Is she having a fit? Should we take her to San?" I asked. The thought of Evelyn lying inert in a tightly made-up bed next to Mademoiselle was obscurely upsetting.

"It isn't a fit," Sophie said. "Fits don't make you float into the air. There's something *wrong* with her."

"Emily," Evelyn said. Her voice was wretchedly weak. I was still clutching her shoulders, straining to pull her downwards.

"What is it?"

"Don't make me, don't let her, I don't want to let her in." It was almost a chant, low and desperate.

"Don't let her what? What don't you want?"

"Violet," she said, her voice rising. "She wants—she's trying—I'm frightened. I don't want her to."

"Violet's—in there?" I felt ridiculous, speaking to Evelyn's still, floating form. I had to go up on my tiptoes to look her in the eye. I felt very frightened that she had gone mad and would never again go back the way she had been.

"All week. I tried to keep her out."

"Why would you *do* something like that?"

"It's a sin," she said miserably.

"You're not making any sense," I told her, but I saw Alice and Dot exchange a rather pregnant glance, as if it did in fact make sense to them. I think, now, that Dot often saw more than I gave her credit for. "Let Violet in, I'm sure everything will calm down if you just let her do what she wants."

"I haven't had a second's peace all week. It's like she's got a hand in my insides and won't stop clutching at them. She wants to *use* me—" She moaned, her words becoming less and less differentiated.

"Just let her," I pleaded. "Whatever it is she wants, just let her. Evelyn, please."

She gave me a sorry look, eyes drooping, mouth tight, like she'd lost the energy to beg me further. Her eyes closed, momentarily, and opened again.

"Hello, Emily," Violet's voice said, and Evelyn's body dropped like a stone, bouncing once on the hard mattress and then settling, her head turned towards me.

"Violet?"

"Gosh, but that was difficult. I didn't know Evelyn had it in her. I've been trying to get through to you for days and days."

"You can't do this to Evelyn against her will," Marion said, furious.

"Can't I really? It looks rather as if I have."

"Marion's right, Violet, we've had a hard enough time as it is trying to persuade Evelyn to do another séance and if you've been . . . possessing her, or whatever it is you're doing, she'll never agree to it again." I hated saying it, I hated defending Evelyn from Violet. I tried to think about it from a purely practical standpoint. Evelyn's feelings, of course, didn't matter to me in the slightest.

"It doesn't seem to me as though I need Evelyn's permission to do much of anything. In fact, it seems to me that I'm right here talking to you now, whether she likes it or not, and I think I had something important to tell you—damn, you've distracted me—it's like a dream, you know, you remember it right as you wake up but the second you think of anything else it's gone."

Evelyn's body shifted, propping itself up on one elbow. Her hair was plastered to her temples with sweat and there was a greyish sheen over her face, but the pose was lithe and unmistakably Violet's.

"It's beyond belief, is what it is. I can't *believe* you're doing this," Alice said. Her voice was dangerously low.

"Just tell us," Sophie said. "You can tell us and then maybe you can leave Evelyn alone for a while. We can try to help her come round to the idea on her own."

"All right, all right, I'm just cranky from being trapped for days and days. It was something about . . . it was about the staircase. The one where I died. It feels like something's going to happen there, like it's a well filling up—oh, I'm sorry for all the metaphors but that's how things are here, they're not very tangible so you have to try to stick them to something."

Marion nodded. Her mouth was still pressed into a thin line, but the more information Violet offered the less she looked like she was going to hit something. "Was that all?" she asked.

"All that effort and I hardly get a hello from you girls. I've remembered something else. You're going to have trouble getting out of here. I can *feel* it, it's an odd heavy feeling, like everything outside of Briarley's gone all quiet. Like you've missed a window, and a door has closed. There I go with the metaphors again—listen, I do feel badly about doing this to Evelyn. You'll tell her I'm sorry, won't you? I just had to tell you—something's coming. I don't know what. I do promise I won't come back unless she lets me, but you've got to persuade her to."

"I'll tell her you're sorry," Marion said.

"Thanks. I'll go now. Only Emily, give me a kiss, will you?"

"A *kiss*?" I said, dumbfounded. I didn't dare turn around to the others. Whatever they were thinking, I didn't want to see it.

"You know—'Kiss me, Hardy' and all. Nelson. Trafalgar. Don't be disgusting, I didn't mean it like that." Evelyn's cheek tilted to offer itself up, her freckles visible in the moonlight. I leaned down, feeling delirious. Somehow Evelyn smelled like the scent Mademoiselle had given Violet. The scent, and the acrid smell of sweat brought on by fear. I brushed my lips against her cheekbone for a second, and yanked myself back up immediately.

"Happy?" I said.

"For a given value," and then Evelyn's arm buckled under her.

"Evelyn?" Sophie said.

"Oh, I feel dreadful," Evelyn said, and leaned over the side of the bed to vomit into a bin, which I suppose she must've hidden there days before. When she lay back down her eyes looked like burnt holes. "She was inside me, wasn't she?"

"Evelyn, you idiot," I said. "Why didn't you tell us what was happening?"

"I thought you'd tell me to stop fighting her," Evelyn said, her voice soft and fretful.

"Well, yes, probably," I said.

"It's wrong. I shouldn't be doing it. It's sinful."

"It's necessary," Marion said, though she didn't sound as if she liked it. "Violet warned us about something. She told us to watch out for the staircase and she told us that it was going to be difficult to leave Briarley. It's important, Evelyn, she's telling us important things. I'm not sure we can avoid it any longer."

"I know," Evelyn said, a choked-sounding sob in her throat. And then she added, nonsensically, "I don't want to leave."

"Marion," I started, although I didn't much enjoy reminding her.

"Violet also asked me to tell you she was sorry," Marion said, with what seemed like great reluctance. Evelyn didn't respond at all, just gazed hollowly past the end of her bed.

Eventually we all retreated. Sophie folded herself up, chin resting on her knees; it occurred to me that it couldn't be easy for her to play nurse to the rest of us. There didn't seem to be much more to say, for the time being. Evelyn was exhausted. I felt certain that the others had plenty to think about, and I could only hope that as little as possible of it was about me.

For my part, I couldn't stop thinking about Violet asking

me to kiss her. She had always been funny about kissing and cuddling, when she was alive. She treated some of the younger girls like they were her pets, and would dispense her affections freely, fussing with them like kittens. I was hardly ever allowed to touch her. I managed in other ways, by plaiting her hair and doing up the clasp of her necklace: practical things that she liked because they made her feel looked after. She was like a child, except for all the ways in which she wasn't. These, among others, were things I was afraid to look at for too long in case they lodged in my mind like a burr and took root there. I felt for one dizzying, awful moment the sensation of falling.

FOURTEEN

NOT MY BROTHER'S KEEPER

"I half expected to be chased about by a gibbering shade, the way she talked about it," I complained to Marion a few days later, when the staircase had remained painfully ordinary and nothing newly terrifying had happened.

"I'm growing sick of it," she replied. Patience was never my virtue, but it was often hers, and for her to lose it really meant something.

She and Evelyn and I were sitting in the common room, where we hadn't been at all since Violet's warning. Sophie was on kitchen duty, and Alice and Dot were off somewhere, doing something, and the less I knew about it, the better. For the most part we'd done our best to avoid the staircase, aside from when we went back to the dormitory in the evenings, which even the biggest threat couldn't prevent. All our manoeuvring meant we'd been getting looks from the mistresses, and I was running out of excuses. You'd think we'd have been afraid enough of the consequences, but the temporary lull in the parade of catastrophes, alongside the fact that we had no idea what those consequences might be, made it difficult.

"Do you think we need to try to leave?" Evelyn said, miserably.

"I don't know if we *can*," Marion replied. "Violet said something about a window closing, didn't she?"

"It was a door, actually," I said.

Marion made a face. "Typical."

"Hordes of girls left the place only a week ago," I said. "I don't see how things could have changed that quickly."

"Is there any point in trying to understand it?" Evelyn asked, not looking at either of us.

"Maybe it's temporary," I suggested. "Maybe, you know, the door will open again."

"Either way I'm supposed to be helping Sophie in the kitchen," Marion said, getting up. "It's all so undignified, having to go to lessons and wash the dishes while we're trying to interpret cryptic warnings. You'd think we'd be allowed out of the ordinary routine of things, given the circumstances."

This left me and Evelyn in a rare moment of détente. With Marion gone and the conversation finished, I had to do something to avoid stewing in worry. I settled for scrubbing the window frames and giving the cushions a good beating to try to air them out. The common room had, for some days, taken on a musty smell. For once the noise I was making didn't seem to bother Evelyn.

"I'm ready to give up on the staircase nonsense," I announced. "If Miss Stevens asks me one more time why I was late to breakfast, I'm going to tell her everything, and then I'll be sent to the madhouse."

"Do you think that's wise?"

"What's wise got to do with anything? If we spend any longer peering over our shoulders I'll *deserve* the madhouse."

"I wish you wouldn't say that," she said stiffly from her seat near the window. She was hardly in any condition to be telling me off. She'd recovered somewhat in the week since the night of her birthday; evidently without the strain of Violet trying to force her way through, she had been feeling better. Still, she was pale and small, though none the less irritating for it.

"I wish she'd just be more clear," I said. "Violet, I mean. Oh, she told us about that suffocating haze she's under, and all that, but first she says we're in for it, then the staircase is a well full of water or whatever it was. I'd honestly rather not be warned at all if she's going to make it impossible to actually do anything with it."

"It isn't her fault," Evelyn said fiercely. "For all we know, it's mine."

"Yours—"

"Because of not being a good enough medium."

I felt rather cowed into silence. I wasn't accustomed to her admitting things like that to me. Really, I'd rather she didn't. "Whatever it is, it's not any use. Even if we had a real professional I can't help but suspect they'd find a way to make it as confusing as possible. They'd put it in a poem, or start speaking in tongues, or something, you know, anything but just telling us in plain English—" I was babbling, but at least I had got Evelyn off a track that led towards an end I felt obscurely afraid of.

"Look, before long they'll decide to tell us more, and then I'll have to tell *you* about it whether I want to or not."

"That's actually a fair point, thanks, Evelyn," I said, relieved to have had some measure of success. She just went back to staring into space, or whatever it was she did with her spare time. She drew her legs up onto her seat and I noticed, quite against my will, the way her stockings creased at the knee, and the fine bones of her ankle.

All our aimless speculation came to a head when Sophie started insisting that she was going to go home.

"Oh, you can't," Dot cried on first hearing her say it. "We all agreed together that we'd stay—you can't."

"I'm sorry" was all she said. She had been tense and distracted for days now—not ill like Evelyn had been, but sort of harried. I hadn't realised that was how she looked when she was trying to keep something secret. I suppose I didn't know her as well as I thought I did.

"Really, Sophie, do please stay," I said. "It wouldn't be the same if we weren't all together. And I think Evelyn'll agree to do another séance if we only wait a little longer." Perhaps this was manipulative, but they do say all's fair.

Evelyn's mouth twitched but to her credit she spoke up. "If it would stop you going, I'll do it."

This was a better outcome than I'd expected, actually. "I say, Sophie, you ought to listen to that, if nothing else—Evelyn wants you to stay so much she's willing to risk her immortal soul for it. Thanks, Evelyn."

"Emily's right," Marion said. "We need you here; you know the most about spiritualism of any of us, and you're a brave friend to have in a crisis. But also we *want* to have you here, because we care for you, and I think we're safer together."

"No reason to think whatever's going on here won't follow us home," Alice said.

"You're very lovely, all of you," Sophie said, and then broke off, staring at her hands in her lap. Her limbs looked longer than I remembered, sort of gangly, as if in a month or so she would have shot up an inch out of nowhere. She was fiddling with the torn edge of a piece of paper from her exercise book, curling it into tight spirals and uncurling it again.

"We're only telling the truth."

"You're very lovely, but I can't stay. I think we should all go, in fact, while we still can. Violet said something's coming, and I think we should stay with our families, where we can be protected."

I heard the others protesting, some gently, some less so. I wasn't part of the discussion; I was thinking. I'd like to be able to say I was having some kind of marvellous realisation, or putting the pieces together in a way that explained everything, but instead I was thinking about how little I associated the idea of family with the idea of protection, and how much I envied Sophie her easy assurance.

"Sophie, don't," Dot said finally, and fell into Sophie's arms crying.

"Shh, it's all right," said Sophie. She stroked her hand over Dot's back in big reassuring circles. "It's all going to be all right. I'm going to write Mumsy and Dad and ask if they'll drive up to fetch me whenever they can. Then I'll be home, safe. I could take you with me, even. Your people are in Norfolk, aren't they?"

"I'm not going anywhere," Dot said, a bewildered look on her face. "I'm staying here with the others so we can find out what's going on."

I thought about Dot's family, and the petty cruelties they showed her, and I thought about the nervous look on Evelyn's pious face during morning prayers, as if she thought God was watching her all the time.

Then I thought about Violet, and Mr. Kirsch. I remembered, with the sick lurch of something shuddering into place, the time he had come to a prize-giving when we were in the upper fifth. Her family and mine had been sat together on a series of benches slightly too narrow for our number; Violet and I were pressed close together and I could feel the long line of her thigh against mine. When her name was called, she leapt up and shimmied past the row of legs to get to the dais on which she was to be awarded a book, for excellence in elocution.

Violet did her elegant little curtsy to Miss Lewis, and came back to the endless adulatory applause that seemed to follow her wherever she went. Then her father leaned in, and whispered something in her ear. I didn't hear it, and she didn't tell me what it was afterwards, but her charming smile dropped instantly. She didn't expend much effort on congratulating the others, after that, until it was my turn to receive the prize for Mathematics and my family hardly seemed to notice that my name had been called at all. I watched her from the dais, the perfect vantage point to look and look and not be noticed, as she half-sprang out of her seat to clap until her hands must have smarted. I hadn't thought about it since it happened: mostly at the time I was just grateful that she was applauding for me.

"I don't know if I much trust our families to protect us," I said. It was something, I only realised then, that Violet and I had in common.

"Emily!" Sophie exclaimed. "They're our *families*!"

"Think about it. We realised that we could hold séances. We ruled out Mademoiselle." (This slightly guiltily, with a thought to her lying alone in San, but it was true.) "We've been protecting each other the best we can ever since Violet died. What do you think would happen if we told any of our parents—yes, Sophie, even yours—everything we've seen and done? We'd be lucky if we didn't get locked up."

Evelyn rested her chin in her hands, looking worn and thoughtful. "Mine wouldn't like it at all. Any of it. I don't know what they'd do to me."

"Then you can stay if you really want to," Sophie said. There were tears welling in her eyes. "I think Mumsy and Dad only want me to be safe. They'd believe me, if I asked them to."

"I hope you're right." Marion drummed her fingers on the windowsill.

Outside, it was raining heavily. November was nearly finished, and the rain had begun to feel like snow, hovering on the edge of something cleaner and colder but never quite getting there, instead covering the ground in puddles that sucked at your heels. The dormitory roof had developed a leak but none of us had the energy to do anything about it, so we shoved an old enamel bedpan Marion found in a cupboard under the spot and ignored it. The schoolmistresses hardly came up there those days.

Despite our hectoring, Sophie posted her letter that afternoon. It cast a pall over us. I secretly hoped that the postman would meet with some accident on his way to deliver it, or at the very least drop it in a ditch by mistake and not realise till it was too late. Evelyn didn't speak to Sophie all evening in revenge. I did, but mostly politely, like asking her to pass the salt when we ate our grim dinner of tinned meat and bitter potatoes.

After dinner, Alice stopped me in the corridor.

"I've been thinking, Locke," she said.

"Really, can't it wait?" I replied, scuffing the toes of my school shoes against the floor.

"I don't know," she said, to my surprise. "So I think we'd better do something about it."

She took me by the elbow—it didn't feel nearly as elegant when she did it; when Violet or Marion took you by the elbow you felt a bit like they were ladies in an Austen novel—and started steering me.

"Where on earth are you taking me?"

"San," she said.

"Oh, no, no, don't. I'd rather not, please Alice, I really don't want to." Her grip was strong, though, and I didn't want to fight her, so I let myself be dragged.

"Things are getting worse here. Sophie's leaving, I'm hoping the rest of us can stay on until we can figure it out, but I don't know if we will. You should—make amends."

It was difficult to say no to Alice, considering that she was five foot ten and exceptionally sturdy, and she was at the time pulling me quite firmly in the direction of San.

"She's not even going to be awake, Alice, I may as well be apologising to a corpse," I said, which was a mistake. Alice's grip tightened on my arm. "Ow! Pax! I'll do it, I'll do it, get off."

We made the rest of the journey in silence. When we got in, it was, obviously, empty of everyone but Mademoiselle and Matron.

"Hullo, Matron," Alice said. "With everything going on, Emily and I wanted to say hello to Mademoiselle. Thought it might give you a chance to take a break and get a cup of tea."

"Dear girls," she said absently, rolling up a wad of gauze and tucking it into her supply cabinet. "Of course. Be gentle with her but you needn't worry about waking her up; nothing seems to stir her. We'll be having a specialist doctor in to take a look at her any day now." She bustled out.

"Will we," I muttered under my breath. The idea of a specialist coming in to figure out what was going on was almost as laughable as the idea of my family believing me if I told them what was happening to us. Alice and I approached Mademoiselle's bed. It was the first time I'd seen her since Lacey died; I was struck this time by how small she was.

I'd grown an inch and a half since Mademoiselle first came to Briarley, a last-ditch (and mostly failed) effort on my body's part to make something elegant out of me. Looking down at her in San, I realised that that put us on par in terms of height, but the weeks she'd spent in bed had left her looking small and almost withered. I could have lifted her with no trouble; the thought that mere weeks before I'd been frightened of her seemed absurd.

"Mademoiselle," Alice said. "I've brought someone to see you."

She slept on. I'd heard that she was conscious enough to be fed soup without choking, but only barely, and as far as I knew she hadn't said a word since her awful warning to me and Evelyn and Sophie. Alice watched me expectantly.

"Well," I said, clearing my throat. I touched her bedclothes only to withdraw my hand when I realised they had the stiff, mildewy feel of linens that had been left for too long. "I'm here to apologise." I glanced at Alice, who nodded. Mademoiselle still lay there, practically catatonic. "I was wrong. I blamed you because it was easier than not having anyone to blame. And I made Evelyn and Sophie blame you too, because it was easier than doing it alone. I wish I hadn't done any of it. I wish I hadn't been right about you and Violet, and I'm sorry that I made things worse when you had lost her just like the rest of us. And thank you," I added, belatedly, "for the handkerchief. I'm sorry I didn't accept it."

Mademoiselle moved restively in her bed on hearing my voice, but didn't open her eyes or speak or anything. Her lips were parted enough to show the tiny gap between her two front teeth. Her hand twitched, like a dog having a dream. I bit at my thumbnail and made something of a vow to myself to become a better person, whatever that meant.

"D'you feel better now?" Alice said.

"Not really."

"Probably worth it anyhow. Always good to clear the air."

"I suppose so," I said, and reached out to straighten Mademoiselle's blanket. "Do you think she heard any of it?"

"No, look at her, she's out cold." Alice was looking at me keenly, as if she'd learned something about me from my apology. I wished she wouldn't—look at me, or learn anything about me. There couldn't possibly be anything good to learn.

A couple of days later, Sophie received a letter—startlingly brief, just a few lines—from her parents saying that they were coming to pick her up as soon as they could, and to expect them at the gates of Briarley at three o'clock in the afternoon that Saturday. If she was disappointed by how curt it was she didn't show it. She took all Saturday morning packing her trunk, meticulously folding the pinafores and blouses she wouldn't have cause to wear at home. I'd spent Thursday and Friday trying to persuade her not to go, making all sorts of promises on Evelyn's behalf about séances. Ultimately Marion took me aside.

"Let her go," she said. "She's going no matter what we tell her, so there's no point working yourself up and making her feel guilty about it." The vow I'd made in San had already begun to feel strained, so I agreed, and didn't say another word about it no matter how tempted I was. It was more of a surprise when it turned out that Evelyn was the one Marion should've been worrying about.

"I just think you're making a terrible mistake," she said, that prissy tone she always used when she thought she was right coming into her voice. Since Violet had promised to wait for Evelyn to agree to it before she came back, the colour had returned to Evelyn's cheeks and she seemed closer to her old self.

"I'm going home where I'll be safe," Sophie said. It sounded like a meditation, or a prayer: something she'd repeated to herself till she believed it.

"After what Violet said? You're kidding yourself if you think it'll work. But be my guest to make your own awful decisions; I'm not my brother's keeper." Evelyn turned her nose up in the air.

"You can be really beastly sometimes, Evelyn," Sophie said and slammed the lid of her trunk a little too hard. She flounced off in a huff.

When Sophie returned, Evelyn was reading her book again, and appeared to be ignoring us all on purpose, which suited me just fine.

"Look, everyone," said Sophie, who had on the peacekeeping face that I realised just then I would miss terribly. "I know you don't agree with me going, but I want you to know I think it's the right thing to do. And I respect all of you for deciding differently. And—I mustn't forget—I'm leaving the book here, in case you can make some use of it."

"Thanks Sophie," I said, around the hard lump in my throat.

"It's the least I can do. I'll be going home to roast beef and fresh fruit, you may as well have anything useful I can give you." As if on an impulse she walked across the room and gave me a tight hug.

"You'll write, won't you?" Marion said.

"Of course—and you must too—"

"As long as the post still goes," said Evelyn, which struck me as rather horrible. Sophie gave her a quick, nervous glance, but no one mentioned the comment.

"Right, I can't see them out there but it's just gone three and the walk down the drive seems to get longer every time I take it," Sophie said, brushing the wrinkles out of the skirt of her pinafore with her palms.

"Goodbye, Sophie," Dot said, her lip wobbling.

"Don't be silly, I'm sure you'll see me after Christmas."

The last I saw of her, she was walking down the gravel drive, her body tipped to one side to accommodate her trunk and her blazer with the Briarley crest on the breast pocket sagging down over one shoulder.

FIFTEEN

NEARER, MY GOD, TO THEE

We found her in the fountain the next morning.

Dot and Alice went for a walk first thing, before chapel, and Dot came back absolutely insensible with terror. Alice's mouth was pressed into a grim line.

"It's Sophie," Evelyn said, with that unsettling clarity she'd picked up ever since she started being a medium. It wasn't really a question, but Alice nodded in confirmation.

I had to see it for myself. I went downstairs and left the building by the grand front entrance, which faced onto the gravel driveway, the fountain with its Adonis statue that we had made so much of when we were younger, and the big iron gates down at the far end that we'd seen Sophie approaching the day before. The Sunday morning light was clear and crisp. It was the second of December, and Briarley had never looked so alien to me. Overnight the temperature had dropped several degrees. The grass had turned to frosty spears and the puddles of mud had frozen over into ugly, dark patches. I tried to focus on the loud crunch of the gravel under my feet.

Even now, the thought of what I saw that morning strikes

me with a particular dread. I dream about it, sometimes: the endless walk up the drive, the whistle of the wind through my blouse. The dream goes on for a long time. But it stops right before the worst of it, and for that I am grateful. The worst of it was the sight of the fountain. The outdoor pipes had frozen so Adonis's jug had ceased its usual pouring. The ice had reached the well of the fountain, too, and spread across the surface with a glassy sheen. The only thing that interrupted it was Sophie's body.

She lay slumped against the statue's legs. We had all been forbidden, in no uncertain terms, ever to go in the water of the fountain, so to see her there was an uncomfortable, incongruous sight that felt like breaking the rules. The lower half of her body disappeared under the water and there was a crust of ice around her waist. It made her look as though she was trapped in there; anyone trying to get her out would have to break the ice. I knew it was useless to try to do anything—worse than useless, even. I didn't want to see her like this, and my legs felt more and more leaden with every step. Still, I couldn't stop myself crossing the rest of the drive. I thought for a second, very stupidly, what an awful idea it was after all to have a fountain out in front of a school—the enormous risk it posed—how if Miss Lewis had had any sense she'd have pulled it down the second she became headmistress. Then I reached Sophie's body, and I didn't think anything at all.

My vision whited out entirely, like I had been packed in cotton wool. I couldn't perceive anything, I just hung there dumb as a post, staring. Evelyn told me later that she'd been watching, and I must've stood stock still for upwards of a minute. I was so still that for a moment she thought I'd frozen, too. But what else was I supposed to do, in the face of that sight?

Sophie was dead. There could be no doubt about that. Her

eyes were open and glassy, staring straight ahead, and her mouth hung open a little to reveal gleaming teeth like seed pearls. Her legs were stuck straight out under the water, and through the filmy glaze of burgeoning ice I could see that she still had her thick woollen winter stockings on. I couldn't see a single mark on her that would suggest violence. She was utterly pristine, only her lips were blue and she was so very definitely dead. It was as if, after she'd reached the gate to meet her parents, she had simply turned around, walked right back down the drive, and sat down in the fountain quite of her own accord. The stillness was the sickest part of all, I think. Violet's fall had been a terrible, bloody shock—Sophie's death was quiet, almost sly, and tinged with a nauseating sense of the inevitable.

By then Evelyn had followed me out. I'm not sure how long she stood there watching before she stepped in line with me, a few feet away from the fountain. She was shaking all over.

"I'm getting Miss Lewis," I said, just to say something, though as the words came out of my mouth they already felt very far away.

"What on earth could Miss Lewis do for us now?" she said softly.

I don't know if what we did after Sophie died will seem very stupid to anyone who wasn't there with us. I have no desire to defend how we handled it, and I wonder if we'd done it differently the end of things might have been very different too. But we were hardly more than children, and we were doing the best we could with what we had, which wasn't much. More than that, I believe that most of what happened was inescapable, one way or another. We were infected, down to the land we lived on and the milk we drank, and escaping that infection by calling the police at the right moment or turning and running would have been no real escape at all. Or, at least, that's what I tell myself.

So we didn't try to leave, or fetch any kind of authorities. Instead we trudged back into the school, leaving a trail of wet footprints behind us, which would have been cause for a black mark under any other circumstances. I couldn't bring myself to care. The big foyer with its grand staircase seemed vast and hollow, any signs of life vanished into Briarley's increasing emptiness. Miss Lewis's office was right around the corner, and with trepidation I knocked on her door.

"Miss," I said. "Miss, there's something you need to see outside." Evelyn and I stood in the doorway, as if we didn't want to bring the news all the way in. I realised I was cold; I had only been wearing my blouse and pinafore when Dot and Alice came upstairs. Miss Lewis must have seen something in my expression, because when she looked up at me her face fell. It was one of the few times I ever saw her hesitate.

Once outside, Miss Lewis stood over the fountain, contemplating the ruin of her life's work. I wanted to stay with Sophie. She had always been shy around Miss Lewis, had found her presence nerve-wracking rather than, as I did, reassuring. I didn't want to leave her alone with someone she had been wary of. If I could have stayed without looking at her I might have, shivering outside with no coat and no stockings, but there was no way around it. Her body was so unmistakably present that I couldn't bear to be near it any longer, so I put an arm around Evelyn's shoulders—recalling, quite unbidden, the last time we had leaned against one another in the face of death—and took her inside.

No one needed to say aloud that lessons were cancelled. The younger girls stayed in their dormitory and did God knew what; we weren't involved. Most of us sat in the common room in silence. Dot wandered about disconsolately, like a little ghost, occasionally reporting back to us on what she'd seen elsewhere in the school. Apparently Matron called her into San and asked what had happened, because no one had gone up to explain things, but she could tell from the hush that had fallen over the school that something was badly wrong. Dot wept and wept to her, and I only hoped that if she let on about what we thought had happened to Sophie, Matron would chalk it up to shock. Watching me tentatively, Dot told us that Mademoiselle had lain inert in the furthest bed in San the whole time, unaware of anything.

After extensive discussion, she went on: Miss Lewis and Miss Parker had brought a clean sheet from the laundry and gently placed it over Sophie's body.

"For her dignity. Or that's what they said, anyway."

"Only so much dignity you can have, sitting in the fountain," I said, and then wished I hadn't. Marion went to the window and craned her neck to catch a glimpse of the fountain, then turned back with her hand pressed over her mouth. I felt a thrill of fear go through me.

"What is it? What did you see down there?"

"No, it's nothing like that," she said from behind her hand. "I suppose I'm trying not to laugh. She's—oh, see for yourself."

The schoolmistresses' attempt at providing dignity for Sophie hadn't worked. With the sheet draped over her head and dipping into the wet parts where the ice was thinnest, she resembled nothing more than a child in a Hallowe'en costume, the sort of ghost that the little ones made with a sheet and a pair of scissors. I couldn't look at it for long without crying or laughing or being sick, so I turned away without saying anything, leaving Marion to shake silently and guiltily in her armchair.

We were told at lunch, which was an unsurprisingly dismal affair, that the telephone had been tested again. In the surprise of the century, it was discovered to be out of order still. I found it enormously difficult to react to the news of the faulty telephone with the dismay the teachers felt it warranted. Evidently they saw this as a terrible blow, rather than the natural progression of events; I would've been much more surprised to hear that anything was working normally.

It was determined that Miss Stevens would head into the village after lunch and fetch the police. Marion stayed behind to clear the dishes and told us later that she'd seen Mildred Allen, one of the few younger girls who'd been left behind, begging to be taken along so she could ring her parents. We exchanged a few horrified looks.

"You don't think—" Alice started.

"Well, we don't know, do we," Marion said flatly. "Why it happened to Sophie. *What* happened to Sophie. Was the letter from her parents even real, were they ever going to come and collect her at all?"

I felt sick, sick, sick. "It's obvious, isn't it? She tried to leave and it killed her." No one said a word about my saying "it."

"Why would anything want to kill Sophie?" Dot said, scrubbing at the sticky tears all over her face. "Will it kill the others too or is it just us?"

"I can't think why it would just be us," Alice said hotly. "That doesn't make any sense, it wouldn't be fair."

"Either way, I think we should stop them leaving, just in case," I argued.

"And what do you think will happen if we tell Miss Lewis that we think everyone who tries to leave will end up in the fountain? Christ, Emily, at some point whatever it is would start running out of space," Alice said. Then: "Sorry, Dot," because Dot had started crying again.

"We can make something up, but I don't think we should let them go out of those gates; we have to tell them *something*."

"I'm not sure we could come up with anything that would prevent someone from going to get the police after a girl died," Marion said, grimacing.

"What if they go and then we find them somewhere worse than the fountain?" Dot said. I hadn't even thought that far. They could end up anywhere. In our beds, in the icebox. In the pulpit in chapel. The way Sophie had died was so obviously unnatural that I felt like the whole school had been loosed from the bounds of reality. I was lost, thinking about it, when I heard faint voices coming from outside. Marion went to look out the window.

"It's too late," she said, quiet and resigned. "They're nearly at the gate already." I followed her: there they were, Mildred seeming awfully young, accompanied by Miss Stevens, who towered over her. Mildred's school hat was sitting neatly atop her head, its navy ribbon angled to the side. None of us had had occasion to wear ours in such a long time; it seemed strange to imagine having the thought *Better put my school hat on*. Like a relic from a faraway time. My skin crawled when I imagined how they'd had to walk past Sophie in the fountain covered with that sheet. There was no way we'd reach them in time to stop them going through the gate. And even if we did, what could we possibly say?

When dusk came and they hadn't come back, Miss Lewis and Miss Stone told us all to stay inside while they picked up Sophie's body and brought it to chapel, which was a cold place that felt less unsanitary than the pantry, and had the veneer of religious sanctuary.

"At last, a benefit to how frigid chapel gets in winter," I remarked to Alice, whom I thought was the only person likely to take it well. She laughed, but only half-heartedly.

At dinnertime, Miss Lewis forbade anyone from going after Miss Stevens and Mildred in case they met with an accident on the road. Motorcars took corners like fiends sometimes, and the tall hedgerows seemed to grow taller in the dark, crowding you in and narrowing the path. Not that any of us in the upper sixth would've gone after them ourselves. We all wilted with relief in the dining hall when Miss Lewis made her announcement; only Miss Stone and the more nervous of the other younger girls, Shirley, seemed to chafe at it. I thought in a pinch we could stand to lose Miss Stone, but I didn't think I had it in me to find Shirley's body speared on the weathervane or whatever would become of her if she tried leaving.

When I thought no one at high table was listening, I leaned forwards and said, quietly, "We should meet tonight."

"Careful," Marion warned, glancing at Miss Lewis.

"Tonight," I whispered. "After lights-out. We need to decide what to do."

"I don't want to do another séance," Evelyn said. She was too loud, loud enough that Miss Stone heard us, and things only worsened from there.

"Girls, may I remind you that you are still at school," she said, standing up from her seat at high table. "These are unusual circumstances, but it is certainly no excuse for poor manners. Whispering at the table is unacceptable."

"Yes, Miss Stone," Evelyn said, and sat up straighter. I sneered at her for her blind obedience, but I was just as startled as she was when, with no preamble whatsoever, Alice made an inarticulate noise low in her throat, picked up her water glass, and threw it across the room.

She was a champion bowler; there was real power in her arm and she could aim like a sharpshooter. The glass sailed through the air and hit one of the portraits on the opposite wall, shattering into countless pieces when it hit the floor. The portrait was one of the old Briarleys, a man in sober greys and blacks with a patrician nose and a cold blue gaze, both of which were now dented and distorted. He had attempted, and failed, to turn the Briarleys' fortunes by investing heavily in sugar refineries back in the 1870s; there was a small gold plaque under his portrait and I had read it countless times while bored during mealtimes, peering up into his small, cruel eyes.

Miss Lewis rose, her chair scraping back with a violent sound. My heart caught in my throat. *What will they do to her,* I thought, suffused for a moment with real fear, *What awful new direction could this day go in—*

In the end, she did something I couldn't have expected: Miss Lewis, shirtwaist buttoned up to her throat, not a hair out of place, picked up her cut crystal sherry glass in one big hand and flung it at Alice, who ducked—but she needn't have. Miss Lewis's fury was belied by the fact that the glass fell short of our table and splintered with an odd little chiming noise on the flagstones.

Alice looked hard at Miss Lewis and then stalked out of the room, her face burning hot and red under her freckles. Dot went after her, the sound of her boots echoing in the silent hall. She looked back once, like Lot's wife, with a fragile, frightened expression. The rest of us were too cowardly to follow them out, dreading the horrors that would inevitably be visited on them: weeks without supper, a hundred whacks on the wrist with a ruler, tortures we hadn't even managed to dream up. But none of the schoolmistresses went after them either, not even Miss Stone. Once Alice was out of the room, it was as if she had ceased to exist, and after a brief, tense pause, all of high table went back to their dinners.

The rest of the meal felt as though it took a thousand years. Every bite of food was an ordeal, which it would have been anyhow, because I was heartily sick of tinned food and if I never ate another vegetable from Cook's decaying garden it would be too soon. Funnily enough, the younger girls and the mistresses didn't seem to mind the monotony and mushiness at that point; it was as though they had forgotten what good food tasted like. Shirley prolonged our suffering by bringing out bowls of tinned satsuma slices for dessert. The whole process went on and on: multiple trips to and from the kitchen, a single bowl shattering on the floor when she'd taken more than she could carry at once. I spooned my satsumas up and thought about spotted dick, blancmange, all the stodgy horrible puddings that I used to groan at, which I'd have given anything to eat a bowlful of just then.

Once we got back to the dormitory, Alice was already in bed, a large lumpen shape. Dot was looking at a magazine with no real sense of concentration. As we moved about, it became increasingly difficult not to notice the space Sophie had left behind. All her things had been gone since she'd left, of course, but her bed felt emptier than it had ever been, standing between Evelyn's and Dot's like a loose tooth. Evelyn seemed inured to it already, but Dot kept leaning away from the empty bed with its neat hospital corners until Alice's voice came from under the covers and told her to come and share her bed. They looked funny there, Alice so tall that she took up more than her fair share of space even when on her own, Dot filling in the gaps.

We lay there in silence for some time. I was struck by how

little comfort the schoolmistresses had attempted to give us this time around. I don't mean to say that I would've wanted to be handed a cup of hot cocoa and told that it was all going to be all right; I wouldn't have believed it for a second. But we hadn't heard a word at all, other than being told not to go to the village and not to whisper at the table. I tried, briefly, for patience: they were in shock just as we were, and things had ceased to seem coincidental. Only it seemed so out of the ordinary, that we were to be abandoned entirely to our loss. I didn't *want* saccharine reassurances, but I felt the total lack of them nevertheless.

I had too much time to think, lying there in the dark and the quiet, all of us too consumed with our own thoughts to talk. Before long I had thought myself into being terribly angry. It was that sort of unfocused, multidirectional anger that could launch itself at anything that came into its path. I was angry at Miss Lewis, for acting like nothing had happened. I was angry at Alice, for walking off and leaving the rest of us to flounder. I was angry at Evelyn, for refusing to do a séance until it was already too late for Sophie and for still refusing now. I was angry at Violet for making everything so complicated and for being so beastly when all I wanted was to have her back. I was angry at Sophie for going and dying when we should all have stayed together.

Finally, the bell for lights-out came. From across the room Marion blew out her bedside candle. I felt as if I might vibrate out of my skin. My blood was up; I itched to do something.

We waited, and waited, seeing who would be the first to move. The only sound in the room was the wind coming in where one of the windowpanes had broken and been inexpertly taped up by Alice. It felt like eons, and to my surprise, it was Dot who spoke up.

"Oh, I can't wait any longer," she said. "Let's go to the common room, where it isn't so frigid. I'll go first and make sure there isn't anybody out there and if Miss Stone's about I'll tell her I was—"

"Going to get some warm milk?" I said. It came out sharper than I'd intended it.

"Well. A cup of tea, anyhow."

Alice kissed the top of her head. "No end plucky of you. You don't have to, you know."

"I think I'll go *quite* mad if I don't do something now," Dot replied, wriggling absently. "If she isn't there, I'll knock twice on the wall of the landing so you know it's safe to come out."

"Bring the book," Marion whispered.

Dot threw a dressing-gown over her shoulders.

"Wish me luck," she said, putting the book under her arm, and she crept out the door. Within seconds, I felt like I couldn't bear to wait for her to come back. It was agony. For one thing, my whole body was desperate to get up and do something and I wasn't sure how much longer I could lie in bed thinking about Sophie without going mad. I'd been forced to stay still for so long that I was losing the ability to keep the sight of her in the fountain from my mind, try as I might, and practised as I was at not thinking about things I didn't want to face. For another, I didn't like the idea of one of us going off exploring alone one bit. It felt like tempting fate. I think Alice felt the same way; once or twice I heard her muttering, "Come on, come on." It felt like an age, but it couldn't have been more than several minutes, when we finally heard two soft knocks on the dormitory door.

"It's her," Alice breathed in relief, and leapt out of bed. I followed her, grateful to be in motion, and we opened the door as silently as we could.

Dot wasn't there. Perhaps, I remember thinking, she had hurried away to keep out of sight. Down the steps—onto the landing—she still wasn't there. Everything was dark; it was a cloudy night so even the moon wasn't coming through. I thought for a moment about the two who'd gone to fetch the police and wondered where they were now, if they were still alive, if they were in the cold and the dark all alone. I turned to look for Dot, and nearly jumped out of my skin when she was right there beside me.

"Dot?" I whispered. Something was wrong. She wasn't waiting for us, ready to shepherd us all safely to the common room. Instead she was frozen in terror, pressed against the wall of the landing. Her breath was coming in little gasps and her eyes were screwed shut. She hardly seemed to notice me. "Dorothy!" Alice was at my side in a second, and her arrival seemed to jolt Dot out of her stupor.

"She's out there," Dot said in an agonised whisper. "Sophie, Sophie, she's out there." I felt the blood drain from me till I was dizzy.

"What are you talking about," said Alice, but it wasn't really a question; she sounded as if she didn't want to know. Dot pointed towards the stained-glass windowpane of the door in the vestibule, which overlooked the lawn. She didn't open her eyes, just raised a hand and pointed. I turned, reluctantly.

"Christ alive," Alice said, and shuddered.

There was a large, girl-shaped shadow silhouetted in the glass. It wasn't moving. It looked like it was waiting. I recognised the way Sophie wore her hair, falling straight down over her shoulders. It was Sophie but it wasn't. It was standing all wrong, shoulders slightly hunched and long arms hanging down loose so it resembled an oddly stuffed scarecrow. The divisions in the glass warped my view of it, leaving it rippled and multicoloured, but there was no denying what we were looking at. I felt as though all the air had been sucked out of me the second I laid eyes on her.

"Don't look at her," I said, with the last of my breath. It was an instinct, more than anything else. "I don't think we should look at her." Marion and Evelyn had caught up but hadn't yet come in view of the shadow standing outside.

"What is it?" Marion asked, coming closer too quickly, and saying again, in an entirely different tone, "What is it?"

"I think it's—Sophie's body," Alice said. She began to drum her knuckles against the wall in a quick, staccato motion: a habit of hers, when she longed to run.

"Her spirit?"

"No, it's not her," Alice said. Dot moaned a little. Her eyes were still squeezed shut. "It looks like her, but it isn't her. It's all wrong."

"I think we should get into the common room as quickly as we can so it can't see us," I urged. I didn't know why it felt so important that it didn't see us. The thought didn't invite interrogation. "We should go now. I don't want to be near it any longer. Don't look at it, Evelyn."

Without deciding it aloud, just by instinct, we formed a queue like children, and filed as quietly as we could towards the common room. For all her pleading, Dot didn't move at first; Alice had to take her by the shoulders and gently push her along. I took one last glance behind me at the Sophie-thing standing outside, only for a second, because I couldn't help it. It hadn't moved. This was good, because I think if it had I would've expired then and there. But its unwavering presence was also bizarrely at odds with what I knew it must have done, which was stand up from where Miss Lewis and Miss Stone had laid it in chapel and walk around half of the school to get to this door. How long had it been there—had it moved with intelligence and intention or was it some kind of puppet—was there anything of Sophie left at all? It was such a violation: Sophie's body, all that was left of her being used for God only knew what purpose, or with no purpose at all, just an instinct or a reflex like a muscle jumping when electricity is applied to it.

Entering the common room was like going into a sanctuary, though how long it would remain so I couldn't be sure. I tried to collect myself, heaving in great shuddering gulps of air like I'd been deprived of it since leaving the dormitory. Alice was the first to speak.

"Horrible, horrible, I can't believe it," she said in a low voice.

Evelyn shifted about. "I'd rather not think about it, if you don't mind."

"I can't not think about it, God, the way she just stood there—" I said, feeling as though I might be sick.

"Can we get started, *please*," Marion said. "Dot, the book?"

Dot, white-faced, placed the book in the centre of the room, where we had unconsciously replicated our séance circle. Sophie's absence throbbed like a wound.

Evelyn snatched the book. "Let me look at it. I don't want to be the medium again but, I suppose"—and she said it with the most extreme reluctance—"there might be something else we can do."

"All right, O high and mighty one," I said, trying not to let on how frightened I felt or how much I resented her for not having seen the Sophie-thing like the rest of us had. It wasn't fair—after all, I had been the one to warn her—but my desire to protect her had risen up in an instant and faded away just as quickly.

"Do you think we should sing a hymn first?" Dot said. "I think maybe we ought to. I don't feel at all sure that Sophie's going to get a proper funeral. It might be like—like we can give her one ourselves, here."

"Look, I have to ask," Alice said. "Before we do the hymn and all. Could we bury her tomorrow night, if they don't? Put her to rest?"

"I don't see how we could, without being found out. And I think," Marion said grimly, "that touching her corpse is more than I could bear."

So a hymn it was: the best poor Sophie was going to get. We decided on "Nearer, My God, to Thee," which had been one of her favourites. Without discussing it, we reached out and clasped hands, just as if we were starting a séance. While we sang I thought of Sophie crying as she told us the story of it being played while the *Titanic* went down in 1912, and then Violet asked whether we were sadder about the *Titanic* or the Great War, which caused a row that lasted most of last February. Then the one time it had ever been the hymn we sang in chapel, we were near-hysterical with laughter except for Sophie, who started sobbing. We were all herded into Miss Lewis's office, given a thorough talking-to, and made to go without dinner. I missed her already. Anyway, I didn't know the words to the hymn all that well, but if I watched Evelyn's mouth hard enough I could follow her, given how hard she overenunciated.

When we finished, Evelyn picked up the book again and flipped through it derisively, leaving the rest of us just to sit there. Finally she put it back down with great prejudice, spine up, pages open to a point about halfway through. She wouldn't look any of us in the eye.

"What did you read?" Dot asked. Evelyn didn't answer. Her teeth were sunk deep in her lip, leaving a white imprint.

I picked up the book, keeping it open to the page she'd

stopped at, just to spite her. It was the chapter about materialisation. According to the book, a talented medium could be made to call up not only the voice but the ectoplasmic body of someone who had died. There were all sorts of stories of people materialising wives and friends and children, seeing them whole and perfect long after their bodies had gone to dust. With language that bordered on the lurid, the book listed the various confinements mediums could be put in to prevent the possibility of fraud (wire cages, velvet collars, strips of calico held together with sealing-wax). Evelyn glanced at me nervously as I read, as if I was going to get ideas. But the book was better for stories than it was for instructions, and while I didn't need to be persuaded of the truth of spirit communication, one account did catch my eye.

It was the story of a man being led out of a collapsing mine by the shining hand of a materialised spirit, who moved with unnatural speed and seemed to know her way through the piles of rubble. *She kissed my hand thrice*, the man said, *with lips at once cold and wonderfully soft. Having felt those unearthly lips on my skin I can speak with absolute certainty of the fact of materialisation, and of the marvellous power of our departed friends, for my own life was saved by the same.*

I read it aloud to the others, my voice catching on the word *kissed*.

"I think materialising Violet might save us," I said, looking around the circle. Evelyn had stiffened, and was trying to disguise it by turning her nose up in the air in condescension. I didn't want to think about how much we were beginning to depend on her.

"I don't know if I think materialisation was ever real," Marion said doubtfully, "or safe—"

"And you'll need me to agree to do it first," Evelyn retorted, and just then, the door to the common room creaked open.

The Sophie-thing, I thought, in a haze of panic. I had my back to the door and it was so very dark. I thought of her icy dead hand touching me on the shoulder and all I could do was struggle away from the sound as quickly as I could.

"What are all of you doing in here?"

It didn't sound at all like how I'd have expected the Sophie-thing to sound. It was high-pitched and supercilious. Whoever it was sounded like they could use a good smacking, which didn't seem like Sophie, either in life or in death. I turned around and saw Ann Turner standing in the doorway in her nightdress. There was a shuffling noise as Marion slid the book under the sofa; thankfully, Ann was too pleased with herself to notice.

"Might as well ask you the same thing," Alice said, scrambling up so her whole big frame towered over Ann.

"I heard a noise," Ann said, in an accusing tone.

I found I was able to speak again. "And so what if you did? Can't you see we're doing something private? Go on, get out of here."

"You're doing something *odd*," she hissed.

Marion stood up as well. She looked ever so tall, bent over Ann's little body with all the authority she had. "I don't think you saw anything at all," she said. "We were singing a hymn. Sophie died today and we wanted to mourn her together."

But Ann looked right back up at her, unfazed. "I think you're a bunch of liars. I think you're doing something wrong in here and I'm going to tell Miss Lewis." She had a glint in her eye that said she was enjoying this; I hadn't heard her say that many words in a row with any success since she'd arrived at Briarley a few years before.

"You little bluenose—tell anyone a thing and you'll regret it," I said without thinking.

"I *am* going to tell!" Ann exclaimed, and took off before any of us could go after her.

"Oh hell," Alice muttered, and sank back.

"Do you think we ought to just go back to bed as quickly as we can?" Dot asked.

"No use, I'm afraid," Marion said. There were footsteps coming up to the common room. We hastily moved out of our circle and tried to look innocent. Miss Lewis's heavy footfall came closer and closer, and finally she was there, a candlestick in her hand. I wondered if the Sophie-thing was still there, if she had felt its malign presence. If she had, she seemed unaffected by it.

"What on earth is going on in here?" she demanded. "I heard voices, and on my way to investigate was met by an extremely upset Ann Turner, telling me you were in here attempting some sort of pagan ritual. An explanation, please, now."

"Ann doesn't have the slightest idea what she's talking about," I protested.

"I heard you," Ann said. She crept out from behind Miss Lewis, whom she had been using as a shield against us. "At dinner, I heard you talking about it, and then I heard a noise like someone was walking around and I heard you *even more*." She sounded triumphant. I hadn't even thought to watch out for her and Shirley at dinner.

"Ann, back to bed," Miss Lewis said, and sighed. "Now, if you will." She turned back and surveyed us. I suspect we hadn't done a very good job of looking innocent.

"Honest to God, Miss Lewis, we were just trying to sing a hymn for Sophie," Alice tried, but it didn't work at all. It was a cruel irony that the night we were found out, we weren't even trying to do a séance. I suppose Alice was only lucky that Miss Lewis didn't seem to remember what she'd done at dinner.

"I am deeply disappointed in you girls. I depend on you to set an example for the younger girls who remain here, and instead I catch you engaging in what I can only assume are un-Christian rituals at all hours of the night. Hart, may I remind you that you are a prefect?"

How could she stand on ceremony, at a time like this? How could she treat us this way, when she had always seemed, despite exterior appearances, to care for us? I was so furious I wanted to break something, to throw something, to make someone sorry. All that anger that I had been waiting to pour into the séance had nowhere to go, and it boiled over.

"I'm sorry to interrupt," I said, seething, "but there's hardly anyone for us to set an example to. We're practically the only ones left here and there's fewer and fewer of us by the day, if you hadn't noticed." The others gaped at me. I wished immediately that I hadn't said it.

"I am going to choose to let that slide, Locke," she said, looking hard at me. "It has been a long and difficult day and I appreciate that the circumstances are trying. But I will not accept such insubordinate, wilful behaviour again. Your actions tonight are a stain on Briarley. If I catch you doing something like this in future, I'll have no choice but to expel anyone participating. As it is, I'll be forced to put a black mark next to your records."

"Miss Lewis—" I started. The thought that the threat of expulsion was profoundly stupid didn't even occur to me, as it does now—after all, where would we have gone? Instead, I felt a pathetic, instinctive terror at the thought of being expelled. Not just the fear of being caught breaking the rules, but the idea of being cut off from the only place I knew, and the only place where I was known. I had a vision of being turned out from the very idea of Briarley and told it would be closed to me forever afterwards, like the gates of heaven being shut against a sinner. Whatever it had become, whatever I had experienced there, I didn't know anything else, and something in me quailed. Even then, I wanted to keep hold of it as long as I could.

"Rest assured I will watch you diligently to ensure you're unable to attempt such a thing again. Tomorrow morning we will hold a funeral for Miss Salisbury and, after that, another group will go for help. With any luck you'll all be safely home before the day is out and the question will be settled." She stood by the door and gestured for us to leave.

Once we were on the landing, I chanced a wary look outside. The Sophie-thing was gone.

SIXTEEN

THE HABIT OF SHAME

The next morning was cold, the sun casting a bright but impersonal light from behind thin clouds. Someone—I assume Miss Lewis—had waited outside our door for what felt like hours the night before. I don't know if any of the others were still awake, but I only heard footsteps heading back down the stairs when the birds started going outside the window. It brought me some small measure of satisfaction to know that as little sleep as I'd had, Miss Lewis couldn't have had much more.

Satisfaction or no, my whole body felt heavy and unwilling, the corners of my eyes sore; the sole benefit, I suppose, of barely having slept was that I didn't have to experience the moment upon waking where I remembered that Sophie was dead. I dragged myself out of bed with all the enthusiasm of a conscript and scrubbed my face roughly with cold water, the only kind reliably coming out of the sink taps by then, which didn't so much help as provide a new and different sort of discomfort.

By the time I was finished in the bathroom, the bell had rung and the others had begun to wake up as well. When we had returned to the dormitory the night before, Dot had crawled back into bed with Alice and they had pressed close together, like sardines in a tin. Early in the morning I thought I noticed their bedclothes rustling, and heard a small soft noise that sounded like Dot coming from beneath, but I didn't have it in me to feel much of anything about it. I simply pulled the covers up over my head and waited for it to end, thinking abstractedly that it might have been nice to share a bed with someone, if only to keep the cold out.

"So what do we think," Alice said, struggling up onto her elbows. "Séance tonight, as soon as we can get away from Miss Lewis?"

"I don't know how we can," Marion said.

"She'll have to look away some time. Unless she puts a guard in the dormitory we'll be alone for at least a few hours. Nix the hymn, sit right in the middle of the floor if we have to."

"We've got to do it," Dot said as Alice combed her fingers through her short curls with a tenderness that made me feel ill. "That—thing—last night, that looked like Sophie? I want Violet's help. I couldn't bear it, seeing it again."

"Or if it tries to get in," Evelyn said, softly. I shuddered. Before anyone could reply, Miss Parker knocked hard on the door and, without waiting for an answer, let herself in.

"Good morning, girls," she said, without a hint of warmth. It wasn't like her; nothing felt as it should.

"Good morning, Miss Parker," we chorused drearily. It was a reflex more than anything else. I didn't think it was a good morning at all and I didn't particularly care to wish one to Miss Parker, but it would've felt stranger not to say it back.

"I think you'll find the bell rang several minutes ago. Why aren't you dressed?"

"I hardly think—" I started, furious.

"We were talking about Sophie," Marion cut in smoothly. "Miss Lewis told us last night that there was going to be a funeral service for her this morning."

"Yes, Miss Lewis told me all about your midnight conversation. We'll meet outside chapel in ten minutes, so you'd better hurry," Miss Parker said, casting a disapproving glance up and down the room. "There won't be time now, but you ought to tidy this place up. Not having dormitory inspections is a privilege; it can be lost." She shut the door hard behind her and went downstairs.

We gawped at one another.

"What's *wrong* with her?" Alice asked. She sounded as if she'd like to march after Miss Parker and give her a piece of her mind. "You'd expect it from Miss Stone—"

"Under normal circumstances," I interrupted. "You wouldn't expect it even from Miss Stone in a situation like this."

There wasn't anything else to say. We dressed once again in our funeral clothes, which by now had got more wear in the past couple of months than in their entire previous lifetimes. My dress hung on me awkwardly after weeks of poor food, though it was still much too short to be dignified. I spent the entire walk wondering what they'd done with Sophie's body, or if it was even there at all after what had happened the night before.

When we arrived at chapel, the others were already standing outside in two neat lines. Only Matron and Mademoiselle were absent. There were so few of them, now; with yesterday's rescue party gone, our numbers felt unutterably diminished. Ann and Shirley were in their school uniforms, which I uncharitably thought was just like them, no respect for the dead at all, and then I looked harder and saw that all the schoolmistresses were wearing ordinary clothes as well. I started composing a furious rejoinder in my head. *Just because it's our third funeral of the term doesn't mean we don't have standards to uphold—the real stain on Briarley*—but before I could finish, Miss Lewis spoke.

"You're late," she said. "We value punctuality in Briarley girls." Not a word about everyone who had gone—Miss Stevens and little Mildred, or even Sophie—just the admonishment, delivered in a flat tone.

"We haven't even had breakfast yet," Alice said, bewildered.

Miss Stone sighed. "We'll have to do this with efficiency, if we're to start lessons on time." I exchanged a horrified look with the others.

We were ushered into chapel with no degree of solemnity whatsoever. I feel somewhat embarrassed to admit that as few of us as there were, we filed in neatly, one by one like the good schoolgirls we hadn't really been for weeks. Chapel was never warm, exactly, but usually there were enough people in there at a time that with our shoulders pressed together, our collected body heat stopped us shivering. Now, though, there were so few of us, and while all of us upper-sixth girls crowded together in one pew, the rest scattered across chapel, seemingly at random. They must have been miserably cold.

I looked up towards the altar, but the normal candles and cloth had been cleared away, and only the gramophone was there, with its big old-fashioned tulip head. I hadn't seen it since Hallowe'en. Miss Lewis came up through what passed for a nave, her face curiously expressionless. We all watched her go, our heads swivelling in bewilderment at her silent, steady gait. There was a sense that we were all poised for something to happen, something that would break the tension. I couldn't picture Miss Lewis starting to cry, or embracing us, but there had to be something—

Dot saw it first. Of course she did; as the upper-sixth girl least able to resist making a scene, it was inevitable that she would be the one to stand at the end of the pew, the one whose eyes would alight first on the shape across the aisle. She drew in a shuddering gasp, then a wail, and then she turned to Alice, clutching at her sleeve and collapsing into sobs. It was only a moment before I saw it too.

Sophie's body was lying flat along one of the pews, white and inert, and I found myself at once desperate to stare at it and repulsed beyond measure. Her yellow hair was lank and washed-out and there was a waxy sheen across her skin that was miles away from anything like life. There was none of the unfeeling malignancy of the Sophie-thing we had seen, but nor was there anything left of the real Sophie, the Sophie I had known for years.

"God—God—" I heard Marion say, in a tone that verged on wonder.

Dot was insensible, and the rest of us were frozen still in the pew. I found myself staring hard at the Bible on the shelf in front of me. A block of its onionskin pages had folded over on itself in a dog-ear that must've spanned all of Leviticus.

"I think we'd better begin," Miss Lewis said. She spoke quickly, brusquely, as though she was announcing a change in schedule. "Lord, we mourn the loss of Sophie Salisbury, who was taken from us too soon. She was only eighteen and had a lifetime ahead of her: she would have made an excellent wife and mother if she had only been given the chance. Sophie was a good, God-fearing English girl, a credit to King and country. We pray she has joined at your right hand. May we follow the example she set for us." She dipped her head and clasped her hands. When we didn't follow suit quickly enough, lost as we were in our reverie of horror, she looked up and said, impatiently, "The Lord's Prayer, girls."

When we had finished, she put down the needle on the gramophone. A crackling rendition of "Abide with Me" swelled through chapel and my head swam at the memory of the last time I'd heard it, at Violet's memorial. I hadn't minded it then, but now it was nauseating. None of us sang along with the record, though our hymn books were right there and even without them we all knew the words well enough. I, for one, was almost trembling with how badly I wanted to cut and run. I wanted to, but there was such an oppressive atmosphere in that room that I couldn't shake the thought that if I tried, I would be stopped. Miss Stone, clutching my upper arm so hard it hurt. Miss Lewis, twisting the thin skin on the underside of my wrist between her bony fingers.

I tried not to look at Sophie, whose hair was limp and full of snarls. In life she never would have let it look like that; she was a hundred-strokes-before-bed sort of girl, rag curls on weekends. I longed to brush it out myself and give her a piece of my mind for being so stupid as to try to leave.

The record ended. More accurately, it juddered to a halt on the old gramophone. There were a few seconds of silence until Miss Lewis picked up the needle again and started the hymn over. I glanced at Alice, who shrugged, though her jaw was hard. For her part, Evelyn was staring straight ahead, unmoving. I wasn't sure if she'd even looked at Sophie properly, about which I felt a curious mix of disdain and envy. I briefly fantasised about getting my hand in her hair and turning her head forcibly so she was looking across the aisle. It was hypocritical of me, I know, to feel so cross that no one was taking action, when I wasn't doing anything myself but standing there dumb as a post. But the desire for someone to be better than me, braver than me—I can't begrudge myself that. Miss Lewis looked out from the altar impassively. I couldn't tell what she wanted from us.

Dot began to sing halfway through the second verse, her quavering little soprano sounding awfully thin in the cold cavern of chapel. We all broke in after a line or two, I suppose not wanting to leave her on her own, but we sounded dreadful. Sophie had been a lovely singer, always picked for solo parts; we were worse without her. It was a familiar gesture to sing a hymn, though, and for a moment it felt like a relief to slot back into the grooves of school life and run along the track set out for us.

That is, it was a relief until the record came to a stop, and Miss Lewis once again picked up the needle and deposited it at the beginning. The words "Abide with Me" had stopped sounding like words and had become a collection of sounds that I knew ought to signify something but instead were blank and hollow. We sang it again, for lack of anything better to do, but on the third go I'd rather lost the thread of the phrasing, and kept finding myself off beat or finishing a line with no breath left. *In life, in death,* O *Lord*—and then it began again. I hadn't been looking when it ended that time and consequently hadn't seen Miss Lewis replace the needle; the result was a queasy sense that the hymn had started over of its own accord, some invisible hand plucking the needle from the record and placing it at the beginning.

Midway through the sixth repeat of the song, Alice started up from her seat towards the door of chapel. She took an awkward route between two pews to avoid coming too close to Sophie's body. I watched her go, envying her uprightness and strength, but then she reached the door and found it had been locked. She rattled it, pulling with all her considerable strength, but it held fast.

"You can't keep us in here," she shouted above the music.

Ann and Shirley didn't even flinch, entranced by the gramophone. Miss Lewis started the hymn over with neither ceremony nor rancour. I heard Dot give out a little whimper next to me, and Alice gave the chapel door a hearty kick (this didn't inspire any kind of reaction, either, which was odd enough in itself). There was something beaten-down in her posture as she returned to our pew. On the eighth repeat, as the trumpets began their escalating drone, Evelyn burst into sobs that shook her whole body, but she didn't try to leave.

I didn't want to turn to look at her—the idea of her noticing me doing so felt impossibly horrible—but from a sidelong glance I could see that her mouth was locked in a wail like the tragedy mask that was embossed on our editions of Shakespeare. Marion reached out to squeeze her shoulder and then withdrew her hand when Evelyn whipped her head around; it was when I finally turned to her that I could see she was crying with fury, not from sadness or fear.

I don't know how long we stayed in chapel. I lost count after the eighth repetition of the record. By the end, I do remember that we were all weeping together, hunched in the pew. Evelyn's hand was clenched around my wrist so hard it hurt; Alice was draped over Dot like a boa constrictor; Marion had her arm tight around Evelyn's shoulders. We were pressed so close together that I couldn't tell whose tears were whose. It had all become a collective mess smeared across our faces. Somewhere in the midst of it, the thought floated into my mind that the way we were carrying on was improper, un-English; our outlandish behaviour did not befit young ladies such as ourselves. I hardly know where it came from. It sounds like utter rot, given the circumstances, but old habits die hard, and the habit of shame is the hardest to break. We were too wrapped up in each other to notice what the schoolmistresses and younger girls were doing, but I have a nasty suspicion that they were sitting perfectly still, listening to the hymn again and again.

I don't much like to recall what can only be described as Sophie's official funeral. It wasn't what she deserved—really she deserved to live, but in the unhappy event of her death she should've had at the very least a competent choir and a charming white and pink coffin. I hadn't even said goodbye to her: I had been too afraid that something snarled and cruel would come out of my mouth instead.

Some time later, Miss Lewis stepped away from the gramophone as though nothing out of the ordinary had happened at all, and walked down the nave without so much as a glance at the corpse in the pew. She unlocked the doors with a key produced from her skirt pocket, and then we were released into the daylight.

I thought back to the day everyone else had gone into the village to ring their parents, and how Miss Lewis had been at once firm and tender with me. I remembered the fond humour in her voice, even as she warned me that she wouldn't lie for me. Miss Lewis had been brusque with us before. She didn't suffer fools and she made it plain that she did, on occasion, consider us fools. But she never crossed the line into cruelty. I thought after Sophie's funeral that even if I couldn't have back the Miss Lewis I had known for years, I'd take the one from last night, who, even when she was admonishing us, had told us she understood it had been a hard day.

I couldn't imagine why she would've done this—to us, but more pertinently, to Sophie, who had been decent, excitable, good at dancing and clever at first aid, dramatic on occasion but always there when you needed her. In fact, I knew that behind her hard-shelled exterior Miss Lewis held a secret hope that we would do something other than slip easily into the roles carved out for us: I knew it because she had told me so, in a glancing, roundabout way when I was fourteen and first told her of my intention to go to Girton. I had said it very shyly, half expecting to be told not to bother, but instead she looked up from the papers on her desk and said that she was pleased, with that same almost-smile she'd given me the day everyone was in the village.

There were no longer enough schoolmistresses left at Briarley to take lessons as normal. Our schoolwork jumped around seemingly at random, with no consistency at all regarding who taught what. The hour-long lessons went back and forth in fits and starts, invariably losing the plot altogether by the end.

"Miss Stone, we were working on algebra before," Marion pleaded, halfway through an afternoon lesson on the magnificence of the spinning jenny, taught for some inscrutable reason not by Miss Parker, but by Miss Stone. Miss Stone had gone on a long and rather disturbing tangent about how the factories of today owed everything they were to the factories of the past, that all the mangled limbs and clotted lungs were the cost of progress. "We have our exams next term, can't I at least do some problems on my own?"

I thought this was rather optimistic of her considering that so far none of us was able to leave Briarley at all, let alone sit examinations and take up a place at university. I suppose she was, in her responsible way, holding onto the idea that in the event we made it out of this alive, it wouldn't do us any good to have completely abandoned our lessons. I, for one, had given up aiming higher than survival.

"Miss Thomas, I think you'll find I didn't ask for your opinion on how this lesson ought to be run. I intend to keep order in my classroom, and that includes everyone paying full attention to the lesson."

"I'm sorry, Miss Stone, I only thought—"

"I do not take kindly to interruptions, Thomas. Go stand in the corner with your face to the wall for the remainder of the hour."

Dumbfounded, I watched as Marion—elegant, poised Marion—slowly got up out of her seat, adjusting her pinafore as she went so it hung neatly, and stood in the back corner of the room. Her shoulders were still and her chin tipped up high but I could see how tense she was even from a distance. The room hadn't been cleaned properly in some time, so she faced onto a couple of cobwebs and a dark, unidentifiable stain that started at the base of the wall and was creeping upwards to about knee height.

"Miss Stone, I really think—" I said, halfway out of my seat.

"That's enough, Locke, unless you'd like the same punishment."

I sat back down, balling my hands into fists. It was the sort of thing the teachers had done to us when we'd been really bad, and young enough that the minutes would stretch by immeasurably slowly. None of us had been made to stand in the corner since we were fourteen at the oldest, and I couldn't remember the last time Marion had done it at all.

I sat in my seat for the rest of the lesson, incandescent with rage. The five of us were the only ones with any grip on reality whatsoever, and that was including Evelyn, whom it pained me to categorise within the sane faction. Or maybe we had all gone insane, and could no longer tell what was supposed to happen when someone died horribly and no one knew why. Maybe this was normal, and it was our expectations that had gone skew-whiff.

Marion was allowed back in her seat when Miss Stone swapped out with Miss Parker, who had never had quite the same fetish for authority. You could see an odd tension at the corners of her mouth as she gave us orders not to speak during the lesson unless we were spoken to. I thought that if Miss Lewis was directing them to behave this way it was awfully hard of her.

Evelyn was clutching at her fountain pen so tightly her knuckles had gone white. It looked like she'd bend the nib of the pen the second she touched it to her exercise book. Her prefect badge, bright green and shield-shaped, winked sunnily at me from her lapel and it sent me into a kind of dizzying fury.

Without thinking, I lunged forwards to rip it off, but she was further away than I'd thought and I didn't quite reach her, grasping at thin air instead. My chair made a juddering noise that brought me out of my stupor; I could no longer understand why I'd thought that tearing Evelyn's badge off might be a good thing to do. For her part, Evelyn looked me up and down with a curious expression on her face. After a few seconds, she hunched back over her exercise book and continued to write. No one else seemed to notice, but when I glanced over at Evelyn again some minutes later her prefect badge was gone from her lapel. I later saw it on the floor, its pin back bent beyond fixing.

In the afternoon we had Comportment, which consisted chiefly of wandering about the classroom in silence with our books balanced on our heads, and then Miss Parker left. Left

Briarley, I mean: Miss Lewis told us she was going to get help in the village. I watched her go from the classroom window, where we were penned in, reading aloud "The Charge of the Light Brigade." She had a carpet bag in her hand, as if somehow she knew that she wasn't just walking to the village and back again. I fancied that if I physically saw Miss Parker go through the gates, I'd learn something from it. Maybe she'd expire then and there, or there'd be a mysterious shimmer in the air and she'd disappear. But nothing happened. She went through the gate and then walked down the road until the hedgerow hid her from our sight. I never saw her again.

I finished the day utterly fagged. The strain of pretending from dawn till dusk to be an ordinary girl in an ordinary school felt heavier than ever when our circumstances became more extraordinary by the hour. We picked at our dinner, having been crowded onto one table so that Ann and Shirley could keep an eye on us, like diminutive spies. Ann was just within reach, so I kicked her as hard as I could in the shins. Despite being an incorrigible goody-two-shoes, her courage from the night before appeared to have left her, and she stayed silent.

"Two thousand," Dot whispered from next to me, her mouth as close to my ear as she could get it. There was something feverish and desperate in her voice. It took me a moment to understand what she'd said; it seemed all too possible that she had started speaking gibberish.

"Two thousand what?"

"Tonight, for a séance. Count to two thousand. Tell Evelyn."

I didn't *want* to tell Evelyn, who would probably say no and slap me for assuming she might say anything else, but I didn't have much choice. Ann was watching us carefully, but there was no way she could've heard. From across the table, Alice winked. When I leaned close to Evelyn, she turned on me with instinctive indignation. But—I had no choice—I yanked at one of her plaits and pulled her closer, until I was close enough to pass the information on. To my surprise, all she did was nod, although there was a look in her eyes like a prey animal trapped in a corner. By the time everyone had been told, Ann was enormously frustrated, in which I tried to take as much satisfaction as I could.

The last thing I wanted to do once the lights were out was haul myself from bed and hold a séance where we'd learn God knew what horrors, under constant threat of being found out and punished. I wanted to sleep and sleep, to make up for all the nights before. But as I counted to two thousand in my head, my body began to come alive with the possibility of using whatever power we had, to prove we weren't as enervated as I felt. I'd got to one thousand nine hundred and fifty-eight when Alice sat up in bed warily.

One by one we slipped out of bed, leaving plenty of time in between each of us in the hope that anything audible could be mistaken for the normal shifting-around of five grieving teenagers during the night. I don't know when we started thinking so strategically; we certainly never sat down and discussed it, but somewhere along the way we had all gained a tactical sense that Field Marshal Haig would have envied. This time, the dormitory floor would have to do.

"Are you sure about this, Evelyn?" Marion whispered.

"After today I have to be, haven't I?" Evelyn replied, gravely.

"Let's skip the hymn, shall we?" I said as quick as I could, in case leaving it too long gave her room to change her mind. "Just to be safe."

Evelyn looked indignant, but rather than saying anything she shook her shoulders out and closed her eyes. It was odd, the change that came over her when we sat down for a séance. For all she told us she hated doing it, as soon as we sat in the circle the tension left her shoulders all at once; you could even see them drop by an inch or two. It wasn't just Violet's presence, I think. It was the séance itself. I have never seen anyone change so much so quickly, as if the channel to the spirit world that was somehow in her had opened, and she was filled with boundless vitality. She hadn't done her hair, and I found myself noticing how it fell over her shoulders in a big copper wave. It looked so much longer when she hadn't plaited it.

"Is anybody there?" she whispered. I shivered. "Is anybody there?"

There was a thirty-second stretch when nothing at all happened, but this time there was no concern in the back of my mind that no one would come. I could feel the power running through the circle like an electrical current, a little fainter without Sophie there, but still very much present. All we had to do was wait.

"Are you looking for Violet? The other one isn't here," a voice said. It wasn't a hundred miles off Evelyn's ordinary voice but it was deeper, a little huskier. I winced at how loud it was; it almost echoed in the dark dormitory. Only then did I stop to consider, stomach twisting, that "the other one" was probably Sophie.

"Yes, we are," Marion said. "Only can you keep it a little quieter, by any chance?"

"Something is in decay," the voice said, ignoring her. Its tone was curiously frank; it sounded rather like it was reading the shipping forecast. "Something else, something ugly, is growing out of its remains. Rows of towering sugarcane, endless ordered factories. A process has begun that will reach its conclusion decisively and inevitably. There is little you can do to stop it now."

We all sat in silence, for a moment. I thought that maybe if we didn't acknowledge what we'd just heard, we could pretend it had never happened, but then the voice came back. Evelyn's head bowed solemnly.

"You don't deserve what will happen to you."

I shook Evelyn's hand a little, in a rather pathetic attempt to jostle the spirit into listening to us. "We want to talk to Violet. Now, if you don't mind." She turned to me. I didn't recognise what I saw in her face; it was devoid of anything but a blankish look, tinged with pity. Then she nodded, once, and closed her eyes.

"Violet?" Dot whispered. Then, after the pause stretched to the point where it could no longer really be called a pause, "Evelyn?"

All the hair over Evelyn's shoulders brought to mind a mediaeval saint, or perhaps John the Baptist, feral and hirsute in the wilderness. I felt in such a dreadful fug following the other spirit's pronouncements that these impressions seemed to float towards me through the ether. I thought very hard and with great concentration about how much I would prefer Violet to be sitting in Evelyn's place, golden instead of red, sharply angled towards me and merciless. Without conscious thought I had begun to stare; it was upon wrenching my gaze away that Evelyn's body shivered. I didn't know what I was about to see.

"Finally," said Evelyn's mouth, in Violet's voice. She brought my hand up to her mouth so she could hide a delicate yawn without breaking the circle. Evelyn's hot breath steamed over the back of it. "I thought you'd never come."

"You kept your promise," Marion noted, her voice dry as a bone.

"I usually do."

"Do you know about Sophie?" Dot asked. I found myself very relieved that the others appeared to be taking the lead, allowing me to hang back and fulfil my silent role as hand-holder and circle-finisher. I didn't want to think about Sophie. Violet hung her head at the mention of her name, Evelyn's curls falling over her face.

"Yes, I know about Sophie," she said bitterly.

"Can you tell us what happened?" Marion said, spooling her words out slowly with a tone that bordered on hostility.

"Just what it looked like, Marion, she tried to leave and she died. If she'd had the sense to ask me, I would've told her not to try it at all. Idiot." Her voice broke a little there at the end, but I let it slide. I didn't like how close I could feel things coming to an argument.

"What killed her?" Alice asked, trying to forestall it.

"I don't know. I don't know. Whatever it was that killed me, I suppose. I don't know if there's a name for it."

"The spirit who was here before you said something was—decaying. Can we fix it?"

"You don't *listen*, do you," she said, sounding almost fretful. "I could shake you. No, you can't."

I hated when she got all truculent like this. Once she got an idea in her head, she'd never let it go. I couldn't help myself and stepped out of my observational posture, regretting in advance whatever I was about to say. I knew full well that it wouldn't be the sort of sweet and winning thing I'd have wanted to say given the chance to speak to my dead bosom friend, in any other circumstance but this one.

"What do you want us to do, then, Violet? You can't just tell us we have to sit here and wait to die."

"Can't I?" she snapped. "At least then I wouldn't have to wait patiently until you all manage to sing a lovely hymn and call me into Evelyn's body." The disturbing possibility that she might prefer us to be dead than alive mingled with the idea that she wanted us—me—to be with her. It was flattering, almost. It came close to temptation. To be with Violet, forever, loosed from the bounds of earth. But even as tempted as I was, it gave me an idea, born out of Sophie's book, and I wrenched myself reluctantly out of my fantasy.

"What if—what if you weren't in Evelyn's body any more?"

"Unless one of you is offering—"

Marion looked at me with dawning comprehension and, I suspect, some degree of horror. "All we know about materialisation is that paragraph you read us from Sophie's book. Just as I said then, I'm not convinced it was ever real, and even if it was, we don't know what would happen if we tried it ourselves. And Evelyn would never in a thousand years agree to it—"

"Materialisation is exactly what I'm suggesting. What if"—and I turned to Evelyn's still form again—"what if you could have your own body again? If what's killing us is something from—where you are—if you could materialise, couldn't you try and stop it, try and get us out?" The more I said it aloud the more I could imagine it. A shining, otherworldly Violet accompanying us down the gravel drive and through the gates, protecting us from whatever it was that had killed Sophie. The thought didn't escape me that if it didn't work, and we went through the gate to meet whatever fate Sophie had, Violet would be right there with us, and then at least I wouldn't be alone.

"Emily, surely you can see that this is *very* dangerous," Marion said.

Violet ignored her. "Materialise. I wonder if I could."

"It seems awfully convenient to suggest doing this now when Evelyn isn't here to say no," added Marion, growing more agitated.

Alice looked concerned. "She's right, Evelyn's going to hate this."

I thought they were being altogether too generous to Evelyn, who'd made a habit of making everything far more difficult than it needed to be. "Evelyn isn't here right now. Do you really want to let all our chances rest on whatever idiotic objection she's going to come up with?"

"Oh, she'll be furious," Dot said, looking a little queasy, but then Violet settled the question for us.

"Be quiet, all of you—I kept my promise not to show up without Evelyn's say-so, but I'm not waiting for her to say I'm allowed to try this. I think she's had altogether too much influence lately over what I do and don't do. I want to see if it'll work. Hold still, will you?" For the first time in a long time, I was grateful for Violet's uncanny ability to shut down debate in her favour. I had missed the feeling. Evelyn's brow set in a bizarre replication of the look that Violet's face made when she was concentrating hard. Her hand squeezed mine. I could hardly breathe.

"Is it happening?" Dot asked, pointlessly.

Evelyn's body shuddered, and her mouth dropped open, too wide, her head tipping back. I experienced the odd intimacy of looking directly down someone's throat. Only there was something there, emerging from her gullet.

It looked at first as though it might be just a wisp of smoke, completely insubstantial. But then it emerged, further and further—first reaching her tonsils, then level with her teeth, then actually coming out of her mouth into the cold air. It became more and more solid, like a twist of cheesecloth dripping with something viscous and faintly pearlescent. We all stared at it, completely dumbfounded. I couldn't tell you exactly what shape it was, but it filled her entire mouth. It was akin to a thick rope, I suppose, only there was something amorphous about it, a blurring around the edges that made it difficult to tell where it ended and the air around it began. The shape became so bright that my eyes ached to look at it, but I couldn't stop looking, either, I was pinned to it, held fast—

Marion's voice broke what had become a collective reverie. "Evelyn!" she exclaimed, too loudly. I tore my eyes off the glowing, floating thing that was still growing further and further out of Evelyn's mouth and looked at Evelyn herself.

Her throat was working as though she couldn't breathe; she was making an uncomfortably guttural clicking sound, and she had begun to slump a little. I couldn't think of anything else to do so I snatched my hand away from hers and broke the circle. The glowing thing—I'll call it ectoplasm, just as the book did, because there was simply nothing else in this world or the next it could've been—vanished in an instant, and Evelyn fell backwards like a marionette with its strings cut.

I leaned over her, being the closest, and pressed two fingers to the pulse point at her throat. It was fast and faint, and her skin was cold. Not for the first time, I wished Sophie were there, so she could tell me if we needed to be worried. Evelyn's chest was rising and falling, but only shallowly, and with effort. I placed my hand onto it, just below the collarbones, to reassure myself that she really was breathing. It seemed to settle her a little, which I can't say I felt particularly good about either; I snatched my hand away after a second or two. Anyway, I wasn't looking for her to break my wrist if she woke up and noticed me touching her.

Just then there was a noise from downstairs. It wasn't footsteps—nothing so bad as that, only a creak, one of the settling noises old houses like to terrify you with sometimes—but I felt my own heart start racing.

"We should get to bed," Dot said nervously. She was right; we were lucky as it was that no one had come to investigate after the sound of Evelyn's body thumping to the floor. "But we can't leave her there—"

Alice shouldered her way in and picked Evelyn up, staggering a little as she stood. I had a queer feeling like I wanted to be very far away from Evelyn, or perhaps very close, and instead of doing either I crossed the few feet over to my bed and let the others take the lead. Once Alice had put her to bed, I heard Evelyn and Marion having a low, murmured conversation about what had happened. It was an enormous relief not to have anything to do with it. Lying there, in the dark, I thought I might never sleep again. The shining form hung in my mind's eye, like the print left behind by looking at a bright light for too long. In reality, I think it was only a few seconds before I fell asleep.

SEVENTEEN

EVELYN

After the materialisation, Evelyn developed a wheeze in her chest and shadows under her eyes like purple thumbprints. None of us had been hale and hearty for weeks, but she looked properly sick, the kind of unwell where in a normal world she might've been sent to San for weeks on end. Some of the others were terribly solicitous; I, for my part, avoided her. To Evelyn's credit, she seemed determined not to acknowledge any of what had happened, and scowled at anyone who suggested she might go back to bed. I longed, trying to think as little as I could about what it might do to her, to try another materialisation, to see if with practice she could graduate from shapeless blobs to hands and hair and bodies.

School life, or whatever passed for it these days, carried on with unrelenting force. Miss Parker hadn't come back, of course. Shirley piped up once during a German lesson to ask if the police were ever going to come, and Miss Stone looked at her as though she'd begun speaking ancient Greek.

"Wasn't Miss Parker . . ." Shirley started, and then trailed off in the face of what could've been a brick wall. There wasn't a hint of recognition in Miss Stone's eyes. "What I mean is, didn't Miss Parker go to fetch the police?"

"I'm sure she did. Our attention, however, must now be turned to German grammar, the state of which is dire in this classroom."

Shirley turned scarlet. "But Miss Stone—she went for the police *yesterday*."

"Miss Parker's movements are none of your concern. If you continue to disrupt my lesson in this way, I'll have to send you out."

By way of response, Shirley lowered her head onto her desk. Her shoulders shook a little, and when Dot reached out to pat her on the arm Miss Stone whistled her ruler through the air, coming down on Dot's soft pale hand with a force I'd never seen her use before. Alice smacked the top of her desk and cried out, but it was too late; Dot was screaming, higher and louder than I had thought her capable of. Then, when she realised what she was doing, she simply broke off and went silent, like a stone. None of us did anything after that for fear of being similarly punished; I looked over at her in concern and made as sympathetic a face as I could, but it was like she didn't see me at all.

I thought about that quiet, furtive conversation I had overheard between Miss Stone and Miss Parker in the vestibule the day the lower years went to the village. They had cared about each other, once, had had the capacity to feel so frightened and overwhelmed that they had hidden away in an unoccupied corner of the school to tell each other about it. I can't pretend that I was ever able to see them as real people, just like we were, rather than avatars of authority—such, I suppose, is the solipsism of youth. Even so, when any lingering signs of the sympathy they had once had for us vanished in that dreadful parade of events, I felt it like a loss.

Morning break came with a sickening lurch. The bell seemed to drill through the bone at my temples and I was so thoroughly done with being cooped up in that stuffy miserable classroom that I hoofed it outside as quickly as I could in case anyone tried to stop me. I wanted to go for a walk, where the cold air would burn my throat and numb the tips of my fingers by the time I had to go back inside for whatever joke of a lesson would come next. I made it out of the side entrance, passed the vegetable garden and the well, and set off across the grass towards the apple trees at as quick a clip as I could muster.

It was all Briarley land—the family had bought up a few hectares centuries ago and half-heartedly planted some apple trees, which had overgrown until they looked more like something wild than an orderly orchard. It was one of the school's few concessions to nature, the rest of the grounds generally being kept at a tidy remove. I'll admit to considering, just for a moment, whether the land beyond the apple trees—where they blended into the sycamores that ringed the outskirts, larger and darker with a comfortingly occlusive shadow—might be a way out. But, of course, it was futile; if there was no way to see the danger through the gates, I wouldn't know I'd crossed some invisible boundary until it had already killed me. I wasn't quite so stupid as to test it, although a not-insignificant part of me wanted to hurl myself into the thicket. Instead, I hung around aimlessly, relishing in the whip of the wind and, outside of that, the silence.

I could only have been there for a minute or so when a twig cracked loudly and I turned around, my heart in my throat at the possibility that whatever killed Sophie—or, perhaps worse, the Sophie-thing we'd still only seen once—had come to find me.

"Emily?"

It was only Evelyn, although from some angles that prospect was considerably more disturbing than the alternatives.

"Honest to God, Evelyn, you can't sneak up on a girl like that. I nearly had a heart attack."

"I followed you out," she admitted, not quite making eye contact, "because I wanted to tell you something."

"Well? Out with it. We aren't getting any younger." Something about the way she was standing made me want to run my mouth; she looked as though she was squaring up for a fight. Her hair was in plaits so tight I suspected she was trying to pull the curl out of it by force.

"It's just—" She broke off as if she was exasperated with me, which wasn't fair in the least.

"Spit it out, Evelyn, come on."

"I think what you're doing is hateful. You haven't stopped for a second to think about anyone but yourself, expecting everyone just to fall in line behind you."

"Oh—I'm sorry—am I meant to be able to read your thoughts? Have you mistaken me for a clairvoyant? That's more your lot than mine, you know. Have a care and enlighten me."

"What I'm saying is—" She twisted her hands around each other until I heard the bones of her wrist click. "What I'm trying to say is that I can *see* you plotting to force me to let Violet take over my whole body and make more of that horrible ectoplasm stuff and you should know that I won't do it, I won't do it, I'm not some kind of hollow thing you can put whatever you want into. I'm sick of sitting by and letting things be done to me." She was practically gasping by the end, crossing her arms in front of her in a gesture that looked as self-protective as it did indignant.

I marvelled at her. "The idea of making this about me and you is the stupidest thing I've ever heard in my life. You're the worst kind of prig and a coward and a wretched little hypocrite. I can't very well help it if I think that your poor, wounded pride is less important than getting us all out of here, and if you think you're going to persuade me otherwise you're even more full of rot than I expected." I felt half-blinded with rage; I couldn't look at her. I marched towards the sycamores.

"Did you ever think for a second how it feels to know that every one of you but me is able to talk to Violet?" I heard her say from a few paces behind me. I turned around and she was right there, close enough to touch.

"Funnily enough, I haven't, because it seemed considerably less important than thinking about how to stop us all getting killed."

She scoffed. "You know perfectly well it isn't about that," she said, her voice icy.

"I won't listen to you talking around things any more, Evelyn, for God's sake come out with it and tell me!" I couldn't stop myself raising my voice even though she'd gone quiet. Evelyn had a way of getting under my skin like a splinter, burrowing her way in and settling there, stinging.

"Do you really think," she said, "really, do you honestly think I might feel all right knowing that Violet was—using my body—not just to talk to you, but to *take* something from me and mould it into whatever she wants?"

"So it's just that you don't want—"

She interrupted me, though how she did it when she was speaking so quietly I really don't know. "And the bit I can't even think about without feeling as though I'm going to be sick then and there—that the rest of you get to see and *touch* whatever disgusting thing she's made out of my own body, and I'm not even there for it—I'll never ever get to even see her—" She pressed her lips together so hard they went white, as if she was afraid of what would come out next.

She looked like she might cry, or vomit, or maybe scream;

I felt distantly terrified, as though we were hanging right at the edge of a precipice and it was only her self-control or mine that was keeping us from falling. My ears were ringing.

"Evelyn," I pleaded, unsure of where I was going next.

"Emily." There was a visible sense of her trying to gather herself back into her own control.

"I'm sorry you can't see Violet too," I offered. "I'm sure it's difficult when the rest of us can." I thought it was extraordinarily mature of me. But instead of mollifying her, it struck something and her eyes blazed.

"Don't pity me," she spat. "I don't want it, I never asked for it."

"What on earth am I supposed to do, then? What on earth is there that I could do that would please you?"

"I want you to admit it." She took another step closer to me. I could see the freckles on her forehead and the purplish circles under her eyes; she looked as though she hadn't slept in a week. I hadn't realised just how much smaller than me she was.

"Admit what?" I said.

"Admit that you loved her like I did, and that there's nothing you love more than knowing you'll be the one to see her again and I never, ever will," Evelyn said.

It was almost a whisper. I hardly heard it at first; I thought I must have imagined it. I felt something in me break open and scrambled to put it back together with an altogether unconvincing little half-laugh.

"I don't know what you're talking about."

"Don't be an idiot. You know what I mean."

"Well, if I'm really thinking about it," I said, raising an eyebrow at her, "I suppose I do understand—in a sense. Violet told me as much."

Evelyn faltered at this. "What did she say? When?"

"Oh, during that first séance when we spoke to her—it was

an offhand comment, really, I didn't make much of it." I turned to walk away, but she grabbed me by the arm of my blazer and yanked me back. She was surprisingly strong.

"Tell me what she said, Emily, tell me on your honour."

"On my honour? Well, then. What Violet told me was that she was—she was *fucking* Mademoiselle and it was all her idea, and that I mustn't tell you because it would make you jealous," I said. I felt myself smile but there wasn't any mirth in it. For a few seconds Evelyn stared at me. "You asked," I added.

Evelyn kept her eyes on me, but I couldn't read her expression. Then the next moment, she pulled back and slapped me. It was a loud slap, and a hard one; I heard it crack through the trees almost before I fully felt it, but when I did, it was as a sharp pain tearing across my cheek. I staggered away a few steps, raising my hand to my face, dizzy, spinning.

"Christ, Evelyn," I gasped. We looked at each other for a moment, and then she launched herself at me with such unexpected force that I overbalanced and ended up on the ground.

Evelyn and I tussled like schoolchildren right there in the bed of mulch and fallen leaves. I got hold of one of her stupid plaits and pulled on it hard, trying to get her off me, but she was like a furious spitting cat and wouldn't let go. She pummelled me over and over until all the wind had been knocked out of me; I did my best to give as good as I got but she had a frenetic energy I couldn't hope to match. One of the ends of her plaits was still in my hand, and when she noticed she shoved one of her hands into my hair, pulling and pulling until I was forced to arch my head back.

Then she bit me—really meaning it, like a feral animal. She ducked her head down and sank her teeth into my throat till I was sure she'd draw blood if she bit any deeper. I tried to scrabble away but she held me fast.

"Evelyn," I whined, not sure where I was going with it.

I felt my pulse thud where she'd bitten me; in fact I felt all my blood flooding through my body, something I'd never been aware of before. She looked up at me, baring her teeth in something that might've been a smile. Her eyes were nearly black from how big her pupils had gone.

"Evelyn," I said again, and she shoved me by the shoulder, pinning me down to the earth.

"Emily."

And then she was kissing me, fiercely, furiously.

I'd never been kissed before. I don't think she had either. We didn't quite know how to do it, and our teeth knocked together hard enough to be painful. By that time, my scalp hurt where she'd pulled my hair, my throat where she'd bitten me, my shoulder that was grinding against a stone on the ground, my belly where she'd punched me, and God only knew where else, so I hardly noticed. I caught myself thinking that it certainly hadn't looked like this when Dot and Alice were doing it.

"I hate you," I said, staring up at her awful, luminous face. Her nose wrinkled and she hit me again, lighter this time but still sincere. Acting on pure instinct I tried to move into it and away from it at the same time, and pulled her—none too gently—so she was half across my lap.

"I don't know how," she whispered, but then she yanked the skirt of my pinafore up and plunged her hand down my knickers, and after that she figured it out pretty well for herself.

I remember, quite distinctly, realising what she was doing. I had never thought very much about what sex might be like before, aside from the vague repulsion I assumed all girls felt when they really considered it. This was something else entirely. All of her obstinate single-mindedness, which I had always loathed, was focused on me at once, her hard gaze keeping me still.

Her hand was cold and very small, but when she pressed another finger inside me alongside her other two, it hurt. It was so good it made my breath stopper up. My feet kicked at the mulching leaves like I was being throttled. Something like a scream kept building in my throat, my thighs, the tips of my fingers, rising higher and higher until before much time had passed at all everything went white and I fell to pieces.

I have always been glad that in those months when I seemed to do one stupid thing after another, I got it right, that once, in letting her touch me.

My uniform was a mess, covered in mud and bits of dry leaves and rumpled beyond repair. There was a tear in one of my stockings—they were the thick wool kind, which never get a run unless you've done something really terrible to them. And there was Evelyn, hovering over me with a feverish, nervous look on her face, her hair coming out of its plaits and a flush high on her cheeks.

"You look frightful" was the first thing she said to me.

"Thanks," I croaked back. Then I shook myself out of my stupor and reached for her, grabbing at her hips and marvelling that I'd never once touched her waist in all the years I'd known her. But she smacked my hands away, and not gently either, drawing her brows together in what looked almost like confusion.

"Absolutely not." She stood up to brush herself off. She'd fared much better than I had, all things considered.

"Let me—" I said, and I staggered up after her. "Let me at least fix your hair." She rolled her eyes but let me undo her hair-ribbons and unravel what was left of her plaits. I combed my fingers through her hair; it was tangled here and there but it reached almost to her waist. With the scowl she wore on a perennial basis she was like one of those dreadful Pre-Raphaelite paintings Miss Parker had always tried to persuade us were great works of art—the one, in particular, of the red-headed girl biting down furiously on a handful of little flowers. She scuffed her toe impatiently while I plaited her hair again and crouched down to tie her hair-ribbons.

By the time I'd finished I felt dizzy again, so I sat back down on the ground rather heavily, and looked out at the school. I could see people moving around inside. I wondered if the bell had gone after all, and we'd been missing for ages, and whether the others were worried about us. There was Alice's tall frame, moving across a window. There was Miss Stone, waiting in the one classroom that was still in use.

"D'you want to talk about it?" I said, instead of anything practical like "Should we go back inside" or "Will you do another materialisation séance for us now?"

"Not particularly," Evelyn said, though she sat down next to me, with a great deal more dignity than I was presently able to muster.

"Did you ever, with Violet—"

"No."

I nodded and found a twig amidst the fallen leaves. I amused myself by breaking it in half, and then half again, and then again until I had a little pile of tiny pieces of twig in front of me and dirt all over my fingertips.

"Did you?" she asked, after a long silence. She sounded tentative, like she wasn't sure what the answer would be. "With Violet, I mean."

"No. No. And—what I said, before. About what Violet told me. Don't be cross, but it wasn't strictly true." I winced preemptively, in case she went for me again. "Well, it was mostly true but she didn't tell me you'd be jealous. She just said you wouldn't like it."

"You said *on your honour*, you brute, you *cad*—!" Evelyn cried. "No, don't, you'll spoil it. I don't want to talk about it, anyway."

"I only thought I should be honest with you about it. I was upset," I said, the consummate adult, "and I was trying to hurt you."

"I said I don't want to talk about it, Emily, I wish you'd learn to listen for once."

"Well, I wish you'd learn to accept an apology, because you make it very difficult to give them in the first place," I said, rolling my eyes. My knickers were soaked through and I was beginning to notice the cold again.

Evelyn sat up even straighter, if that was possible. "What's that?" she said, pricking her ears like a hunting dog.

"What?" My heart started hammering in my chest. I wished I had any idea what I looked like. I thought Miss Lewis might quite literally murder me if she saw me in this state, supernatural terror be damned, and the thought of the others seeing me and reaching the conclusions I was certain they would reach made me nauseous. Evelyn shook her head.

"It's just Alice," she said, pointing.

Alice was lolloping across the grass on her stocky, strong legs. Any relief I might've felt at it being her evaporated when I saw her face; as she got closer I could see her chest heaving and her features contorted in terror. I exchanged a look with Evelyn, who had clearly seen the same thing. Then her gaze snagged on my neck and she ineffectually flipped the collar of my shirt up to hide what I assumed was an impressive set of her own teeth marks.

"You've got to come—come quickly," Alice panted, once she was within a few yards of us. "It's Mademoiselle. She's dead."

EIGHTEEN

SOME FIGHT

Mademoiselle was lying exactly where Violet lay after she fell from the landing. It was the same down to the details: the pool of blood at the back of her head, spreading through the mess of Mademoiselle's tangled brown hair rather than Violet's flaxen plait. The angle of her neck, which looked terribly wrong and off-kilter. Even the ghastly sight of the bone emerging through the white, wasted flesh of Mademoiselle's shin wasn't new to me. The only real difference was that instead of a bottle of scent, she was clutching the lilac handkerchief, embroidered with her initial or mine, that she had tried to give me so long ago.

The others had got there before us, arrayed in a horrified arc around Mademoiselle's body.

"What happened?" I asked Alice, whose face was blotchy.

"She was just lying there," she said in a strangled voice.

Marion stepped in. "When the bell rang, we realised you two weren't with us, so Alice thought she'd go and find you before Miss Stone came in and noticed you were gone. We all came running when we heard her scream, and found—well, this."

Evelyn looked at me warily. "Did we—curse her?"

"Are you joking?"

"Not in the slightest."

"What are you two whispering about?" Alice asked, looking at us with a curiosity I didn't intend to indulge.

"Nothing," I said, quick as I could.

Clattering footsteps came from down the hall.

"Élodie? Élodie?" It was Matron's voice, sounding winded, and it took several seconds for me to remember that Élodie was in fact Mademoiselle, that the woman who had become a cipher for me over the past months had been a real person, with a name of her own. Matron came around the corner in a rush, no grace whatsoever, and stopped dead when she saw us all arranged around Mademoiselle's corpse. "Oh," she said simply, and dropped to her knees to administer first aid, as though it weren't obvious that there was nothing at all to be done. Her hands shook a little as she unbuttoned the wrists of Mademoiselle's old-fashioned nightgown.

It was only then that I understood how awful it must have been for the teachers to see one of their own number lying catatonic in a bed in San for weeks on end. For my part, Mademoiselle had been an object of affection—then an object of jealousy—then an object of hatred—then an object of guilt. I had never really managed to see her for what she was, which was a woman who could've been no more than five years older than we were. After a few minutes of worrying at Mademoiselle's pulse points and leaning down to check her breathing, Matron was bloodied up to the wrist and Mademoiselle was still lying, limp and staring, on the floor.

As if she was released from a spell that had kept her standing utterly still next to me, Evelyn broke into motion. She knelt beside Matron and felt for Mademoiselle's pulse at her neck, in the exact place where minutes before she had bitten me. Then she placed her hand on Matron's shoulder in a gesture more tender and adult than I'd ever seen her make before and said, coaxing, "You did all you could." Matron nodded, and then looked up at us as if noticing our presence for the first time.

"Girls," she said, stricken, "you shouldn't be seeing this. Get along with you—fetch Miss Lewis or Miss Stone. Go!"

I almost appreciated the naïveté of her thinking that there were sights left that might disturb our young, impressionable minds. It was sweet, in its way. I liked the idea of preserving our innocence in Matron's head, if only there. I was glad, at least, that she had got there first; she had been less harsh than the others, of late. So I turned around and went back upstairs to the classroom where we were supposed to be, and the others followed.

When our little group reached the room, easily fifteen minutes later than the bell dictated, Miss Stone was standing at the head of the class, right by the blackboard, like an actor waiting for his cue. I saw her first through the glass in the door. She was still as anything, staring straight ahead with no discernible expression on her face. She didn't move a muscle until I opened the door, and then she was right back to what I had begun to think of as the new normal.

"Where have you been?" she exclaimed, and raised her ruler threateningly, in a gesture that made me think of an automaton that had just had its lever pulled, in the groove of its familiar movement.

"Please," I said. "You've got to come downstairs. Mademoiselle Lefèvre is dead."

"The bell rang to mark the end of break easily a quarter of an hour ago. If you think you can disregard the bell, Miss Locke, you are sorely mistaken—" She spat my name out as if the very thought of me disgusted her.

Marion strode into the room, patience run dry, and grabbed her by the wrist. "You've got to come now, Miss Stone. It can't wait for lessons." She pulled Miss Stone out the door like a recalcitrant child being dragged to school. I had never seen anyone be so bold. We all followed them in amazement, but not before I glanced behind me to see that Shirley and Ann were also sitting in the classroom, occupying their seats in total silence.

Matron slumped a little in relief when she saw we'd brought reinforcements.

"Alethea, it's Élodie," she said, gesturing redundantly at Mademoiselle's body. This seemed to cause some spark of recognition behind Miss Stone's eyes.

"Someone bring me a pail of water," she commanded, but at least it was the normal sort of command, not the kind that felt unmoored from reality. Honestly, there was nothing I wanted to do less than stay there and continue looking at Mademoiselle, dead, and probably so because of me. I ran off to fetch a bucket but I hoped with all I had that someone would be willing to carry it back for me and let me stay, alone, in the cool dark of the kitchen. I filled the bucket from the tap, and when I turned around Alice was waiting in the doorway with an odd expression on her face.

"Locke," she said. "You and Evelyn." Her tone was neutral, but I couldn't bear it regardless.

"Oh, don't. Please don't."

"If you're trying to hide it, you're not doing a very good job of it," she said gently, gesturing towards my neck. I suddenly realised the collar of my blouse had fallen back down. My face burned. I didn't want to touch it; it felt so obvious.

"Evelyn and I got in a fight." I braced my hands against the cool porcelain of the sink. "That's all."

"Some fight."

I scowled at her.

"Look here, you don't have to—I understand it. You might take some advice from me, Dot and I've been getting away with it for years."

"I don't know what you're talking about but I'm sure whatever is happening between you and Dot hasn't the slightest thing to do with me and Evelyn," I said thinly.

Alice sighed. "Don't listen to me if you don't want to. Just thought I'd let you know you can talk to me about it if you do."

"I'll keep it in mind, thanks ever so, now will you do me a favour and take the water up to Matron and Miss Stone?" I foisted the pail on her before she had a chance to say no. Water sloshed over the edge in my haste and stained the front of her pinafore. She shrugged and walked away with it, not saying a word.

As soon as she was gone I felt like I might scream, so I set my teeth in my own wrist till I thought I'd break the skin. The marks came away damp and pink and I couldn't stop myself thinking of Evelyn's teeth, Evelyn's cheeks flushed hot with blood, Evelyn's hair clinging to her temples with a sheen of sweat. I stamped a foot so hard the impact reverberated painfully through the heel of my shoe, and closed my eyes against all of it.

The day, inexplicably, carried on. I made an overture towards Evelyn as soon as we could hang back from the others and was firmly rebuffed: in her words, "I don't think we ever ought to speak of it again."

Once in the common room, we watched Matron and Miss Stone from our position huddled at the window, carrying Mademoiselle's body to chapel, where I could only assume they laid it in a pew alongside Sophie's. We were lucky, I suppose, that it was cold enough for there to be no smell yet. For all I knew, chapel was thick with flies. We went back to lessons in a dull, disbelieving way. Miss Stone delivered the driest lesson any of us could remember, divorced even from such indulgences as "English" or "History." Instead she read inscrutable fables aloud from an old book titled *The Youth's Moral Miscellany*. When she turned the pages, you could see that her hands were scrubbed red and raw.

We regrouped after dinner in the common room, though going by the suspicious look Miss Lewis gave us as we walked up the stairs, I suspected we might not be allowed to use it for much longer. In the absence of the dozens of girls who used to occupy it, Briarley Manor had transformed into a series of rooms that we congregated in, and the stretches of corridor that connected them: no longer an irreducible whole, more than the sum of its parts. Just rooms, which we tried to fill even with our diminished number, to keep the cold out. Alice made a fire, and we pushed our chairs together as close as we could. For the first time, I noticed that there were mouse droppings in the corner and a long, feathered crack in the paint on the wall. I glanced around at everyone's faces—how exhausted we all looked: shadows under eyes, hair lank, nails ragged.

"Feels like we're heading towards something, doesn't it," Alice said roughly.

Dot nodded. "Something bad," she added. We sat there for a while. I watched the flames flickering until I couldn't stand it any more.

"It's my fault," I said. "Mademoiselle. It's because of me and Sophie and Evelyn that she collapsed. If she'd been awake—" Evelyn didn't say anything but she had a look in her eye like she was thinking hard about something. I wished I couldn't guess what.

"I'm not going to absolve you of all responsibility," Marion said slowly. "I didn't agree with you doing what you did and I think it made things worse for Mademoiselle, who didn't deserve it."

"I wasn't asking for forgiveness," I said in a rush. "I didn't mean—"

"Let me finish, will you? I'm not absolving you of all of it, but I don't think you should feel responsible for her death. Sophie was perfectly awake when it killed her. I think—if it wants to, it'll find a way." Unsurprisingly, this didn't do much to make me feel better about the situation.

"Please can we change the subject?" Dot said. "I feel like we're fighting and I can't bear it. Can't we just all get along and be nice to each other, please, all of you . . ."

Really I probably did deserve to be fought with at least a bit, but Marion smiled at her, tensely. "What would you rather talk about?"

Dot's eyes flickered around, as if there was something in the vicinity she could catch onto that wasn't somehow awful. She seemed to come up blank, and propped her chin on her knees like a child, saying nothing.

"I think we need to do something," Evelyn said. I jumped at hearing her voice; I don't think she'd said a word since before dinner. I had to stop myself saying something snide about our row earlier, because I wasn't sure I could manage it without betraying everything that had happened afterwards on my face.

"Like what?" Alice said.

"Another materialisation. Like you all said. I suppose I haven't much choice in the matter."

"Evelyn, for the love of God, how many times do we have to tell you we're not going to force you?" I said.

She fixed me with a glare. "I meant that I don't suppose we've got much choice, considering the only way any of us can think to get out is with the help of a spirit, like the book said. I wasn't talking about you."

Marion spoke up. "Look, you know how I feel about this. But I saw the—the ectoplasm as much as the rest of us did, and I'm beginning to think it's our best hope. Only I'm not sure it'll do us much good to keep producing just bits of it. We're going to have to try to get it to become Violet's body, somehow. Maybe Sophie's book will have something useful." She looked at me and Evelyn while she spoke and I dug my nails into my palm, hoping Alice hadn't told her anything.

"I don't need that book," Evelyn sniffed. "I haven't needed it before and I don't intend to now."

"You can be as independent as you like, but we do need Violet. I don't much like it either, but the thing you managed to materialise last time isn't going to get us out of here."

"Well, Evelyn was fighting it last time," I said. Evelyn flinched. "No, I'm right though, aren't I? You didn't want it to happen—you didn't want to let her in. It was all Violet's intention and none of yours."

"She's right," said Marion. "Violet probably had to push and push to get through your defences. If she's wasting all the effort there . . ."

"I suppose Evelyn ought to rest," Dot offered. "So she can build up her energy."

Evelyn didn't look at her. "So there's more of me for her to use." I glanced over—I couldn't help it—to see a carefully neutral look on her face, her gaze directed at a fixed, empty point on the wall. Her hands rested limply in her lap, as if she was already practising letting Violet in. The thought of coddling her produced a sick wrench low in my stomach. Feeding her rusks soaked in milk; plaiting her hair for her; fattening her up for the slaughter.

We decided, in the end, to wait a few days. Having the excuse of Evelyn needing rest was a relief—after all, everything we had read in Sophie's book had told us that materialisation was exhausting for a medium and doing it wrong could even kill them, which was the last thing we needed, even if it would've made some things more convenient for me. Throughout this reprieve, Evelyn and I barely spoke, as if saying anything would puncture our uneasy peace. I told myself we had far too much to do to bother ourselves with petty feelings but actually, in private moments, it didn't feel petty at all; I was frightened that if I confronted her about it she'd pretend it never happened.

I kept turning over in my mind what she'd said right after we'd seen Mademoiselle's body: did we curse her? I wasn't utterly deluded; I knew what we'd done was wrong. But the sense of responsibility I had over Mademoiselle's death was related exclusively to the real wrongs we'd done, not the kind where the only person you're ruining is yourself. My feeling was, by this point, what self did we have left to ruin? But Evelyn shuddered every time we had morning prayers (in the dining hall, now, not in chapel) and whenever Miss Lewis made an uncharacteristically brimstone-ish reference to hell, which had begun to happen rather frequently.

There were other things, as well. One day Evelyn brushed past me in the corridor on the way to lessons, determined not to be late even though it surely no longer mattered. I was irritated at her: a teacher's pet for teachers who'd mostly left or vanished, trying to make it before the bell that ran our lives regardless of whether there was any sense in it. I think I made an indignant noise, to which she turned halfway around and scoffed, before taking her usual place at the front of the classroom, ready to be taught something incomprehensible about physiognomy in a lesson usually reserved for poetry. But for the rest of the day, I felt the glancing pressure of her against my shoulder like a constant weight. I wanted to reach out and touch her just to see what happened, even if it was only being slapped away.

We did look after her, in the slight ways we could, although I deliberately took as little part in it as I thought I could get away with, marking my distance. I feared what might happen if I got too close to her: what she might do to me, what I might want to do to her. Alice looked askance at me when I declined to make Evelyn's bed or do her hair. Dot was usually there to step in, a benign, pleasing presence who didn't seem to raise Evelyn's hackles in the way I did.

I found ways to care for her, though. I gave her the best of all my food, the few carrots that hadn't gone soft and the thin milk skimmed off the top of my glass, so as to avoid lumps. I liked this way of doing things because it meant I didn't have to look at her or touch her too often. Really, if only Alice had given it some thought, perhaps she would have realised that my withdrawing from Evelyn was all that was keeping some semblance of order among us. Being patient with ourselves and each other became an ever more time-consuming task, with no help from the teachers, who seemed to have devoted themselves to making everything worse.

From time to time, something punctuated the gloom: one day, Matron left for the village against Miss Lewis's express orders, and we never saw her again. The tinned food started to take on a sharp, metallic taste. Marion sliced open her tongue on a bit of metal that was left in her corned beef, leaving a cut that refused to heal properly. Two days later, she bit down on it wrong and choked on the stream of dark fluid that came out, like blood but not, with a rotten smell to it. She hadn't complained once, had just nursed herself quietly as her tongue swelled and it became harder and harder for her to speak, until the abscess burst and she finally let herself weep.

On post day, which in ordinary times represented letters from home and even, on occasion, a box of chocolates, the heavens opened. I felt apocalyptic about it. The postie's arrival had begun to feel like our only connection to the outside world. The newspapers had stopped arriving around the time Sophie died, which couldn't bode well. If he cancelled his route, if he decided it wasn't worth it—but he did come, one arm raised to shield his face against the downpour. I thought briefly about yelling for his help and then thought better of it: who knew whether, once he'd entered through the gates, he'd be trapped here like the rest of us?

In the end it didn't matter. He came right up to the gate where the little red postbox stood, but he didn't do anything after that. He stood there, staring, not at the postbox but through it. Not at Briarley, but through it.

We'd all clustered around the window with the best view by then, and morning break was rapidly coming to a close. Then the bell rang, and we were forced out of the common room and back to lessons. *Please let him do something to help us*, I thought to myself. I was making all sorts of bargains, then: silently appended onto the end was *and I'll never touch Evelyn again*.

But when we got out of our lesson and rushed back to the window, the postman was still there, exactly where we'd left him. He stared vacantly into nothing, one hand in his messenger bag as if he'd been reaching for something inside. The rain was collecting in his hat and pouring out in a steady stream over his face. I wanted to beat on the windows and scream at him, or better yet run down the drive and drag him through the gates myself. It looked almost like he was mocking us, or at least *something* was, which I couldn't bear. I didn't want to be toyed with. He stayed there at the gate, unmoving, until we went to bed. I could see him out of the dormitory window, a dark, familiar shape silhouetted by the moonlight. By morning he'd disappeared.

NINETEEN

KISS CURL

"It's been long enough," I announced. "Séance tonight?"

With the schoolmistresses on the warpath, it was getting harder to discuss these things. I didn't trust Ann or Shirley as far as I could throw them, so mealtimes were out. We were left with morning break, when we'd flee in search of as much privacy as we could find, or just before bed.

"If we must," Evelyn said. "Though none of us has any idea what we're doing."

"Oh, no, but you *are* good at it," Dot cried.

"We're running out of time, so we're going to have to try," I said.

"Emily, have you ever heard the saying about catching more flies with honey than with vinegar?" Evelyn said. "I'm only asking because I thought you might not realise that actually I preferred the compliment."

"I had no idea! So false flattery and futile hope is the way to your heart? I'll make a note of that, thanks." Evelyn looked alarmed and I bitterly regretted my choice of words, but Alice rescued us.

"Arguments aside, we should find out what happens if you're not trying to stop Violet. If you go into it knowing what you're trying to do."

"I think maybe I read something about a cabinet? Apparently they used to put mediums in a cabinet and that's how they did it," Dot said. In Sophie's absence she had taken to reading the book in quiet moments, and was becoming the closest thing we had to an authority.

"I'm not doing a magic trick," Evelyn scoffed, though I didn't know where she thought she was getting the right to reject any of our suggestions.

"Oh, and the book said sometimes they tied mediums up, you know, with bits of thread or even handcuffs, to make sure they weren't faking it, but maybe tying them up did something, and that's why the materialisations were so good—"

"You're not *tying me up*."

"If you know so much about it then let's just try it tonight, see how far you get," I suggested, figuring that if she succeeded we'd be one step closer to getting out and if she failed it would at least be very personally satisfying.

I suppose one hidden benefit of our days-long wait for Evelyn to gather her strength was that in the intervening time, the surveillance being conducted on us fell away somewhat. We became so utterly boring during that period that the teachers stopped watching us as closely as they had been before. It was as though it—whatever it was—wanted our inaction, preferred us still and complacent and beaten-down; we were rewarded for our docility by something like a cessation in hostilities. Lessons carried on in the same suffocating way, sometimes so difficult that my head ached afterwards, but more often bizarrely facile. Miss Lewis and Miss Stone took subjects seemingly at random, reading aloud from *Boys' Own* adventure stories or making us do hour-long dictations in French or German, usually from impenetrable political texts that none of us could get our heads around. They couldn't seem to keep to one subject for long, skipping back and forth from one thing to another, sometimes with lassitude, sometimes hectic energy.

At least they were content to let Ann and Shirley take the lion's share of the questions, and Ann and Shirley were perfectly happy to answer them. Just our rotten luck, to be stuck with two inveterate teacher's pets as our only other company. In fact, Ann and Shirley seemed more and more able to anticipate and understand the logic of the questions we were being asked, even as the rest of us found them utterly baffling.

That afternoon, the final lesson of the day that we had to get through before our séance, Miss Lewis looked down at us with a vague fogginess in her eyes and demanded we tell her which empire was the greatest, without specifying when or why. Just as I was suppressing the urge to ask for some specifics, Shirley said, "Ours," with a beatific smile. That was perhaps the worst of it: that they were somehow able to understand each other.

What I didn't realise at the time was that it was the last lesson I would ever have at Briarley. As endings go, it was an ignominious one.

That night, when we assembled in our familiar circle on the dormitory floor, it felt like coming into place, clicking together like a magnet. Only Evelyn looked uneasy. Whether that was to do with the materialisation attempt that was to come, or having to sit next to me and hold my hand, I didn't know.

"Is there anything we ought to discuss before we start? Evelyn, are you sure you don't want to look at Sophie's book?" Marion asked.

"I'd rather just get on with it, if you don't mind," Evelyn said.

She was sitting so close to me that our cross-legged knees

touched. Waves of goose-pimples kept rising all down my leg. I was rather dreading having to hold her hand as well, if I'm being honest. It felt too acute of a reminder of the last time she'd touched me and how desperately I wanted her to do it again.

"Of course," said Dot solicitously. "We mustn't keep you waiting. Let's all join hands and see what happens."

Holding Evelyn's hand this time around was about as bad—or as good—as I had imagined. She seemed reluctant, but there was no way around it; as she touched me something settled, unexpectedly, in my chest. I saw her eyes flicker to mine, and before I could stop myself I was looking at her mouth. Wanting Evelyn was a terrible experience. It didn't stop me finding her profoundly irritating, a habit formed of over six years' practice, and it didn't stop her mouth from pursing in annoyance when she looked back at me. Worst of all, that didn't stop me wanting to kiss her.

"Shall we begin," Evelyn said, a little stiffly.

"Time's a-ticking," I added, which was very embarrassing.

She rolled her eyes and then closed them.

I had the chance to look at her, then, without her looking back. There was more colour in her cheeks and she had lost the gaunt, hollow look that had begun to frighten me.

"Violet, are you there?" There was a pause, and Evelyn's brow furrowed. "Well, we'd like to try another materialisation. If you're willing." She shifted where she sat, and I thought she clutched my hand a little harder, though it's difficult to tell if that was real or my imagination, considering how hard I was thinking about it.

"Should we do anything?" Dot whispered. Evelyn didn't respond. She had gone very still. While we waited for her to speak, something pale and pearlescent began to drip from one of her nostrils. I nearly leaned forwards to wipe it away before realising that that would've broken the circle; it was odd to see Evelyn, who was ordinarily so fastidious with her appearance, not even flinch as the substance reached her lips, slipping in between them and eventually reaching her chin.

"What is that?" Alice said, in fascination and disgust.

Then Evelyn's mouth fell open, and masses of the stuff started pouring out. It was thinner and finer than last time, somewhere in between crinoline and candle wax. That doesn't sound right at all, but the substance was not of this world, and so you'll just have to believe me when I say that's what it was like. Evelyn, although her jaw was hanging open as far as it could go, didn't seem to be in distress, or at least the ectoplasm didn't appear to stop her breathing. It didn't have weight in quite the same way as something earthly would, and it took longer to fall and start pooling on the floorboards than you might've expected. It hung suspended in the air, as though it didn't have to follow the same rules of gravity as everything else.

Once it did reach the floor, though, it knit itself together until it began to look more substantial. And then right where it had hit the floorboards it articulated itself into fingers, which grew longer and more real-looking, and then those fingers were attached to a hand, and then a wrist.

"Oh my God," Marion whispered. "Is it—"

Of course, there was no way to tell for certain whether it was Violet's hand. It had that same strange blurriness as the stuff Evelyn had produced last time. But there was something—an angle of the wrist, maybe, an insouciance that looked familiar. I wondered what would happen next: would an arm and shoulders appear, then the rest of her, bit by bit? Would Violet's torso grow from the ground, or would she appear out of order? Would she be whole, in the end?

The hand moved in a slow circle on the floor as if it was

feeling out its surroundings. It flattened completely, palm down, then glided towards me. I almost flinched and had to stop myself. Ectoplasm was still pouring from Evelyn's mouth, though the pace of it had slowed. The hand moved in a way I can only describe as *creeping*. It brushed against the place where Evelyn's hand and mine were joined together. The movement was nonchalant, an insinuation. It was cold, really cold, and slimy, but there was something vital to it that made it feel like more than a piece of fabric or rubber. It moved with intention.

We were all absolutely focused on the motion of the spirit hand, so I didn't make much of it when the ectoplasm coming out of Evelyn's mouth flared up the way a fire does when it catches a new bit of kindling and goes huge and hot for a moment. We didn't notice anything, really, until Evelyn swooned, a good, old-fashioned swoon where she went limp and fell to the side. Her hand slipped out of mine and she ended up—because, with my luck, where else would she have gone?—squarely in my lap.

With the circle broken the hand disappeared, melted right away into nothing. Or, I should say, almost nothing. I looked down at Evelyn, who, I must stress, was very much in my lap, and realised her hair was coated with something sticky and wet. I couldn't see much, but her plaits were full of it, and when I reached out a hand to touch it, it felt cold, just like the ectoplasmic hand had. It was all over my fingers, webbing between them and glistening in the moonlight.

"Oh, ugh," I said. Then I remembered that much more importantly, Evelyn had fainted.

"Evelyn," I tried, and then I slapped her cheek gently. Doing this made me feel a thrill of something awful, so I determined not to do it again. She did sigh, though, which felt like a good step forward. Dot scurried over and started chafing her wrists, which Sophie had once told us was good to get people out of a faint. Not for the first time, I wished Sophie were there. Evelyn opened her eyes.

"Emily?" she said. I could see the moment she realised that she was looking up at me from my lap and her eyes filled with something akin to terror.

"It's all right," I said. "You fainted. But before that—you almost managed it." She blinked and came to herself a bit more.

"The materialisation? Did you see Violet?"

"Just her hand," Marion said.

"It was her, wasn't it," Alice said. "Thought I recognised it."

Evelyn's face fell. "That's *nothing* like almost. I thought you were going to say she appeared but couldn't speak or something."

"Come on, Evelyn, buck up," I said. "It was incredible. It was so clear compared to last time, really obviously a part of her body—"

"And then I fainted," she said disdainfully.

"You need practice!" I exclaimed. "Look here, it was so much better than before, and it'll be even better next time."

Evelyn looked sceptical. She raised a hand to her plait, about to twist the end of it as I'd seen her do a thousand times before, and drew it back in horror. "What's *that?*" she said, and scrambled up from my lap. "Oh, it's all over my hair, it's disgusting! Is it—ectoplasm?"

"How should I know what it is? We've only just started, for all I know this happens to every medium from time to time."

"Horrible, it's horrible," she muttered, and ripped the ribbon off the end of her plait to try to massage some of it out. The more she touched it the stickier it looked. "Get it off, someone, please, I can't stand having it touch me."

"We're making too much noise," Marion warned.

"I'm not going to sleep with this stuff in my hair," Evelyn insisted. "It's revolting and I'm not convinced it won't turn out to be poisonous." She pulled at her hair again, but only succeeded in making it worse. It was matting together as the substance dried, going from a sticky mess to an angry snarl.

"Should I fetch the scissors?" I asked.

"Oh, you brute, of course you want to cut all my hair off," she said, her eyes round as saucers.

"I don't have to—"

She looked down at the ectoplasm covering her fingers and seemed close to tears, swaying dizzily. "No, do it, but do it fast so I can't think about it."

She didn't seem to entertain the possibility that anyone but me might cut her hair. Evelyn was so distraught that I thought she oughtn't have to be in front of the others any more; her sense of propriety was too strong.

"We can go into the bathroom," I said, helping her to her feet. "As long as we don't run the taps I don't think it'll wake anyone up." She nodded weakly, making a thin, humming sort of noise like she didn't trust herself to open her mouth. Dot fetched her scissors for me, thankfully without passing comment on Evelyn's choice of hairdresser. We made our way to the bathroom with Evelyn's entire weight hanging off my arm. Somehow I didn't mind being a support for her: I didn't need an excuse to touch her because I already had one, and she had one too, and I was no longer at risk of being swiped at like an angry cat if I indulged myself.

Once in the bathroom, I could see by the marginally better light that her cheeks had gone crimson.

"Please will you hurry up," she said, not looking at me, and when I took hold of a hank of her hair she let out a sharp exhale.

I had to wipe off the blades of the scissors every few cuts, because the substance in Evelyn's hair was getting thicker as it dried. Evelyn sat very still, as if she thought I was going to slip and nick her if she moved a muscle.

"You can relax," I told her. "I'm nearly done." And I was: lots of her hair was now littering the bathroom floor in limp, wet piles. When I'd cut it, her curls had sprung tighter, no longer being dragged down by their own weight, so it had turned out shorter than I'd intended. It hung above her shoulders, giving her an angular, elfin look. Her face seemed clearer, now, without all the masses of hair around it, or the tautness at her temples that came from how tightly she did her plaits. I noticed for the first time that her face had character: the fine turn of her brow, a certain clarity in the grey of her eyes, the way her chin tilted stubbornly.

Evelyn didn't say anything for a while. She ran her fingers through what was left of her hair, which did make the whole effect look better. Finally: "It could be worse. Thank you for doing it," she said, turning to me. The gratitude looked like it was causing her a great deal of discomfort.

We returned to the dormitory, where the others were still sitting in the remains of our circle.

"You're ever so stoic," Marion said, drily. "I'd be in gales of tears if it were my hair."

"Hang on a second," Dot said, leaping up. She licked her thumb and forefinger, leaned forwards, and swept the shortest strand of hair right at the front of Evelyn's face into a kiss curl. "Now it's perfect."

None of us said much else. It felt better to leave it till morning, leave all the rest of it till morning, the danger and the ectoplasm and the uncertainty. Alice and Dot climbed into bed together, having given up the pretence that Dot would move back into her own bed when the wound of Sophie's death was less fresh. In the moonlight, I watched Dot touching Alice's forehead, sweeping her fingertips along her temple and down to her chin, whispering something in her ear.

TWENTY

SOUL BY SOUL, AND SILENTLY

The next morning, the last morning I would ever wake up at Briarley, we weren't awakened by the bell, but rather by music. It was faint, coming from downstairs, but it was such a singularly bizarre sound to hear at dawn that it jerked me awake in a second. I strained to hear what was playing.

"Can you hear that?" I asked the others, who'd started sitting up and rubbing their eyes too.

" 'S the gramophone," Alice said blearily. "Dunno why."

"What's it playing?" said Dot. "I wish it'd shut up." Ordinarily Dot was much politer than this, even in dire circumstances, but waking up early was her Waterloo.

"It's 'Rule, Britannia!' " Marion said, putting on her dressing-gown. "Though why that would be playing at this hour is anyone's guess."

"Oh, turn it off," Evelyn groaned. "My head feels like someone's pounding nails into it."

"Must be the materialisation, you're probably exhausted," Alice said. "Will you actually, though, Marion? It's dreadful."

"Sorry, but someone's going to have to come with me. I'm

not going alone, I don't want to end up—" Marion said, not finishing her sentence, but not needing to, either.

I heaved myself out of bed to join her. "All right, all right," I said. "I volunteer, if only to give us all some peace." I pulled on my dressing-gown as well and winced at how cold the floor was. It must've been around seven o'clock; dawn was starting to creep in through the windows.

Marion and I slipped out the dormitory door and down the stairs. The sound of the gramophone got louder and louder as we went, blasting the verse of "Rule, Britannia!," which you only ever heard at the Proms or when the King appeared at the horse races. The music echoed and rebounded against the walls; Briarley was so empty now that there was hardly anything to absorb the sound.

"If this is what killed Mademoiselle and Sophie it looks like it's determined to drive us insane," Marion muttered. We made it down to the dining hall, where the music was loudest. I had a sudden unsolicited thought, and tried to suppress the laugh that bubbled up hysterically in my throat. "What?" she said.

"Nothing, nothing," I said. "Only—have you realised it's Christmas soon?"

"Oh, God. It can't be. Really?"

"I've stopped paying much attention to the date but it's definitely—well, it's been December for a while, hasn't it?"

"At least a week, maybe two," she agreed. "I suppose we've not been keeping track." We crossed the dining hall together, and I located myself around the side of the gramophone so I didn't have to have my ear right next to the trumpet while it was playing at full volume.

"I hate this thing," I said. "I wish we had a wireless instead."

We'd never been allowed to touch the gramophone before, on pain of—if not death, then something equally unpleasant.

My parents had one at home, but it was a newer model; this one was old and creaky and gave a distinctly scratchy sound to any music it played, which didn't do the recording any favours.

"Is there a switch to turn it off?" Marion asked. I felt around the back, but it was curiously smooth. That couldn't possibly be right. There wasn't even a handle you could turn, implying that the gramophone was somehow powering itself.

"None whatsoever, I think we might have to wait till it finishes—oh, hang on, I'll just take the record out altogether." I lifted the needle and there was blessed silence. I left the disc of patriotic songs on the floor, figuring that I didn't much care if it got trodden on.

"Promising," Marion said, but then some rather weepy violins started going and "I Vow to Thee, My Country" began. We both started in surprise, though at least this one was drippier and less obtrusive. I found myself hoping, without knowing when I had started prioritising her well-being, that it would be better for Evelyn's headache.

"How is it doing that? It shouldn't be able to do that."

"I know better than to ask," Marion replied grimly, glancing over at the gramophone, which was spinning happily and playing the hymn full blast. I sat back on my heels in defeat. Trying to get to the bottom of it felt like a waste of energy.

"I'm not listening to that all day," I warned her.

"Wait here." She walked out, scrubbing a hand against her temple. I sank down against the wall and listened to the tinny wailing choir going on about how we should lay the dearest and the best on the altar of our country, and waited for Marion to get back. I could hear her footsteps clattering around, and cupboard doors opening and closing.

Marion returned, holding, of all things, a cricket bat. You

could tell it was Alice's because of the red tape wrapped around its handle with more enthusiasm than precision.

"What are you—" I started, and then it became very clear what she was doing when she raised the cricket bat high above her head and brought it down on the gramophone with a resounding crash.

The first blow didn't do much. It came down on the big metal trumpet, a morning glory–shaped thing, and put a huge dent in it, but the music kept going. After she'd hit the gramophone, the sound distorted; it became all hollow and echoing like we'd gone through a tunnel. I stood up in haste to avoid being in the line of fire when she tried again.

"For God's sake," Marion said, and brought the cricket bat down again, harder this time. She missed the trumpet and hit the body of the gramophone. The needle flew off and part of the case was smashed to bits, the varnished wood looking terribly fragile. Throughout our years at school, Marion had always been a dab hand with a cricket bat. The choir was singing about how *soul by soul and silently her shining bounds increase*, which felt like a horribly ironic joke.

A moment after she'd hit it the second time, I realised there was something coming out of the trumpet. I didn't dare get too close, but Marion, who was braver than me, leaned towards it, clutching the cricket bat for all she was worth as if she could beat whatever it was to death as well. It was dark, the sort of blackened colour that had once been brown, and it moved slowly, spattering onto the floor with a sticky sound that echoed through the dining hall. As it left the furrowed depths of the gramophone and reached the light, I realised it had a stink, too, the smell of something sweet that had been hidden away and rotting for a long, long time.

"Oh my God," I said, and clapped a hand over my nose and mouth.

"This is horrible," Marion said, in wonder.

It was coming faster now, and the smell was starting to fill the dining hall. Something about the way it moved, its slow creep and its viscosity, brought to mind the awful obverse of the ectoplasm that had poured from Evelyn's throat just the night before.

I didn't know what it meant, and I didn't have time to work it out, because just then there were footsteps outside, and Alice's voice cheerfully announcing, "What on earth are you two doing?" She broke off when the smell reached her and added, "Ugh, that is *rank*."

I looked up to see the others clustering in from the doorway, still in their nightdresses. Evelyn had a hand pressed to her forehead and looked like she was regretting leaving her bed.

"We thought we'd come to see if we can help," Dot said, edging closer in her slippered feet.

"I'm not sure if there's much anyone can do," I replied. "The music wouldn't stop even when we took the record out, and then—well—this happened." I gestured to the thick sludge spilling onto the floor from the mutilated gramophone.

I can't express strongly enough how badly it smelled. The closest I can get to describing it is that it was like if you've ever had a mouse die somewhere in your house, behind the cupboards or under the floorboards, where you can't get at it. Before long the stink starts filling the whole space and you can't get away from it, and searching for its source drives you to distraction. It was much worse than the mouse-smell; there was an edge of something oily and cloying to it, like sugared butter gone rancid. But it was, unmistakably, something dead and rotting. There was no doubt about that.

"Oh, it's disgusting," Evelyn said. "Give that to me." She took the cricket bat from Marion and gave one hearty swing, completely at odds with the way she played actual cricket, which was with notable indifference. This final swing broke the trumpet off entirely, sending it clattering to the floor and leaving a splintered wound where it had been. For some reason, that did actually stop the music playing, but the sludge oozed on.

"Good morning to us, I suppose," Alice said.

"I hate it here," said Marion suddenly. "I really can't bear it any longer. I wish the whole place would go up in flames; I would almost rather die than stay here another day."

"Oh, Marion, don't say that," Dot pleaded.

"I do mean it, though. It isn't tolerable." She took the cricket bat from Evelyn and stalked around to prop it against the wall, but first she looked as though she might take a swing at the walls of Briarley themselves, futile as that would be. The image of it was tempting: Marion, knocking the place to pieces armed with nothing but Alice's old bat. "Do you know, I hate this whole stifling country altogether."

Only very recently, I would've gone to the ends of the earth for Briarley. It had been my home, or the closest thing I had to one. I had done everything I could to keep the others there with me, in what was increasingly looking like a death trap, because I had thought there was something worth preserving. It wasn't as though I had anything else, either: returning to my family home after all that had happened would have been like going back somewhere where you'd once spoken the language, years before, and finding that you could barely read the street signs. I'd never exactly been Pollyanna but I had, of late, grown into something else altogether. To go home to suet pudding when I was good and my father's belt when I was bad, piano lessons and junior dresses, books with morals and boating-parties—

it was as though somewhere along the line we had entered a new world entirely, and all of a sudden I could see the seams and patched-up places in the old. Even if we got out, I would have nowhere to go.

But the things I had loved about Briarley, the things that had made it something like home, were falling away piece by piece, until there was nothing left except for my friends, whom it seemed I had doomed by begging them to stay. It was an irony that didn't bear thinking about.

Evelyn spoke up, startling me. "I hate it too," she said, which I wasn't expecting. "I always felt—better here." Her eyes were fixed on the stinking sludge, which by then had slowed to a trickle. "And now it's suffocating. As though we're being embalmed alive."

"I don't want to go back home, I just want to get out," I said, by way of agreement.

Dot bit her lip. "Do you know," she started, looking to us as if we could offer any comfort, "I'm frightened that the whole world's like this now."

"Do you mean if it's not just Briarley? Being haunted, or whatever this is?" Marion asked.

"Yes! Imagine if it's our parents, too. The whole world. Only if it's just Briarley then I can't stop thinking about what we did to deserve it. I can't work out what's worse."

"Dot, no," Alice said, more out of an instinctive repulsion from the thought than with anything useful to add.

"I just thought, what if it's us? What if we're the reason this is all happening?" Dot's voice spiralled upwards, high and fearful.

"Could've been one of the old Briarleys. Got a witch to put a curse on the place when he realised he couldn't keep it," Alice offered, in an attempt at levity that didn't come out as funny as I imagined she was hoping.

"Ugh," Marion said. "Maybe it's something in the soil, or the water."

"Or we're dangerous to whatever it is," said Dot. "Do you think that's why it's trying to kill us?"

"I think it just is," Evelyn said, "and always has been."

The doors to the dining hall burst open.

Miss Lewis led the charge, with Miss Stone and Ann and Shirley close behind. They looked ridiculous. Their faces were red, their chests were heaving; they looked like they'd run a marathon, just to find us standing perfectly still in the dining hall. I braced myself for Miss Lewis to shout and gesticulate, maybe to tell us she was disappointed in us or to expel us from the school we were unable to leave.

But that never came. Instead, Miss Lewis opened her mouth wide and made a baying noise, like a hound that's caught the scent, which should've been silly but was so full-throated and sincere that my blood ran cold to hear it. I'd never heard anything like that coming from a person's mouth. It didn't seem possible, it was too much, it was outside the bounds of behaviour that I understood to exist in polite society. I wondered what the others were thinking, whether they were hearing this too or if I had finally gone mad, as I had feared all along. The space between us and them seemed to crackle with potential.

And then they rushed at us.

They moved with an awkward jerkiness, like puppets being danced inexpertly. The noise of their shoes against the flagstones shocked me out of my daze. Acting on pure instinct, I went for the nearest thing I could find, which was the fireplace, and the heavy iron poker and shovel that hung there. I tossed Marion the poker, which she caught in an elegant arcing motion. Alice went for a nearby dining chair, Evelyn snatched up the cricket bat. Only Dot was left without anything, her face crumpling.

"Just get behind me," Alice ordered her. Dot nodded, white-faced.

The group of them reached us at last. Miss Lewis came towards me first and I closed my eyes and swung the shovel at her. I thought I might bottle it at the last second if I had to look at her while I did it. It caught her on the shoulder and she staggered a few steps back. She didn't seem to be reacting to the pain in an ordinary way. She didn't say a word, didn't clutch at her shoulder or anything, only made a high keening sound and lumbered around as though she wasn't capable of proper thought any more. Miss Lewis, I thought stupidly, *Miss Lewis, are you all right?*

I'd bought myself a few seconds and glanced towards the others. Dot was still behind Alice, but had snatched up the needle of the gramophone and was clutching it in her fist. I hoped she wouldn't get close enough to need to use it.

"Anyone who's got something you can keep them off with, get to the front," Alice shouted. Captain of the cricket team, indeed. I was full of gratitude that she was taking over. "Me and Dot'll stay at the sides—got to get out of the hall, there's only the one exit."

Miss Lewis was hurtling towards us again, but it was Shirley who got closest to me this time, her ringlets bouncing absurdly. She looked rabid: that's the only word for it. She was nearly a foot shorter than me, and she launched herself at my waist, trying to knock me down. I raised the shovel and brought it down on her head, just enough to strike her off me. It felt desperately unsporting, going after a child like that, but some hind-brain instinct in me knew she was trying to get me onto the ground, and she wouldn't hesitate to kill me if she had the chance. She detached from my waist like a limpet being pulled from a stone; there was blood running down into her eye from a cut on her forehead, the only damage I had caused. It had got into the white of her eye, staining it crimson, and when she bared her teeth at me anything human in her expression was completely gone.

"Are the rest of you all right?" I called, panting.

Alice grunted and I heard splintering wood, then "I am now," and looked over to see Miss Stone trying to get up from where she'd been hit with the chair.

We had been edging nearer all this time to the doorway. I tried to keep as close to the others as I could, remembering from a long-ago Latin lesson the diagrams of Roman soldiers' formations, how they looked like a turtle or a hedgehog with spears bristling in all directions.

Evelyn clutched the cricket bat like it was the last thing on earth, bracing herself as Ann hurtled forwards and onto her. She was prepared, but not enough; she was small, and exhausted from the séance the night before, and she went down hard.

I heard a roaring in my ears and I flew towards Ann without thinking, conscious only of the need to hurt her. I jabbed her as hard as I could in the neck with my shovel. I didn't hold back like I had with Shirley. The generous explanation is that I was being selfless, that to save Evelyn felt more vital than to save my own skin. Sometimes I wonder if in fact I still resented Ann for ratting on us to Miss Lewis, which is a much worse reason to do what I did. Either way, Ann fell backwards, her mouth in a perfect O. She didn't even clutch at her throat like a normal person would have, she just fell, and flopped like a fish on land.

"Thank you," Evelyn said.

I tried to say something back, but my heart was beating so hard I thought it would come right out of my chest and I just gasped at her.

Ann was starting to climb back up.

"The door," Alice cried. "Get to the door!"

We were close enough to it now, and I squeezed through just behind Evelyn. The teachers and Ann and Shirley were right on my heels. I felt a hand grasping at me; it plucked at my dressing-gown and pulled it halfway down my shoulders, then off completely. It was Miss Stone, her face contorted with rage and her hand reaching out to grab me again. There was a vein pulsing hard in her temple. Looking back was a mistake. It allowed her to gain on me, only by a stride or two, but it was enough that she was able to scrabble at my shoulder, her nails scraping my skin till it stung smartly. I thought she had me and my stomach dropped, but I was half a step too far away from her. She reached for me and came up empty, tripping over her own feet and holding up the rest of them as we broke through.

They fell in an ungainly heap around the doorway to the dining hall, too addled to untangle themselves easily. Only Ann managed to stagger to her feet, and as we surged and ran for the stairs that led to the Long Gallery, she came after us, scrawny legs sticking out from under her pinafore and a blank expression on her face.

"We can lock her in—the Long Gallery, I reckon," Alice called back to us.

"D'you think we can force her in?" I shouted.

Ann was finding the stairs difficult, it seemed, pitching forwards onto her hands, her feet slapping at the steps. I couldn't remember these stairs ever feeling so steep or so numerous; my throat burned from dragging in gulps of air.

"Five of us, one of her. We'd better be able to."

Evelyn darted a nervous glance down to the doorway, where the things that had once been Miss Lewis, Miss Stone, and Shirley Carr were disentangled and shambling towards us. They were looking the worse for wear, Shirley still bleeding freely and Miss Lewis's dress torn from where the shovel had caught it. She was moving oddly, and I wondered if I had hit her harder on the shoulder than I'd thought. It seemed possible that even if I'd broken something she'd hardly notice, would just keep hunting us through the school as her bones grated against one another.

"We need to hurry," Evelyn said. "Once she's in there, do we kill her?"

I stared at her. "Evelyn, you bloodthirsty little—we *lock her in*, tie her up, I don't know."

Ann had nearly caught up to us; she was now on all fours, like an animal.

"What next?" I asked Alice.

She had the same look she had on the cricket pitch when she was about to tell us to do something that would win the game. "Let her follow us in," she called, and we piled in after her.

Ann came through the door seconds later, her posture all wrong, hunched and brutish. She crouched dumbly in the doorway, and for a moment we could hardly hear the heaving breaths and scrambling feet of the others, coming up the stairs after us. Ann was bathed in early morning light, which streamed through the windows and shone on her like a beacon, as if to confirm that for once we'd made the right decisions. The whole thing felt like a stroke of pure dumb luck, until it didn't.

What happened was this: we started towards her, and she changed. Ann went from a vacuous nothing to a whirling, spitting hellion the second we approached. Her hands curled into rigid claws and she dug her nails into any flesh she could reach. She gouged a bloody runnel out of Alice's cheek, and whipped her head around to sink her teeth into Dot's forearm when she got too close. Dot howled and tried to shake her off, but Ann's jaws were locked tight, the frantic grip of a dog with a bone.

"Get her off, get her off me," Dot wailed. Marion and Alice each took one of Ann's arms and wrestled her away, leaving a spittle-soaked imprint of her teeth glistening wetly in Dot's soft skin. It looked as though it was taking all their strength just to hang onto her, and I was about to try and find something to tie her up with when the others made it to the door of the Long Gallery.

Evelyn saw them first and let out a high shriek. After that it all went so fast I can hardly remember it.

It comes back to me chiefly through impressions: a figure darting at Dot, who screamed once and put the gramophone needle right through Miss Stone's eye, spearing through sclera and fluid and whatever lay beneath, and then screamed again when she realised what she'd done. Ann lunging for my ankle, and me kicking her in the face so hard that a lone baby tooth came loose and hung drunkenly from its socket. Finding Evelyn in the melee, knowing her not by sight or sound but by the feeling of her, grasping her by the wrist and yanking with no thought to how rough I was. I was so focused on dragging her out of the door behind me that I barely saw what happened next.

It looked for a moment like we'd managed it, after all, against the odds. Dot came out just after me and Evelyn. She was clutching the gramophone needle, which was dripping with blood and something grey and jelly-like that didn't bear thinking about. Marion beat Miss Lewis away with a hearty whack from the poker and put her hand out to Alice, who should've been right behind her.

"Alice!" she called. "Alice!" Alice whipped her head around and saw an opening, a single corridor of space. She dropped the dining chair she'd been using to keep them off and dashed towards the door, her long legs pumping. Marion was standing by, hand on the doorknob, ready to swing it shut behind her and trap them inside.

Alice should've made it out. There were a thousand possible worlds in which she did, the fastest of any of us, the best at any sport she put her mind to, brave, vital Alice with her broad-shouldered frame and her gruff voice. But in this one, she didn't.

She was a step or two away from the entrance and then she tripped, falling into the door itself. It slammed shut with the weight of her. Marion frantically jiggled the knob and shouted to Alice on the other side, who said, "Don't—just bar the door—don't let them out—" Her voice stopped abruptly, replaced with a terrible crunching noise and a ragged scream, and Dot howled. I realised I'd never stopped clutching Evelyn's wrist, so I let her go and beat on the door instead, shouting Alice's name. There was nothing in response. Wishing that I were doing anything else in the world, I crouched down and put my eye to the keyhole.

I had a narrow range of vision, and Alice was slumped against the door so I could only see her legs. I thought, incongruously, of the Wicked Witch's feet sticking out from under the farmhouse in *The Wonderful Wizard of Oz*, which I had read as a child and been terribly frightened by. Miss Lewis and Shirley were hunched over her, more animal than person. Ann and Miss Stone were just out of view, but I could see Ann's bony ankles, and Miss Stone's severe navy dress pooled over Alice's scratched-up knees. I didn't want to know what they were doing, but I couldn't look away. Miss Lewis bent over further and opened her jaw wide. She sank her teeth into the meat of Alice's calf; I saw it happening like it was in a dream. She worried at the flesh, shaking her head from side to side. After a moment, she withdrew and there was a piece of Alice missing. Her teeth and chin were smeared with blood.

She looked up, then, right through the keyhole, and met my eye. There was nothing there. Nothing to suggest she understood what she'd done, nothing that implied a shred of sentiment, just a fathomless hunger that I had only ever seen before on the face of Violet's father, the day of Lacey's memorial service. I tore myself away from the keyhole and pressed my back against it. I didn't consider then that I was a mirror image of Alice, on the other side of the door, but I have thought about it ever since.

"What do we do?" Dot said. "How do we get her out? We have to get her out. We can't let her stay in there with them."

Evelyn's eyes were big and wild. "We can't get her out. You can feel it, can't you?"

Dot said, "No," sounding lost, and then she sat down against the wall.

There was a beat where no one said anything, and then I felt something sticky and warm seeping out from the crack under the door. It touched my hand and I wiped it off on my nightdress almost absent-mindedly, before I had a chance to look at it. A scraping sound came from inside the Long Gallery. I thought about the suit of armour, imagining its sword arm rising, ready to batter the door down, and said, "We have to do what Alice told us. She said to bar the door."

Marion stood and ran downstairs, returning with a dining chair just like the one Alice had been holding moments before, and jammed it under the doorknob. "That'll hold for a while," she said. "Is that—"

She was gesturing at the smear of blood down the skirt of my nightgown. I nodded, sure that if I said it aloud I would begin to scream and never stop.

TWENTY-ONE

GONE

Dot was pretty much insensible after that. Her hair was all over her face and she flinched whenever we came near her or tried to speak to her.

"Dot, please," Marion said softly.

But Dot didn't move, just stayed curled up against the wall. I could hardly blame her. Alice wasn't the sort of person you could imagine torn out of existence, just like that; she was too warm and solid. The thought of death didn't suit her. The one time I ever saw her really, truly frightened was when she slipped and fell playing hockey and broke her arm so badly the doctors told her she might never play again, and even then it wasn't the pain that had disturbed her but the prospect of boredom and stillness. The thought that she would never move again, never speak again, never clap you on the shoulder when you'd done a good job at something—I wanted to protest that it couldn't be countenanced. It just couldn't be possible. But, more pressingly, there was Dot, sitting like a china doll, her cheeks red and limbs frozen awkwardly in place. I couldn't quite picture Dot without

Alice, couldn't quite imagine the way she would move through the world.

The chair under the doorknob rattled, and Marion and Evelyn and I jumped.

"Come on, Dot, Alice would have wanted you to get out of here," I said, crouching down to her level. She raised her tear-soaked face to mine, her expression only a shade away from baring her teeth. The wrongness of it made me feel ill. "It's why she did—what she did."

"You're only saying that because we left her in there to die," she said, her voice cracking. "I don't want to live without her. None of us deserves to live without her. She stayed here for *me*, she could've gone back to her family ages ago, and now we've just left her to die."

"I'm saying it because Alice was giving us the best chance she could. She wanted us to get out, that's why she told us to bar the door," I said. An awful slavering noise came from inside the Long Gallery. I didn't want to say that Alice was, probably, already dead. "Look here, we've done our best with the door but it's not going to hold for long."

I grabbed her by the arm. She just sat there so I pulled as hard as I could. At that she rose up about an inch and then flopped back down. She'd gone all boneless and limp, like a child refusing to be taken somewhere it doesn't want to go. Could I blame her? I sometimes wonder whether Dot had it right, then, and it would have been easier to cut our losses and give up. "Dot, come *on*."

She made a sniffling noise that sounded promising; a snotty, weeping Dot was better than one that wouldn't move at all.

"I want to go to the common room," she said, in a small, truculent voice. "I won't go anywhere unless it's the common room."

"Why the common room?" Marion sounded like she was

trying very hard not to let on that she was frustrated. "I'm not sure it's the best idea, Dot."

"Alice left her captain's badge in there yesterday and I want to get it for myself, to remember her by. Please can we go, I can't go on without it, please—"

I looked at Marion, who shrugged one shoulder, with a sort of swift desperation. I had an attack of nerves over the idea of trapping ourselves at the end of a corridor, but we couldn't stay where we were, and we couldn't leave Dot there, either.

It was bizarrely unchanged in the common room. Evelyn's copy of *Jane Eyre* was resting on the arm of the sofa, a bookmark slotted carefully into its pages about two-thirds through, with little chance of her ever finishing it. There was even an empty cup, chipped around the rim and tea-stained on the inside, that I suspected with an unpleasant lurch had last been touched by Sophie, whose hands ran cold in the winter.

I thought of the whole of Briarley stretching out, the same as it had been for decades except for a few interventions: the smashed gramophone, whatever carnage had happened in the Long Gallery, the bodies in chapel. The common room stood as it always had, a little washed-out in the early morning light. Violet's drapes were open. There were ashes in the grate from the last fire we'd made, and with that there was a wave of roiling bitterness coming with the memory of Alice stoking the fire, as she always had.

Dot trudged to the fireplace mantel. Sure enough, on the baize covering, Alice's badge sat between a little pot of dried flowers and a class photograph, taken back at the beginning of term, when we were all still alive and everything had been different. In the photograph we were in two rows, Evelyn, Violet, and me sitting on stools at the front and the rest standing behind us. Violet was at the centre, as she always was, of everything, looking as if she had come out of an advertisement or a painting rather than real life. Evelyn and I were each turned slightly towards her. I couldn't remember whether that had been posed intentionally by the photographer or whether it was simply an unconscious habit. You could just make out Briarley in the background, a large, looming presence, ordered and monumental.

The word CAPTAIN was emblazoned across the red enamel badge in gold, on a proud diagonal. Dot picked it up, pinned it to her nightdress over her heart, and slumped onto the floor, as if that exertion had been all she had the energy for.

"She'd want me to have it," she said, defensive, as if any of us were arguing with her.

"Of course she would," Marion said helplessly.

"What are we going to do?" I said. I don't know if I thought there was an answer to the question. "What do we do now?"

"I can feel her," Evelyn said. She was standing by the fireplace and all of a sudden bent double, clutching at her midsection; when she spoke it was in a low whine, as if the words were being forced from her mouth. "Violet's here. I don't know if I can—oh—I don't feel well at all—"

She staggered to an armchair and slumped into it. Her eyes were closed, and she took in short, sharp breaths. I rushed to her side and pressed two fingers to her neck; her pulse was fast, but strong. Without thinking I took her hand; she held mine very hard.

"Violet, please" was all she said, before she went still.

I wasn't afraid, not of this; what we had seen in the Long Gallery was worse than anything Violet could do. I took the opportunity to look at Evelyn. She hadn't been injured, which felt like a miracle. There she was, like the hymn went, entire and whole and perfect, to whom I offered service. When her eyes were shut you could properly see her rust-coloured lashes, which gave her a startling pale look. The sunlight came through her hair and—if you'll permit me saying this, because I know Evelyn wouldn't—lit it up like a halo.

And then, the change happened before I could notice it beginning. Evelyn's hand flexed in mine, and she rolled her shoulders, and I wasn't worried about Dot any more, because I had bigger things to think of.

"It's you," I said.

"You don't much stand on ceremony any more, do you, girls?" came Violet's voice. Evelyn's nails had stopped biting into my hand, and I found I missed the bright focal point of pain.

"No time for that," Marion said. "You're the one who forced her way here." She was kneeling in front of the armchair; Dot was curled up beside us with her forehead on her knees. I suppose we made something like a séance circle, but one that was unsure of itself, like a body newly missing a limb.

"It's not going well, I understand."

"Rather," I said. "Alice is gone. It's only the four of us left. The teachers are—they aren't themselves."

"They killed Alice," Dot said, her voice rising.

"Tore her apart," Violet said distantly.

I felt a shard of pain lance through me, and tried to hide it. I had been the only one to see what was happening in the Long Gallery, though I was certain that the others at least had some suspicion. "Christ, Violet, don't."

"I don't see any reason to sugar-coat things." Violet's voice sounded morose, but Evelyn's face appeared as though she'd had the last three months wiped from it. I hadn't much thought about how worn we'd all started to look, and I suppose we hadn't exactly been bothering with mirrors of late. Without Sophie, we were a group mostly unaffected by vanity, aside from Marion, who was more concerned with being neat than pretty, anyway. But seeing Violet's coquettish pout, which it seemed she was still capable of doing even under the worst imaginable circumstances, painted across Evelyn's mouth made it more obvious than ever that we looked dreadful.

Marion gave me a look, which I hoped didn't mean she'd seen me staring at Evelyn-Violet's mouth. "I think we need you to materialise," she said. "If you don't think it's hopeless."

"The thing is, Marion darling, I haven't the slightest clue what would happen if I tried walking you out of those gates. I can't see beyond them as it is—but at least I don't think whatever it is haunting Briarley—"

"Aside from you," I added despite myself.

"Well, yes, aside from me. Whatever it is, I don't think it can hurt me. One small benefit of being dead, I suppose."

"But you don't think it's impossible that you could get us out," Marion pressed.

"No, I don't think it's impossible. But I shan't have you blaming me if we try and you wind up like Sophie. Your judgemental streak has got significantly worse, Marion."

"I really loathe you sometimes," Marion said, with something akin to wonder.

It felt then like it came out of nowhere, but when I think back I can't believe it took her so long. Six years of competition, being second best to Violet's charisma. Little snipes on Violet's part when Marion was in earshot—*Oh, Marion's always wanted to be the best at dance, it's a shame how tall she is*, or *Don't you think Marion would make an excellent schoolmarm, with brains like that?*

"I do, I loathe you," Marion said. "I always have. You have always been capable of the most astonishing cruelty, when you want to be, and the fact that you don't always want to be cruel makes it worse when you are."

"I wouldn't be so quick to say such things to my only chance of getting out," Violet said, although there was a little uncertainty in her voice.

"That's precisely what I mean. We haven't any other choice but you. This is all we have, and it'll probably kill us, and you can't bring yourself to be kind about it even for a second. I *hate* you, Violet, and I don't have it in me to pretend otherwise any more. If you want to be begged, you'll have to get it from Emily, not me."

Evelyn's head snapped to me, with more speed than felt quite natural. "Well, Emily?"

I looked between Marion and Violet-Evelyn, and Dot, who hadn't reacted at all to Marion's admission that we most likely wouldn't make it out of the gates alive. I didn't know what to say. For a moment, I found myself wishing that Evelyn were there, only to see what she'd do.

"Please, Violet," I managed, at last. My voice sounded hollow and artificial. "Please. You're all we have. And if it doesn't work—"

"If it doesn't work, we'll be together," she said, and I swear to God she batted Evelyn's eyelashes at me. The thought occurred to me that only a few weeks before I would have jumped at the chance of forever with Violet, even in death. I can't say the idea held no appeal at all, even then, when I should have known better.

"Don't. Please don't."

"Lucky Marion, that Emily was willing to ask me for it—though you didn't give her much choice, did you? And you call me cruel—well. We'll just have to see what Evelyn can do." Her voice was light and pleasant, and a second later Evelyn's face went slack. She slid off the armchair and onto the floor, head bowed.

"Come on, come on," I muttered, and then I spotted something at the side of Evelyn's head.

A trickle of ectoplasm was dripping out of Evelyn's ear, which was pink and almost pointed at the top, something I'd never noticed before. But it was all we got: there was an unholy racket coming from downstairs. They'd finished with Alice, I caught myself thinking, with a bloodless tone that startled me. Dot shut her eyes and whined, high and wordless.

"Oh, *blast*," Marion said.

"Do we wake her up—try to get out of the building while we can?" I said. "It's not far at all to the Long Gallery. If they're really out they'll be up in no time."

"Oh, oh, please don't let them," Dot whimpered. Downstairs there was a clattering, which must have been the chair we'd shoved against the door coming down, and a splintering, which I suspected was them breaking through the wood of the door.

"We don't have much time," Marion warned.

"Right, that's it. We can't stay in here," I said, and with one last look at the pearly stream coming out of Evelyn's ear, I dropped her hand. The ectoplasm vanished, sort of skittered across the floor like water droplets on a hot pan and then melted away. Evelyn sagged. I put one arm under her shoulders and the other under her knees and scooped her up. She was easy as anything to lift. "Marion—the door, will you?"

"Can you carry her all the way?" Marion asked.

"If she hasn't woken up by then I suppose we'll have to find out."

Marion put her arm around Dot and shepherded her out, holding the door open for me and Evelyn. I took a glance over my shoulder at the common room as if to fix it in my mind. I didn't think I was likely ever to see it again.

Neither of us uttered a word about what Marion and Violet had said to each other. We made our way down the corridor that connected the common room with the landing. Evelyn was still clutched in my arms, one hand slung around my neck; my hand supported the backs of her knees, which was a new and surprising intimacy. It was a part of her that I'd never touched before. In that moment, two things happened. First, Evelyn woke up and absolutely wrenched herself out of my arms, with an indignant yelp very much at odds with the fact that I'd probably just saved her life by picking up her limp body and carrying her about. Next, there was another crashing noise, and then the sounds of panting and pounding footsteps.

"Oh, hell," I said. "Evelyn, can you walk?"

"I'd better," she replied, with a curious look.

We didn't move as quickly as we should have. Evelyn could walk, but she wasn't yet up to running, and chivvying Dot along wasn't easy. The corridor stretched before us, looking longer than it ever had before, and the sound of footsteps up the stairs was getting louder. There was a moment when I once again longed to drop everything and give up, let them tear me apart or do whatever it was they wanted with me. We were too young: we were naïve, silly children and we'd been through enough already. We ought to have been thinking about frocks, and going to the pictures, not this. Surely now that everything bordered on hopelessness we had licence to curl up and wait to die. Nothing more could be expected of us. I ran over these thoughts in my mind the whole time we were stumbling and limping down the corridor, and then we came out onto the landing and I looked around the corner to stare directly into the vacant eyes of Miss Lewis.

The timing was uncannily bad. They came up the stairs just as we rounded the corner, and for the first time we met them without the advantage of numbers. The route out of the building was an impossibility; they were in our way. Miss Lewis headed the party, moving with an awkward shuffle, one arm swinging rather uselessly at her side. She was closely followed by Miss Stone, who had only one eye left after what Dot had done with the gramophone needle. The space where her left eye had been was now a mess of blood and tissue, gazing out at us as blankly as her intact right eye. All of their mouths were crusted around with gore, and my head swam as I imagined what Alice's body would look like. Dot moaned.

"Nothing to do but run," Marion panted. The stairs up to the dormitory were right there. I didn't think of giving up any more. I didn't think of anything, really, just scrabbled for Evelyn's wrist to bring her with me and ran full tilt across the landing.

I don't know when Dot fell behind. She was ahead of me at first, doing an admirable job of keeping up with Marion. It was Evelyn I was most worried about; she was weak and depleted and the closest to Miss Lewis, who was hot on our heels. But then I took a stride and Dot was level with me, and I took another and she was behind me, and I reached back to grab her and missed. My fingers closed on a bit of her nightdress, but she pitched forwards and it came out of my grasp.

Evelyn screamed something and turned around, but was confronted with all four of them, who were beginning to gain on us. Dot was already being set upon by Miss Stone, whose face was red and contorted, with a strange blankness shining out of her remaining eye. I've never seen anything at once so empty and so full of rage. It was as if all the things anger was supposed to be supported by—resentment, or fear, or wounded pride—had fallen away, leaving only a hollow shell of fury. Evelyn reached past me and got hold of a corner of Dot's sleeve and was tugging as hard as she could, but she didn't dare get closer, because Miss Lewis had turned away from Dot to go after her. It was useless, anyway.

Miss Stone crowded Dot into the balustrade, and was reaching for her throat when Dot just—went. Her body tumbled over the edge like it was nothing. Alice's captain's badge caught the light as she fell. All of us—even the four of them—stopped in our tracks and watched her go. It felt like it was happening very slowly, though it could only have taken a second. Her dark curls flew up and half-covered her face while she fell the fifteen feet to the floor, but what I could see of her expression looked serene. Her hands stretched upwards, grasping at nothing, or reaching for something we couldn't see.

Watching her fall, I remembered something from when we were younger, perhaps thirteen. Alice and I had been climbing trees. There were a few good climbing trees on the school grounds, the sycamores especially. They were old and had trunks so wide my childish limbs couldn't reach all the way around, so the game was in finding knotholes and protrusions you could balance on or shove your feet into, until you reached the branches and were able to scramble gloriously high. Once up there, you could see around for what felt like miles. Alice and I had gone as far up as we could, and were dropping whirligig seeds from our hard-won vantage points. They wheeled down with abandon, dipping crazily, their acceleration slowed by their lightness and shape so that they seemed to be flying.

Dot appeared at the bottom of the tree and had to bat away the seeds, several of which caught in her hair. She wore it long back then, tied in pigtails with red ribbon. She begged to come up and join us. I didn't think she could do it, and said so, but Alice talked her through it the entire way up, telling her where she could put her foot or where to reach with her hand until she was safely on a branch adjacent to ours. Dot beamed with the pleasure of exertion and achievement, and Alice reached out as far as she could towards her, a tender touch that brushed at Dot's cheek. But Dot was surprised by the motion, and before we could do anything, she started and lost her balance. Her eyes went huge, she hung on only by her hands, but her grip began to slip on the wide branch. She wasn't used to it. She didn't know how. Alice and I picked our way towards her, trying not to fall ourselves, ready to reach out and pull her up, but before we got to her she had given up and let go, finding it easier to fall, which was at least certain.

On the landing, Dot didn't fall cleanly, like Violet and Mademoiselle had. She must have been at an angle—there was none of the spooky neatness in her death that there had been in theirs. The curving banister that led down the staircase broke her fall at first. She bent backwards over it with a resounding crack, which on reflection must have been her spine breaking, and then slumped off it. There was a thud as her body hit the floor, a curse from Marion, a scream from Evelyn, and then we all came back to our senses and hurtled up the stairs to the dormitory.

I had never hated the founders of Briarley more; the avarice that led them to build the pokiest, narrowest staircase imaginable for the housekeeper a century and a half before felt like a personal insult. We went as fast as we could, Marion and Evelyn and I, slipping down onto our hands and knees more than once, nearly kicking each other back down the steps just as often. Whoever had exited the dormitory last had left the door open, which most likely saved our lives. I wish I knew who it was. I skidded into the room and wheeled around, slamming the door behind Evelyn, who came in looking deathly pale.

"Go sit down," I ordered her. "Do it now, I'm not having you fainting on us."

For once in her life she did what I told her and placed herself on her own bed, looking for all the world like an ordinary schoolgirl in an ugly flannel nightdress who'd woken up from a nightmare.

"Did I—" she started, and collected herself. "Did Violet materialise?"

"Almost," Marion said, and then moved swiftly to the doorway.

The teachers had made it up the stairs; I could hear them moving against the door. They weren't beating on it, just moving against it; the fabric of their clothes rustled like the wings of a cloud of insects. Marion braced herself against the door, and held the knob fast.

"Get the nearest bed," she told me. "It'll hold them better than the chair did; we'll have more time than when they were in the gallery."

I complied, though dragging the cast-iron bedframe on my own was almost too much to manage. I thought, with a smarting feeling in my chest, how good it would have been to have Alice there to help. Once the bed was partway across the door Marion helped with the rest of it, sliding my trunk underneath and stacking hers and Evelyn's on top to weigh it down. Neither of us cared to touch Dot or Alice's trunks. There were still scratching noises and the occasional sound like a fist coming down on old wood, but having a good solid barricade in between us and the others outside felt much better. It was when we finished blockading the door, however, that whatever resolve we had managed to keep in our headlong rush up the stairs fell away.

"They're gone," Evelyn said, quietly.

I felt something wild bubbling up in my chest. "I think Dot—"

"Don't," Marion said. "Emily, don't," and when I looked

over, she was tearing at the skin around her fingernails until it was raw and red, something I hadn't seen her do in years, not since we were children. I sat down heavily on the nearest bed, and some moments later realised it was Violet's, neatly made and untouched for months.

The fact that I hadn't noticed it was hers the second I touched it sent me sobbing. I couldn't tell you when I'd stopped being perpetually aware of everything that had belonged to Violet. There had been a time when so much as picking up her blazer instead of mine would inspire a thrill within me; I suppose it's too late now to be embarrassed by the fact that I sometimes did it on purpose. She caught me once, when I had brought it up to my face to breathe in the smell of her just as she walked in. I thought she might shout at me, which she was given to do when anyone touched her things without permission. All she did, though, was laugh, not unkindly but not with much humour either. Oh, Emily, she had said, *if you wanted to know what scent I was wearing you could have just asked.*

"Oh, no," Marion said, as I wept, and came to lay a hand on my back. It felt wrong to be touched by her. I could sense the whole outline of her hand like a brand. Evelyn was looking at me from across the room. We stared at each other for a moment, till Marion took the hint and, with one last squeeze of my shoulder, retreated to her own bed. Evelyn wiped tears off her cheek.

"They're gone, and there's nothing to be done about it but try to get ourselves out," she said.

Her face had come out in scarlet patches where she'd scrubbed her hand across her pale skin. I wondered how it would look to slide my thumb over her cheekbone, whether it'd go white and then pink, how hard I would have to press.

"She's right," Marion said to me gently, and I shook myself.

"We ought to do it now, oughtn't we," I said. "While there's still time." Evelyn nodded and stood up from her bed. She looked out of the window. It was fully light by then.

"What's that?" She leaned over, peering out. "There's something out there—look—"

Marion and I followed her. There *was* something out there, something dark and shadowed, but the thick, century-old windowpanes blurred and distorted it so I couldn't see its boundaries. I hoisted the sash up, and all three of us squeezed in and peered out.

There was something spreading out from underneath Briarley Manor, creeping across the frosty morning grass. I recognised it instantly. It was the same sludgy, poisonous substance that had leaked from the gramophone. It moved outwards, slowly but surely, an inexorable wave of sickness and decay. It was killing everything in its path; I knew it without knowing how. Nothing good could survive being smothered in it. The lawn was nearly swallowed up already, and before long it would reach the vegetable garden, then the apple trees where Evelyn and I had fought. It would obliterate everything I knew and had cared for, turn it all bad and rotten. I thought of it carrying on and on and on, reaching the gates, eating up the fields and the whole county and further, until there was nothing left of England at all.

TWENTY-TWO

NACREOUS

"No time to sit and stare," I gasped, tearing myself away from the awful sight out the window.

"What's the point?" Evelyn said. "Look at it, it's—"

"I've seen it, Evelyn, thank you, I just think we ought to do something rather than sit here and wait to die."

"We'll never find out what it's doing or if we can stop it if we let ourselves be torn apart by the things out there," Marion said with an air of finality.

I thought of her with all those sisters, whom she might never see again, breaking up fights when she'd rather be left to get on with things herself. I still felt as though I wouldn't be satisfied until I had scrapped with Evelyn, or worse, kissed her again. But we were running out of time. They were still right outside the door, rustling and scratching, ready to kill us the second they could make their way through. So I relented, and sat on the floor alongside Marion.

"Before we start, I think we ought to decide on a plan," she said.

"I don't know how we can decide on a plan when we don't

even know if I'll manage to materialise Violet properly," Evelyn protested.

"I'm not willing to entertain the possibility that you won't," Marion said, as archly as she could under the circumstances. I was glad she didn't tell Evelyn that Violet had made me beg her to come at all.

"Well, it's simple. We follow her out, fast as we can, and try to get through the gates before they reach us," I said.

"Simple," Evelyn said, drily. "And if that doesn't work, I suppose we fight our way out."

"Sounds like as good a plan as we're going to get," I replied.

"It's a terrible idea," Evelyn retorted, but she sat down nevertheless. "Hold my hand. Let's get it over with."

"Pax." I stuck out my hand and she shook it once, then deftly turned our clasped hands over and rested them on her knee.

The three of us were sitting very close together: a consequence of our séance circle being reduced to three. I imagined us from the outside, our heads bent together, Evelyn's hair shorn short and Marion's escaping from its hasty morning chignon. Evelyn drew in a deep breath and let it out again.

"You're practically a professional by now," I said to her.

"Don't distract me," she whispered, but her mouth twitched into a smile before she closed her eyes. It felt like we were hanging in some delicate balance and the slightest touch could ruin it all.

"Violet," Evelyn said. "Violet, now, please, if you can."

I waited, wondering if Violet would come and talk to us first. We didn't have time for much conversation but you could never hurry her; she was so easily offended by any suggestion that she didn't have your full attention. She didn't come, though, not like I was expecting, an incongruous voice inside of Evelyn's familiar mouth. No—it was better than that.

Ectoplasm began pouring out of Evelyn. It came from her nose, pooling over her cupid's bow; forcing its way between her lips, collecting in the hollow between mouth and chin and dripping to the floor; from her ears, her nostrils, even at her hairline there was a thin trickle of the stuff. It was a nacreous, mother-of-pearl substance. I leaned in and saw that her eyes had started to gum shut with it. It was beautiful, really, if I could have got over the discomfort that prickled at the back of my neck at how viscous it was and how thoroughly it was coating Evelyn's face. Her chest rose and fell steadily despite how much of it was coming through her nose and mouth.

There was so *much* of the stuff pouring out of her, but her back was still straight. Typical Evelyn; she always prided herself on her posture. The ectoplasm started soaking into the hems of our nightgowns, cold and sticky. The three of us were pressed so tightly together that it began pooling between us. If I'd had a hand free, I could've dipped a finger in it almost up to the first knuckle. I thought about it seeping through the cracks in the floorboards and making its way into the structure of Briarley itself. I wondered what would happen if it touched the oozing rot outside.

"Emily," Marion said urgently, and inclined her head. Almost imperceptibly, the puddle of ectoplasm had changed. I couldn't say exactly what shape it was becoming, not yet, but it was drawing together, becoming more compact and solid by the second. I looked up at Evelyn; her face was serene even as her mouth was being forced open a little by the stream of fluid coming out of it, which was knitting together before it even hit the ground. There was a shimmering coalescence, a process that didn't make sense to the human eye, so I found myself rather skating over it, waiting until something more explicable was happening to take it all in.

This was the part that Sophie's book had never really had an answer for. Perhaps there was a reason why not many people did materialisation séances any more. It had gone out of fashion in favour of more plausible manifestations: voices, automatic writing, things that didn't defy belief in the same way. Our rational, scientific, twentieth-century minds could no longer handle the transition from substance to presence, amorphous fluid to individual solid. There were plenty of reports in the spiritualist papers—I've read them, in the intervening years—of talented mediums manifesting wisps of ectoplasm, or protoplasm, whatever the vogueish term was at the time. But maybe the materialisation of a real spirit was best left to the Victorians—and us.

All of a sudden, Violet was there.

I won't say "in the flesh," because that wouldn't be right. She was perfectly formed and yet intangible. I suspected that if I reached out a hand to touch her, my fingers would slip through her body like it was nothing. It wasn't at all like the illustrations of ghosts you'd find in a book for children. She looked like herself, only glowing from within by a queer unearthly light, her skin pearly and almost translucent. Her hair was in the loose plait I'd put it in the night she died, which made my throat stopper up with the ache of things past. I couldn't take my eyes off Violet, but from the corner of my eye I could see that Marion's mouth had fallen open in an uncharacteristically inelegant expression.

Violet's spirit raised a hand. It looked like she was stretching out towards some faraway horizon, and then she turned her hand around as if to inspect her fingernails.

"Evelyn really managed it," Violet said, with no little surprise.

"Jesus Christ, Violet," I breathed.

I wanted to kiss her. I'd never managed that when she was alive. I had wanted her with such an unnameable, unbearable desire for so long, and now that I had the words for it, I didn't even know if she could be kissed. And then that desire was lanced by the memory of kissing Evelyn and a guilty feeling of disloyalty—to Violet, to Evelyn, I couldn't tell in what proportion—bubbled under my ribs.

"I wouldn't go quite that far," she said, and I marvelled at how her voice sounded the same coming from her own throat as it had from Evelyn's. "But thanks for the welcome anyhow."

"How do you feel?"

Violet smiled. I hadn't seen her smile on her own face in three months; it was radiant, dazzling. She tossed her hair. "Marvellous," she said. "I can't tell you how marvellous. Disembodiment was the pits." When I saw her like this, forced to crane my neck to look up to where she was standing, all my fears melted away. I couldn't imagine how there would be a thing in the world she couldn't do if she set her mind to it. She had that effect, I suppose, in death as in life.

"It's good to see you," I said, which was the understatement of the year. She dropped to a crouch so she was on a level with us, crowded into the negative space left between me and Evelyn and Marion. Evelyn just sat there, utterly still, eyes closed.

"Darling Emily, it's good to see you too," she said, looking right into my eyes with an intensity I didn't think I could bear for long. She came closer and closer, till our noses were nearly touching, and then she looked, for a second, at my mouth. "Only—oh! Now we'll be making Evelyn jealous in two directions at once. It seems too cruel." She drew away.

"You're an awful tease," I whispered, and Marion made a face.

"I'm here for something else anyhow," Violet said, resting her chin in her palm. "I'm getting you out of here, aren't I? If I can."

"If you can't—" Marion started.

Violet's face went grave. "Dot. And Alice. I'm—sorry, about them." My head swam with the effort of not thinking about Dot's sweet, blank face, shining up from where she lay at the bottom of the staircase.

"And I'm sorry about how we left things," Marion said, "last time."

"How very generous of you." The silkiness in Violet's voice seemed to vanish, briefly, before she started again. "You've seen what's out there, I imagine."

"Do you know what it is?" I asked.

"I said before that it was too big," she said, "and if anything it's only got bigger. It feels as though it's going to blot out the sun, the whole world—it feels like something's ending, or just beginning. Like something's ending so that something can begin. Oh, I don't know. It all looks so different, down here. Not you, though," she said fondly. She even turned to look behind herself at Evelyn's still form. Evelyn, to my relief, was still upright. "You all look much the same. More tired, I suppose. Older. And Evelyn's *hair*—well, I wouldn't have recommended it, but I suppose what's done is done. Really, though, it's funny seeing you all like this; it's as though nothing has changed at all."

"I can't say I agree," Marion said, but she didn't argue, either. I hoped their little détente would last. "So what do we do from here?"

"I think I can hold them off," Violet said, a little distantly. "I hope so. I want to, anyway. If I could I'd destroy them altogether, the loathsome things. Burn the whole place down and them with it. We're sort of—opposed. Like oil and water, you might say."

"Can you keep them away long enough for us to get out?"

"We'll have to see," she said. "We don't have much of a choice in the matter." I was struck how, when she was between a rock and a hard place, she sounded an awful lot like Evelyn.

"Is letting go of Evelyn going to break the circle? Is she even going to be conscious?" Marion said.

"Marion, ever practical. You could always leave her up here. Draw the attention away from yourselves, you know."

This time I didn't bother protesting; I just looked at her and the hardening of her expression told me she understood that things had changed.

"All right, we won't do that. Let go. We'll just have to see what happens," Violet said. She nodded towards our clasped hands. The thought of letting go of the others was faintly repulsive to me. I felt as though if we held onto each other hard enough I couldn't lose either of them. And if what I feared did happen, if none of us made it out at all, I couldn't stand the idea that I might never again get to feel the thrumming current of power running through us. Worse, I couldn't bear thinking that it might be the last time I ever touched Evelyn.

"Come on," Marion said, gently, as if she could hear my thoughts. I held my breath, keeping hold of Evelyn's hand for just a moment longer.

Nothing happened when we broke the circle. Violet was still there. Evelyn stayed upright, though her eyes remained closed.

"That wasn't so bad, was it?" Violet asked. I ignored her.

"Evelyn?" She didn't stir.

"You might need to give her a good slap," she added, directing what I can only describe as a malevolent wink at me.

"Ugh," I said, and leaned over to shake Evelyn gently by the shoulders instead. She blinked.

"What on earth do you think you're doing?" she asked, which I thought was a bit rich coming from her. Then she noticed Violet. "Oh" was all she said.

She sounded like she hadn't been prepared for the prospect of actually seeing Violet face-to-face again, and also like she might have been losing the last remaining tenets of her religion all at once. The thing about Violet was that she had always inspired a kind of spiritual devotion, so it must have been very complicated indeed for Evelyn in that moment. She raised a hand as if to wipe the last of the ectoplasm out of the corner of her eye, but it had already vanished, drawn into the making of Violet's unearthly body.

"Terribly rude of Emily not to give you any warning," Violet said in mock indignation. "Can you stand, Hart? Ideally, can you run?"

"If I have to," Evelyn said, still staring at the vision in front of her. It occurred to me that she'd never been present at one of our séances before. I hadn't really thought about what it must have been like for Evelyn. She had done her best to tell me, in the orchard, but I hadn't been listening. There was so much of the past few months that she simply hadn't seen. I felt, though you couldn't have got that information out of me on pain of torture, a brief flare of terror that Evelyn would never look at me again, now that she had Violet back. I imagined how it would feel for Violet to have been on her pedestal still; I couldn't compete with that.

"Well, you will," Violet said. "We're breaking out."

"Violet thinks she can hold them off, at least for a little while," Marion explained. "We just need to run as fast as we can and get to the gates."

"I'd like to get out of here nearly as much as you would. On reflection—which I have more than enough time for, now—good old Briarley was never as much of a sanctuary as you made it out to be, Emily." Violet's voice went all vague. "Something about the place always brought out the worst in my father, you know. Like it was filtering out the good in him and leaving only . . . He'd snap at me over the smallest things and paw at me in the hallway. Once he called me a little bitch because I didn't care to put on a weepy act and follow him back down the drive when he dropped me off."

Evelyn winced at this, hard enough that Violet gave her a sharp, appraising look, but she didn't say anything. I did, though, which was stupid of me. Violet had never liked being coddled; she thrived on a certain amount of petting and fussing but if you went too far she would snap at you like a trapped animal.

"Violet, I'm sorry I didn't—"

"No. No, I don't want to talk about that. I wish you'd shut up, Emily. I wish I'd never said it at all." Then she shook her head, a motion that blurred her features momentarily. "Anyway, I'll be right behind you to help you through the gates. Hopefully."

I chose not to dwell on whether she meant hopefully she would make it to the gates with us or hopefully we would get through them without dying. Neither option was particularly comforting.

There was a scratching noise at the door, which provided an unpleasant reminder that the others were still waiting for us outside. I jumped.

"Violet," Evelyn said.

"Yes, Evelyn?" Violet said prettily, and for a moment there she was the picture of innocence. She looked like an angel on a gravestone.

"Thank you for coming to help us when I asked." Evelyn said it rather stiffly, as if it was a formal obligation.

Violet laughed it off. "Oh, Evelyn, I'd never resist the call of a lady in need," she said.

"Really. I'm grateful." I wished Evelyn would stop pushing. I didn't feel at all certain of where it would go.

"It's really just nice to feel needed!" Violet exclaimed. "Especially considering that you and Emily have each other now. It's lovely to know there's still a place for little old Violet in your hearts."

Evelyn looked furious, and then cowed, and then sort of sad in quick succession. As for Marion, at first she made a face like she was about to see what would happen if you hit a ghost, and then she pinched the bridge of her nose as if she had a headache.

"Anyhow, you'll have to be responsible for getting all that out of the way." Violet gestured towards the makeshift barricade we'd put in front of the dormitory door. "On account of, well—" She glanced down at her insubstantial form.

"I don't remember her being like this when she was alive." Evelyn's tone was sort of wondering. She addressed me alone, as if Marion and Violet weren't there at all. I suppose the most impressive thing was that it took so little time for the scales to drop from her eyes. Another thing to admire her for, however reluctantly.

"Get to it, then," Violet said, a little frostily.

With some of the urgency we'd had running through us on entering the dormitory gone, dragging the bedframe and trunks away from the door was a much more arduous task. I was sweating by the time we reached the last trunk, despite the cold weather. None of us wanted to slide the last one away, understanding implicitly that when we did so the penultimate barrier between us and the mindless automata that had once been our teachers and schoolmates would be gone. I thought, distractedly, *Why them and not us?* And then I recast the question: *Why us and not them?* Perhaps there was something protecting us, Violet's influence from beyond the grave, maybe, or we were protecting ourselves, somehow. Perhaps there was something about us that meant it couldn't reach inside our heads in the same way, the ultimate violation and a terror I could hardly comprehend.

"Are you ready yet?" Violet asked.

"As ready as we'll ever be."

She started towards the door. It was almost difficult, watching her walk across the room; she moved with a strange weightless drift that left her shimmering. I reached out as she passed me to touch her—in case, I thought, it was the last time I ever could. She was cold, and her shoulder collapsed underneath my touch as if she hadn't any bones, just a beautiful, crushable exterior.

Marion gave me one last, worried look, and then, together, we pulled the final trunk away from the door. It felt like rolling the stone away from the entrance of the tomb, only the tomb could well become ours any moment now. Immediately there was a noise at the doorknob, as though they'd figured out that it might work to open the door. I didn't want to think about what it might mean if they were becoming capable of complex thought.

Evelyn, Marion, and I were poised to run. It was a short distance we had to make, all things considered: down the stairs, over the landing, down the next flight of stairs and across the vestibule, out the door, around the building, down the gravel drive and—when Violet had caught us up—through the gates. It was a route I'd taken countless times since I'd first arrived at Briarley six years before, though, of course, never under such circumstances.

The doorknob turned first one way and then the other. It jiggled a little and then—there, they had managed to figure out the mechanism through whatever was addling their minds. The door swung open, and I caught a glimpse of the four of them poised on the threshold, their faces frozen in inhuman snarls, blood all over their mouths and foam between their teeth.

"God," Evelyn said, hollowly, and then Violet's spirit rushed at them. She was no headstone angel, now. She was something avenging, more akin to St. Michael with her golden hair and the look of cold fury on her face as she flew at our attackers. They seemed baffled at first, but the second she touched them, they recoiled. She was right; they were like oil and water. Their faces contorted further and then slowly, stumbling, they began to retreat down the stairs.

The three of us were still poised in the doorway to take our chance as soon as the teachers and pupils had dispersed enough for us to make it down the staircase in one piece. It could only have been seconds but my legs ached with tension as though I had been standing for hours.

Violet sprang towards them in an arcing, elegant motion. Loosed from the prospect of injury, she moved with total freedom. In death she was like a silvered fish or a plume of smoke; the easiest comparisons were inhuman, elemental things. She dove into their mass and they scattered. Whatever she was made of was anathema to them. They couldn't touch her, it seemed, or they were afraid of her. They staggered down the steps, and it was then that we took our chance. I was at the front as we thundered down the dormitory stairs as fast as I'd ever gone in my life. I heard a sharp cry from behind me, and turned my head, trying not to slow down in the process, to see Marion. She had rolled her ankle on the stairs, and she was clutching the balustrade as if it was all that was keeping her standing. Her face was set in a white grimace.

"It's fine, I'm fine," she said, her voice strained. "Keep going."

We made it to the landing. I didn't ever want to see that

landing again as long as I lived, which I felt certain wouldn't be much longer, but there we were nonetheless. The faded Persian rug was rucked up against the wall, but the balustrade gleamed as it always had, untouched by the months of deterioration we had all experienced. That's the thing about an old house: no matter what else happens, parts of it will always look much as they did when the place was built.

Marion was limping and slowing down; I could hear the unevenness in her gait. I held back a little to grab her by the elbow and take some of her weight for her. There was still a clear path for us, just. Violet had them cornered and it felt like a miracle. There was a high, silvery laugh, and then I heard a loud thump as Miss Stone fell to the floor, dead, blood still trickling out of her eye socket where Dot had stabbed her. How Violet killed her I don't know. Once she went down, we were no longer outnumbered, for the first time since Dot had fallen. We got across the landing and rounded the corner to the stairs. And then we made a mistake.

None of us had considered, really considered, that Dot's body would be there in the vestibule, waiting for us. We had needed to push away as much of the pain of her death as we could, because to feel the agonising weight of it would have kept us trapped in the dormitory forever. But she was there, just as we had left her. Her eyes were open, staring blue and unseeing up to the ceiling. She was crumpled against the bottom of the stairs, back bent at an unnatural angle. I suppose it was a small mercy that there was hardly any blood.

I never worked out why that spot became a site of such pain and terror. It had felt innocent, once, the only thing remarkable about it being that it was a good place to slide down the banister when the teachers weren't looking. Maybe it was like something from Sophie's book, an old injustice revisiting itself upon the living, or maybe it was nothing at all.

I saw her first and nearly skidded to a halt, bile rising in my throat.

"Oh no, oh no," Evelyn chanted behind me.

We kept going, but there wasn't enough slack to slow down even for a second. That's what ruined us. Shirley slipped away from where Violet's spirit body had penned her in. She took one wild swing and hit Evelyn in the head, right at the base of her skull, and sent her flying down the stairs. Blinded by rage, I whipped around without even thinking and caught Shirley in the stomach with my elbow. She was smaller than me, much younger and short for her age besides, and although she didn't cry out, she doubled over, staggered back, and sat down heavily, winded. Marion cursed loudly from somewhere behind me, and I took the stairs three at a time to get to Evelyn, who was sitting up but looked dazed. There was a trickle of blood coming from a gash on her temple, and she was clutching her wrist, which hung at a sickening angle.

"Please don't stop for me," she said, eyes like saucers, when I got to her.

"Don't be an idiot," I told her roughly, and hauled her up by her good arm.

Evelyn swayed. "No, look, they—" She broke off and looked past me, back up the stairs. Marion was nearly at the bottom. She was clutching the banister and leaning most of her weight onto it. I had never seen her look weak before.

"Marion, hurry up, we've got to get out," I said holding out my other hand for her. I was prepared to drag them both with me if I had to.

"Emily, look," Evelyn said, and at last I looked properly. Up on the landing, Shirley was staggering back to her feet and Miss Lewis and Ann were approaching the stairs.

There was no sign of Violet.

"I felt her go when I went down the stairs," Evelyn whispered to me. There were tears streaming from her eyes but she didn't sound as if she was crying. "Like a cord snapping. Let me go, I won't make it, you and Marion should save yourselves."

Miss Lewis and Ann were three steps down, Shirley close behind them. Marion had nearly made it to us, a few steps up from the base of the stairs.

"No," I said, and tugged on Evelyn's arm, trying to pull her with me before they caught up with us. She held fast. They were gaining on us now. I spared just a second to wish I had seen Violet one last time, before she disappeared.

"Honestly," Marion said in a thin voice, looking us up and down. She was exhausted, done beyond all comprehension. Before I could stop her, she turned and took off back up the stairs.

"Marion!" I cried, but she was struggling up them faster than I could follow, not with Evelyn hanging onto me, anyway. She was clinging onto the banister but otherwise showing no care for her injured ankle. It was the kind of strength you can only expend when you don't expect to live much longer. Miss Lewis, Ann, and Shirley swivelled their heads like they had caught her scent and stopped in their tracks. She kept going; I watched dumbly as she reached the point of no return, after which she couldn't help but sacrifice herself for us. I know I should have stopped her somehow, or at least turned and run as soon as I realised what was happening, but I remember thinking—*I can't let Marion do this, or if I can I have to bear witness, if she's going to do this she shouldn't die without anyone there to see it.*

Evelyn and I clutched each other. She was hanging onto me with her good arm. I was brought back, for an instant, to the moment when she leaned on me after Violet's memorial, and wished bitterly that we still hated and hardly knew each other, so we could be spared all the rest of it. But then Evelyn turned her face into my shoulder and set her teeth into me to stave off a sob, and I understood that not to know her like I did now would be unbearable.

So I watched as Marion kept on climbing till she had surpassed Miss Lewis, Ann, and Shirley, their heads still turning as she went. I suppose they were trying to react to something incomprehensible with what little intelligence they had left. Predators, I imagine, aren't used to their prey delivering itself to them conveniently. She took one look backwards as she reached the landing, her gaze falling on me and Evelyn with an unreadable expression that I thought might be pity, or frustration, or sheer tiredness. Then she limped painfully across the landing and up the dormitory steps, and it was there that they caught up, and went for her.

I think—I hope—we stayed until the moment of her death. They set upon her like carrion birds, all three of them on her at once so that most of her body was obscured. Only her arm jutted out, all five fingers flexed so that each bone in the back of her hand stood out. A second later her foot slipped on the stairs and there was a flash of her ankle, which would have swollen and purpled if she'd lived long enough. They were a swarm, a hive, and we could hardly see what they were doing, for which I was grateful. She would've hated the indignity of it. I don't think I ever saw her admit to being hurt, neither that day nor in the six long years of our acquaintance. Marion was like a cat, in that way: she simply took herself off to deal with injury or illness alone.

There were a few seconds when Marion maintained her usual self-control, and then she let out a last choked cry that cut off abruptly. Evelyn and I turned tail, then, and I only hoped Marion was already gone so she didn't have to see us take her sacrifice for the gift it was, turn our backs on her, and go out the door on the other side of the vestibule. Not fighting harder for Marion is an act of cowardice that makes my stomach churn still. I try to persuade myself that we were doing what she wanted, just like we told Dot about our leaving Alice, using the time she bought us to save ourselves rather than throwing it away. I wish I believed it. Evelyn and I shut the door behind us and emerged into the thin December sunlight.

TWENTY-THREE

SCRUBBED RIGHT OUT OF EXISTENCE

I have never been able to decide which of the stupid, catastrophic things we did in those last days hurts the most. I worry at all of them like an aching tooth, running across them over and over until I can't tell whether what I'm feeling is the original hurt or the result of all my pressing and prodding. I try to remember that the litany of mistakes we made was a product of our circumstances, which were about as bad as they could have been. The oldest of us were eighteen; we were barely out of childhood. We were so young, exposed to terror and grief far too early, forced to make all our decisions for ourselves without any kind of guiding hand. Of course Alice didn't try harder to get out of the Long Gallery once she was trapped there. Of course we allowed ourselves to be herded up and up into the highest point of the school, making our route back down all the more fraught. Of course I made us stay, in the only place I had ever considered my home, until it was no longer possible to leave.

I wonder, sometimes, whether by the time we realised something was wrong, any of us would have been allowed to make it out alive, or whether we were doomed from the start. From the moment Violet died, I was—we were—in no state to be making strategic decisions. And still it all hurts, because even if you provide a laundry list of reasons why we did what we did, the fact remains that all of them were killed.

The only part I can look back on wholly without shame is what Evelyn and I did once we made it outside. We slammed the door behind us, so hard that a pane of stained glass shattered. There was a crate full of empty milk bottles by the door, a relic from weeks past, when milk could last more than a day without spoiling, and I hauled it up and shoved it against the door in case that provided a little more protection. Evelyn's whole body was very still; she had always been the patient one of the two of us. She had that look of queer clarity in her eyes, like dawn breaking. I waited for her to speak, knowing I would do whatever she told me.

"We have to burn it down," she said suddenly. It was the first thing either of us had said since we watched Marion struggle up the staircase. "Like Marion said, and Violet. All of it. We have to do it now, before they—finish with Marion's body."

I looked over at her. Her chin was tilted high in the air and her eyes were fierce.

"Are you certain?"

"Certain."

I nodded and squinted out at the landscape, rolling hills and the vanishing lawn under its blanket of thick dark ooze. It wouldn't take long before it spilled out into the rest of the world.

"We'll go around to the front," Evelyn said decisively. "We can get down into the kitchen that way. Cook kept kerosene and matches down there."

"And then we torch the place."

"If you insist on putting it that way, then yes, we torch the place."

Getting to the front of the school was more of an undertaking than either of us had really considered. We were barefoot, after all. The whole miserable day had started with that God-awful gramophone, and none of us had thought to put on shoes.

"I've got to be honest, I don't want to touch that stuff," I said. "I don't know what it'll do to us."

"It's us or everyone else," Evelyn pointed out. "What do you think happens when it spreads outside of Briarley?"

I wasn't feeling brave. I wish I could've said that Marion's sacrifice, or Alice's, or anyone's had inspired something selfless in me, but I simply didn't want to touch whatever that substance was. I hadn't wanted to in the dining hall and I wanted to even less now, when there was so much of it that you couldn't tell how deep it was. I imagined stepping out onto it and feeling my whole foot sink in up to the ankle, then the knee, being swallowed up whole, like the quicksand you read about in adventure novels for children. *What if it got in my mouth,* I found myself thinking, *what would it taste like, would I choke on it?*—the sort of frantic cascading thought that makes action feel impossible. In the end, it was the force of Evelyn's glare that got me to move.

"Your wrist," I started, trying to delay the matter. She looked at me scornfully.

"It doesn't change what we need to do."

"At least let me bind it up before we go?" She rolled her eyes but didn't refuse, which was as much assent as I was going to get. I knelt, and, tugging as hard as I could, tore along the hem of her nightgown till I had a good long strip. She thrust out her wrist, though the motion looked as if it pained her.

"Hurry up, please," she spat, and I took her hand in mine and wrapped the strip of flannel around and around as tightly as I could. She went grey when I first touched the bones of her wrist; her eyes squeezed shut and she visibly fought down a reaction. I was being as gentle as I could, handling her like she was precious and breakable.

"You need a sling," I said, and made for the hem of her nightgown again.

"Absolutely not, I'm not having you take more off mine. Use your own." Her voice was high and strained. I rolled my eyes and ripped off as much fabric as I could from my nightdress till it was long enough for me to loop around her neck and tie together.

"Better?"

"Acceptable," she said, and we stepped out into the blackened pool.

The smell was overwhelming. It was the smell of something old: something putrescent, sickly, with a burnt-sugar undertone. It was all around us now, taking over the frosty, clean air and replacing it with something unwholesome. I wondered how long it had been brewing under the foundations of Briarley. From the smell, it could've been there for as long as I'd known the place—for as long as it had existed, even. It felt awful under the feet. I hoped there weren't any cuts or scrapes I hadn't had time to notice; the idea of the sludge getting into my blood was more than I could handle. There wasn't any sound from inside yet but instead of feeling comforted, I imagined them tearing the flesh from Marion's bones.

"We need to move," I said. "Can you go any faster?"

Evelyn adjusted her makeshift sling and resolutely began to run, wincing with every step. I followed her, only a step behind. The muck sucked at my heels with every footfall. I wondered at how I'd made it through unscathed so far. I didn't deserve it. I wasn't any cleverer or any less clumsy than the others, including Evelyn, whose wrist was in all probability broken. The side of her face was tacky with blood but we hadn't time to do anything about it. My body was strong and alive, and it was my responsibility to use it to destroy Briarley. I thought about how I would be burning up Marion's body, and Dot's, and Alice's, and even Sophie and Mademoiselle's bodies if we managed to burn chapel too. It was a terrible thought, but it would be a clean break. The idea of letting something get inside them and wheel them around like puppets was a betrayal I couldn't countenance.

Evelyn and I made it around to the front. The steps up to the front door were left unscathed from the stinking substance that had reached nearly everything else. I hated them for looking so clean. Smearing our dirty footsteps over the spotless stone was a small satisfaction.

"Down to the kitchen," Evelyn said. She didn't look well at all, but I thought if I tried to stop her now she'd bite my head off. "Cans of kerosene—splash it around as much as you can. I can't carry them but I'll fetch the matches."

We ran down to the kitchen, where hours ago Marion and I were supposed to have scraped together breakfast out of whatever we could find. Where I'd made a failure of a birthday cake for Evelyn, what felt like so long ago.

I didn't have time to think about what I was doing, just picked up the two big cans of kerosene and poured a thin trail through the kitchen and back up the stairs. Evelyn trudged behind me, uselessly, given that the only job she was capable of was lighting the match at the end. I thought, almost hopefully, that perhaps she didn't want to let me out of her sight. I tried to maintain an unbroken line of kerosene, imagining a clean wall of flame licking its way through the manor, until the whole place was overwhelmed. The dining hall, the classrooms, even the old governess's turret. The oily smell rose into my nostrils until it overtook the rotting scent of the muck that Evelyn and I had tracked in.

We didn't speak as we went; I can only assume that she, like I did, said silent goodbyes to each room we passed as I splashed across the floorboards and the portraits and the curtains. So many of those rooms had accumulated layers of memory like sediment. A classroom in which I'd cried upon learning about Latin declensions, then later had passed notes with Violet during lessons, which finally had become a site of shame and bewilderment as we were punished for things at random, in those painful latter days of Briarley. The dining hall, where Alice had once instigated a game of "Would you rather" so rowdy that we were all sent straight to bed with no pudding, and which was now slowly filling with the rank seeping substance that continued to ooze out of the gramophone. Even a side passageway where, only days before, I had seen Evelyn pass through a shaft of afternoon light, and was so struck with the urge to kiss her that I had clawed three neat pink lines in the flesh of my forearm.

There were rooms we wouldn't be able to bid farewell at all. The common room, our dormitory. On balance, I had hardly got to spend any time in the upper-sixth dormitory, the secluded privacy of which had been something to look forward to since we were eleven. The prospect of it had felt so achingly grown-up. We gave the Long Gallery a wide berth, in the unspoken understanding that it would be a mercy not to see what had been done to Alice's body. I longed to burn the landing where Violet had died, and which held Dot and Marion's bodies as well, but I had to hope that we'd done a thorough enough job with the kerosene that the whole place would go up. I didn't want the landing to exist any more. I wanted it all scrubbed right out of existence.

"I wish—" I started. It was the first thing I'd said in what felt like forever.

"So do I," Evelyn said shortly. "But we can't."

Chapel came last. To avoid jolting her wrist further, Evelyn sat on the stone steps out front, waiting for me. I didn't want to go alone but it had been a kindness for her to come through the school with me, and there was a wan quality to her that I didn't like the look of. So I steeled myself, dropped the empty can of kerosene that I'd finished in the main building, and stepped back out into the mire. It felt worse with every step I took. I tried not to think about how even if we got out of here, we might be poisoned forever, or worse, we might track the poison with us, letting it grow wherever we went next.

I made it to chapel and opened the door. I hadn't been in there since Sophie's funeral, and since then Mademoiselle's body had been left there too. I was hit instantly by the stench, which had finally developed and was strong enough to cut through the chemical smell of the kerosene and the foul muck outside. This was the odour of decaying flesh, which wasn't something I'd have expected to be able to identify, only there was something unmistakable about it, an instinctive animal feeling of wrongness. I raised my arm to cover my nose.

"I'm sorry," I said aloud. I didn't have it in me to open my mouth for any longer than that, although there was more that I wish I had said. The smell was so thick that I could almost taste it, a bad, fruity sweetness at the back of my tongue. There was no way this place could be suffered to stand any longer.

I splashed kerosene over the pews, including the one where I had sat with Mr. and Mrs. Kirsch during Violet's memorial, trying not to look at the parallel pews where Sophie's and Mademoiselle's bodies still lay. Then I moved on to Fish's carved wood pulpit, and the altar, and even up the stark whitewashed walls. I briefly considered whether it was a sin to burn down a church, and then decided that I was so far gone in every other aspect of my life that one more transgression couldn't possibly be what tipped the balance.

When the whole place stank of oil and my head had begun to pound rhythmically from the fumes, I left chapel, feeling unsettled at the thought that it would be for forever. As I went I poured a thick trail of kerosene behind me, striping the rotting lawn with it on my way to fetch Evelyn. She looked like she was moving in and out of consciousness, sitting there on the steps, but when she saw me she shook her head and affected a curled lip.

"It took you long enough." When she saw my face she added, softer, "It was bad?"

"Bad," I said, distantly, not good for much other than parroting back to her.

"Shall we get it over with?"

I nodded and she reached out to me with her good hand. I put mine in hers, and felt her familiar grip, the dig of her fingernails that she never seemed aware of. We trudged through the mire together, hand in hand, the last of the kerosene streaming freely from the can. The blackened substance that was eating up all the life around Briarley had spread almost all the way down the gravel drive. It had even surrounded the fountain, leaving Adonis the sole survivor, cresting out of the thick sludge with his water jug. Nothing was pouring out; the pipes had gone.

Evelyn and I wiped our feet off on the very last of the good grass. It was dewy; I thought it must still be morning. It felt right to clean ourselves off as much as we could. Then, without any kind of ceremony, we stood at the very edge of the infected land, and Evelyn struck a match. She flicked it into the air and I watched it sail to the ground, where it caught the trail of kerosene and went up instantly.

I had been standing too close. I hadn't expected it to catch so easily. It flared up, creating a momentary, magnificent burst of flame that licked at the frayed hem of my nightdress and set it alight. The heat was a shock, and I cursed, crouching down to beat it out and burning my hand in the process.

"Are you all right?" Evelyn asked, but she wasn't looking at me, just staring out at the fire. I peered at my palm where it had blistered and reddened. The pain, I suspected, would come later, if I lived long enough to feel it.

"Fine, I think," I said, a little breathless. "Or I will be, once we've managed to find some ice and a bandage." This, finally, was what made her look at me, with a curious, appreciative expression on her face, as if she was relying on me to carry on believing for the both of us that we would make it far enough to find such things. Then I looked up and saw that nearly the whole lawn had gone up and was burning clean away, leaving razed nothingness in its stead: a dry, clean blank that lacked the foul smell that had been there before. The fire was tracing down the trail of kerosene I had left with incredible speed, faster than I could've imagined. If I'd spent any more time contemplating my burnt hand I'd have missed the moment it reached the building.

When the fire did reach Briarley Manor, it multiplied a hundredfold in size and intensity, searing a path up the steps and over the threshold, licking at the big old oak door and racing into the entrance hall. The gravel drive was so long I could hardly see a thing once the fire had made it inside, but the building was beset on all sides by the burning remnants of the rotting ooze, which was flammable beyond my wildest hopes. It didn't stand a chance. The first part to go was the windows. The front-facing ground-floor windows exploded all at once, the antique bullseye glass panes we had been forbidden from approaching as children blowing out into splinters. You could see, through the gaping holes where the windows had once been, that my trick of splashing kerosene on the curtains had worked, and the flames reached up and up towards the ceiling, till all that was visible was a violent orange glow.

I needn't have worried about the fire not spreading sufficiently through the school. Once started, there was nothing that could have stopped it. It was as if everything brittle and old in Briarley had gone up like dried-out paper crumpled in the grate. In just a few moments, in the suspended place between breaths, the fire spread to chapel, and to the wing of the school where Marion and Dot's bodies lay, and where our dormitory had been. I tried not to listen for screams over the crackling of the flames. Soon enough the whole thing was burning.

I glanced down and noticed that sometime during all of this Evelyn had picked up my hand again, the one that wasn't burnt. I looked over at her, saw her face illuminated by the glow from the school, proud and finally unafraid. Her left temple was bloody but she stood, straight-backed, her arm hanging in the makeshift sling. We turned to each other, her good hand in mine, and I stepped forwards and kissed her, jolting her injured wrist so that she gasped and bit me hard on the lip in surprise, and then we walked out through the gates of Briarley for the last time.

TWENTY-FOUR

OURS ALONE

Some years later, with an ill wind in the air and a bad taste in the backs of our throats, we took the train to Sussex and walked to where Briarley had once stood. It was early September. We hadn't planned the coincidence, but Evelyn pointed out as the train rattled into the station that the date was within two weeks of the day Violet died. September was always a good time for that part of the country; the trees still had all their leaves and there wasn't yet a bite in the air, but the sunlight glowed like something on fire. I stepped onto the platform and reached out a hand to help Evelyn off, and then there we were, the train going off to its next destination and leaving us stranded. I thought, briefly, that it felt like an abandonment.

Neither of us had been back since the fire. There had been a rush of headlines about the tragic deaths of several schoolgirls and some of their teachers, although from one publication to another the numbers seemed to vary: nobody was quite sure how many of us had died and when. They were in agreement that the first exodus of girls had made it home safely, and there were reports that Cook had retired to the country, but the whole affair seemed veiled in an obscuring fog. In the face of this uncertainty, most of the tabloids decided to lay the blame on unmarried women being unfit to take proper care of their charges, and the broadsheets decided instead to run sombre stories about a joint funeral held for us in London. My family did not attend. When Marion's mother drowned herself in 1931, there was another brief flurry of headlines, but on the whole we have largely been forgotten.

Walking through the village, I found there was something satisfying about seeing Evelyn around all our old haunts. She had never grown much taller, and really she hadn't lost that cygnet look she had had all those years before, but the way she moved wasn't the same at all. There had been something furtive about her when we were younger, a nervy, awkward way of approaching the world, but now she went across the cobblestones with a sort of irritable confidence. She walked so quickly that I was forced to scramble to keep up, hanging perpetually a step or two behind her like an eager dog.

The village had expanded in the half-decade or so since we'd left it. There was a cinema now, and all the shopfronts had been re-done. It had always been an old-fashioned place but modernity was making its inexorable way through the countryside whether anyone liked it or not, and Briarley Village was no exception. When we passed where Mrs. Northcote's house had been I shuddered despite myself; it had been turned into neat, dull flats. I wondered whether Mrs. Northcote had thought of us at all after the fire. If she might even still be alive, in one of those well-appointed new builds with all the modern conveniences. Thinking in this direction, I registered a flare of nerves that someone in the village would recognise us, even after all these years. Evelyn seemed to read my mind.

"We won't hang around," she said, blinking into the midafternoon light. It was the first time either of us had spoken since we'd stepped off the train. "I don't want anyone noticing us."

"Whatever you say," I replied, though really I was grateful that we weren't taking the risk.

Sometimes I wondered—and still wonder—whether if we had friends, they would caution me against her. Her carefulness, which forces us to move to a new flat every couple of years; once, when a neighbour asked her to go to the theatre with him, she sent in our notice to the landlord the next day without even asking me. Her unending need for control in all things, her inability to show simple affection. Her refusal, ever, to brook discussion of Violet: it took years of trying on my part, met with a chilly, uncomfortable silence, to learn that it was easiest just to give up and keep my thoughts to myself.

But the idea of anyone—these hypothetical friends of ours—disapproving of Evelyn is almost laughable to me. Our life is constrained, but it is a life, and without her I wouldn't have it at all. I love her fervently: her clarity, her willingness to take charge, her deft hands and the sardonic turn of her mouth. What I have come to understand, over time, is that even if I didn't love her still, we would have no choice but to stick together. Once, after the worst of our fights, I stormed out of our flat into the cold unlovely street and thought about leaving her for good; then I realised that neither of us had anywhere to go. I slunk home in ashamed supplication and she took me back without a word. She and I, for better or worse, are the only people left in the world who could ever understand each other.

As we approached the edge of the village, I found myself torn between relief to leave it and a blank misery upon reaching the road to the site where Briarley had stood. There were a few tastefully built houses on the outskirts, and everything seemed awfully clean, but otherwise the further out you got, the more it had retained its character despite everything that had happened down the road. I couldn't work out whether this felt like a consolation, or an insult.

I felt grateful beyond belief that Evelyn was with me, but I didn't mention it: mentioning things was always a risk, with her, in case she faced up to herself a little too cleanly and in response retreated into her shell. Still, she allowed me to put a hand around her waist once we were far enough down the road that we couldn't be seen. The feeling of her body moving underneath the crepe of her dress was almost enough.

With my free hand I reached out and snagged a blackberry from the hedgerow. It was out of instinct more than any intention. Realising that it was a motion I had completed a hundred times or more during my school years was a queer, ghostly sensation, the idea that my child-self was still lying dormant within me a disquieting thought.

"I wouldn't eat that if I were you," Evelyn said, her grey eyes fixed ahead of us. I jumped.

"Oh, Christ, do you think—"

The point was moot; I'd crushed the blackberry between my fingers when she startled me. Its juice seeped under my nails, ringing them with purple. Nothing came out. No maggots, no rot, only the last of summer. I put my fingers to my mouth and sucked the sharp, bright taste off them, and then Evelyn grabbed my hand and bit at my fingertips, half in apology for surprising me, half out of her own inscrutable needs. Her teeth were as sharp as ever.

We neared Briarley, at last. The land where the foundations had been remained untouched. The grass had grown back, and the ruins of the manor cleared away, but the gate was still there, separating the road from the nothingness within. Somewhere in the back of my mind I realised that for all these years I had imagined what we'd burned as being replaced by a hard, glassy surface, something unending and impermeable. Seeing it as it was, all grass and weeds, nature having been permitted to take her course, was something of a let-down. Evelyn let out a short breath. I reached for her.

The rest of it, I think, is ours alone.

ACKNOWLEDGEMENTS

Self-indulgently, I'd like to start by thanking the dead people who made this book possible: the mediums, séance sitters, and spirits who in the most surprising ways imagined another world.

On a more practical note, I owe endless thanks to Imogen Morrell, my agent, whose belief in my work has meant so much to me. Thank you to everyone at Greene & Heaton, who have been so kind and welcoming, and also dealt with my tax forms. An enormous thank you to the many other people who have been involved one way or another in helping this book to publication: Steph Delman and Elizabeth Pratt, indefatigable champions; Rhian, who understood just what I intended with all those hyphens; the many people whose names I don't know but whose labour has been invaluable. I am forever indebted to my editors and their colleagues, who have all been terrific: Jasmine Palmer, Ana McLaughlin, and the rest of the team at riverrun; Carolyn Williams and everyone else at Doubleday; and Sarah St. Pierre along with the rest of PRH Canada (and Lauren Park, who was there at the beginning!). It has been such a pleasure—thank you in advance for all the new things you will have done by the time these acknowledgements go to print.

Thanks also to my parents, John Curran and Kristen Frederickson, for their love, support, and tolerance, even as I refused to let them read this for a very long time; to Anna Parker, for making it all happen; to Abi Palmer, Jay Dalton, Freddie Kölsch, Sarah McCarry, Rowan Wilson, Mikaella Clements, and Onjuli Datta, for reading this book at various stages and saying nice things about it, usually at times of great need; to Claire Heseltine, for reading it first. To Rosalie Bower and Julia Armfield most especially, the best of friends, whom I could never thank enough even if I had a hundred thousand years in which to try.

And finally to Martha Perotto-Wills, for everything, always: I love you as the copper to the zinc.

ABOUT THE AUTHOR

AVERY CURRAN studied history at university, where she first became interested in spiritualism, and then worked at a publisher and archive centred around a Swedish mystic. She is now midway through a PhD on queerness in nineteenth-century spiritualism. She was born in New York City and currently lives in London with her girlfriend and their cat.